cluck

cluck

murder most fowl

eric d. knapp

Cluck: Murder Most Fowl
cluckthebook.com

© 2007 by Eric D. Knapp
All Rights Reserved
ISBN: 1-4196-8264-4
EAN-13: 978-1419682643
Library of Congress Control Number: 2007908890

Visit www.booksurge.com to order more copies.

Cover art and interior illustrations by Ian Richard Miller, IRM-Arts
irmarts.com
Book Design by Ian Richard Miller and Eric D. Knapp

This book is dedicated to the ones that the fox got, for they all deserved better, and to Prince Talizar, for proving that chickens are capable of love.

about cluck

"Cluck" was written as a work of independent fiction. It was written, designed and produced by the author, Eric D. Knapp, and the illustrator, Ian Richard Miller. By purchasing this book you are promoting the "indie scene," and are thus entitled to feel a bit hip. At the very least, you should have a warm and fuzzy feeling.

The interior typeface is Adobe Garamond Premier Pro, with chapter titles being adorned by the fine fontography of Brittany Wigand, using type that is whimsically named "Anywhere but Home."

The cover and chapter illustrations are by Ian Richard Miller. The cover is a digital compilation of photographs, scanned textures and hand painted art.

The story is mine, though it owes much to the world of dreams, and to the beauty of Star Island; the two are both magical places that inspire the soul.

cluck

cluck

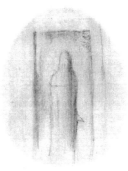

prologue

Evil was about to happen, in the gloomy hours of the night. A shape, made amorphous by the dark, moved slowly through twisted hallways and climbed crooked stairs. Old wood creaked occasionally as the figure advanced, and on each such occasion the figure halted, listening for any indication that the floorboard's small complaint was noticed amidst the backdrop of chirping insects and vociferous night birds. Each halt turned into a pause, and then into a patient moment where awareness strained for any indication of discovery. Eventually satisfied, the sinister silhouette crept on with shallow breaths and steady, careful steps, until at last it came to a door. The dim outline of a hand stretched forward, and took hold of a cold marble doorknob. The door, too, moaned softly in protest as it was pushed carefully inward. Steady breaths became staggered and agitated as adrenaline began to surge. A pulse quickened. The door opened. Pent-up moonlight from the room's large dormers spilled outward, darkening the outline of the figure as it crept inside. As the intruder moved slowly across the room, a brief glint of sharp steel reflected the otherwise peaceful moon.

Knapp

As the door fell closed again, new sounds joined the choir of whip-poorwill and owl and cricket. Nothing so dramatic as a scream, or a crash; simply the sound of cold metal muffled by soft flesh, barely notice-able above the persistent rattling of ancient shutters and the soft whine of the night breeze. The pulse was now pounding, the breath heavy, and the cold *thunk thunk thunk* of the blade was accented by the soprano squeaks of old bedsprings, and then—just as suddenly—all was quiet. After another pause, the footsteps began again. Louder, hasty, less caring of discovery, the figure fled back through door and away into the night.

The night—unconcerned with the goings-on of man—crept on, intent on finding dawn. In the distance, oblivious to the disturbance and confused by the brightness of the moon, a rooster crowed.

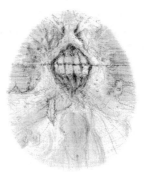

chapter 1   the mouth of hell

There was something foul at the mouth of Hell.

There was resistance, reluctance. A heaviness brought the air together with a humid, foreboding defiance; a slow and barring exhalation reminiscent of a woman's ire as she blows smoke into the face of unwanted company. There was the faintest of grins on the Hell-mouth's lips that would have sent chills down anyone's spine, if anyone had been there to see it. There was no one there, however. No one alive, at least, to witness the face of evil as it twisted itself into an unmistakable expression of *"no"* before it withdrew, and snapped its jaws shut against entry. The mouth stood closed, teeth clenched.

There was a soul, rebuked and forlorn, standing before the entrance to the underworld, awash in brimstone light, drawn to the devil's teeth by some unknown instinct. Perhaps it simply found its way to this dismal pit of despair due to the cruel inevitabilities of chance, or some ill fate. Sometimes, a soul is pushed by the living, through suggestion or impression, at the very moment of demise, leading it to this place.[1] The Hell-mouth was used to that sort of thing, and it was both experienced with and accustomed to the arrival of unwanted, misguided souls.

Typical.

The soul standing now before the gates was all of these things and more: a creature of instinct, certainly; misguided, most definitely; pushed away by the living, absolutely. It was also completely and profoundly confused. There was no clear memory of how it had arrived, or why. Whatever force had led the wandering spirit to this spot urged it forward still, towards the menacing maw of eternal damnation. *Go into the gate*, said the force, *discover what lies beyond the teeth.* Was there a tunnel? A light? The siren call of disembodied voices, promising shelter and warmth and food? Food sounded good. The spirit liked food, but the point was profoundly and theologically moot: however the spirit had arrived there, the mouth was now closed. The teeth clenched. The way was shut.

It wasn't that this thing, this pneuma, standing there before the very mouth of Hell, wasn't worthy. It had, in a rudimentary way, performed its share of 'evil.' Arrogance, greed, gluttony and pride were among its sins. Hell had no problems with this. It was Hell: home to evil, dementia, lies, decay and pestilence. Hell welcomed evil. The entity standing forlorn before the barred gates had an irksome goodness to it, as well, but this wasn't the problem, either. After all, if it hadn't deserved in at least some small way to spend an eternity in the land beyond the river Styx, it would surely have found its way to a kinder shore, to a gateway of a different sort.

---

[1] "Go to Hell" being a popular modern utterance towards the soon-to-be deceased.

cluck

The problem was that the entity standing stubbornly before the closed mouth was something that was so unwanted and so dirty at such a base level that it was almost ... innocent. That was the paradox.

"Innocence doesn't belong in here," thought an ancient will, and the teeth clenched more tightly against entry. Despite being the biggest and most savage of its kind, and despite a suitable resumé of sins, this soul did not belong. Most of its crimes were little more than acts of instinct, and instinct is hardly born from evil. The soul approached again, and once more the mouth of hell shrank away; it was denied.

The denial, and the logic behind it, was little more than rationalization on the part of Hell. The truth of the matter is that the gateway was a *mouth*. Even a thing designed to contain the most egregious essences of evil had standards when it came to what it would and wouldn't put willingly into its own mouth. While not as odious as many spirits in terms of its morality, this one took the prize in raw physical pungency. There was the *other* thing, as well—this soul had been touched by some power, and was even now linked strongly to a destiny that spanned the eternal rift between life and death. Deep down at the very bottom of this soul, down with the silt and scum, there was a *clause*, a fine-print so secret and small that Hell couldn't quite make it out. Hell, knowing a thing or two about twisting a lien, wanted nothing to do with it. Even if Hell had arms and hands with which to hold a ten-foot pole, it wouldn't touch this soul. The teeth squeezed closer together still.

Unable to fully grasp its rejection, the unwanted entity hobbled closer. It wasn't exactly large, though it was larger than the rest of its kind, and it wasn't exactly smart, although it was brilliant relative to its species. What it was, was determined. The spirit had, during life, a rather tough time of things, and had always persevered. Its few faint memories—mere wisps of earthly recollection—held little more than hurt, hunger and hate. It stared at the mouth of Hell, confident that it would enter. It seemed like it could fit between two of the larger teeth if it just squeezed a bit, and because thought of any kind was rare, it felt that this thought must be a good one. It lacked the sense to realize that squeezing into Hell probably wasn't a good idea under any circumstance, and so it limped closer. With a bit of effort the wretched thing squirmed through, and was lost for a moment in the eternal darkness of pain and torment. There was a further moment of silence, what could have been a few moments or a few lifetimes; there was no knowing in this timeless, evil place. If there had been anyone around to witness it, they might claim that Hell itself recoiled. The mouth puckered. There was a universe-shattering noise that sounded more than a little bit like a whimper.

Then: a sigh.

In the time (which again could have been an instant or an eternity) after the mouth of Hell had been violated, something else occurred in the cosmos which brought a great sense of relief to the underworld. Tiny letters began to glow. The microscopic terms that clouded the fate of this sour soul grew potent. They were being read. Something else was calling the thing back. The mouth smirked in a "told you so" kind of expression. As it suspected, this soul was linked strongly to a destiny that did not involve the underworld, and whoever or whatever was at the other end of that link was pulling at the soul, reeling it in like a reluctant bass. *As it should be,* thought Hell. *It does not belong here.* Without ceremony the mouth of Hell pursed its lips, a thick and ancient metaphorical tongue sucking at the roof of a rotten maw cloying with the slime of lost souls, and it spat.

Whatever wants it, can have it, thought Hell, as the tiny ethereal shape sailed away through the air. It tasted terrible.

The disembodied thing, wet with the spit of Hades, rolled to a stop. It was confused, certainly. It had barely comprehended the world around it during life, and was even more confused by death—never mind trying to understand concepts so sophisticated as Good and Evil, or Heaven

cluck

and Hell. With the saliva of the forever damned still dripping from its soggy self, the rejected soul stumbled to its ghostly feet. It was no longer surrounded by the furnaces of the nether-world, but it wasn't sure where else it could be. The smell of brimstone was gone. There was a slight breeze, and the distant hooting of an owl, and a slight glow upon the eastern horizon. It seemed an infinite distance away from the gate, standing again on earthly soil. It cocked its deceased head from side to side, attempting to get its bearings, and then wondered for a moment why the ground was blackened with fire and smoke. It pondered for an even briefer moment why it was that it felt naked and cold despite the pain that coursed through its body as a result of its suddenly burnt and smoldering flesh. Despite its abrupt dismissal from Hell to this barren, earthly place, its thoughts lingered mostly on a much simpler question: it was hungry, and wondered if there was anything nearby to eat.

It cocked its head again and a faint memory finally coalesced. It knew this place. Yes, it was back in familiar territory. Home? Perhaps, for the memory brought with it the feelings of comfort and safety that are associated with one's home. The memory continued to manifest itself, providing more detail, and the soul felt strong, powerful, *royal*. Yes, it was a King, it remembered, but ...

Something was different, for it also felt disconnected and alone. It felt the cool night breeze stinging places where the touch of air should have brought comfort. The pain was hollow, cold, *deep*. The thing looked down and saw itself. Two sturdy and strong legs: one intact and one bloodied; one supported by three strong and sharp talons, one with nothing but a burnt stub and one sharp claw. *That's not right*, the thing thought, though it didn't seem to mind the deformity. It scratched at the earth expectantly, raising a small wisp of ash. It didn't think to wonder why there might be ashes here, so far from the burning gates of Hades, or why its own body was so suddenly burnt, when the fires of eternal sin had left it untouched. It never drew the connection between these disturbing details and its own sense that something had changed. It took things in stride, confident in itself despite the pain and confusion. It flexed a wing, and then another, feeling the strong muscles ripple upwards through its frame as it stood in the grayness of predawn.

Inevitably, over the rambling line of an ancient rooftop, the sun appeared and warmth washed across the thing's inexplicably damaged body. The light was a thin slice of brilliant power that cut the darkness like ... *fire*.

It remembered.

There was a huge and devastating fire. Not the same as the brimstone of Hell, visible through the gates just moments before, but something real. Something earth-bound. Something that burned more deeply because of the circumstances of the blaze. The new light showed the scene more clearly with each passing moment. There had certainly been a fire, there was no doubt now. Where there was once a bounty of worm-filled soil, there was nothing more than a splotch of char, and bones, and stench. The thing would have been shocked, if it weren't so hungry. The smell of the burnt corpses surrounding it awoke the hunger further. It smelled like barbecue. The thing scratched the earth again, and then scratched at the bones, but there was nothing left to eat.

This thing, defeated, was not capable of weeping. It was not capable of crying out, "Why? What have I done? Where am I?" Impotent, it was unable to thrust its will into the spiritual places of the world to demand an answer. It once had power—it was an exemplar of its species. Now, it wasn't really capable of much at all, and it was alone. There had been others before, but now all it had was instinct, and—forgetting its hunger for a brief moment—it succumbed to one such instinct. An instinct that was primal, unavoidable and as certain as the progression of spring into summer, autumn into winter. The urge became irresistible as the sun emerged fully from over the rooftop and cast the new day across the scene of carnage. With the light came another, more distant memory,

cluck

of lights and warmth and food and sleep; a distant image of a foggy past that ripened into a collage of stink and confinement and pain and—

Losing itself in the moment, memories were cast aside and the lost soul pointed its scarred and scaly face towards the sky. In the silence of the morning, the sound carried through the nearby house and woke the people there, as it had many times before. The echoing *cock-a-doodle-do* sounded somewhat hollow, and despondent, and uncertain.

In the house, a man was yanked from sleep by the noise. He'd heard the sound so many times before but he knew he shouldn't be hearing it now. He sat up, sleepy and confused. Perhaps he had imagined it? He looked at his wife, who was only barely able to throw him a hateful look before she rolled away back into the comfort of the large feather bed.

Cock-a-doodle-do! The sound continued, persistent, determined to call in the new day. The sound was stronger now, full of feigned conviction, like a man boasting his courage through terror and tears.

The farmer and his wife had no choice but to wake; the farmer's confusion kept him from sleep. He jumped from the bed, the wife's foul mood growing hotter as she was forced awake by his noise and activity. Inside the old farmhouse, though angry and argumentative, life began to stir.

Outside, the rooster continued to ponder the faint memories, as it wondered what had happened. It had a decent life at first, and a tail to be proud of, but that hadn't lasted long. There was a ribbon-flash, and things had changed. It remembered being unstoppably strong—omnipotent, and yet ... sad. Somehow it had found the Mouth. It had found itself before the gates of Hell, with no recollection of how it had gotten there. It hadn't understood what Hell had been. The poor creature was too simple-minded to grasp the simple fact that it had approached the gateway to the underworld, boldly entered against invitation, and had for some reason been turned away. It threw back its head and crowed again, oblivious of its own lifelessness, reveling in the light of the day.

Knapp

cluck

chapter 2   bird and boy and bastard

Long ago, before the incident at the mouth of Hell, in a small box of aluminum scabbed over with straw, lay a single, speckled egg. It lay in a crust of filth, kept warm beneath the downy belly of a large plump white bird. As nature dictated, the consistent warmth of the hen inspired, in time, a small crack to form in the dappled shell, as the infant chick within sought freedom. Chicken trapped within box, egg trapped under chicken, chick trapped within egg. It was an ignoble birthplace, but typical. Stacks of similar nests stretched away in each direction, three boxes high, each with a small opening in the front and a latched tin door in the rear. It was through this door that rough human hands collected the few items of which a chicken might feel pride: eggs for food, chicks for perpetuity. It was through this door that the ever-cycling population of enslaved fowl was either nurtured into existence, or, as sometimes happened, fried with bacon. They weren't slaves, exactly, but something worse: they were *domesticated*; beaten down and driven dumb by generations upon generations of unthinking servitude. The ones who were earmarked for breakfast were the lucky ones. Fortunately for chickens, they never saw it coming, having the relative awareness and attention span of a crack addict in a kaleidoscope factory.

The egg's eager fracture widened and a tiny beak appeared, followed by something wet and brown. The egg shifted itself under its mother as its inhabitant wiggled about. A few rows down, the clatter of a tin door catalyzed a wave of squawks and ruffled wings. The first hen, spooked by the noise, fluttered and screamed as if all Hell had broken loose, spurring its neighbor to do the same, and so on down the line. At the source, one hen protested loudly as she was lifted and then replaced. The door clanked shut. The birds calmed.

"Must be too early, I've got nothing ... *still*," a voice called down the row.

"Stop whining, you're almost done. We've got to check them all." The new voice was barely audible over the racket of wings and clucks, which filled the distance between the two men. Another door opened and closed. The brown spot of down pushed harder, the beak striking eagerly against the fragile bits of shell around the widening fissure. A flat, metallic clink indicated the opening of another door, and then another. And then there was light.

The chick's eyes were shut, but the tiny speck of barely formed brain matter knew that something spectacular had happened. A rush of air ran over the soggy down like oil across a surface of water. The light cut through the protection of tiny lids, sent synapses along miniscule optic nerves, and flooded the pinhead-mind with unbearable light.

"Figures! We've got one here, but it's wrong." The infant bird was lifted roughly. It was squeezed tight by mighty hands ten times its size, and buffeted cruelly by the mad flapping of its mother hen's wings.

"Wrong? How can it be wrong? If it's dead, chuck it. If not, bring it to the incubator." The words grew louder and were accompanied by footsteps. A second set of hands palmed the chick, held it up to the blinding light. "Looks fine to me."

"Except it's *brown*. This whole row is supposed to be *white*. I keep telling Doc that this free breeding stuff is a bad idea. Hell, these eggs should already be in the incubator. You leave 'em to hatch out on their own, and all we get is dead chicks, bad eggs and cross-breeding."

The world spun, lights shifting around the hatchling, confusing its limited newborn senses, which had yet to develop into limited adult senses.

"Yeah, yeah, but you know Doc. Hmm, definitely not a leghorn, but looks healthy. Big too. Already. Shit, we don't have any ostriches hanging around the place, do we?"

"Funny."

"Well, shit, look at the size of the thing. Must've been when Jim left the gate to the heavies open. Looks like a game bird. Cornish maybe. Crappy layers."

"Maybe its got enough leghorn in it to fix that. Anyway, might as well throw it in with the rest of the mutts."

"It should be in there already. All of 'em in the oven, hatching the natural way. Not out here shoved under these stupid chickens." His tone was that of frustration and contempt. It had been a long day of doing things in what he called "the hard way."

"Are you kidding? This is the natural way, stupid. You think wild chickens lay their eggs in incubators, do you?"

"Ain't no such thing as a wild chicken," came the retort. "And they should, 'cuz then I wouldn't have to grope their damn butts every day looking for eggs!" The two continued to bicker as they walked together to the end of the rows and through a heavy swinging door to the incubator room.

There the tiny life was placed into a warm and humid place, where it was cared for by a new set of hands, only slightly gentler than the first.

In the warmth of its new home, it slept and grew. Eventually, it opened its eyes and saw the world for the first time. Next to it, nestled in the soft pine shavings, was another—a hen—even tinier and more fragile, with the faintest nub of ruby-red under her beak. She was shaking, whether from the cold or from the shock of life, it could not tell. Chickens aren't much for thought, but this little chick was something special from the start, and it huddled against the shivering hen, offering its warmth to her.

As if protected by some invisible shield of luck, this small, noble bird grew larger, stronger, smarter than the rest. While other roosters were unceremoniously thinned from the flock, this little bird showed promise. At just six weeks, it had already grown a tail like a Phoenix, so dark that each feather radiated a different color—just a hint—before sinking into dull black. It was stout and beautiful. It was, thought the elderly farmer called Doc, good breeding stock. So, at the start of life, things were good. That is, if 'good' meant living in a cramped commercial coop, forced to live in your own feces, awaiting the inevitable eventuality of the soup pot.

Chickens had long ago lost any capability for organized thought. Decades of inbreeding for fat breasts and large eggs had taken its toll on the mind. This bird, however, did have a thought; paper thin and only partially coherent, but a thought just the same. Somehow, this rooster was able to know that life could be good. It played its part, and kept itself clean and fit. It protected the fair hen, its friend from birth, which had grown into a beautiful, fertile concubine. Together they produced eggs for the farmers, who came to view the pair as pets more than livestock, and who would bring them scraps from the table in silent gratitude for their worth.

cluck

Far away from the tiny rooster, in a small suburb of Detroit, another babe was born. A man child, fully sentient and anything but domestic. There was no shell, no rough hands, no rude violation of the mother. The delivery occurred at home, amid a pile of pillows and over-packed bags that were the result of a well planned but poorly executed trip to the hospital. A terrified almost-mother and a nervous almost-father crossed the thin line into actual parenthood with no casualties other than one cream-colored carpet, which had needed replacing anyway. Since that very first day of the child's life, he and his mommy and daddy all fared exceptionally well. The boy grew quickly and seemed both healthy and remarkably intelligent—he was able to drool and make nonsensical noises better than all the other infants and even a few of the toddlers. As he continued to grow and develop, the small house in the small suburb of Detroit was surrounded with nothing but happiness.

Time passed, and the blessings continued. The boy walked early, and was quick to potty train. He was a bright and fit young boy, who never spoke in baby talk but jumped straight from the nonsensical noises into complete, appropriate sentences.

His first words were, "Mom, I'm tired."

"Did you say something?" mother said to father, and then there was a commotion as they realized it was their son who had spoken. "Oh my lord, did little Arnie just say something?" They were so shocked, having expected something more along the lines of "purgle?" or "dat!" that they completely forgot to photograph the event.

Little Arnie rolled his little eyes. "I said I'm tired," he affirmed to the two stunned parents. "Can I take a nap?"

From that point on it was no surprise when Arnie learned to ride a bike—without training wheels—with just one try, or when he was reading before kindergarten. He would squirrel away behind the sofa with books he'd stolen from the bookshelf in the den, working secretly through the symbols until they became recognizable, and then organizable, and finally understandable. It didn't surprise his father when he asked to open a bank account, or complained that his first-grade teacher seemed a bit lazy, or when he asked his parents to please stop calling him "Arnie," because he really preferred "Arnold."

One accomplishment after another, Arnold continued to amaze, but rarely astonish, his parents. Everything went uncommonly well for several years. From the time of his birth—a brief if unplanned labor that lasted less than an hour—until well into his pre-teen years, the boy's parents had absolutely nothing to complain about. He was smart, and polite. A tiny gentleman. Everything was so easy with him it was almost unnatural.

Arnold had been named after his father's uncle, once-removed, who had been a doctor of medicine and quite successful in his time, although he didn't hold a candle to the brilliance of the boy. Arnold was a wiry, wily and strong boy from the moment he entered the world, and he seemed to be blessed with good fortune. Or something like that.

Another life, in yet another place, paced back and forth along the length of an old farm porch. Unlike the chick and the boy, this man had been born for quite some time already. His skin was leathery, as if the alligator skin of his elbows and knees had performed a *coup de grace* and usurped the soft skin on the rest of his body. He slouched a bit, and made a habit of running his hands through his thick hair.

The man's mind raced. That is, each thought came quickly upon the heels of another, although the thoughts themselves were thick and dull—mostly due to lack of exercise and a few too many beers. He paced along the rail because he was nervous. His mind was racing because he was trying to make sense of a complicated situation, while fighting off a nagging sensation that he was about to make a huge mistake.

cluck

Without breaking stride, he paced off the porch and out into the gravely dirt drive and turned to look back at the place. It was huge, bigger than he and Janice could ever need. Hell, they didn't even have kids. If they started right away, it would still take years to fill this place with enough brats to make it worth the trouble of upkeep. The windows leaked, as did the foundation, probably. It needed painting. A lot of painting, he thought, as he scanned the almost never ending expanse of clapboards.

The deal was damn good, though, he was sure of that. If he could put a business together here, he knew he'd be able to write off most of the meager mortgage, and almost all of the phenomenally high taxes. Thinking of taxes made him spit; Uncle Sam was taking almost as much as the bank on this place.

"What am I getting myself into, buying this stupid shit-hole of a house?" he asked no one in particular. A stiff breeze picked up, blowing sand into his eyes and forcing him to cover his face with his arms so that he didn't see the car pull up, although he could hear the crunch of the tires against the unpaved drive. He squinted, and saw the heavy door of a tan Caddy swing closed, revealing a pair of stubby legs in a stocky brown pantsuit. It housed a stern and ambitious looking woman, who was squinting at a bundle of papers.

"Bobby Ger ... Gerfun—

"Garfundephelt," the man said, wiping the sand out of his eyes as the breeze quieted as unexpectedly as it had arisen.

"Ah," she replied, resisting the urge to add a trite "Gesundheit." Tucking the mass of papers under one arm she extended a hand. "I'm Nancy, Boombard and Swallows Realty." She shook his hand and he could feel the greed through her skin. It suddenly occurred to him what was worrying him so much: it was the whole deal, everything was just too good to be true, too easy. This is not what buying a house is supposed to be like. This should be difficult and twisted, full of tricks and snares and red tape and never, ever, not in a million years should it be this simple.

"Nancy, nice to meet you," and then with a bluntness characteristic of Bobby, "so this is for real, huh? I mean, what's the catch?"

Shark-like real estate eyes flickered to the house, and to Bobby, and back to the house. She hefted a folder and produced a pen with the grace of a matador, preparing to spear another big, stupid bull.

"No catch. Honestly, I don't know why this place goes on the market so often. I mean, it's a bargain. Must be because it's just so big. Though I understand you're smarter than the rest and you're going to put this thing to some *real* use." She was referring to the obvious history of failed industries that the farm had seen in its past. Bobby, being a big stupid bull, caught the woman's saber of flattery full in the face. Mixing analogies like an amateur bartender mixes drinks, Bobby swallowed her words hook, line and sinker. "It is awful big ..." he finally managed.

"It contains, in all, some twenty acres. That is, well—no wait, here it says seventy. It seems to contradict itself on a few points, but nothing a quick survey can't sort out. The house itself is very big. A veritable castle!"

"Hmm. Castle. Dracula lived in a castle."

"Did he?"

"Yup."

"Well, I can assure you that this is just a house. There are no vampires here." She stifled a nervous laugh, determined to regain control. Stepping back, Nancy Boombard of Boombard and Swallows Realty made a show of examining the beauty of the property. As she hoped, Bobby's eyes followed hers, taking in the entirety of the estate. Having recovered the situation, she then steered the conversation back in the direction of a signed sales agreement and a fat commission. "It is spacious, certainly. Plenty of room for opportunity, in a house like this." Bobby hesitated.

cluck

" ... and there's this solid stone wall that surrounds it all." She added, hopefully. Bobby looked around, following the fieldstone wall until it disappeared from view.

"All the way around? Around all of it?" It was hard to believe that such a wall could exist.

"Yes, I think." There was an uncomfortably long pause. " ... and there are many, um, trees." Nancy finished feebly.

"Well, so there are. So there are. Trees, a wall, and ... what was the other thing?"

"Opportunity, Mr. Garfundephelt. Lots and lots of opportunity." Bobby's skepticism faded against the growing brilliance of his greed. It did have potential, this place. It had the potential to make him a heap of money with (and this is important) minimal effort.

More words were exchanged. Papers were signed, and the tan Caddy lumbered away, leaving Bobby alone, the proud owner of an impressive historic piece of farm property. It could have been the light of the fading day that made the house look, well ... *pleased*. The beginnings of a sunset reflected from the aged, leaded windows, making them glimmer like the eyes of a happy child. The sagging roof of the porch looked almost like a grin, which was ridiculous, as everybody knows that houses can't grin. Especially wide, wooden, shit-eating grins like this one.

Arnie never went to Hell. Nor did Bobby—at least not entirely. Neither saw the red-hot glow of damnation, never smelled the acrid burn of despair. The boy simply grew, finding his way through life as boys do. It was a normal life at first, and then less normal, and eventually it was anything but normal ... but it was still life. The Rooster, lacking the necessary essence to do the same, did the best it could and made a parallel journey through death. Of course, "death" is not necessarily accurate, as the Rooster was even less dead than it was alive. It was somewhere in between, stuck painfully between worlds like a nut caught in a zipper. It found itself picking its way through the afterlife, learning how to survive in a world that was built for the living. It settled into the world, learning to interact with solid things, to manipulate the physical world. It learned, with some effort, how to channel the infinite and uninhibited powers of the spectraverse into the more mundane land of the living. In short, it grew just as Arnold did, though its existence was never anything even close to normal.

Bobby Garfundephelt: there was nothing normal about him, either. His life had been ordinary enough for a little while, until the day that the Rooster crowed, waking both he and his wife unexpectedly—for it was his misfortune to be the owner of the very farm that a very special rooster called home. Thus the three began their slow spiral of convergence: the normal and the abnormal; the living and the dead; the good, the bad and the ugly.

While time is a fickle friend when life and death become interconnected, it could be said (in earthly terms) that things happen in a certain order. The Rooster, for example, was first alive, then something wonderful had happened to it, making it exceptional among its kind. In a cruel twist of fate, it then died, and then un-died. That is, it became un-dead and un-alive and generally un-happy. The boy, too, began as most do and grew as most do, although he maybe did it all a bit better. Until, just like the Rooster, something special happened that made him exceptional among his kind. It happened at about the same time, although unlike the poor Rooster the boy was spared the uncomfortable bit about being partially dead. Bobby ... well, Bobby had something special happen to him, too. Sorry sonofabitch.

cluck

chapter 3   one helluva flu

The vision first occurred to the young boy named Arnold when he was no more than ten-and-a-half years of age. He didn't have visions like the ESP-flashes of television detectives, or the feigned precognition of the crazy woman who loitered around the arcade. His sight simply evolved. It happened just after a fever had kept him from school for three entire days. It should be noted that Arnold's parents were not the type to coddle. Arnold had never needed coddling, being self-sufficient practically from birth. Even the worst flu would not gain him any pity nor mercy from the onslaught of chores that all parents seek to inflict upon their offspring, and his parents held extra comfort in the knowl-edge of their son's exceptional constitution. This particular illness, however, was different. It had oomph.

His mother, a kind and beautiful woman who looked much younger than she truly was, was running late after a restless night full of odd dreams. After waking well past six o'clock in a cold sweat, one particu-larly vivid dream stayed with her.

She was driving a truck down a long and featureless highway ... There was some sort of crash, and a blazingly bright vortex appeared out of nowhere, swirling and spitting. It was a storm of some sort, full of electricity and fear, and she was driving straight through it! Arnie was there, when he was still a young child who would tolerate the pet name. He was playing with a rubik's cube, belted next to her in the car. The wind was strong, and the windows in the car were down, and in a cacophony of events that only dreams can foster, Arnie was sucked from the passenger seat, swept away into the swirling wrath of air, leaving the intact seat-belt still fastened.

She woke cold and damp, breathing heavily, and looked nervously at the clock. There had been more: something about a duck ... and a plane crash ... and custard, but as her thoughts turned to the real world, the meager details of the dream faded. They were soon forgotten as she scrambled out of bed to prepare for the hectic day ahead.

She had no way of knowing there really had been a storm that night, of sorts. A mysterious, mystical storm.

"Arnie, you need to get up or you're going to be late for school," his mother called through his closed bedroom door as she hurried to get herself ready. The day was not much different from any other day, consisting of the unavoidable necessity of school, and a young boy's instinctual desire to sleep through it. The day wasn't about to change on her behalf, simply because she was running late. She called to Arnold again on her way back to the kitchen, and then again as she rushed past his room on her way to find her purse. There was no response from young Arnie. Not the first time, nor the second, nor the third.

After a brief moment filled with matronly concern, the door opened, and his dear mother entered, a little perturbed and a bit flustered. She watched him lie still, like death. It's a truly amazing thing how young boys can sleep and sleep and sleep ... "Arnie?" she called. He didn't stir. Not at all. She stepped closer. "Arnie? Did you hear me?"

cluck

"Mom ..." he whined, finally managing to twitch a little, yet barely disturbing his blankets. He stretched the simple word into several wavering syllables. He mumbled something else, which sounded like "Please don't call me Arnie."

"What?" His mother wasn't going to fall prey to the wiles of her son. Not so easily, anyway. It was spring, and she knew all too well about how boys grew tired of school well before the snow had fully melted. "You've got to get up, you'll be late for school."

"But I feel like—"

"Arnie—" she warned, sensing the word that was about to follow. He'd been picking up swear words at school. He'd been picking up bad habits in general lately. She knew she'd had it easy up until now, and he was over ten years old. It helped knowing that she'd had a solid decade of good behavior, while other mothers had gone through multiple hellish phases of development. She also knew that he would soon be eleven, then twelve, and then after that he would transform into a dreaded "teen." The occasional expletive wasn't much to worry about compared to sex, drugs and who knows what else, but she remained determined to stem them off, if possible.

"I feel like a turd," he finished lamely, with a bit of last-minute censorship. He rolled towards his mother. He looked sunken, and dark. His damp, pale gaze looked past the woman into the eyes of some invisible stranger as he pleaded with her, as if she were one foot to the left and behind where she was standing. Arnold always made a point of making his mother happy, and that usually meant respecting her desire for clean language, but he was in a mood.

"I mean, I really do feel like shit." He managed a grin and then slowly—as if with deliberate effort—he pulled his focus back to see her where she truly was. Only this time he looked down, ashamed. He'd been playing, swearing directly in the face of his mother, testing limits—a joke born of defiance and only let loose from his inhibitions by the fever—but he knew he was wrong. He did feel like shit, but now he felt even worse.

"Arnold—oh my God," she hurried closer and knelt down beside his bed, leaning over him, and only then, after she was motionless by his side for a moment, did he manage to fully align her with his stare.

"Arnold? Are you all right?"

Little Arnold stared at his mother. She looked weird. Well, not weird—she was a fairly typical-looking woman in her early forties. She stood about five foot four, with hair that sometimes looked blond but was really more of a sun-bleached brown. She had brown eyes, too. Even her complexion was earthy, making her look natural overall, though she was far from it. She had always scoffed at farming, especially disliking the smells that occasionally wafted through the small suburb from that "dirty remnant of a farm" that was just a few miles down the road. She didn't even tend a garden, and denied possessing any affinity or connection with the Earth, although she always gave the impression of being a nature-lover. It was what attracted his father to her; Arnold had heard the story many times of how his father had been drawn to her natural beauty, only to be trapped by the coy city slicker hiding within that shroud of earthly gauze.

His father was a bona-fide hippy. He had adapted to a middle-class life and a middle-management job, but he never really belonged anywhere near Detroit. He loved his wife and was happy to be by her side, no matter where they went. While he never complained, there was always an extra glow about him when he stood outside in the sunshine, breathing what little fresh air there was to breathe.

It was his mother who was glowing now. Not with any natural radiance, though. She was literarily glowing, with a very faint blue light. Arnold squinted, and the light formed misty halos, like when dry eyes stare at a streetlight in the rain. It was hard to focus on the refraction of his mother. The ghostly afterimage wavered around her. It was clearly

cluck

her, but it held a slightly different posture, a slightly more concerned expression. It was as if some amateur film-maker had been playing with double exposures, superimposing this ethereal-blue woman on top of the mother that he knew. The technique was imperfect, and her blue double jiggled haphazardly around her. Arnold continued to stare.

With some effort his eyes focused more clearly upon her, and then looked to her left, her right, behind her, searching for something. Arnold found the answer: the effect was not random at all. The blue-mother was simply preceding the real one, by just a few seconds, as she rushed to his side. Armed with this discovery, he was able to finally track his stare correctly, and he looked into his mother's worried eyes. "I don't know Mom. You look weird. Like you're ... glowing."

"Glowing?" she gasped, as if she had never heard anything more shocking and terrible in her long, good, god-fearing life. She stood back, and continued, more quietly and to herself, "Dear lord, he's delusional."

A flu could be overcome with pills and hot soups, and some fresh air and exercise, but Arnold's kindly mother knew nothing of how to deal with delirium, and so the boy was bound to bed, missing not one but three whole days of school. Like with all illness, the boy eventually began to feel better. His fever broke, and everything should have gone back to normal, but it was still three full days before she lifted her protective wing fully and let him return to school.

"He's delusional," she repeated, over the course of those three long days. "He says he can't see it anymore, but he's lying—I can tell. Look into his eyes," she whispered to his father when she thought that Arnold couldn't hear them. He could hear them, of course. Heck, they were right outside his room, after all. Did she really think he was so far gone that he couldn't even hear her? Each day the whispered conversations grew more frequent and more concerned, the words becoming a mantra of her worry. The sounds of his mother's muttering and pacing echoed about inside the small house. Not unsurprisingly, Arnold withdrew further. He would no longer look anyone in the eye, and was reluctant to speak. Was he going crazy? Maybe he was. He couldn't explain the glow, which was still there whenever he opened his eyes. Even though he no longer felt physically ill, he couldn't avoid the fact that he was still seeing things.

On the second day, he'd been rushed to the emergency room, where he stayed overnight. They took blood, performed x-rays and scans and ran tests of all sorts, but they couldn't find anything wrong with him. Other than being slightly dehydrated (no doubt a symptom of his recent bout of influenza) he was in perfect health. If he could really see the "glow" that he described, they felt it must be the result of some astigmatism or other ocular condition. An appointment was made for the following week with an optometrist, and it was expected that Arnold would be fitted for glasses. Until then, he would just have to deal with his "vision." When he returned home, however, he was sent to bed as if he were still sick. When he refused to stay still, he was repeatedly sent back to bed, under threat of being grounded.

"Mom," pleaded the boy, not for the first, nor last time. "I really don't feel that bad anymore. Maybe I could go to school later?" He was almost eleven, full of youth and vim and vinegar and life, and he was bored. Now that he knew he was healthy, excitement replaced ennui, and his confinement became harder to bear. His fear, caused by all the worry and fuss, had been replaced with relief. Wearing glasses would suck, but at least he wasn't "deranged." He wanted to revel in his sanity and to see his friends. If he had to wear glasses in a week, he wanted to relish every moment of his two-eyed life until then.

"No, you're not ready, not at all," was the reply, "you're obviously still sick, if you're telling me that you *want* to go to school."

"But I'm bored. Can Matt come over? After school I mean? Please?" His eyes turned as puppy-dog-pathetic as he could manage, but it was a hopeless effort. Rumor had gotten around to the parents of all

cluck

Arnold's friends that he was the victim of some horrible plague; they would never approve of a visit, even if Arnold's mother eventually gave in. Arnold was stuck with nothing at all to do. They didn't even have any good cable TV channels.

"Maybe I could go ride my bike later? My headache is looong gone," he said with extra flourish to indicate he hadn't had a headache for days. It was mostly true: it was getting much easier to deal with the dull, tired feeling behind his eyes—to the point where he barely noticed it anymore.

"You can't go riding your bike if there's something wrong with your eyes. You'll crash," she began, but quickly changed her track when she saw the disappointment on Arnold's face. "I'll tell you what. I'll call your friend Carl's mother. They're closer. Maybe we can have him bring by some more of your school work later—but he can't stay." It was a sorry excuse for a compromise. Arnold had effectively been trumped with the homework card ... he still hadn't finished the earlier batch of work, which his father picked up for him while he was in the hospital. Dejected, he returned to his room and closed his eyes against the light.

The next day, he was finally allowed back to school. Once Arnold returned to the humdrum of his public education, he quickly found that his classmates and teachers were illuminated with the same bizarre blue iridescence. A week later, he went for his eye exam with the specialist. Arnold saw the strange light surrounding the Optometrist, too, but he kept his mouth shut and read the letters as best he could. He did end up with some weak-powered glasses, but they didn't stop the strange lights and so he rarely wore them unless his mother was around. The mysterious light continued to precede everyone that he knew as if it were some sort of pre-shadow; a shadow of light, not darkness, that walked in front of people, and not behind. His father, who was rarely home, had a similar glow. As with his mother the first time the glow appeared, each of these subsequent spectral pre-flections moved slightly ahead of their real counterparts. It was almost as if Arnold was seeing a short moment into the future. He saw people's lips begin to move and, reading their ghostly lips, could see the words before they were spoken. The light only appeared around people, never around cars or chairs or trees, making everyone around him stand out brilliantly.

When the glasses failed to help him, some of the fear returned, but Arnold wasn't stupid, so he told no one. Around his parents he pretended to be cured. With concentration and practice, he was able to force himself to look at the solid form and not the lighter, spiritual form that it followed. Over time, he learned to suppress it and ignore it.

He didn't hide it perfectly, though. He honed the skill over time, but it was difficult. The newness and brightness of the effect was a distraction, drawing his attention. It was as if there was a buzzing fly, constantly at the edge of his vision. For months after returning to school he was constantly being accused of attention deficit. When he would look at people wrong, sometimes focusing on the glow, sometimes speaking towards an empty spot on the floor—knowing that his listener would move there—it was seen as some sort of reclusive behavioral problem. Sometimes, he would wave to a friend before they entered a room or clip a classmate as he stepped around the light only to collide with its source.

These occurrences grew less frequent with time, and with practice and patience on Arnold's part, but the damage was done. He developed a reputation at school because of it—a reputation he would never be able to fully shake free of.

Interestingly, though, he was rarely if ever ridiculed. There was a certain respect among his peers that surrounded his odd condition. It was as if he were some ancient oracle and not a ten-and-a-half year old boy at all. He was not an oracle; he was simply a child who perceived things differently, but to children of that age, it made him special. Special enough to become amazingly popular at school. Although his wandering gaze was definitely seen as strange, he learned to amaze the boys

cluck

with predictions of who would come out of the girls' bathroom next. He grew much more adept at athletics, as well, and a young boy is often judged most intently upon his sportsmanship.

At tryouts for little league football, his abilities had shone through enough to counteract his slightly soft upbringing. The faster people moved, the further ahead of them their spectral shadow would emanate. He was able to see where a pass was being thrown well before the ball was ever released, and no amount of careful planning or sophisticated play could stump him. As his prowess increased with exercise and experience, he grew formidable on the field. By the time he was thirteen, he had a different sort of reputation, and all the opposing school's teams knew him. After all, he denied them of victory after victory, game after game.

In short, Arnold got by. Things were okay. He had his health, his family and his friends. He learned to ignore the rest.

Knapp

cluck

chapter 4 something winged this way comes

Sometimes planets align and shape our destinies, sometimes moons. Groups of stars, joined into pictures of men and beasts by our active imaginations, predict our fate in the back sections of cheap tabloids as they move through the night sky. Perhaps it was an event of astrological significance such as this that called the ribbon flash from the heavens and sent it screaming across the world to change the lives of man, chicken and child. Maybe it was some stronger portent: not a mere constellation, but something built from entire galaxies, or perhaps even something more than galaxies. Whatever caused it to appear, the Inter-spectral Rift was a sudden and mysterious coincidence of celestial proportions. Though visually impressive—like a towering sheet of liquid glass, soft and supple, bending away into the sky as it shimmered across the land, reflecting the light of the sun like a circus mirror—it was noticed by few. The Rift first intersected with the Earth just outside the middle of nowhere, flashing out of the heavens with the spasmodic agility of a cornered rattlesnake. It was first seen near the western border of South Carolina, where it crashed steeply into the ground and then angled sideways along the dusty countryside. It wobbled, fighting itself as if forced against an opposing magnetic field, yet somehow holding fast as it changed course sharply, never slowing. From the deep south, it zigzagged rapidly up and across the American continent, taking only a few moments to travel from fields of cotton, to amber waves of grain, to neat rows of tasseled corn. It rippled like a giant glistening ribbon that was so thin it might only have occupied two dimensions, and would disappear entirely if viewed directly from its edge. It undulated fiercely, however, splaying its shimmering light in all directions as it sped across the planet. To the few who witnessed it, it appeared to be nothing more than a trick of the light; a brilliant flash of color, as if the Aurora Borealis had been ripped from the northern skies and planted within the earth. No one noticed it because, as brilliant as it was, it moved incredibly fast. It seared across state lines, moving rapidly and erratically but leaving no trace of its passage. It moved steadily northward, until it finally dwindled and dimmed into nothingness.

It hadn't drawn much attention, so there were few accounts with which to help track its course. Luckily, the exact path was unimportant, save for two points of special interest, both of which occurred near Detroit, Michigan: the first, in a small typical home in a small typical suburban neighborhood, where a young boy blinked away a sudden burst of light and was stricken with a mysterious yet enlightening flu; the second, a few dozen miles outside of the western edge of the city, along a nondescript section of highway that would shortly intersect that very same neighborhood. Neither place was special, other than to mark the only two points at which the mysterious light intersected with a living being.

cluck

A truck driver drove his rig eastward through the early morning mist, listening to an old radio that was turned down so low it was barely audible. He was a stout man, tanned on one side to an extreme and pale on the other (a hazard that all professional drivers face). He had dark black hair and narrow eyes, and was so evenly divided between light and dark tones that from one side he looked to be of Mexican decent, and from the other he resembled a Boston Italian. The hair on his head was thinner than that on his back—a fact that was evident due to his attire: a too-thin white collared shirt made of cotton, with no undershirt. He barreled down the interstate oblivious to many things: the speed limit; his own fatigue; the safety of other motorists; and the sudden flash of light—which was extremely bright but only lasted two-thousandths of a second—that washed over the extensive trailer of his rig, weaving around and between the cargo.

The truck carried poultry, and was headed east into the city, then south and then east again. The truck driver whistled along to the faint tunes on the radio, happy to be approaching the city early, while the traffic was thin. He'd set out even earlier, when most people were deep asleep and the roads belonged to truckers like him. The morning haze was also unusually thin—enough so that he was making good time; at this rate, he'd be through the city and approaching Toledo in time for lunch. He'd find a place to stop there and get something quick to eat, and if his luck held with the traffic, he'd be able to skirt Cleveland and be in Pittsburgh early enough to catch second shift at the Motel Ten. It was a small local place that he preferred, not because the rates were low but because the girl behind the counter would sometimes have a drink with him after her shift was over. Traffic was tricky in these parts, and if things turned wrong it could add hours to the drive. If that was the case he'd head straight east and bypass Pittsburgh altogether. If he was going to miss her anyway he might as well start trekking into the more secluded roads towards the eastern coast.

Knapp

The truck, a metallic color that lived somewhere between maroon and purple, was meticulous. Inside the cab things were sterile except for a single travel mug, which might have been used to benefit several branches of biomedical science. The upholstery was clean, although the springs were sunken and tired, forming a deep cup beneath the driver's munificent form. Outside, the truck's chassis glowed. It was washed and waxed far more frequently than the driver, and glistened from bumper to hitch, from which point back it turned steadily from gloss and gleam to varying degrees of dust and stink. The cab pulled two long trailers: one a commercial produce trailer, consisting of dozens of aluminum cages riveted in rows along a sturdy steel spine; the other a common flatbed, piled high with slotted wooden crates. Each cell, metal or wood, was stuffed with anywhere from a half dozen chicks to a full score of smaller birds, and with such a cargo it was impossible for anything downwind to hold a shine.

The sudden arrival of the shimmering Inter-spectral Rift flashed a million colors of prismatic light as it cut through the cargo and then jolted away—all in a matter of microseconds. Luckily, the Rift didn't dislodge any of the clucking and fluttering cargo: it left no indication of its presence on the trailer, or on the wooden crates, or even on the taut nylon straps that held it all in place. It did leave its mark on one small form, crammed into the topmost crate at the rear of the second trailer.

It was one crate of six, and it held one rooster of six. They were the elite: the finest half-dozen specimens of their kind, held separate and safe for transport. Each had been selected by the same men who previously nurtured one rooster so well that it actually developed a fondness for the approach of heavy boots, and the touch of warm, featherless hands. One of the six, however, held a very noticeably special rooster, which had just seen the light of eons flicker through its soul. It had no reason to suspect that anything had changed, though it was suddenly aware of an icy wind pushing its way through feather and down, chilling each of the captives to their very souls. Yes, even chickens, who are mindless and often senseless, have some sort of spirit to contain.

For the most part, the other birds were crammed together without luxury. They were livestock: nothing more, nothing less. They stretched away, row after row, front to rear, side to side. Below, the lower stacks grew more crowded still, dark and thick as the upper layers blotted out both light and fresh air. They cowed predictably to the Alpha Six, who were so obviously superior that even they, in their limited mental capacity, recognized their place. The one rooster, however, surpassed them all, in many ways. It was smart (for a chicken), and it was strong (for a chicken), and it was wise (for a chicken). It was a full-grown cock among yearlings, and therefore outweighed the others by a good deal, which would have been enough to satisfy the normal rituals of Leadership Through Dominance, though in this case there had been no struggle at all. For one thing, each of the roosters were held apart, each in its own crate, with no hope of one attacking another. For another, the one rooster had an aura of kindness about it. Yes, kindness. It was just as proud as any rooster could be, and just as cocky, and just as capable of tearing out the eyes of a challenger, if it were to come to that. It did not. Five of the Six bowed in subservience, letting the One rule benevolently and with care. The others should have wanted its throat as a matter of Darwinian obligation, but the truth was that they liked their leader. The largest of the six prize roosters, which had been so carefully packed—best of the flock—side by side atop endless rows of crowded, filthy boxes had that one quality that so many other chickens lacked: it was *likable*. It was obviously the leader among leaders, and none dared or cared to challenge it (although they remained cautious and alert, regardless).

When the light cut neatly through their master, they watched with some compassion, and less comprehension. A barely noticeable spark of starlight divided their master with a curtain of light before flashing away into infinity. Though it looked like the brilliant cut of a knife, the bird remained fully intact, though it shook and fell, blinking against the magnificence of the Rift. It quickly staggered to its feet again, trying to maintain poise as it shook again, violently, as if struck with a sudden chill. Soon things returned to normal: the Five, being chickens (and roosters, at that), quickly forgot the incident. The One raised its head, shaking its proud beak at the rest, wobbling its high, bright comb at them.

"Do not fear," it said to them, "I am not hurt." It shook first one leg, then the other, and then stretched its impressive wings to their full span, and gave them a flutter. The bird's five brothers tilted their heads in unison, pointing one eye suspiciously towards the spectacle of a talking chicken. One hopped back and forth, from one talon to the other, agitated. Another knocked its beak against the wooden slats of its cage. From below, the lesser birds—hens and cocks alike, which had been stuffed together in groups of ten, without mercy, into even smaller cages—peered up stupidly.

"What are you all looking at?" the one rooster asked of them. "I've done my best, and have always been kind to you, and now you look at me as if I am a newborn chick, worthy of suspicion and scorn." It stood as tall as it could while it spoke, pushing its breast so far forward that the feathers of its chest splayed outwards. It searched the masses below for a sign of its love, Helena (*Helena? Was that her name?* It did not remember any chicken ever having a name before, not having even been aware of the concept of nomenclature, but the name Helena came to mind when thinking of its true love). It wore a dark suit made of shimmering feathers, and had a gamey appearance, as if it shared ancestry with wild pheasants and fowl (which it did, to a degree). It had a comb and wattle so red and grand that they perfectly framed the long, powerful beak and bright, clear eyes. The five subordinates, in contrast, were only a few months old and were noticeably shorter and weaker, with stubby beaks and dull peacombs. It, however, was unique and grand, and it wanted desperately to

cluck

find its dear Helena, who was raised by its side since the hatchery, and who had a coat of downy pearls.

"Has anyone seen Helena?" It asked. "You would remember her, I'm sure. She is well built, though petite, and has such opalescent plumage! Her beak and wattle are both crimson red, and luscious, and her crop stays flat even when she is full of grain. If anyone has seen her, please tell me." The nervousness in the nearby crates increased, but there was no reply. The rooster pondered this, scratching at the sides of its cage as it did so. Eventually, another rooster ventured close, peering through the double-layer of chicken wire that separated them.

"You can speak?" the frightened rooster asked (in Chicken, which consisted of scratching at the ground in a confused manner while shaking its wattle). *"Interesting,"* it would have thought, if any other chicken besides the one special rooster was capable of organized thought. Instead, it trembled a bit, and hurriedly backed away again.

"Of course I can!" It was obvious that it could talk, all chickens could talk—and then, suddenly, the newborn awareness, which had been placed into the unsuspecting rooster by a thin ribbon of celestial power, grew. *I am the only one that can speak,* it suddenly knew. *I am the only one that can think,* which was true. Though benevolent and kind, it was still a rooster, and so its new intellect quickly reached another conclusion: *I am the only one that can rule.* The newly appointed King of Roosters looked around, surveying itself and its surroundings. The King noticed many things: it noticed that it was noticing things, which was an accomplishment for a brain the size of a garbanzo bean; it noticed that it was even bigger and stronger than it remembered; it noticed that things seemed to be glowing brilliantly, although being a chicken and therefore not very good with colors, it couldn't tell that things were glowing blue. It noticed that the sharp chill flash of light that occupied its soul just an instant before was fading, like the glow of a red-hot iron as it is removed from the heat. The Rooster also noticed that it was growing—rapidly, although at a slowing pace that corresponded with the ebb of the lingering soul-fire. Finally, it noticed that it was very angry, and frightened, and perhaps more importantly that it was aware of being angry and frightened.

The most immediate thought to form in the Rooster's new intellect was: *We are trapped.* It, and its kin, were in cages. In many cases, they were packed into cages that weren't fit to lay an egg in. There was a terrible wind that, upon reflection, seemed to move opposite of their direction of travel. A sudden awareness of physics confirmed that they were traveling at high speed, in cages, attached to some unknown beast of burden. The conditions were savage at best, and—by the smell of fumes and the unnatural texture of things—they were man made. The King was growing larger, too, and was at risk of filling its entire cage, but it managed to turn and twist enough to look down, and back, and to the sides; a sea of chickens were being scratched and battered as they fell against each other, but there was no sign of Helena. As all roosters are wont to do, it turned its attention inward, to itself: it was still growing, and it was strong—stronger even than before. A new thought formed: *escape.* Their prisons were tethered by thin straps, stretched tight across the tops of the crates, and the King bit into them, where it could reach through the wire, striking hard with its sharp—*it had never been this sharp before!*—beak.

Looking around, the King noticed they were rushing past an area of wide fields dotted with a number of high, painted man-coops. It was the outskirts of a distant suburb. Grass turned quickly into thick areas of brush and small copses of evergreens. In the distance—and approaching fast due to the speed of the truck—a denser neighborhood appeared on one side of the highway, and what looked like a strip mall appeared on the other.[2]   Further ahead still, the glassy spires of distant skyscrapers could be seen. "There are fields all around us, full of food, if we hurry," the King said, attempting to put the other birds at ease while it formulated a plan for freedom. The others looked at him with stupid indifference

"Now," the King urged, fearing the worst, "I will free you!" They reacted only with cautious indifference. How dull they were, compared to the shining splendor of the Rooster King, but they were its subjects, and so it would fight for them. That is what roosters do! The beak tore away the nylon strap, and it soon began to fray, and then split, until it finally snapped. The King looked up in what was meant to be a pose of triumph, but it had grown even more in the past minutes, and was now forced to crouch within its confines, its long black neck pushed backwards and down. When the restraint was removed, the crates began to rock and bounce with the turbulence of the road, and the King began to feel afraid again. *Suppress fear,* it thought, *you are the King!* Willful courage, however, did not account for the poor quality of midwestern highways, nor did it expect to see the crate by its side, which contained one of the King's elite brothers, topple over the side of the truck. There was a loud crash that was quickly carried backwards and away into silence, drowned by the rush of wind and the sounds of the road. It was gone.

The truck driver hummed to himself as the truck continued on its way towards the city. There was a good deal more noise and commotion than normal among the cargo, and a few more feathers than usual were caught up in the rushing wind. The topmost crates, near the rear of the trailer, began to bounce around, but he didn't notice—not even when a resonating "cock-a-doodle—" was cut suddenly short as the recently

---

[2] The Rooster wasn't sure what a strip mall was, but it had a sudden craving for pizza, bargain shoes, some fried rice, a karate lesson, a new pair of seat pants—in that order.

freed rooster, a prize bird, fell over the top of a roadside fence and rolled, broken, into oblivion.

The driver, whistling now, noticed just in time that he had missed the exit for a mandatory weigh station. Checking his rear view mirrors for policeman's blues, he failed to notice the distant spray of feathers and a bloody wing, barely visible in the breakdown lane. He stopped whistling and craned his short neck to make absolutely certain he hadn't been seen and failed to notice the rather spectacular cloud of feathers diminishing into the distance. There were no cops, so he turned his attention (if you can call it that) back to the road before him and started to whistle again.

"Steady, my brothers, steady!" the King commanded, barely keeping its composure. "If you jostle now, you'll fall over too!" To itself the Rooster wondered, *what have I done?* Thinking that perhaps the power of intellect, being so new, should be treated with less haste, the Rooster tried to relax. The box was getting smaller, or rather the Rooster was getting bigger. Its head was pressed into a corner now. Rotating its beady eyes upward, it could see its own beautiful comb, pushed against the thin octagonal holes of the wire, a thin trickle spreading along the filament. It tried to move its legs, and managed to wriggle into a slightly more comfortable position, its head pointed nearly straight down—and there she was, barely visible through the throng, several rows directly below: Helena! Just as suddenly, she was gone again, hidden by the poultry horde as they milled about.

"Helena!" He called, but she did not answer. Like most of the others, she didn't know how to, or even care. She and the other hens scratched at the open wire at their feet, as if the instinct might raise up a tasty worm or grub. They seemed barely aware of the world around them, and were oblivious to their King's pleas. He wriggled again, staring through the pack of filth and feathers, joyful of those brief moments when a space opened through the trapped bodies to show another

cluck

glimpse of his love. He barely even noticed that his growth was slowing (and a good thing, too, for there wasn't a free space left). Reflecting on its condition, the Rooster wondered what had happened. It remembered a happy chick-hood, for the most part (though its memories, at least those prior to the ribbon-flash, were cloudy). When it did try to remember, thoughts like *warmth* and *food* and *shelter* surfaced, giving the overall impression of happiness. And there was a man, a warm pink hand that had sheltered it since it first poked its wet downy head through the sharp broken shell of its incubation. There were also boots, which carried food, and even a stubbly face that would occasionally look deeply into the refuge of the coop, checking for signs of disrepair—housekeeping, if you will. Occasionally the face would peer intently at each bird in turn, checking for disease, and there were hands to give aid when there was need. And then without warning the warmth and shelter and food were gone, replaced by hard crates and biting wire and the endless wind and rumbling of the road.

Resigned, barely able to point its beak enough to crow, the sound of the rooster's sad cry echoed against the turbulent wind of the speeding semi. It was a resonating cry that carried the weight of both passion and perception. It could be heard for miles by anyone who cared to listen, which of course nobody did, and the driver, whistling, didn't even notice.

Knapp

cluck

chapter 5   Three boys and a corpse

Matthew Bilks, Nate Young, and Carl Hoss climbed the dusty burm that separated their small suburban neighborhood from the danger and noise of highway traffic. It was a climb that had been made by the trio nearly every day for the past two years—at least during summer, when school was a forgotten torment and the days, long and hot, found three adventuresome boys outside with energy to burn. They were adolescents, aged fourteen, fourteen and fifteen, respectively. They were good enough boys, which kept the labels like "punk," "hoodlum" or "hooligan" from sticking, although they all applied to a degree. They were boys. They were teenagers. They had dreams and they had drive—a combination of traits that had afflicted them around the same time that they had developed hormones, and subsequently earned them the courage needed to cross four lanes of speeding traffic. It was a necessary risk if they wished to escape the relative protection of their parents, and of their sheltered *cul-de-sac* neighborhood.

Their goal was simple—the back lot of their town's lame excuse for a mall. It was just a rundown collection of pizza, Chinese food, mega-discount shoe and "fashion" stores, and one of those athletic supply stores that didn't actually sell any sports equipment or paraphernalia, but was a great place to browse for oversized sweats and team-branded hood-ies. There was a Kung Fu studio that had been out of business for about six thousand years, though the neon sign in the window still shouted "OPEN!" to anyone passing by (and causing its share of local gossip around who might be paying the electric bill), and a small storefront that was usually either the campaign headquarters for some local electorate wannabe, or a seasonal purveyor of Christmas gaud, made-to-order teddy bears or Halloween costumes. The best among them (at least to a teen) was the pizza parlor, with its retro decor, square pizza and questionable health certifications. There wasn't even an arcade. There was a huge back lot, though, separated from civilization by the cluttered back-rooms of retail hell on one side and by the speeding highway on the other. It was the perfect place to hang out, spit, tell jokes about girls' tits, and all the things that make a young boy's day go by. Where the front of the place was full of activity and brightly lit signs, the back was desolate and dark and held only unmarked doors and several collections of large green dumpsters.

Today, the game was supposed to be dodge ball, but as there was no ball, they played with small bits of broken tar from the edge of the lot. After a few hard hits, which stung like hell and left nasty welts, the game evolved into a chase, and the three youngsters raced up and down the length of the lot, leaping over speed bumps without pause, glad they were boys and not cars—glad there was nothing in the world that could slow them down, until finally they crashed side by side, hands outstretched, into the green dumpster in the far corner of the lot. Nate and Matt were in the lead, and Carl (who was less athletic than his friends) followed at

cluck

his own leisurely pace. It was he who noticed the box, as the others fought to catch their breath beside the dumpster.

"Look at that—Nike." He observed, pointing the shoe-box out to the others. For some reason it stood out from the rest of the litter. For a start it was mostly clean and looked new, and the logo showed clearly that it was intended to contain Nike shoes. It lay a bit apart from the trash, partially squashed beneath a box, built of wooden slats and chicken wire. It was soggy at the bottom, so that the proud swooping logo of the sneaker seemed to rise from the damp cardboard. Beneath the wooden crate and the half-crushed shoe-box was a puddle, although the parking lot—and the day itself—was dry as a bone. There was something distinctly ominous about it, but to a teen the only immediate observation was that of the box and the label, and the deduction that a salvageable pair of Nikes might be had for free.

"What is it, Carl?" Nate asked, probing the situation nervously, not noticing the box and still regaining his breath from the sprint. Carl pointed again to the wet prize. Fascination forced them forward, to discover what was in that box, but something else held them back. A chill hung in the air, sudden, foreboding. The boys, despite the brightness of daylight, felt as if they were standing in a mist. Nate shuddered as if against a cold wind. Matt rubbed his hands together against a nonexistent cold. All three boys were held frozen, their youthful, adventurous (and greedy) spirits held in check by inexplicable fear and repulsion. Stepping closer, Carl—who was older and a bit braver—peered into the dark space between the slats. At once the cold damp feeling left them as a waft of hot air washed across the back corner of the lot, choking the two boys who were panting, and causing Carl to step back and cover his nose.

"It smells like—holy shit!" Nate used the curse to carefully stifle a retch. He kept his lunch down, turning away and swallowing hard. Whatever was in that crate smelled dead. Long dead.

Knapp

"You're both pansies. For chrissake, I'll do it," said the third of the friends, moving in boldly and kicking the soggy shoe-box out into the open, freeing it from beneath the weight of the crate. The crate, no longer held aloft, tipped forward. With a squelch the small box tumbled clear of the puddle, spilling a new (but squishy) pair of sneakers onto the pavement, but the prize was upstaged by the crate as it continued to topple. The wooden crate tipped over, and a hinged lid—barely held in place by a few twisted staples—fell free. From within, something rancid dribbled onto the pavement, and a decayed mess flopped outwards, being held for a moment in the delicate balance between gravity and the lingering strength of a few tormented sinews. Moving in quickly to kick the lid free had been a good move. It gave Matt enough momentum that his last-second cowardice couldn't stop him, and he was able to save face in front of his friends. For a moment. Shortly after the carcass had been revealed, Matt heaved and a lunch of bologna sandwiches boiled forth onto the ground.

"Hey *Ralph*," the others mocked, "did you buy a *Buick*?" The words were exaggerated to mimic the sounds of retching. Two of the three giggled, but the third, Matt, was too busy trying to spit the taste of bile out of his mouth.

"Shit, I caught a load of that stink, is all."

"You are a load of stink, Matt," Nate added.

"A butt-load," appended Carl.

"What in the heck is a dead … *thing* doing behind the mall?" Nate finally asked. "And on top of those shoes, too!" he added, as if whatever the corpse had been had no right to decompose all over *his* sneakers. Matt was fishing in his pockets for some gum, but found none. "The hell do I know?" he muttered angrily. Trying to regain his status as a bad-ass pre-teen, he tested the air gingerly and approached again. He prodded the box with his foot.

Squelch, Squelch, went the box.

cluck

"Don't get any of that crap on you, Matt. Your mom has a nose like a bloodhound. She'll kick your ass if you come home smelling like that."

"I can handle my mom, thanks." He finally found the gum and stuffed piece after piece into his mouth until it was gone. He considered putting a piece in his nose as well, but thought better of it in the end.

"Yeah, but we gotta deal with her too."

"She'll call both our parents just to know she's still the biggest bitch in the world," Nate predicted. He was right too, she would call their parents, and she was a bitch. Even Matt knew this. She had taken many similar opportunities in the past to make the boys suffer. It seemed as if she had nothing else to do than to spy and sneak on them, to find fault in something (innocent or otherwise) and then overreact with some loud and rash punishment. It had gotten to the point where it was almost funny, and she had become a legendary character within the group's various jokes and stories. In their adolescent minds she represented everything fat, mean and terrible. They had names for her like "ogre" and "porkenstein."

"She sure is a bitch, isn't she? But you two don't have to live with her." There was a general nod of consensus. The hardship that Matt had to endure by being the son of the ogre was much sympathized, and had elevated him within the group. "I mean, she'd be okay if she wasn't so completely goddamned crazy." They laughed, as they often did, at her expense. They didn't consider that they were often getting themselves into trouble of some sort or another, and usually deserved their punishments. In truth, Matt's mother was as likable and caring as any other parent—she was just perhaps a bit smarter.

"How'd she get like that?" Nate ventured. Hatched from an egg, he thought, or found pale and slimy under some rock.

"Born crazy. I don't know." Carl punched him squarely in the shoulder. "Bet it's hereditary," he teased.

"Shut up, ass-face!" Matt rubbed his shoulder and made indications that he was going to return the blow, only harder, when he stopped suddenly as the decaying mass rolled further out of the crate and pressed against the side of his foot. Matt froze, concentrating on the flavor of mint.

Squelch—

The thing oozed further, spreading towards him, causing him to step back. "You're calling me an ass-face? You're the one with Chicken Dead-Nuggets all over his feet. Fuck nut. Why don't you stop kicking that thing around so we can get outta here?" As often happens with youth, some small intangible thing turned playful banter around and pushed it softly across some invisible but ever-present line. Matt's face turned red. He spit again. He balled his fists.

"Shut up! It's moving on its own. I'm not doing it!" the significance of the words were drowned out by the other boy—Nate Bilks—who wondered loudly whether it was the remains of a dog or maybe a sheep. "That's a farm crate," he said, ignoring the brewing fight between Matt and Carl. "They ship farm animals in boxes like that. It's pretty big—maybe it's a sheep ..." but he didn't believe it entirely. It looked familiar, but not like a sheep. There seemed to be a wing, crooked and with what looked less like hair and more like crusted feathers.

Squelch—

This time Matt's foot was nowhere close, and the others finally stopped and took notice. The carcass—for it was definitely the rotted remains of some animal or bird—had rolled again, contrary to gravity, towards Matt. The wet eery noise it made as it heaved itself towards him was more evident now that the boys' bickering had ceased. It was the sound of a boot sucking out of deep mud, followed by a soft hiss and gurgle. They stood still and quiet, staring at it. Waiting for it to move again. Waiting for the *squelch*. A wing was clearly visible now. "An

cluck

ostrich," Nate decided. "It must be an ostrich. It's as big as a sheep, but it's got wings."

No one paid any attention to Nate as they fixed their attention on the corpse, waiting for it to roll forward again. Waiting for the sucking sound of mud and decay. After an awkward moment of staring slack-jawed and afraid, Matt's unrelenting foot prodded one final time. The movement and sound that followed was nothing like before. Instead of a lazy, wet, flopping roll the thing hunched up, as if it were alive and suddenly on guard. In place of the soft, wet sound, there was a loud and crisp noise that filled the back lot like a scream. It was at once familiar and yet entirely out of place. The three, as if they were one, jumped back and then froze again.

"Was that a rooster crowing or have I gone fucking crazy?" Carl asked. Whatever spasm had moved the thing relaxed, and it slumped back into inanimacy.

"I thought it was ... maybe there's another ostrich around here somewhere. Wherever this one came from ... maybe there are more. Maybe they miss the ol' bird!"

"Maybe it's Matt's mom." It wasn't a funny joke, nor a tasteful one, but to the teens it was solid gold standup material. The joke also demystified the grotesque oddity before them, removing the uncomfortable trace of what they all feared—that the thing was somehow *not* a corpse, that it was still alive somehow. Like Nate said, it was nothing more than a big ostrich or an emu or something, probably fallen from one of the big livestock trucks that raced up and down the highway on a regular basis. It looked enough like normal chicken meat found behind a deli counter, only full of dirt and rot, that there was nothing left to be afraid of. It wasn't moving, other than to ooze forth from its overturned cage as anything in its condition of decay might. Far from being frightening, it was suddenly hilarious, and they laughed. Their laughter was awkward, but loud enough to mask the sound of footsteps, so that when another boy spoke from behind them they all jumped.

"Step back," Arnold said. The words were not a command, but they were uttered with such irrefutable confidence that after the initial surprise of Arnold's presence was past, they each obeyed. Matt, Nate and Carl stepped back, their eyes darting now between Arnold and their pitiful plaything. Matt's eyes also darted to the original prize: a dirty pair of Nikes just on the other side of the fetid pile.

"Hey Arn, look what we found, it's—

"Back further. Don't you see it?" Arnold looked strange. Scared? Confused? It was hard to tell, but there was an inner struggle within this boy that no soul of such a young age should ever be forced to experience. Matt and the others couldn't understand what was going on: the events so far were odd enough, and now Arnold had appeared, acting heroic and brave as if the jellied remains were some monstrous enemy that had risen before them. To them, who had so recently passed through their own initial fears, Arnold's serious tone struck them as being ridiculous and misplaced.

"What's the matter Arn?" Matt's words went unanswered as Arnold leapt forward and put a hand on Matt's shoulder. He pulled the older and larger boy back. "Don't be stupid, I said get back!"

Monstrous. Enemy. These words, though unspoken, were true ... at least to Arnold. Where the others saw and smelled nothing more than moldy meat, Arnold saw a huge and terrifying creature stand up from the puddle of death. He had trained himself not to see with his other sight, but he could not ignore this angry coalescence of blue. He pulled Matt back from it as quickly as he could, retreating as it shook its large, powerful and iridescent wings. A long serpentine neck rose from its midst, crowned with a ghastly comb and pointed into a large, sharp beak. Having risen to its full height, Arnold could see it more clearly than ever. It was not an ostrich, as Nate had suggested, but a rooster. A rooster

cluck

larger than any that stood before it, tall and strong and bright and wild. A magnificently plumed bird, with a broad breast and a pendulous, full crop. It scratched the ground, bobbing its head about, as if trying to gain its bearings in the world after a long deep sleep. Arnold pushed Matt back further and stepped backwards himself, not daring to turn away.

"Listen, I'm gonna kick your ass, Arnold." It wasn't a threat; it was just the way things had to be, between boys. Matt's arm cocked back, his juvenile hand bunched into a fist. Arnold still had his hand on Matt's shoulder, and he used it to turn him around, so that instead of getting punched by Matt, his friend could see. In the middle of the pavement, the chicken squelched once more, moving further from the upturned crate and the pair of near-forgotten Nikes. A limp neck, unnaturally long, was exposed. A broken eggshell of a skull topped it, a cracked beak and two lifeless black pits for eyes were exposed. Everyone was watching as it moved again, and then turned. A wet, rubbery spasm rippled up the thing's neck. It looked up at them. Matt stood frozen, and then slowly lowered his hand, relaxing his fist.

Squelch—

Matt had already thrown up once, and he nearly repeated himself. Teenage boys possess amazing amounts of bravery and cowardice, wrapped together in a pubescent free-for-all, fighting for survival. Arnold had started to rekindle uneasy feelings, tipping them again towards fright. For now, their internal adolescent battle un-won, they all remained still. All except Arnold. Arnold looked forward towards the beast, towards the angry blue aura. He did not hesitate, but strode forward. Kneeling before it, drawing closer than the others had dared, Arnold earned the temporary respect of his peers. His hand slid on the vomit as he leaned even closer, and whispered, "Your time is over. Go ..." he searched for the words, "Go home. Go away."

The bird turned towards him and stared at him resolutely. It nodded, and relaxed, and Arnold leaned back again. His relief, premature, was short lived. First swelling, as if with the intake of breath, the thing grew huge, and then in a long putrid sigh it deflated, shrinking with the acrid hiss of expelled gases. The chicken, now flopping about in its newly deflated sack of rotting skin, hobbled forward as it began to draw power into itself. Where the others saw black pits, Arnold saw red eyes of fire, growing hotter with newly summoned abhorrence. It leapt. The shrieks of Matt, Nate and Carl were a reminder that within every little boy there was something of a little girl. The sound could have shattered glass.

Arnold ducked and rolled, just as the fluttering mass of wet and sticky feathers bore down on him, and he caught it neatly by its neck. It struggled, wriggling in an entirely unnatural way.

"Why are you fighting it, Arn? I think it's already dead—" Nate cried, but somehow Arnold knew otherwise, and he twisted his hands, and twisted again. There was eventually a snap, and the bird succumbed to an overdue death in his grip. A cold gust of air escaped from the wet lump of the corpse as it hung limp in his hands. Startled by the chill, he dropped the empty shell and shook the vomit and decay from his hands. Turning back to his friends, he saw the ebbs and currents of the unnatural breeze flow towards them.

"Do you see that?" Arnold asked, but the others, his classmates and his friends, were looking at him with shock. They hadn't seen anything, thought nothing of the slight wind that rose up around them.

"Who are you?" Arnold demanded, loudly. He was speaking past his friends, into empty air, frightening them even more. "Where are you?"

Dried leaves and dust danced about, mocking him. Matt shivered and began to back away, the movement drawing Arnold's attention to him.

Stupid boy ... think! No, don't think, look. Look with your eyes, and look beyond your eyes. Don't suppress it, but see—and no sooner had Arnold torn down the wall of his true sight than he saw what he was look-

cluck

ing for. From near Matt's right sneaker emanated the eerie blue glow of
the unwanted soul. It swirled in and amongst itself, like a constantly
imploding cloud of sin. He stepped forward cautiously as it pulsated
with anger. "Matt, hold still—

"What the fuck, man? Don't come near me!" Nate was gone, and
Carl was edging further back. It was a showdown between Arnold and
Matt; Arnold trying to calmly approach, and Matt jerking away like a
frightened woodcock. "I said FUCK OFF!" Matt yelped, and the fists
came up again.

"Listen, Matt, I'm not going to hurt you but you need to stay still ...
it's right behind you—" and he lunged past Matt to one side, grabbing at
the empty air. He didn't have the time to explain himself before rushing
to the aide of his friend. Matt, being not just a bully but a terrified bully,
reacted accordingly. Mistaking the lunge as an attack on himself, he re-
taliated; the boy's shoe caught Arnold right in the gut, doubling him
over and sending him tumbling back in the opposite direction. It should
have ended there, but to everyone's surprise, Arnold kept moving. He
was sent skidding across the pavement in an unnatural, exaggerated slide.
He was thrown back almost to the edge of the grassy incline, nearly
twenty-five feet away. He rolled, and skidded, and bounced like he was
the victim of some poorly directed martial arts flick. He was thrown
back with such force that a thin trail of blood lingered in the air for a
moment, marking Arnold's path, before it spattered to the earth. It was
as if Matt's worn sneaker had been a mighty dagger, cutting Arnold and
throwing him back in one awful, deadly strike. Matt stared slack-jawed
with awe at his foot as if it were possessed by some godlike force. From
somewhere above them, a single feather fluttered down, circling within
eddies and currents of soft summer air.

"Shit ..." Matt was otherwise speechless. His right foot was covered
in blood, and there was something stuck to the front of his laces. Somehow, *he* had done this to his friend. His creepy friend, sure, but he hadn't

intended to hurt him. Not badly, anyway. He looked up from his feet, following the wandering red line with his eyes until his gaze came to rest on Arnold, who was writhing on the ground, screaming. Did he really do that? Man, he was going to be in real trouble. He followed the descent of the drifting feather as it lazily settled to the hot tar. He looked back at his sneaker, reddened with Arnold's blood, at the thing stuck to his foot. It was a feather too. A bloody, sticky, dirty feather.

"Shit!" Matt said, again, though it was more of an exclamation this time, as Matt was shaken from contemplation by Arnold's scream. Arnold continued to writhe upon the ground, jerking about as if being pulled and thrown by some invisible monster, and there was more blood. A lot more. Something was cutting Arnold still, over and over, spattering the parking lot with droplets of red. Blood speckled his face and his forearms, small gashes opening here and there as he continued his struggle with emptiness. Arnold could see it, of course. It was wrapped in blue light, shining bright against the dim light of the living. It was the rooster, determined to resist its exile from life. The thing was massive; the size of a dog, even larger than its rotten corporeal form had seemed. It pecked and kicked out at him as he fought to control it. The pain was unbearable, too much for Arnold's fragile and untrained mind, but he was able to strike at it one last time before he slipped away into darkness. The battle ended in Arnold's favor, his final blow being enough, finally, to kill the one that was already dead. The mighty bird vanished, leaving Arnold victorious and unconscious, close to death.

Arnold didn't go back to school for a whole week. Matt still felt bad, thinking he had been the one who hurt his friend. He had kicked him, but—hell, they'¹ known each other for years, grown up together even. He never meant to hurt him. Not like that. Even worse: Matt had visited Arnold in the hospital, and later at home, and there was something different about him. Something had happened that nobody but Arnold could understand, and it had changed everything.

cluck

Needless to say, all the boys were grounded. They'd been forced to call the police, and as Arnold was rushed off to the hospital the others were left to come up with a semi-plausible story for their parents and for the cops. Sure ... a dead chicken in a box they would believe. It was still there, after all. But the rest? Matt kicking a kid his size across the parking lot like some super-samurai video game warrior? Arnold rolling around and thrashing while new wounds continued to appear out of nowhere? Right. There was only one thing to do, and that was to lie. Being teenage boys, they lied badly, but it was enough. They made sure to visit Arnold when they were allowed, so they could tell him their fable. He would need to corroborate the story if he was questioned, but by the time they got there, the questioning had been long over. Luckily, Arnold had lied too, and had kept the details sufficiently vague, so his story didn't entirely discredit theirs.

What he said was this: He had been standing with his back to the highway, talking to his friends, when he saw their faces and one of them—Nate, he thought—screamed. The next thing he knew, he was on the ground, and there was pain. He didn't know anything else, he told them. He guessed maybe he'd been mugged, but he wasn't sure.

But he did know. He was the only one who did know. He could still see the huge rooster in his mind.

He stared off into the distance and his mind was full of the creature; an almost prehistoric looking bird that was built of power and hate. He looked straight past his friends as they stood there beside him, and wondered if maybe the thing was still out there somewhere, and if maybe it would find him again. Sometimes, as he stared into nowhere, he thought he saw a figure there. A man. Was it God? He wanted it to be God, so he could ask what all of this meant. Why could he see things? What did it have to do with Chickens? Why *him*? If there was anyone there at all, it couldn't be God, because the figure remained silent, and his questions remained unanswered. God had failed him.

The room was silent for a long time, with Arnold gazing fixedly into the corner. Matt, Nate and Carl weren't sure what to do, so they just watched their friend stare mindlessly past them.

"Arnold?" Matt finally probed. It was obvious something was wrong and a boy can only stand so much guilt. "Arnold, I'm ... I'm sorry," and after far too long of a pause, Arnold turned to look at him, but Matt couldn't look him in the eye, at least not for long.

"It's all right," Arnold whispered, and then looked off into the corner again. Nobody could rouse him this time, so they eventually left. Subsequent visits showed a gradual improvement, but Arnold was never quite the same again.

As the days drew on, the image in his mind faded, and the bird became little more than the blue outline of his whacked-out second sight. That too began to fade as he built up fresh walls, learning again to ignore it. Eventually, the incident was blocked completely, conveniently removing itself from his mind.

It wasn't long before another chicken related incident occurred, and then another. After Arnold's parents continued to find their son amidst suspicious circumstances, each involving some sort of poultry, they began to fear the worst. Was he in some sort of cult? The term "Satanic" kept cropping up in conversations—first with his therapist, and then amongst themselves as they grew more certain that some unholy obsession was involved. Mr. Thurmond was his first therapist. Mrs. Holmes his fifth. A string of shrinks examined him and spoke with him for hours on end, but none found anything wrong with him. In Holmes' own words, Arnold was "a remarkably well-adjusted young boy," who'd been caught in some compromising positions, sure, but disturbed children usually fell into a few set behavioral patterns, and had predictable responses when confronted with their deeds. Arnold was logical and compassionate. When he had been caught with the second dead hen, he said that he had heard something in the bushes while he was walking home from the bus

cluck

stop. When Arnie investigated he found a dead chicken and had picked it up, intent on burying it. His route took him past a small section of town where suburbia bordered the far edge of some distant farm, so the presence of a chicken, while a bit odd, wasn't surprising. His lack of concern over *Salmonella*, *Campylobacter* and *Staphylococcus* was another issue, but his lack of hygiene didn't indicate any psychosis as far as the best psychiatric minds of middle-class Detroit were concerned. He didn't try to draw attention to the act, nor did he try to draw attention away from it. There was no hint that it was an "act" at all, it was simply something he'd stumbled upon. There was no reason to question the truth of his testimonies, for there were none of the telltale indications of a lie.

The third incident was even more innocent on his part. A poultry truck, presumably from the same farm and destined for some metropolitan meat market, passed him on the road, and two young birds managed to escape their cages and hurtle towards the road. Arnold had been there and buried the two birds. There was no ritual, or collection of parts, or any odd or obsessive behavior at all. Other than a string of incidents involving dead chickens, it seemed that there was nothing unnatural or unwholesome about the boy.

Then again, there were the bites. Small wounds on his hands. He was always able to explain them away: he fell off his bike while racing down the big hill towards the library; he was in a fight at school, trying to protect Carl from one of the many "bad kids" that liked to pick on him; his hand was stepped on by another student during a game of football. He'd used every excuse other than "I fell down the stairs." His mother knew he was lying. Those wounds were bites and she knew it. They looked an awful lot like the wounds he'd received that day behind the mall, when the four boys were attacked. Some details never fade from a mother's memory.

Being extremely worried about him, and finding no other recourse, there was only one thing left for Arnold's mother and father to do.

Knapp

cluck

chapter 6 dang gum!

"God-dang-bammit! Noisy Chickens!" hollered Bobby, through the last mouthful of a dry tuna sandwich. Bobby was far too old to go by the name "Bobby," but he was a farmer and was therefore expected to. There was no hyphenation in this particular redneck appellation, like "Bobby-Ray" or "Billy-Bob," but he would have been okay with that. What really bothered Bobby, as he lounged in a slightly flea-infested sofa on the long porch, which wound around the entire front facade of his new house, was the racket being made by his chickens. It should have been a peaceful scene: it was a bright summer day and there was a white rail along the porch's edge, which was covered almost completely by a fragrant and ancient flowering vine. Through the brilliant foliage and the slats of the railing, however, the small dapples of bright summer sun splashed across several piles of accumulated junk, the old sofa, and Bobby—enough to ruin any scene. And of course there were the chickens.

"Can't get no peace even in the sun-shine with all thems racket!" He said "sunshine" like it was two words. Two words that each required concentration. Bobby wasn't really dumb, he was playing a role; a farmer who lived as far out in the country as he did had a certain image to up- hold. It made no difference that he was far from anyplace where such a fostered regional accent would be appropriate. It was a facade that he promoted for the benefit of his aspiring enterprise; Bobby assumed, rightly so, that people would be more likely to part with their money if they felt they were dealing with some poor ignorant hick. If they felt they were cheating him, he would in turn be able to cheat them. Despite the subtleties of his master plan, however, his fruitful returns refused to ripen: time had passed, and the business had yet to open its doors. In- stead of working a profit from the clever ruse, Bobby had simply fallen further and further into the role until his playacting became less of a performance and more of a predilection. Now, despite his education and upbringing, Bobby was firmly stuck in the part of the redneck.

"Git! Git! You good-fur-nuthin' birds!" He waved a hand towards the group of hens that had gathered just on the other side of the chicken- wire fence. The farmstead was enormous, and formed a huge jagged "U" built of rambling outbuildings and in-law homes. While portions of the estate trailed away in other directions as well, the majority of the collec- tion of buildings slowly wrapped back around to form an open entrance to the main drive, which snaked its way into the heart of the estate. The drive itself eventually spread out into an archipelago of smaller paths that plunged into several bays of the largest barn, as well as into various other carriage sheds— enough room all together to park a dozen or more full- size cars. The effect on a newcomer as they entered the drive was that of driving through a narrow tunnel or perhaps a fjord that was cut between deep edifices of architecture. At the outer edge of the drive, closest to the long farmer's porch upon which Bobby now sat, there was a narrow point. It was at this point, which was formed by the protrusion of a makeshift storage shed and the outer edge of the "U" (which happened to be an old cobbler's workhouse), that a length of chicken wire had been

cluck

stretched tight. Everything behind it in the interior courtyard had been given over to the birds, an enormous area where they were allowed to range freely. It was filled with nooks and alcoves formed by the many oddly arranged pieces of the farmstead, and in the center a small but adequately sized coop had been built. For some reason, despite the extent of their yard, the chickens insisted on pressing as close as possible to Bobby whenever he sat on the porch. They pressed against the wire, flapping their inefficient wings in a pathetic but noisy attempt to fly over the wire and escape.

One of them had a brilliant plume of white feathers on her head like a crest. Most of the other chickens knew her as "Feather-head" (or at least they knew her as a collection of scratches, glances and clucks that roughly translated to 'Feather-head'), though she had another name as well: Helena. She was a beautiful example of her species, and was known among the flock as being extremely clever. She was always the first to find food in unexpected places, such as when she alone thought to overturn the small piles of scrap lumber to reveal the juicy crickets hidden there.

"Food?" she asked (in chicken). She looked directly at Bobby as she made this request, but Bobby ignored her. To him it was just more scratching and clucking. He stared intently at the fingernails on his left hand, contemplating his life. The other chickens watched with interest; to them, food was a valid subject and they were keen to see if the request would be fulfilled. They were very hungry.

"Food?" another hen eventually joined in. Chickens were not good at ideas, it simply wasn't their *forté*, but food was a good idea even to a chicken. After all, Feather-head usually knew what she was doing and was worthy of imitation. Bobby was sometimes known to throw things into their yard, and sometimes the things he threw were edible. The risk was worth it, to a chicken.

"Food? Food? Food?" demanded a growing collection of greedy ladies. A small rooster wandered in, tiny but proud, richly plumed like the chapeau of a Bonaparte general.

"Food!" he demanded.

"Food?" another hen hastily added, eager to contribute.

For Bobby, the chickens represented a real problem. The problem being that they were loud, distracting him from his important thoughts of ... well, distracting him from his thoughts, at least. He considered feeding them for a moment, but decided against it. That would have meant getting up, walking back into the house, through the kitchen to an old milk rook, down the stairs into the cool basement pantry where the grain was stored, and then back up again. It was far too much effort on such a sunny and—apart from the raucous behavior of the flock—peaceful day.

"Shadhup, will ya!" He howled. He looked around for something to throw, but to the chicken's collective disappointment, the only thing within reach was a can of beer, and he hadn't finished it yet. He certainly wasn't going to throw that at them until it was empty.

He was for the most part irresponsible, irritable, and inclined towards laziness. He had inherited the flock along with the purchase of the house, but he had no idea what to do with it. Their papers said there were seven roosters and almost forty hens, but Bobby never cared enough to count. If he had, he would know that their numbers had dwindled to only four roosters and twenty-two hens, but content in his ignorance he knew only that there were "a bunch of stinking chickens." They were all different sizes and shapes. There were Silver Penciled Wyandottes and Minorcas, Sultans and Silkies. There were even a crested duck; to most people it looked like a penguin that had swallowed a ping-pong paddle, but to the trained fowl farmer it was a prize. The variety of feathers and colors was amazing—and indeed they impressed many visitors; but Bobby thought they were nothing more than smelly farm birds.

cluck

They all looked the same to him: ugly and dirty. Except for one of the roosters—a big black bird that was easily twice the size of the others, which looked almost prehistoric. He never jumped at the fence like the others, but always lurked in the darker recesses of the yard. Sometimes when Bobby was trying to feed them, that damn black rooster would attack him, jumping out at him and fluttering its wings menacingly. That sole rooster was different, somehow, and it gave Bobby the creeps. It was one of the reasons why he hated going in there to feed and water the damn things.

"Stupid birds. Ugly too, 'specially that black bastard. Mean lookin' summabitch," Bobby once complained.

"They're not stupid or ugly, and that 'black bastard' is a sweetheart, the way he protects his lover from the rest," Janice insisted, pouting. "And look at Aramis! He's a handsome bird." She indicated the small, demanding rooster. It was true, the miniature rooster was rather fanciful; a pale fawn bird with highlights of rich brown feathers.

"What did you call him?" Bobby wasn't well read—he was nearly as poorly read as he was poorly bred—so he didn't catch the reference.

"Aramis. From the Three Musketeers."

"You named him?"

"How couldn't I? See how his little tail stands up so high?" As if on cue, the small bantam's tail rose straight up like a decorative, feathered hat. "There's two more just like him. Over there is Athos, and Porthos is around here somewhere. The Three Musketeers, get it?"

"I get it, I just don't understand it." Bobby shook his head, dramatizing his disbelief to cover up his ignorance. He couldn't understand why anybody in the world would want to name something as low on the food chain as a chicken. It was like naming a cow; these animals weren't pets, they were livestock. They existed to serve. Literally. On the dinner table. To Bobby, such an inferior status should remain incognito.

Anonymity made for easier digestion. He'd come to expect this sort of sappy behavior from his dear wife, however.

"They don't need names," he insisted, against his better judgement. "They taste the same no matter if they got names or not."

"I've told you plenty of times already, Bobby, we're not eating them. You can only eat their eggs." She stared intently at her husband for an uncomfortably long moment, and then laughed. It was in her nature to find the light side of things. "—and I wish you'd stop talking like a hick," she added. "You sound stupid."

"Well, I *am* a farmer now," was his only reply, but he made an effort and let the accent drop, a bit, to appease Janice.

"Only just."

"Well, but you know my family. I really am a hick, you know. At least by breedin'—see! I can't help it, it's in my jeans." Bobby patted the seat of his dungarees.

"The word is *genes*, with a '*g*,' you fool," she said, stifling another laugh.

"How can you tell how I'm spelling when I talk?"

She turned, throwing him a flirtatious look over her shoulder as she skipped back to the house. Any warm-blooded man would have followed her, but even in those happy early days Bobby's love for his wife had become tainted by his hate for the stinking, filthy, smelly birds. Three musketeers and all.

"Besides," Bobby called after her, "who the heck is Aramis? I thought the three musketeers were Porthos, Athos and ... what was the other one? Dar-tan-yun ..."

"*D'Artagnan* wasn't a musketeer, stupid, he was ..." but her voice was lost as she disappeared inside.

Things went downhill from there. Bobby turned back to the flock just as the huge black beast of a rooster entered the yard, stepping between the feather-crested Helena and the smaller rooster. Aramis backed

cluck

away as the bastard black bird approached the fence and stared deter-
minably at Bobby. It didn't call for food, like the others. It simply stared.

Creepy, he thought, *and worthless. Stupid, filthy, creepy and worthless. Nothing good at all from them, except the eggs.*

The eggs were enough, though. Especially the little blue ones,
which his wife said were laid by a small clutch of prize "Araucana" hens,
whatever the heck that meant. He didn't know nor care which chicken
was which. He was satisfied to understand that the colored eggs were
supposed to be colored, and that they were edible, not spoiled. There
were green eggs, too, and of course the typical brown and white, but the
blue ones were definitely his favorite. Bobby was not inclined to eat
things out of the ordinary, but the blue eggs were just so dang tasty, he
was able to get over it.

While some might recognize the value of the flock, which was significant, appreciating the collection would have required a good deal of
extra effort on Bobby's part. He didn't like extra effort, being the lazy
bastard that he was, so he was content to dislike them.

"Dang blasted things are more trouble 'n they're worth!" He made
this proclamation to his wife Janice on a regular basis, but unlike extremely rural farmers, extremely rural farmer's *wives* were allowed to
sound a bit more educated and even-keeled. She always had a level-
headed and logical rebuttal, and persisted in finding the bright side of
things ... which irritated Bobby even further.

"They're not too much trouble, Bobby. They're not any trouble at
all. You only have to bring them food and water once a day," was her
typical reply.

They required two daily trips out to the coop, for one thing, thought
Bobby in silent defiance. Even in winter. Not to provide food and water
when they needed it, but when Janice insisted that they looked hungry
or thirsty. Bobby had tried several easier methods to feed and water the
chickens. One involved simply sloshing a bucket of water and dumping a

bag of chicken pellets out of the side hall window every few days. That stopped because it attracted the chickens closer to the house, making them louder and the house dirtier. Then a skunk had discovered the feed pile and had moved into one of the basements through a hole in the foundation. So it was back to doing things the hard way. Bobby's complaints of how hard the work was would always be trumped with Janice's quiet declaration, "Well, *I like them*! So take good care of them for *me*."

"But what good are they?" When defeated by logic, the last resort was always whining.

"Eggs, remember? The eggs you stuff your face with every morning? And don't forget that a Bed and Breakfast needs lots of eggs." Another good argument, rooted in Janice's stubborn desire to turn the place into a profitable Inn, despite the business's stalled momentum. Still, Bobby hated the birds and wished for nothing more than to be rid of them. Yeah, the eggs were good, but he knew what that meant, too. Collecting the eggs every single day, and washing the "dirt" off of them.[3] It was simply more work. If you got lazy and waited days in between, there was always that risk of cracking open an egg to find more than breakfast waiting inside. One suspect egg, in Bobby's mind, was enough to taint them all and he was happy to throw out a hundred eggs to avoid the risk of being grossed out in front of the frying pan. As far as Bobby was concerned, you could buy eggs from the supermarket with less work (which made perfect sense to him because Janice did the shopping).

What he hated most was carrying things to and from that henhouse. It wasn't that the food, water, eggs or whatever payload he carried was exceptionally heavy. It was the way the stupid things would always get under foot, complicated by the fact that Bobby insisted on wearing high waterproof rubber boots whenever he went "into that filthy place." The first winter they were there, he managed to slosh an entire bucket of cold

---

[3] "Dirt" is a well-known farm euphemism for "shit."

cluck

water down one of those boots while carrying it out to the henhouse. He had to walk all the way back with a boot full of ice-water. That was the last straw and Bobby had decided to just stop feeding them altogether. Two weeks later, there were still almost twenty hens but there was only one of the three musketeers left, and of course the dominant, black rooster. The rest were dead in the coop, discovered by Janice while she investigated the smell that had started to drift through that side of the estate. Bobby slept in front of the TV for three days after that. Feedings had resumed afterwards, on a clockwork schedule, carefully monitored by Janice.

"It's not so much that you murdered those poor animals," she had scolded him, "but that you actually pretended to go out there every morning. Just to deceive me. What did you do? Walk around the corner and then just stand there for ten minutes? Honestly, Bob, sometimes I wonder about you," and a small part of her typically gentle and forgiving nature chipped away. "I mean, really. How would you like it if someone murdered you?" she asked with a darkness in her voice he never heard before. The words scathed him.

He really hated it when she called him "Bob." Regardless, he transferred all the blame onto the chickens, and didn't feel much guilt about it. To tell the truth, he was more than a bit jealous over the attention they were given, and Bobby was never able to forgive them that. Never.

Knapp

cluck

chapter 7   oh mon dieu!

Although Arnold was young, his eyes had a deepness and hardness to them that was anything but young. They were once soft and kind and innocent; before the change they were like any young boy's eyes. Long ago, his mother had seen a bit of herself in those eyes, and a bit of his father as well, and she loved them dearly. The world that the younger, soft-eyed boy knew was full of summer and breezes and running barefoot through the grass. That world was full of color and joy. As Arnold grew older, his world changed with him, and it was now as dull and lifeless as this room; with grey suspended ceilings in place of blue skies and long fluorescent bulbs in place of clouds. His mother, after all, had cast him out of that better world. She had done it under the guise of helping her son, but he suspected it was more because of her own lack of patience and understanding. She simply couldn't stand to live with a freak like he had become. She couldn't live with someone who was delusional, crazy, criminal. When she turned him away everything that was soft began to crust over. His eyes were deep with wisdom beyond his years, yet dry and cracked like a river bed in the height of drought. He had calloused and become hard in order to survive. His mother, so long ago, was always worried about him, always caring, but despite her concerns he grew reclusive after the visions had started, and she grew distant in return. A mother's love and concern had been rebuffed too often, and the trouble became more frequent. The neighbors asked questions and the perfect family in the perfect house in the small suburb of Detroit developed an unwholesome reputation. It was his fault, of course. He was the one who changed. He was the one who was always surrounded by death. She couldn't possibly understand; she felt her son's strange behavior must have been a reflection of something that had frozen within his character. She feared it might have been a reflection of her own inadequacies as a mother. So she did what she had to do. He was so very, very young. He went with her, hand in hand, to Michigan Central Station.

Arnold looked up at the train schedules, printed in large plastic letters that flitted with a rapid succession of clicks as the train numbers and arrival times updated themselves. He was glad that his parents had at least come into the station with him to make sure he got on the right train. "We'll ask the man at the ticket counter," his mother had suggested, and ask she did. She bought the ticket and handed it to Arnold with the assurance of the kind man that they would take great care of their boy and make sure that he arrived safely.

"Now you be safe, and behave," she told him as she kissed him goodbye and handed him over to his new steward. The man was tall and wore a clean uniform that clearly indicated he was a manager at the station. "When you get there, look for Father Beaumont. He'll be waiting for you at the station."

cluck

"Father Beaumont? You don't mean Father Beau from the big church just outside Blackwater Missouri, do you? I think his full name is Beaumont. Yeah, it might be." The manager's question took Arnold's mother by surprise. She was unable to regain her composure in time to prevent a dark blush from covering her face.

"Yes, that's right," she said. "How did you know that? Do you know the Father?"

"I'm from Missouri, originally. I've worked some of the north-south lines from there for a long time. I only know the church because I grew up near there. To answer your question, no I don't know him personally, but Father Beau's pretty well known. Famous, even." At this he turned to Arnold, "You're going to the church, are you, boy?" and then back to his mother with a grin. "What'd the little tyke do?" He asked the question innocently enough, but both Arnold and his father winced; Arnold was certainly far too old (and proud) to be called a "tyke," and his father resented the implication that his son was a bad egg.

"That is none of your business!" Arnold's father answered, stepping in front of his wife with poorly practiced confidence. Arnold couldn't remember ever seeing his father make a fist before.

"I didn't mean any offense, sir. No, sir. Please calm down, sir, it's just that Father Beau is known for helping out people in need, that's all—but I see that your son here couldn't possibly be one of those boys. No, sir. I see that, now. Looks like a fine young gentleman, now that I look close." He held out his hands, offering to take the boy's backpack. "Let me get that for you, son. You two don't worry, we'll get him there safe as can be." He helped Arnold onto the correct train, and true to his word, the young boy was delivered safely into the hands of Father Beaumont, who called Arnold's parents to tell them all was well.

Arnold had quickly developed a reputation for being odd because of the cock-eyed way he would often look at people, but at Father Beaumont's church he fit in well enough. Religion wasn't new to him—

he had gone to Sunday School and attended church regularly with his parents—so he felt fairly safe and comfortable there. Knowing that he was different, that there was something wrong with him at some level, he understood why he was being abandoned to this new life, and was even somewhat resigned to it. He was not allowed to grow comfortable, though.

The incident happened within two months of his arrival. His rooms were downstairs from the church hall, behind a group of rooms that were used as function halls or for choir practice or other gatherings. He heard a noise in the middle of the night, a clacking noise that echoed heavily in the hollow acoustics of the place. Thinking that someone must be wandering around the cloisters, Arnold went to investigate only to witness a ghostly, glowing blue light as it danced around outside of the stained glass fixtures. Being one floor below ground level, the small decorative windows were set high on the walls, so Arnold couldn't see much through them, but he recognized that light.

Without thinking, he climbed the stairs into the back hall of the church and went outside through the handicapped-accessible side entrance to get a better look. The church was built of stone, set high on a hill that overlooked the town from its front entrance, and loomed over a distant farm to the rear. Typically, the view of the town was full of folksy bustle and small-town charm, while the sprawling expanse of the farm provided a peaceful border of serenity, full of the scents of field grass and wildflowers. What Arnold saw as he emerged from the confines of his cloister, however, was different. The farm was currently dancing with light as if a grand and morbid ball was being held. First the sapphire glow would pulse and grow, and then suddenly flash and swirl in a chaos of color—an organic rhythm of festival lights that cut through the still night air like a carnival. The light shone brightly enough to hurt Arnold's eyes, as if gazing into the sun, even though Arnold had been subconsciously suppressing his vision for so long. He knew, at once, that

cluck

something was terribly wrong. He knew the roller-coaster patterns of brilliant blue were souls.

People are dying, he knew. So much light—it couldn't mean anything else. His eyes widened in terror as the lights continued to dance from far away, down the hill, and he could feel the pain, again and again as lives were ended. It was a searing heat through his eyes and into his head, a throb that saturated every nerve, and a dull ache that infested his heart.

Arnold screamed, stirring the others in the place of silent worship with the sudden explosion of noise. He was caught. He was questioned. He tried to warn them—to tell them about the massacre he witnessed from afar ... At the same time his thoughts turned inward, and his mind filled with questions. Would he be punished? Would he be sent home to deal with his mother? Worry combined with the lingering pain that had struck him so severely, and the sensation mottled into nausea, nearly causing Arnold to empty his stomach. The last thing he expected was to be taken into a private cloister by Father Beau himself, where the kindly old priest sat him down and looked him in the eye.

"So, you can see spirits, can you?" It was like running a too-hot shower that had suddenly turned cold. Nobody, not even his parents, had ever suggested that what he saw were people's spirits. He had figured it out on his own, of course, but he had never told anybody. Never.

"Father," Arnold began. He leaned forward in his plastic chair, shaking. "If you know what I saw, then—Father, people were dying. I could see it! I—

"Nobody was dying, Arnold. You can relax. You are mistaken."

"I'm not, Father, I could *feel* it. It was everywhere. The blue light was everywhere!" The shaking became a bit more frantic, and Arnold gasped for breath. Father Beau knelt down beside him and soothed him, convincing him with the calm demeanor of his priestliness to slow his breathing and relax his mind.

"You're a real interesting boy, Arnold. I knew that from the first moment I saw you. I thought then that you might have the sight. Yes, I've known a few before you who could see people's souls. Rarely like this, though ... you thought you felt people dying, did you?"

"I ... I felt it. I did."

"Tell me, Arnold, what did it feel like? To sense the very moment when a life ends?" The kind eyes were bright with honest interest, a juxtaposition of the priest's pure intent and somewhat uncomfortable curiosity. Arnold looked up at Father Beau, insecure in his ability to put the experience into words. "Try," Father Beau urged him with a whisper.

"It, well, it hurt. In my eyes. I mean, not just the light burning my eyes, but also ... well, it burned all inside me. Everything felt dark."

"Dark? Dark as in a deep sleep, or as in—

"I don't know ... dark. Cold. Empty. So empty that I felt lost, and—I'd rather not. I'm sorry, Father, I really don't want to talk about it. Please?"

"No, my son, it is I who am sorry. I shouldn't have pressed you. You're obviously upset." He stood and paced, and sat down again. "I'm afraid you'll have to forgive an old priest for desiring whatever look into the next world might be had. An infliction that is common among men of the cloth, I'm afraid. It's a bit of an occupational hazard. Please, forgive me." At once the tension eased. Arnold's shoulders relaxed and he slumped exhausted into his chair. The rush of adrenaline left him and the shaking subsided, then stopped completely.

"Well, Arnold, I have some good news for you, at least. Now that I've scared you even more than you were, I at least owe you that. Those weren't people, Arnold, the ones you saw die."

"I really did—" Arnold insisted, straightening up again, alert.

"Oh, yes, you did. I don't doubt that."

"Then ... then you believe me?"

cluck

"Oh yes, I believe you. Partially. I believe that you saw something, but ... well you see, that farm is a *turkey* farm. Sometimes, at night, they operate the slaughter house." Before Arnold could protest, he continued, "I've already called down to Earl, and sure enough everything is fine down there. That is, unless you're a turkey."

"So I saw ... turkeys? I—" Arnold began, but then silenced himself again as Father Beau launched himself from his chair and began to pace again.

"—Yes! Which is interesting, mind you, because not many people can see the spirits of animals. Fewer still ever build the sort of connection that you seem to have built."

"Connection?" Arnold was used to strange things happening, but talking about his infliction, sharing such a taboo subject with a priest, of all people, confused him.

"Your connection with *birds*. Or maybe not all birds, maybe only poultry ..." He gestured at a file that lay on the small desk. "Yes, I know what you've been through. Chickens, before, now turkeys. It's not unheard of—people can develop spiritual bonds with animals, such that they can see, if you will, into their very souls ..."

"I can see people too, sometimes." There was a pursed silence.

"Interesting ..."

"Mom always made it seem like a disease. I wish it would stop."

"Do you want it to stop, really?"

"Of course I do! I want to go home, and be normal. I don't want to be the freak anymore, and I don't want ... I don't want to see things that other people can't see. All the pain, and the ... and I want my mom and dad to ... to love me again. I want to be normal!"

"Arnold, you can see things and do things that other people can't. That makes you special, doesn't it? Not abnormal. It could be considered a gift. A gift from God."

"It's not. It's just not, okay? God couldn't have anything to do with it, because it's not ... it's not right. It's ... evil."

"Evil? That's an interesting choice of words."

"Why do I have to be the one to kill them? I'm telling you it's *not right*. I don't think God gave me this. I think it was the devil. It *is* evil! What I see, and what I ... do."

"Oh, not a disease, no. And it's not evil. Not at all. Arnold, *you* are not evil." Father Beau had the practiced look of assurance and compassion that only a career priest could possess, and it did calm Arnold, if just a little. "Please try to understand, Arnold, that there is absolutely nothing wrong with you. Everything is just fine, everything *will continue to be fine*. There's nothing wrong with being special.

"You have a gift—yes, a gift, even if it doesn't seem like one to you now. Even better, I think I know how to help you. If you're up to it, I think you just might be ready for a change in your life, boy. Something better." Arnold sat, overwhelmed and confused. "Tell me, Arnold. Do you by any chance speak French?"

The memory faded with the flickering of fluorescent lights. Arnold blinked, and rubbed his fingers together; the sensation of his mother's hand lingered just a moment longer as he held onto their last moment together. The light flickered again, and it was gone: he was on the train, moving south to the priesthood, and then back out of it again. He had fulfilled his mother's wishes, but the path she had envisioned for him had changed tracks along the way. Where he ended up was far from the calm monastery that she imagined. The place where Arnold was sent was the headquarters of a small, underground order that was unknown by most. Certain farmers, those who had a keen memory and a habit of telling the tales of the old-timers, knew of the small group of men. Certain priests

cluck

like Father Beau knew of them—if they were both old enough and had open minds (which is a rare combination among priests, whose minds tended to close further with every sermon). They were forces of light, yes. They dealt with good and evil, yes. They knew there was such a thing as Hell, certainly. They weren't associated with any commonly known religion, though. In fact, they weren't really a religion at all; there were no hymns, or teachings, or commandments or communions. There were no crusades or condemnations of man or inquisitions or smiting. There was a deeply rooted belief, but it was not a faith, *per se*. In contrast to the beliefs of faith, these beliefs were founded in experience, the culmination of generations of firsthand observations and physical evidence, well documented in secret pages and hidden libraries. They dealt in spirits, yet they held no obligation to any God. They had their own power, or at least that was the general idea. There hadn't been any new evidence of actual power in some time.

After he first arrived, Arnold wasn't exactly sure where he was or why he was there. He had been put on a plane to France, had been picked up in a black car by a stout man with sweat stains on his shirt who didn't speak a word to him, and who deposited him unceremoniously in front of what looked like a run-down old office building. Far from the majestic stone facade of Father Beau's mission, this new place was ugly, nothing more than a collection of rundown buildings, where walls were built from painted concrete blocks and the floors were hard and scuffed. It was more like an old school campus than a monastery, and Arnold's room wasn't too different from a classroom: there was poor light, a low ceiling, and little furnishings of any kind. Not surprisingly, the others who lived there didn't take to Arnold. Those who spoke English still only rarely spoke to him, and he was helped in no way to discover the secret of his visions (as Father Beaumont had suggested they would). Each day two meals were delivered to him on a brown plastic fast-food tray. The rest of the time he either wandered around trying to stay out of the way, or he simply sat in his room on his small bunk and waited.

There were a few other men who lived in similar rooms, and although they wore no real uniforms he understood they were all part of the same group. They whispered among themselves, sometimes in French but often in English. Since he had little else to do, he would listen carefully to these conversations whenever he could. In this way he was able to piece together snippets of dialogue, and get a fairly good understanding about what was going on. He learned that this group—they called themselves *The Order*—was relevant to his situation after all. They were a secret group, and the best Arnold could tell, they were used as some sort of secret police force to solve problems in the neighboring towns.

Once, while exploring the various fluorescent-lit halls, Arnold passed a group of important-looking men, and overheard the word "ghost" amidst the whispers of their hushed conversation. Arnold, not thinking the conversation was private, interrupted and asked excitedly if they could see people's souls, too, like him. *They must be like me*, he thought, excited at the thought, at the brief taste of association. *After all, hadn't Father Beaumont told me they would be able to help me? That they would know?* Arnold didn't even pause for breath. He'd had little contact and no conversations since his arrival, and once the dyke had been broken, the boy rambled on about souls and lights and ghosts—everything he could think of, every unasked question suddenly spilling forth. He was sure that these men were high up in The Order; they were much better dressed and spoke more intelligently than the others (and in both English *and* French). One of the men in particular was important, for Arnold had seen him giving orders—always in a polite but confident way. It made him seem like a natural leader to Arnold—who better to finally confess his anxieties to? Surely this was the man who would

cluck

understand Arnold, explain things to him, tell him why he was there and what was expected of him?

I'm finally going to know ... Arnold believed.

When he finally ran out of things to say and grew quiet, the others simply stood there, staring at him in disbelief and—for some reason—contempt. He was given an angry look, and then another, and then a third. To his surprise and dismay, Arnold was not given any answers at all. Instead, he was locked into his room for an entire day.

Another time, feeling bolder, he had cornered the same man and demanded to know why he was there. The man ignored the boy at first, until he started screaming and asking to see a lawyer and threatening to call the police.

"You're not a prisoner, here," the man protested, uncomfortably. "You're here to ... learn."

"What am I learning? I just sit around all day doing nothing. Nobody even talks to me." The man's features softened a bit, and he looked contemplative.

"I suppose you're right. We don't really know how to treat kids around here, you understand. We figured you needed to be a bit older— maybe eighteen—before we told you what was really going on, but I see we can't just leave you hanging around until then, can we." He looked at Arnold as if he really hoped that they could.

"How come you got so angry before?" Arnold demanded.

"What?"

"I heard you talking about ghosts, and you—you locked me in my room ... remember?"

"Oh, you mean when you were talking about seeing souls? Well, you see, we get enough of that kind of thing from the general public without hearing it from you. If you're going to make fun of people, you need to expect them to get angry at you, don't you, kid?"

"But I wasn't making fun of you!"

"You said that you can see ghosts, kid. Went on and on about it. I mean, who the hell do you think you are, anyway?"

"But I really *can* see ghosts. Well, souls, and that's the same thing isn't it? They're blue and they glow a little. Father Beaumont knows."

"Well, maybe ... Father Beaumont knows a lot of things."

"And he said that you know, too. That's why he sent me here!"

"Oh. *That's* why he sent you here? Oh. Christ." The man rocked back onto his left foot, and then forward onto his right. He swayed stiff-legged like that for several moments. "Are you *sure?*" He asked.

"I'm—that is, I'm pretty sure ..."

"Listen, I've known old man Beau for a long time. He's old and wise and smart and all that, no doubt, but don't think we don't know why you're here. Beau runs a home for delinquent kids and criminals—a charitable service to society but that doesn't mean—"

"I'm not some punk kid, I was sent here, because ..."

"Because?"

" ... because there were chickens. Dead chickens, not once but a few times—but I didn't kill them, they were just always—I mean, I could *see them!*" Arnold shook with the angst and rage of a boy who was, truly, alone.

"You could see chicken ... ghosts. Sure. I mean, can't we all? I think maybe you inhaled too much off one of the bigger kid's joints and *thought* you saw chicken ghosts. Christ. I've heard it all before. The jokers like you who think we're so funny."

"I don't do drugs, and I'm not joking. I don't know—I mean, he told me you would help me. When he found out I could see them, he told me you would be able to help me. But I guess you can't, after all."

"Kid?"

Arnold was silent, his eyes to the floor.

"Shit," the man said, suddenly recognizing that the boy was telling the truth. "You're serious? I mean, you really can?" They exchanged a

cluck

quick, thoughtful look. On the man, it read, '*Holy shit what the hell did that old man send to us?*' and on the boy it was simply the look of desperation, a yearning to belong.

"Tell me about it, kid." The man, who was significantly taller than Arnold, crouched down beside him, touched the boys arm to reassure him.

"Re ... really?"

"Really. I want to know what you saw."

"Well, there were all these blue lights that I saw from the poultry farm, and I screamed when I saw it because I was scared, and then he talked to me and he said he knew I could see them, and so he sent me here." Arnold was relieved to be telling his story, finally, but there was still an edge of mistrust and anxiety in his voice. "He said you were going to help me. That my life would get better. Well, it hasn't. I don't like it here."

"You don't like it here ... well, I suppose we can do something about that. We can try, anyway. I mean, this is no palace, it can only get so good. We'll have to make sure to include you a bit more, though—don't look so excited, kid, you still have to understand that we're an isolated group, built around secrecy, and it goes against everything we know to share secrets with outsiders. But I think we can find a solution for you."

"Solution?" Arnold asked, suspicious of what this man's—this place's—idea of a solution might be.

"Well, we do share some of what we know with the new recruits. You're a bit young, but I suppose, if we made an exception on account of Father Beau, we could initiate you. Then we could tell you, a little at least. Maybe more in time. Hell, it's not like we've got people lined up to get in here, we could use some new blood. Sound good?"

"I suppose. Yeah."

With that, Arnold became a part of a new and radically different world.

Once initiated, Arnold's days consisted of French lessons, meals in the common room with the others, and a job. Slowly, things became more bearable. He became familiar enough among the men that conversations no longer halted abruptly upon his arrival, and he was no longer motivated to stay hidden in his room. Though he still wasn't being taught much directly, he learned quite a bit.

There was some sort of gathering that happened every day. It was held in a small auditorium in the rear of the building, and Arnold adopted the habit of loitering around the doors while it was in session. Unfortunately there was an air-conditioning unit in the locked utility closet in the corridor just opposite the doors, and it was difficult to over-hear much over the humming of the conditioner and the rattling in the overhead ducts. He still managed to catch a few intriguing phrases, however. Such as when Joe (a small, fat, sweaty but amiable man) hollered back into the room to one of the others, "I'll be damned if I'm fly-ing all the way to Canada just to wave my arms about and scare off some old ladies' hallucinations!" or when another skinny fellow (Arnold didn't know his name), said what sounded like *"Vous ne pensez pas qu'il y a réel-lement un vrai ordinateur de secours là, vous? C'est ridicule, j'avais fait ceci pendant trente années et non un des poulets a été vrai encore!"* Every newly discovered piece to the puzzle pointed towards the same truth: that this was a group of ghost busters, or some sort of religious police force de-signed to quell spiritually delinquent souls. It took him a while to trans-late the French, especially considering he was trying to remember the words phonetically and from memory, but he eventually learned the gist of it. *He was saying that there wasn't really a ghost. That in thirty years he had never seen ... chicken ... ghost ... ridiculous ...*

Memories came rushing into his head again. Chickens. Ghosts. The Nike box, the terrible wounds received from the ghostly talons of a rooster. The pain and the anger and the mystery of those curious wounds—it had all been suppressed, just as his vision had been

cluck

suppressed. The many incidents that all seemed to return in some way or another to chickens. Most recently, the terrible glow from Earl's turkey farm in Missouri, and the sinking feeling that overwhelmed his soul during the slaughter. Now he had been sent here, to others who were like him? Only these men were not like him. They talked about acting the part, and Arnold had certainly overheard mention of rituals and exorcisms, but he had always imagined something a little more *X-Files*—that is, a little more sleuthing and less actual ghosts—and he had always imagined they were more concerned with human ghosts and less so with the ghosts of livestock. Was it possible this entire order revolved around the pursuit of and extermination of undead chickens? Was that why he was sent here? Was that why—

With a gut-wrenching realization, Arnold suddenly understood why he felt so different from the others. Unlike the poseurs that filled this "order," Arnold could actually see. He could actually feel. *He possessed the power that they coveted.* He'd been accused of teasing them when he first declared he could see spirits. Was it because they didn't fully realize he actually held those powers? Was it because they did realize, and were jealous?

Determined to get to the bottom of The Order within whose walls he slept, Arnold worked harder to integrate himself further. He talked them into letting him attend their meetings, as an apprentice. He stopped mentioning anything about his powers, anything that might upset them, and worked hard to become an expert in their ways. He learned everything academically, through books and words. He saw the men leave on missions, and return chuckling about the crazy old farmers who thought they were haunted. Very few ever encountered anything real.

At first.

Almost two years after his arrival, there was a huge commotion among The Order and an emergency session was held in the noisy old auditorium. One of the senior agents had returned badly wounded, with huge and deep gashes across his chest and face that would not heal. His clothes were in tatters and his feet had been pecked and scratched in a manner that was all too familiar to Arnold. Arnold eventually learned the man's name was Jacob, and that the man had no family to speak of. There were questions about what to do with him should he die as a result of his duties.

Five days later, there was a knock on Arnold's door. "Arnold? You're wanted in the inner sanctum. Ten minutes." It wasn't a voice that he recognized, which meant it was probably one of the clerics from the restricted areas around the inner sanctum. Arnold's mind raced. The inner sanctum wasn't really much more than an old auditorium that was converted into private rooms, but symbolically it was the most important area of The Order. It was only used for audiences with the eldest of their sect, Master Biddeon. Arnold quickly combed his hair and, after a brief sniff, decided to throw on a clean shirt, too. After all, the Master was old and was rarely seen by the others, even the most senior and trusted agents.

What could he want with me? Arnold thought, as he hurried to the sanctum. Once there, Arnold was told to wait, and he passed the time examining the various paintings and scrolls and stacks of old books. They looked ancient and powerful, and yet, like everything in this bizarre place, they were hidden behind chintz. In this case, cheap plastic frames and flat-pack particle-board bookcases. He longed to pick up a book and look through its pages for a clue as to why he was here, but—though he waited for nearly an hour outside the Master's chamber—he lacked the courage to touch them.

When the doors finally opened, and he was ushered inside, Arnold saw his master for the first time. On a plain hospital bed, slightly inclined, lay the husk of a formerly powerful man. Sinuous muscles stretched tight across thin forearms, wrinkled skin hung in loose folds

cluck

from sunken shoulders. His face, too, was weary and stretched; a prominent, boney chin protruding proudly from beneath the deep skeletal sockets of his eyes. The eyes themselves, however, were bright and sharp, and spoke that special dialect of wisdom that only the aged and experienced can tell. He turned to look at Arnold, the effort causing him to open his lips a crack to permit a deep inhalation. Their eyes met, and in a moment that may have lasted one minute or a hundred Arnold felt himself being analyzed, studied, judged. Arnold's escort eventually broke the silence with a nervous cough as he shifted his weight to his other foot, and the Master broke away from Arnold and turned to him instead.

"This is what I suspected," said the old, frail man. He was an Englishman, and spoke with the accent of Arnold's childhood hero, James Bond. The agent who stood beside Arnold—not the tuxedoed gentlemen of MI5, but a shabby agent of The Order—snapped to attention at the sound of Master Biddeon's words.

"Use the boy ..." the old man continued, before laying back again, and closing his eyes.

There was more waiting, more men shepherding Arnold to more places, making him stand outside in the corridors as hurried conversations were whispered behind closed doors. Eventually, he found himself in the charge of a tall man who he knew by sight, and who had a kind voice with a thick French accent. This man had been given the job of watching over Arnold before, but there was never much in terms of conversation between them. Arnold had no reason to assume this man was an ally or a friend.

Eventually, after more shuffling to and fro, Arnold was brought outside Jacob's room, where he stood waiting again. He strained to hear the conversation, eager to understand what he could possibly be expected to do to help. *"Il a dit d'utiliser Andrew,"* Arnold heard, which he understood to mean "He said to use Andrew." Arnold didn't have long to wonder who Andrew was, as the deeper voice responded in English, "I know, but that's not his name. It's Arnold. That's just what he called him, but he meant Arnold." In contrast to the first man, who was obviously French, the deeper voice was unmistakably cockney. Straining to hear, Arnold could barely make out the first voice again, " ... he's pretty old ... called him Armand once, and Archie ..." the first voice then muttered something about senility when the deeper voice suddenly rose far above a whisper, causing Arnold to step away from door where he had inadvertently been leaning close.

"Vous ne pouvez pas laisser ce garçon à l'intérieur ici! Oh Mon Dieu!" and then in English the same voice added "It is all I can do not to vomit, looking at him, it is too much for a boy!" and then the voices returned to a whisper, forcing Arnold to lean close again to hear. There was more French that Arnold couldn't make out, and then " ... clean up some of this blood," he heard, and he could hear them moving about, presumably changing bandages, but the conversation was over.

A few minutes later, the door opened, and he was directed inside by his original escort, the tall man with the kind voice. The second man was at a sink in the far corner of the room wringing out a cloth under running water. In the center of the room was a hospital bed much like the one in Master Biddeon's room, and on the bed lay a man, naked, although his legs and torso and much of his face were covered almost entirely in bandages. There was a bag of clear fluid and one of blood hanging beside the bed, feeding Jacob intravenously. A deep red spot was already welling up through a spot near the man's stomach, as he bled uncontrollably. He was lying still.

Arnold looked at the man named Jacob, lying still in a bed that was newly made, though faint red stains remained where bloodied fingers had tucked in the clean sheets. Arnold knew this man, he'd seen him before, one of the younger agents who was always coming and going at odd hours, and one of the very few who would take the time to throw Arnold a glance, a nod, perhaps even a kind word. Moving closer to the

cluck

bed, he could see Jacob's features more clearly, eyes tense with pain despite his obvious sedation.

As he drew close, Arnold could feel it. Carefully, he let his other sight surface, and as he did so he could see the clear aura of an unwanted soul. Something was lodged under the man's bandages, near the increasingly wet spot of red. Something that glowed blue, brighter than Jacob's own soul, which was dim and grey, struggling to survive. Arnold reached out towards the spot, but was held back by a firm hand.

"You probably should not touch him," warned the thick French accent.

"No—remove the bandage," Arnold said to him, pleading. "There's something in there!" He struggled free, and started ripping at the bandages.

"Aidez-moi ici, volonté vous!"

"Whoah, kid!" the deep-voiced man said in response to the urgent yelp of French, and he rushed to the aide of his fellow, pulling Arnold back.

"There's something in there! It's killing him!" Arnold shouted. Tears were streaming down his face. Kind-voice shot deep-voice a look that said *the Master told us*—and then reluctantly began to remove the bandages. Underneath, pale skin was rent deeply with scratches and darkened with bruises. What caught Arnold's attention, however, was a small hole that dribbled blood as if it were a leaky faucet. Protruding from the hole, like a beacon, was a shining blue shape, streaming up from the wound like a flame. It writhed and fluttered about angrily, but was rooted deeply within Jacob's guts. Arnold struggled to reach him again, but he was still restrained, held back.

"Take it easy, relax ... okay? Okay?"

Arnold calmed down a little, and as he did the man's grip loosened. He let Arnold go, but he did so reluctantly.

Knapp

Shaking, crying, Arnold reached forward and took hold of the light. To the others it seemed as if he were grabbing empty air above the poor dying man's body, but then Arnold shook violently, and he was thrown back onto the floor. He had something in his hands that was struggling to get free, and as he rolled around on the floor fighting against it new spouts of blood appeared. Arnold's face was cut deeply, and his hands were covered in blood. Not knowing what to do, the two agents of The Order crowded close, not knowing if they should try to restrain the boy again or not. In their moment of indecision, however, it was over, and Arnold lay panting and bleeding on the floor. In his hands he held a single, black feather.

"Oh Mon Dieu!" the kind French voice exclaimed, staring in wonder first at the boy, and then at the feather.

"Holy Shit!" the deep, English voice boomed in agreement as both men turned their attention back to Jacob. The dark, bloody channels were closing up, disappearing before their eyes. Amidst streaks of red blood, on the cold cement floor, Arnold shook, his own eyes clenched shut against the terrifying sight of the lone, black feather.

One of the men touched his fingers to his forehead in some superstitious gesture, and said in quavering English:

"Leave no black plume as a token of that lie thy soul hath spoken!"

The words didn't mean anything to Arnold at the time, but they were spoken with such reverence and dread that they scared him even more than the screaming, and the blood, and the pain. Not knowing why, he imitated the man, and put two red fingers against his forehead.

Things changed after that. They changed a lot.

chapter 8 The exorciste de Volaille

Many years later, in a dark room far from the awareness of normal men, a young man leaned over a frail and aging form.

"Come closer, my boy." The words hissed upwards from dry lips. The old man was lying flat on his back, as comfortably as an old man could when he was dressed out on a large stone slab like a piece of meat waiting to be seasoned. While the stone was carved with mysterious and ancient runes, the effect was lessened by the folding function table it was perched upon. Although it was covered with a white cloth, it was still obvious that the table had been reinforced with two-by-fours to hold the extra weight, and the overall effect was culinary, rather than ceremonial. The words were aimed at the young man who stood by his side, though the old man's mouth and gaze faced upwards, unfocused and hard like the stone itself. He wore dirty clothes; a striped collared and buttoned shirt with yellow stains in the armpits and a pair of ragged chinos—and yet there was a definite feeling of ceremony about him, despite the attire of a high school retail worker. The entire scene held a similar note of

discord between old and new. An ancient rite amidst the modern working class. A stone ceremonial slab perched upon a makeshift table at the
center of a dingy auditorium that spoke more of intramural sports than
of holy writ.

"Come closer, I said."

The boy hesitated, but eventually obeyed. He didn't want to. He
was afraid. The man before him had been the only thing in the past years
to make his life bearable. When his master had finally accepted him into
The Order, still so young and impressionable, he had finally found a sense
of purpose. A sense of destiny. He only had a handful of years of any real
training, and he knew very little, but the relatively kind and trusting
Master Biddeon believed in him.[4]   The boy had been "special" now for
slightly less than a decade, which was most of his life. He didn't fully
remember the first years, before he changed, before his parents turned
him away. His life was filled with rejection and misery because of his
ability, only coming close to happiness once the Master took him under
his wing.

Now, Arnold was frightened again, unsure. The old man lay before
him, stretched and pale. Arnold was frightened because, on so many
occasions, this old man had been his protector against prejudice and
punishment. Even though he only ever used it to help The Order, whenever the boy's power manifested he was treated as a troublemaker. Master Biddeon looked upon Arnold's "delinquency" differently. He embraced Arnold and any mention of his power was, for a welcome change,
met with praise. The old man looked upon Arnold as if he were his son,
and he took joy in watching the boy grow.

For example: though The Order always talked about power, if the
boy mentioned that he actually *could* see spirits, he'd be beaten soundly

---

[4] No one in The Order was *entirely* kind or trusting, being, on the whole,
a big lot of bastards.

cluck

until he had bruises all over his arms, shoulders and head—unless of course the Master or one of the other higher-ups were there. When he was caught daydreaming in one of his many French classes, and he innocently confessed that he was distracted by the odd blue aura that was swirling around his instructor's feet, he had been exposed to a flood of new French words that he still did not know the meanings to (and probably never will). He was then locked up in solitary confinement in his rather uncomfortable room for telling lies. When he overheard two of the elders discussing something called a *poulet*, which he knew by now to be a chicken, he would enthusiastically contribute his thoughts about chicken ghosts, zombies and ghouls. He would sometimes ask, skeptically, "You can see them too?" but it was never received well by any of The Order, who would slap him against the head and curse him openly—unless the Master was near.

Now the Master was dying.

Arnold had no reason to be afraid. With the loss of this man, he would be alone again, friendless, but he was used to that. At least this time he would not be cast out alone into the world. This time he had a place he could call home. Looking around the room, he could already see that the looks of contempt in the eyes of the others were being carefully masked behind obsequity. He thought he heard someone mutter "… I can't believe that he chose the boy …" but even a protest as weak as that was quickly hushed. For they all knew what was about to happen. The old man was dying. Even without seeing the man's blue light flickering like a fluorescent bulb, it was clear. The old man had chosen Armand (for he continued to call Arnold by that name) to stand by his side, and to perform the rites. It sent a chill up more than just Arnold's spine as those in the room contemplated the demise of the eldest of their order. They all knew what this meant. The ritual meant a new boss. Uncomfortable changes in the way things worked day to day. Nobody wanted that.

Knapp

The ritual was called "The Passing of The Charge." They had all been taught about this rite of passage, this ceremonial succession where one master stepped down and another took his place. This, and the many other rituals of The Order were taught to each recruit with diligence, although it meant little to most of them. They all held secret knowledge and—to some extent or another—certain so-called "powers," but the true meaning of it all had been long lost under decades of bureaucracy, paperwork and, of course, rituals. To Arnold, The Passing of The Charge was different, and meant much more. He could see the power shifting. To him, it was more than just myth. It was more than practiced rites and word-of-mouth histories. It was real.

"What is it, Master?" he asked, drawing only a tiny bit closer as he did so. His cheek trembled, the small muscles of his face defying his efforts to remain calm.

"I said closer, boy. I'm dying, don't make me shout." More than ever, the eldest of The Order looked … *normal*. He seemed slightly disoriented, as if whatever power held him together had already begun to separate itself from him, but overall he looked, well, *human*. He was still Master Biddeon, however. His eyes, though cloudy, held a mischievous glint; like that of a distant uncle who hopes to trick an unsuspecting nephew into pulling his finger one last time. His skin was so dark and wrinkled that the smooth white cloth, folded neatly and draped across his forehead, contrasted strongly against his visage. In the center of the cloth was a small metal badge, embossed with an emblem. It was a circle built of down with a single upright feather, the type of feather that is made into a writing quill, or that might be used to decorate a hat. In the center, the letters "EV" were embossed, and then some tiny illegible inscriptions that had long ago been rubbed away. Like the man beneath it, it was worn and dirty. The boy leaned even closer, as ordered. He could smell something chemical coming from the cloth. He could smell more than that coming from the old man.

cluck

"Boooooy ..." he exhaled the word, and his eyes relaxed like a great weight had been lifted. "You must not fear. You must not ..."

Arnold couldn't hear, so he leaned even closer. The old man's breath smelled like bananas.

"You must not fear them," he continued. "Guilt is what gives them life. Fear is what gives them power. That is all you need to remem—" and he was silent for a moment.

"—Always look with your soul's eyes. Always see ..." he managed, but then fell silent again.

The boy thought maybe he had died, but the eyes were still looking at him. "Not yet," those eyes said. "I'm not dead ... yet," but he was on his way, and the boy knew what to do. He had been trained for some time now for little else but this. He cast a quick glance around the room, seeking some indication that he was mistaken, but none came. The old man had chosen him, and though it was unorthodox to choose one so young, it was a choice for no one other than the elder to make. Moving around the makeshift slab so that he was standing directly behind his master, the boy was able to see the others more clearly. They were all dressed in their finest, which wasn't saying a whole lot, and were arranged around the room, standing with their backs against the wall in a posture of mixed reverence and boredom. Most looked away when Arnold turned his eyes to them. A few looked back at him. One even smiled.

Yes, he thought, *it might just work out after all.*

When he reached the spot directly behind his master, Arnold leaned down—closer and closer—until his own forehead barely touched the white cloth. It felt oily, and he could feel the cold disc of the small badge just above his eyes. Above, a fluorescent bulb flickered in concert with the sputtering blue light that was his master's soul.

This close to his master, only he could hear the old man's next words.

"You really can see, can't you?" he said, and for the first time in his decade of service to The Order, Arnold saw the miserable old wizard smile.

"I don't want to see."

"But you can. That is enough."

"Master, please tell me how to stop it—"

"You don't. You can't. Hell, without you, The Charge would be nothing ... a memory. It would stagnate in the minds of silly old Frenchmen."

"But it's not right."

"Isn't it?

"No, who are we to commit—"

"What?" The Master's eyes brightened for a moment, pulling back from death to shoot an accusing glare at Arnold.

"—genocide." The word came out slow, weakened by the force of Biddeon's stare, but come out it did. The old man sighed, exhaling so much disappointment that he seemed to shrink down into the stone.

"They're already dead, boy. It needs to be set right. It *needs to*!"

"But aren't we the ones who make them? I mean, we make them come back, in the first place, don't we?"

"If we do, then what we create we must undo." It was a trite answer, in a tone that clearly said it was the wrong place and the wrong time to be bothering with such fears and concerns.

"It's not like they're dangerous," Arnold pressed. "Not really. Mostly they just shamble around. They're a bit gross, but they're not hurting anyone." Surprisingly, the dying man's smile returned.

"Is that so ... It really is amazing ... I always knew that you could see, that you understood the things that we only *think* we know. It really is amazing. Even now, you see me as no other person can. Do you know what this means?"

cluck

No. The boy didn't know. He suspected, but he didn't know. He shook his head, pushing the white cloth back and forth with his forehead as he leaned over his master.

"It means that for the first time in a very long time this ritual is going to work. You will actually receive ... The Charge ..." and the old man died, no more than an inch below the boy's face. He saw the blue light fade. He stood there, unmoving, for a very *very* long time.

Then, awakening from the frozen silence, something else began to happen. Something that was both expected and yet a complete surprise—for no amount of book learning could ever have prepared him. Arnold stood and tried to curse, to stem back the rushing flash and the blinding pain with obscenity, but no sounds came out. Some lessons had been taught too deep. "Zoiks!" he finally managed, suppressing harsher words in tribute to his mother. The pain subsided a bit. He could hear his master's words in the air around him: "closer ..."

The wide-eyed young boy leaned closer over the oddly quiet brow of the rough elder. He knew that, as his forehead touched the white ceremonial cloth again, there would be another spark, and so he was not surprised when he saw the quick lights jump up to greet him again. After the initial shock and pain he'd felt a moment before, he flinched a little, expecting it to hurt, but all he sensed now were tiny pinpricks. They weren't electrical sparks, and they certainly weren't the sparks of romance. They were the sparks of insight. Around the room, where the others had stood in still reverence, there was suddenly a flurry of commotion and a mummer rose as each man whispered to the next. Arnold faintly heard the word *la prophétie* ... What did that mean? The prophecy. What prophecy? In his years of training, he had never heard of a prophecy before, but there was no time to dwell as his thoughts were pulled inward again, and the pain increased.

The boy had not expected any of this, of course; nobody had. They all knew how the ritual would unfold, who stood where and who said what, but no living being had ever seen anything like this. They only knew that one would be chosen, and the holder of "The Charge" would pass the gift to the chosen one at the moment of his death. It was metaphorical: this way, the "power" of "The Charge" would remain a part of their sect, embodied symbolically in their new leader. This way, they would always have a hero. The holder of The Charge was not always an elder, but it was often the case. The holders simply tended to choose their successors from the more experienced of The Order. Even among the oldest and wisest of The Order, none remembered anything to explain the flickering lights, the sparks, the chosen successor wracked in pain. Only as the electricity surged into his skull did Arnold fully realize what was happening. The events that were about to unfold were suddenly familiar. It was if they had always been known, ever since he was born, long before he had first begun to see with his second sight, and long before he joined the old man and this Order, so many years ago. He knew that his master was dead, and that, leaning over him, he was now touching foreheads with his master's corpse. He also knew there was something left alive, deep within his master's husk. He waited, bracing himself, for it to surge upwards into him.

The murmuring grew louder and several people drew in closer to see what was happening. If the ritual were nothing but metaphor, what in the devil was going on with all of these sparks? One of the men almost pulled Arnold away, fearing he was in danger, but he was unable to summon the courage to reach closer towards the ghastly light that now enveloped Arnold and his master both. Arnold himself nearly drew away, nearly shut his mind against the sudden brightness of intuition, and the blistering pain of sudden realization. Until he remembered, *"You must not fear."*

The words were still fresh, he could almost feel the breath of his ailing mentor as he recalled them. Is this what he meant? Did he mean not to fear this strange feeling, this blinding pain? Did he mean to warn

Arnold not to fear the surge of thoughts and experiences that were racing into his mind? Not to fear the small metal badge that was burning against his forehead with the friction of an entire life's memories and emotions? Although they were well indoors, a wind picked up, blowing his hair wildly about his head as the enveloping halo of light grew brighter still. His head ached, and his eyes bulged behind tightly closed eyelids.

When he finally stumbled backwards, it was over.

He'd never been told what to do next—the ceremony had never been described to him beyond this point—but he knew. He took the badge, and clipped it to his boot. It was a dirty boot, but that's okay. There was little pomp or ceremony involved in this religion, he knew. He knew everything now.

Around the room, shocked faces looked back at him. The room itself was suddenly a great ritual hall of ages past, full of power and magnificence. Old desk chairs pushed against cement walls became pillars of stone. Steel support beams across the low ceiling grew upwards and outwards becoming elegant buttresses. Near the back of the room, near a large rubber bin that had for an instant become a glittering pool atop a marble dais, a meticulously dressed gentlemen gasped, "Christ almighty, look at that."

Arnold's eyes bulged again, this time so wide they looked like they would roll out of his skull. He looked forward into what was once the unknown but was now suddenly clear. He stood up straight, and looked carefully about him. He looked under the stone slab. Turning quickly, as if to catch something unawares, he looked behind him. With his new, mystically acquired knowledge, he was suddenly suspicious of everything.

"Holy [poop]!" He exclaimed, and was surprised at the words. Just moments before he had tried to curse, and had deliberately restrained himself (with some effort) into uttering a slightly more polite euphemism. This time the words weren't his at all. He simply wouldn't have said that a moment ago. Poop? Nobody says "poop." There was enough adrenaline coursing through him, and enough of a shock to his sensibilities, that he would have tossed aside his normal restraints and used another word—a word that also stood for the fecal matter of humans, but was appropriately rude, even derogatory. However, he did not. He could not. He wasn't alone anymore, and the decision was no longer his alone.

"What in [stinking] [heck] did I get myself into?" He stumbled, and finally someone worked up the nerve to step forward and steady him. He looked around the room, from face to face, examining the crowd. This time, there was no expression to be seen other than shock, amazement, wonder. Where neat rows of men stood idle before, there was now chaos. "Why the [heck] can't I talk right anymore!" He yelled.

It was a distinctly odd sensation to have your consciousness invaded by some other mind, some foreign soul. He could feel that there was something deep inside him. It wasn't a physical feeling. He didn't feel fat, or stretched, or violated in any way. He did have an unshakable feeling he was being watched. From the *inside*. He summoned a few memories from his past to see if he was still himself. Yes, he could remember the day he caught that spectacular pass in his senior year. He remembered his first kiss (he ought to, it was his own fist he was kissing). He remembered when he was fifteen, and his dog Boomer was hit by a car. Boomer was a heavyset bloodhound, mostly made of skin, fat and nose. There were eyes in there too, but you could barely see them under the permanent shroud of his warm, drooping folds of forehead. Boomer, like most scent hounds, had a singular mind when confronted with a new smell. Boomer had smelled something that day, probably a fox. One of the nuisances of living so close to the country-end of suburbia was that on occasion the fox, raccoons, and even sometimes bear would wander in from the fields. They didn't know better. They, like Boomer,

cluck

were following some odorous trail that promised them an easy lunch of ripe garbage or the spilled seed from neighborhood bird feeders. They left their own trail in turn, and Boomer picked it up, and followed it. He followed it for no more than thirty yards before it took him into the road and a collision course with a black-haired housewife driving an old Dodge Caravan. She was driving a bit too fast, as busy moms tend to do on weekday afternoons, and she never saw Boomer until it was too late.

The boy saw the whole thing. He saw the dog cock his head to one side, and raise his nose to the breeze. He saw the initial bound that allowed the dog to move its floppy bulk forward. He saw the approaching mini-van, heard the screech of the tires and the sudden yelp, smelled the wet stench of fresh blood as Boomer fell. He saw something else too: he saw a bright blue shadow of the dog stand up from the pulp of his former friend, and lift its nose to the breeze. It wasn't an angry shadow, or a sad one ... only slightly distracted at having been interrupted from its fun. The blue glow that was Boomer loped off again, fading quickly as he crossed the road until at last he was gone.

"What was that?" He thought, trying to summon the memory more clearly. He was familiar enough with the blue shadows that proceeded every living thing he encountered. But it was that time, with Boomer, that he first thought the lights were people's souls. They must have been. But he never dwelt on that thought, too frightened to think it through to conclusion. Now was different. He wanted to know.

"You were right all along, of course," came a voice inside of him. It wasn't inside his head, like the voices you hear while reading a book or remembering things that you've heard. It was inside of him. All the way inside. *"They're the souls of those around you. You've got the gift. You can see people for what they really are. You've been told that before, but you never really believed it."*

"So, there is someone in there with me. I thought I felt you. You're not the old man, though. You feel younger."

"I'm old, all right. Very old. I'm not him." The image of the master rose to the front of Arnold's mind. *"He's dead now. I was inside him, though, just as I'm inside you now. You're a lucky boy. None of the others have ever been able to sense me. Not for generations ... you are very lucky indeed ..."*

"You're an arrogant voice," he thought and then immediately regretted it. If it was inside him, it could read his thoughts easy enough, whether he intended it to or not.

"Not arrogant, just experienced. You have that experience now. Try it out, you might like it." There was a pensive feeling. The voice was waiting for him to do something. Not knowing what was expected of him, he did nothing.

"Take the cloth," the voice urged him, *"and tie it into a knot."*

"What kind of knot?" the boy asked. There were all kinds of knots. Square knots and slip knots, hidden knots that were difficult to undo. The boy could see clearly the many choices before him, and pondered the delicate art of joinery.

"I bet you didn't even know what a hitch knot or a splice knot was before, did you?"

"No, I didn't ..."

"Well, I did. See, I told you that you were lucky. Arrogant my ass."

The boy saw the truth in that. If he had some inner voice tagging along, at least it was going to be a helpful one. Leaning back against the slab, he closed the eyes of his master. He took the cloth from his forehead, folded it lengthwise until it was long and narrow, and then tied it neatly into a Chinese sliding crown knot before placing it gently on a small shelf next to the primitive alter. *"Not too bad ..."* the voice said, impressed.

There was a crypt already prepared for his master, the boy knew. He knew where it was, and he knew where to find it. He had to see to the body first, and then he needed to get out of there. His voice was making that clear now, as it continued to whisper things at him in the core of his being. He had things to do. He had a war to fight. He was a soldier now. Ironically, when his mother had sent him to the priesthood long ago, she had specifically *not* wanted him to be a soldier. Fate must not have liked her much. He looked down towards his boot at the badge that dangled there. The raised letters were darkened by years of packed dirt and wear. E.V., *Exorciste de Volaille*.

The young man, his forehead blackened by sparks and his hair frayed and wild, had lost all awareness of his surroundings as he held this inner conversation. He hadn't heard the pleading words of the others as they tried to wake him from his haze. He felt them shaking him now, and he turned to look into the eyes of a man. It was the gentle one, the thin man with the kind voice. "Arnold ... Arnold, are you alright?" he asked.

"I think I prefer Armand," Arnold said. And then, out of curiosity, the boy turned his thoughts inward once more.

"I have to ask," he thought to his new half, "why did you stop me from swearing? You seem to curse quite a bit yourself."

"Simple, Armand my boy. Because not cursing is important to you. Your mother raised you well in that regard. Me, I couldn't give a shit."

Knapp

cluck

chapter 9 The country road to perdition

The street was thin and pocked with potholes and debris. There hadn't been a storm in months, yet litter from the overhanging maples made the small country road a maze of fallen branches and leaves. Despite the lack of rain, there were damp trails across what was left of the pavement, dark lines drawn by trapped humidity and dew. The air smelled of damp peat and greens, the type of smell that was as welcoming as a northern spring. The road itself was a fairly typical country road, lined with stone walls and once-noble trees. Only the trees were no longer proud, drooping morosely where they were once as straight as flagpoles. The quaint stereotypical country setting had become tainted with neglect, as if the peaceful, bumpkin cliché had been somehow confused with something more sinister. Where soft ferns should have stood in neat feathery rows, there were only spots of cold mist lingering in the dark among the thorny underbrush. The lichen upon the ancient stone wall had long grown discontent with its boundary of vertically piled fieldstone, and had begun to creep across the small margin of sand and weeds into the road itself. A slow breeze stirred the mist, and the comfortable springtime scent would occasionally give way to a whiff of bog.

It was no longer a friendly road.

A frail and bluish car broke the solitude of the scene. For the first time since their descent, the fallen branches were disturbed; crushed bits of wood, half-rotten and moldy, marked the small sedan's trail down the lane. The brightness of the headlights, diffused by the crawling fog, slid across the mossy trunks of birch and maple. It had been black once, the car. Black, and shiny and full of firm energy and courage. Over time the car, like its driver, had been weathered by a hard life. Hinges that once swung heavy doors with the graceful ease of well engineered luxury now hung loose. An engine that once operated with smooth and silent efficiency was now prone to rattles and squeaks. Where chrome once glittered, only dull metal remained, scratched and grey. It had a hard life indeed, this weary automobile.

To the car, a hard life meant long drives down many deserted roads—some like this one, some modern and flat, some rural and others frighteningly urban. It meant being left parked in the elements, sometimes for many days, waiting for its tired owner to turn the key and persuade it into yet another loud and rumbling trip home. Yes, for a car it had a hard life. Not as hard as the man who sat within it, though. Compared to his life, the car had it easy.

It turned a corner and the road somehow managed to grow even thinner and more neglected. It followed a quaint little brook now; a shallow trickle of water that was dotted with smooth stones. It might be more accurate to say that the brook had the *potential* to be quaint, if it weren't for the unshakable unease that had settled all around it. For at that moment, in the darkness, it was swallowed and befouled by the same eery feeling that consumed the area. As soon as it had appeared the little brook burbled away again into the mist, just as the road began to rise a bit, and then turn and fall away in a new direction. The country road

cluck

meandered in the way that only country roads can, as if it had been paved by a drunkard or an idiot or both. The car, chuttering along, slowed a bit. The engine coughed. It was a nervous cough.

"Easy now, fella," said the voice of the driver. "We won't be staying long, I don't think. Just up ahead now, and a quick look is all. *Reconnaissance*, that's what this is." The voice was rough and slow. By the sound of it you could easily imagine the texture of the breath upon which it was uttered; hot and thick like old coffee. The speaker was obviously an English speaker, though the accent on the word 'reconnaissance' was that of well-trained French. Despite the battered condition of the voice, it had confidence in its sound. It was a voice that possessed enough strength and courage to be self-sufficient and completely independent of its host, if the need arose. It turns out that the need arose so often that the voice had developed a habit of taking charge of the man's mouth, acting as a sort of gatekeeper for the driver's otherwise unchecked stream of curses. Unlike the driver, the voice had developed a modicum of control, at least. It should have, it had seen enough in its time to be able to stay slow and calm even when the body it belonged to was scared out its brains. As a voice, it had learned from a young age that a certain level of propriety should always be maintained, and so it kept itself and its body in check. While it typically only spoke internally, within the man's thoughts, it would occasionally use the mouth to break the silence when its body was lost in thought.

"Ah, there it is now," the driver added. The car noticed too, and started to slow even before the driver had lifted his foot. An old farmhouse emerged from the mist ahead.

That's funny, the voice thought, relinquishing control of the mouth back to the driver, *there's a lot more fog all of a sudden. Not a good sign.*

"That's funny," Armand agreed, and then just a moment later, "Bad sign." He was typically more verbose, but the somber mood asked for less. The mist had indeed turned to fog, and had grown unexpectedly dense as the car crept a few hundred feet closer. The fog was like a dirty blanket of cotton. The farmhouse loomed up from the baleful cloud in the way that only venerable old farmhouses could loom. The car stopped, and the door opened.

The legs and then the backside of the driver emerged from the open door; his top half remained inside the car for a moment, rustling around in a small ocean of empty coffee cups and crumpled papers. Finding what he was looking for, the driver came fully out of the car and stood straight. The face was immediately blocked by an old-fashioned instant camera, but you could easily tell from the bits that showed that the driver was not a handsome man. The edges of his face—the only part that showed around the sides of the camera—were pitted and grey. The hair that protruded at odd angles couldn't really be called a beard. The whiskers stuck out every which way, and seemed to grow in different lengths from different places—all seemingly without any rhyme or reason, and certainly without any attempt at grooming.

Another day at the office, Armand thought, gazing through the greasy viewfinder.

Since the day when he'd first adopted his new name, Armand's life had been hard. It couldn't be seen in his face, being blocked by the camera, but what showed in the *edges* spoke volumes.

The breeze picked up again, and the mist cleared for a moment. It was willful; as if the house was trying to get a look at the man, and had brushed aside the fog to get a clearer view. Maybe it was Armand's will at work, for he truly *wished* that he could see through, and as Armand had aged his will had grown almost as potent and independent as his voice. Even his car seemed to have a mind of its own. Things seemed to develop qualities around Armand, most likely due to some paranormal survival instinct. The camera clicked, and a pale square of film slid from the front. It at least was content to perform its mundane, mechanical task without undue cognizance.

cluck

Click—whiiiiiiiir, went the camera again.

Another square emerged, and the first dropped towards the ground only to be silently plucked from the air by Armand's free hand. Unlike the soft hands of his youth, each was now a set of leathery and cracked digits, calloused with use and years. The hand stuffed the photo into the pocket of the man's battered coat. The garment was made of oiled canvas—or maybe tattered and dirty tweed – but the design was hard to make out in the mist. Like the car and its driver, the coat had seen many years and lived through many trying times. It hadn't started to talk yet, which was a plus, but it was thick enough with grime that it could practically stand on its own.

Click—whiiiiiiiir. Click—whiiiiiiiir.
Click. Click. Click—whiiiiiiiir.

Each new photograph, like the first, was caught and jammed unceremoniously into the pocket. The camera clicked and the photos were stuffed until the film was finally spent and the last photo, still hanging from the camera like some sort of tongue, was pulled free. The camera was tossed back into the chaos of the car's passenger seat, revealing Armand's face fully for the first time. The fog closed in again. It didn't want to see this.

The face was worse than one would imagine, having only seen the edges. It wasn't really pitted, but the effect was the same due to a thick covering of tiny scars that zigzagged about the skin. There were a few larger disfigurements, as well, and a sole champion of scars, which stretched from under the left side of his chin, across his mouth, and all the way to his right cheek, where it ended with an odd star-shaped pocket. He'd lost a big chunk of skin from that one, and the scar tissue hadn't been enough to fill it back in fully. Where the scar crossed his lips it was staggered as if his face had been twisted when whatever had caused the thing had happened. Above the scar, past a nose that bent several times in many directions, in front of two slightly wobbling eyes, the photo was held fixedly. The picture began to take shape and grow clearer as its composition mixed with the air and caused it to develop.

Damn things take forever, Armand thought, although the almost magical process still secretly amused him, even after all these years. Though he'd seen things that would make most people question every aspect of life and science and even religion, it is sometimes the small things that impress. Pushing aside his amazement and respect for the technology, the man opened his mouth and blew hot breath across the film impatiently. The breath was as dismal and serious as the man who made it, yet it did nothing to speed the films development.

"You need to get a digital camera," his voice suggested, politely inside his head. It took Armand somewhat by surprise, but not because it spoke on its own. He was mostly taken aback because he wasn't really sure what "digital" meant and was rather fond of this old instant model anyway. Speaking out of turn was bad enough, but it was always a bit disconcerting when his own voice, which was hundreds of years his senior, made suggestions that made him feel old and obsolete.

His surprise was upstaged by the developing image, though, as it eventually clarified before him. Armand held the picture up before him, to compare it with the real thing. He tried to curse, but his voice intercepted it and applied a cold calmness to the words that gave him a calculating and menacing air.

"[Poop!]" he exclaimed, wishing that his voice would cooperate just for once. This was certainly worthy of a lot more than *poop*. He tried again, attempting something even harsher but this new word didn't come out at all, leaving him with his mouth open feeling foolish. If his voice was going to censor him, he thought, it could at least choose better words than *poop*. As far as Armand was aware, you would never hear the word "poop" from any of history's formidable heroes, fictional or otherwise. Can you image the legendary James Bond uttering "poop" as he stumbled into the midst of a dozen Russian spies? He decided he would

cluck

need to have a word with his voice about the matter. His reputation deserved better, and the photograph warranted something stronger. Much stronger.

Stretched to all four edges of the picture, the same expansive old farm could be seen. It really wasn't so much of a house as it was a collection of houses, each new structure branching away from the original. Outbuildings, barns, sheds and porches had been glued together piece-by-piece, generation after generation. The largest structure was a huge and peeling old barn, easily big enough for a commercial cattle operation. All fairly typical, individually, but extraordinary as a whole.

In the small instant photo, the story was somewhat different from what one might expect of a wealthy family-owned farm. When the photo was held up in a calloused and grubby hand and compared to the real thing, there were distinct differences. The same meandering farm was there, but in the photo the monstrous barn was buried even deeper amid several Cape-style expansions. One long edifice with tiled, multi-paned windows could clearly be seen in the photo. A squat old stable with slatted doors and crumbling clapboards was also clearly depicted in the picture. Looking past the small square of instant film, to its mist-shrouded subject, these elements disappeared and were replaced by dark, unfriendly woods. As if to hide its true expansiveness behind a blanket of foreboding, the farm had been wrapped in illusion. Viewed from the road the farm looked decrepit; a collection of condemnable buildings upon a foundation of rot, surrounded by unnatural fog and chill. While certainly uninviting, the farm appeared to be something fairly normal out of early American history. The photograph, however, showed a property so expansive that it would have been almost impossible to construct, even with endless generations of construction and unlimited funds. There were so many roofs, arranged at imprecise angles off into the distance, that it was hard to make sense of the estate. Many of these roofs sagged, and several of them were dotted with rusting weathervanes and lightening rods. Close to the road, facing Armand, was a particularly striking oxeye dormer which looked as if it had been pulled out of a fairy-tale book. It also looked more than a little bit like a real eye, which was looking at Armand in a more than casual way.

The furthest buildings may have stretched all the way to the horizon, but it was impossible to tell. The edges of the estate were lost in shroud and mist before their limit could be determined.

"Well, isn't that interesting ..." muttered the aged and worn man who was once a clever and special young boy named Arnold. "Very interesting indeed ..."

While Armand stood surrounded by eddies of thick vapor, there wasn't any fog at all in the picture. Not even a tiny bit of haze. Where the huge pale moon hung menacingly before him, the photograph showed nothing but the normal darkness of an overcast night. The farm in the photo didn't loom, either. It just sat there looking like it needed a good coat of paint and maybe a little bit of love. Looking up away from the picture, the real farm was definitely looming, and it looked like it needed *plenty* of love. The windows peered outwards like the multifaceted eyes of a spider. The shutters groaned in protest against mysterious eddies of wind. The light of the moon swept past the impressive structures of the farmstead and cast blurred shadows into the fog, but it was all a ruse. The oxeye, in the picture, was just a normal window.

Photographs don't lie, Armand thought, lowering the picture. Lost in thought, he crumpled it into the same overcrowded place in his coat where the other photos were waiting.

" ... still haven't figured out how to trick a camera," he said, but he was at a loss to explain the situation fully. It was standard practice to check out a new haunt with film, but the results typically revealed far more subtle differences. He had expected to see the real farmhouse much as it appeared to him now with his naked eye, though with less darkness and dread. Why would the illusion bother to extend so far as to

cluck

alter the appearance of the place to such an extreme? "Something odd about this place," he concluded, and just then, in the distance, a rooster crowed.

"No time for a rooster to be crowing," Armand said to himself as he pulled a remarkably shiny watch from a remarkably shabby pocket. "It's only ... half past two in the morning? [Jeeze!] Where does the time go ... but [heck], even if the moon really *was* up, it's not the right time for crowing." He patted down the coat as if looking for something that might be lost within the bulk of the garment. "And here I am without my kit." There was no need for the man to be surprised. He purposefully and habitually left his gear behind on what he called "reconnaissance missions" to stop himself from blundering headstrong into a situation and getting himself in well over his strong head.

He began to walk slowly towards the house, one step at first, and then another. Each time his foot hit the old road, it was with deliberate caution, as if something terrible was expected at some unknown point. Each footstep was a test. Each of his hard leather boots was a chess pawn, moving him steadily forward with no chance of veering away until he either reached his goal or he was taken. It was as if there was an invisible line, marking the edge of safety and of sanity, the edge of the chessboard. Once this line was crossed, the universe would reject him. It would twist the road and pitch the hapless man into some unknown fate. Another step, and another ...

Armand used his *other* vision to scan for some spiritual clue. He expected to see something—though he didn't know what—with certain, sudden clarity. He was not disappointed: as he stepped closer, something *did* happen. As he stepped over some invisible threshold, some hidden point of demarcation, the universe exploded with light. His eyes grew wide in surprise and then quickly pressed themselves closed again, shutting out the burning blue radiance.

Knapp

"Christ! Turn out the lights, will ya? Are you trying to blind me!" complained his voice against the sudden effulgence. It was as if a blinding light had hit him as he emerged from a dark chamber, flaring and brilliant and almost beautiful ... but also painful. Where clarity was expected, there was the opposite, a myriad swirl of light and shapes and energy that forced the man, with a slight intake of breath, to take one step back across the invisible line, to safety.

"It's all right," he said to himself, to his car, perhaps to no one. "It's perfectly all right. Can't see the forest for the trees, is all," and he stepped backwards again, back towards the car, and as the wind picked up he ducked quickly inside. "This one is going to be a doozey," he added.

"Tell me about it, I'm still seeing spots ..."

The car didn't want to start, but then again it never did. He coaxed it a bit, and said a few kind words, and then turned it around sharply and hurried away back the way he came. The mystery glow of the illusory moon vanished as they turned the corner and left the quaint little stream behind. The engine picked up a bit, as if relieved, and it carried its driver away.

chapter 10 haunting bobby

Bobby wasn't feeling very well. He was scared. It wasn't a mortal fear, for he would have welcomed death. Even a painful death. Even a prolonged and agonizing death. It would have been better than one more day in the living Hell that was his life. Ghostly encounters, it would seem, are not isolated incidents that only surround crazy Frenchmen in secret chicken-obsessed societies. They often surrounded Bobby, as well.

Bobby gibbered a bit, and cowered. He was alone, for now, but they'd be back. He knew it. Something had drawn them away for the moment, but they'd definitely return, probably soon. He scratched at the back of his head and realized there was some pain mixed in with the itching. He straightened a bit and looked up. There was blood on his hands, but that didn't bother him so much; there was always blood. You begin to overlook certain details when you live with them day after day, year after year. Like when you become accustomed to a foul smell to the point where you no longer notice it at all, Bobby barely even registered such happenstance details as blood. It was strangely quiet, so he tested his voice.

"S—" he began, and then started to cough, attempting to rid his lungs of the dust and stink that filled the air around him. Bits of down flew from his mouth, making it look as if there were a pillow fight happening inside his head. He cleared his throat and tried again. "S—sorry," he managed. Bobby's voice, unlike the clear and commanding voice of the scar-faced Banisher of Bantams, was weak and unsure of itself. It had been strong once, but not anymore. Not since *they* arrived. The thought of *them* sent him scurrying backwards on all fours, kicking and scrambling towards the perceived safety of the loft's corner, where he gathered himself together and then pulled himself quickly to his feet. Yes, he had been cowering on the ground. That's why there was so much blood. It was bad to be on the ground. He had to stay on his feet. He looked around, taking advantage of the sudden calm and quiet to get his bearings.

He was, indeed, in a loft. There was stagnant and sordid hay in small piles around the floor, not really much more than straw now that the years had bleached it into dead yellow. The smell of it stained him with its musk. *Piles* may not be the right word—they were what had once been piles but had at some point been scattered around into a shallow carpet of desiccated mess. Mess. There was lots of that, too. Feces, that is. As the exorcist might say (though he'd try hard not to), *poop*. The floor was covered in it. That wasn't right either, but it didn't surprise him. They were filthy beasts. Just about as filthy as they come. That's why they never would have been allowed into the house. Certainly not in the new section—

The new section. Yes, that's right. There was a new section. It had been built not too many years before. Just before—

The thought was lost. He tried to recall. He remembered the house, sort of. His mind suddenly flashed with memories of clean

cluck

country breezes, and the soft feeling as he held the hand of a woman. The smell of fresh-milled pine asserted itself, and the warmth of sunlight. He focused on the memory of the woman, trying to remember her face. He had been in love, he thought. It wasn't a dream, it was a real memory. He had been in love. Something had happened, he remembered, and then the feeling of the woman's soft hand suddenly eluded him. Something happened and she was gone, and all that was left was pain and blood and dust. Desperately, like a drowning man struggling to swallow the most meager gulp of air, he tried to get the memory back.

It was a long time since he was allowed to think about anything, as it was hard to concentrate these days. He tried harder and harder to remember, his face twisting up in concentration. He could see that he was in a loft ... a hayloft. He knew there were several such lofts throughout the place. There was one in an old part of the attic even, and several in the barns. Most had hay, but not the lofts in the new guest rooms. Is that where he was now? For some reason thoughts of the new construction jumped to the front of his mind again. Maybe that's where he was? He felt it was, though he couldn't explain why there would be so much hay inside the newest sections of the house. He could be anywhere, really. It was too dark to know for sure. It was always dark. He scratched his head again, and his legs. He clawed at his face and eyes to peel away the feeling of itch and dirt and blood.

"I'm sorry?" he said again. Sometimes, by apologizing, he would satisfy them for a while, hold them at bay for just a moment longer. He was, after all, paying penance for what he had done. Janice wasn't here to help him, this time. He was utterly alone, and he was being punished for his sins.

His meek request for forgiveness was more of a question, this time. A probe. Where were they? Apologies or not, it was unlike them to leave him alone for this long. They should be here, encircling him, closing in ...

Knapp

As best he could tell the agony had been going on for what must have been three or four years. He wasn't sure how he was even alive, but he knew he must be alive. If he was dead, he'd have to be in Hell, and he didn't believe in Hell. Regardless, he knew he had to get out. He knew that for sure. It was always the first coherent plan to enter his brain, whenever he was given a few minutes to think, but he never seemed to be able to escape. Like a sheepdog herding its flock, they had a way of moving him around. Usually it was because he would panic and run wildly in the opposite direction whenever he saw them, losing himself in his fear and, in turn, losing himself in the labyrinthian house. He had to try to remain calm. He had to focus on the good things, on his memories, on anything that would keep him from panicking. His eye began to twitch and he clawed at his face again. He wasn't crazy yet, but he was sure as heck on his way.

He panicked.

As Bobby ran senselessly through the house, Armand drove steadily away from it. He was making good time back to the motel where he'd set up a temporary office, and was uncharacteristically glad.

"Chick-chick-a-chicken, chick-chick-a-chicken, chick-chick, cha-rooo ... Another day, another chicken." Armand's adaptation of Marry Poppin's *March Over The Rooftops* was slightly flat, largely off-key, and hugely disturbing. He fidgeted in the slightly sagging seat. Though he had stopped singing, his voice continued to hum the tune inside his head.

He was in a good mood because he'd just seen something rather terrifying and he now had a dangerous challenge ahead of him. He'd been in a bit of a funk lately. He was bored of kicking daft dead birds about, tired of the same old routine.

cluck

"You're in a good mood today. I don't think I've ever heard you, um, sing, before. That was singing, right?" Of course, unlike Armand's voice, which could speak freely with Armand inside of his head if not otherwise inclined to take full control of his vocal cords and speak audibly to the world, nobody could hear the car. Its words simply echoed around the ethereal spaces of the spirit world. The car always wondered why Armand couldn't hear, being so spectrally tuned, but if he could hear he never gave any indication of it. Perhaps mysterious, self-developed sentience is hard to hear over normal engine noise? If only the car could make its thoughts stronger, perhaps it could move the air, forming little ripples of noise; sound-waves that could be heard by others. It strained. The tires wobbled a bit.

"Maybe this one will be the last," said the tired exorcist, his mood swinging alarmingly back into the doldrums. The car sputtered, the sun visor slipping free and swinging in surprise: it cracked against the window.

"The last what? You're not talking about retirement, are you?"

"Retirement ... it's not that I'm getting old, but there's more to life than this, isn't there? I mean, how many people do this?"

Did he just reply? He never replied. Never, not to the car. Sure he talked to everything in the spectra-verse, but never to the car. Overjoyed, the inspired sedan steered itself lithely around a pothole that Armand hadn't seen. The car didn't want to get its hopes up, but if he'd replied, that meant that he'd heard. The implications were huge; if the car just concentrated enough, burned enough gas (and a bit of oil), Armand could hear. This was a ... a conversation!

"I'm so glad I really can't tell you how long I've waited to speak, I mean, well I always speak but to be heard is different from just talking and—"

"I mean, Christ, look at me, now I'm talking to myself. Driving down the middle of the road in the middle of nowhere, talking to myself.

I must be going nuts." He often questioned weather he was slipping over the fine line between a rational, sane chicken exorcist and a raving madman. It was a very fine line. Microscopic.

"You're not going nuts, you're already nuts," his voice answered inside his head, and then out loud it added, "I mean, if you're going to talk to yourself, at least talk to me, if you know what I mean." The car began to pull to the right in silent protest against this blatant show of communicability, while it remained mute and moot: jealous that the voice, who is no less quasi-sentient, again took front seat.

Ignoring his voice and oblivious to his car's silent yearnings to be heard, Armand drove on. A question burned inside his head, born from the same doubt as always. Why has he spent most of his life hanging around with weird Frenchmen and/or the walking wisps of chickens past? It was a good question, but Armand wasn't very strong when it came to inward reflection. The need to self-analyze was usually pushed aside in the face of duty. Duty was all he'd had, after he was thrust away from family and friends. He couldn't talk to anyone about it, either. You can't walk into a therapist's office and unburden yourself of the weight of this particular career and expect to walk back out again. Not with your arms in open-ended sleeves, anyway.

The car, which was slowing as it approached a stop sign, decided to stall; the vehicle chugged to a halt at the nondescript junction between two nondescript roads, at the outskirts of some nondescript town in this nondescript world (incidentally, not far from the most concentrated center of spectral activity to ever occur unnaturally).

"Look," said the car. *"Just because you apparently can't hear my thoughts doesn't mean I can't hear yours. I'm so embarrassed, stammering on like some school kid ... So go blank, will you? For years I've been driving you from every corner of this stinking coop of a country, the least you can do is keep quiet, or turn on the radio, at least."* Defiantly, the car clicked the radio on itself as Armand fumbled with the ignition.

cluck

"Hell, what else am I supposed to do? I've got no skills." Armand clicked the radio off again.

"You've got skills, you moron. Of course, you can't hear worth a crap, but you kick more ass than James Bond ever could. You never even have to use a gun. Of course, you don't dress as sharply, and I've never seen you with a woman, [5] but there's no denying you've got skill."

"You've got me," said Armand's voice.

"Oh great, rub it in." The car purposefully hit a bump. Hard.

"I guess I'm stuck cluck-busting 'till the day I die," Armand concluded, and then turned off the switch of self-reflection just as the car switched the radio back on. To the car's delight, Armand's voice kept quiet, too.

"Ah, sweet silence." The engine turned over, finally, and they drove on, turning left towards destiny. As always, there was a ragged collection of cheap novels littering the car's floor-mats, and the industrious automobile turned its attention to the adventures of agent 007. The car loved to read, as did Armand, who thankfully was also a bit of a slob; there was always a discarded paperback left in, on, or under the backseat for the car to enjoy.

Armand looked at the dry vinyl of the dashboard. "That's a good boy," he said, patting the instruments as if his car were a dog (or worse, just a car). "I bet you're glad you don't have to worry about things like life ..."

"No, I'm glad because I usually have a driver who can go for hours without saying or thinking anything. Now be quiet, I'm trying to read."

Sometimes the largest ironies went unknown; unnoticed even by those who've played them out. Of course, in a way, the car *was* alive.

---

[5] Actually, the car had never seen a woman at all, and wondered what was so special about them. The explanations provided by the stories concerning agent 007 lacked sufficient context to be understood by such a humble, non-biological machine as this.

In a way, it was because of Armand, too, and yet neither of them really knew what it meant to be alive, and how special that was. Outside of a four-minute spit of contemplation every ten years or so, these two lives were given very little thought. Armand simply lost the will to try; he'd left it behind when he'd packed his bags and left France, and the car simply took life for granted. Machines are like that; they lack context and perspective, and tend to ignore things outside of their intended operating environment.[6]

There was a sudden noise from about a half-foot above the floorboards as Bobby ran recklessly down a once-familiar hallway. The hay-littered loft was now far behind him, and a long barren hallway stretched out before him as he ran. There was something there, half hidden in the deep shadows of the hall, for there were no lights or windows. It stood low, with a serpentine neck and a small bobbing head, turning this way and then that, alternating the aim of its two dark red marble eyes. It was standing near the doorway to a side room and had come close to being kicked by Bobby as he fled with as much energy as he could muster in the completely wrong direction. Startled, it jumped up and wildly flapped its wings, filling the hall with a cloud of dust and feathers but unable to achieve flight. It hit the wall with a *thunk*, leaving a wet red mark before falling back to the floor. It scratched at the wood angrily and let out a slow clucking groan.

It was a hen. Most of one, anyway.

"There's something that ain't quite right about that thar hen," Bobby would have thought, if he had stumbled across it years ago. He would

---

[6] Unlike life, the car had a deep, well-formed philosophy concerning oil viscosity and proper engine timing.

have thought it odd, and probably would have stopped to shout, "Why the hell is there a dang-gum chicken in the house!" or something equally as eloquent. Then, if he had looked a little closer, he would have said "She-it! What in the hell's wrong with the fuckin' thing, anyhow?" After all, chickens shouldn't be transparent, for starters. This one had a long length of thin chain—complete with rusty padlocks and strings of cobweb—draped over its back, which was also odd. If that wasn't enough, its beak was missing, as was most of one wing and part of one leg. Unfortunately, it wasn't years ago, and Bobby had not stopped to look. He knew already about the chicken, and was trying his best to get away from it and the others like it. He scrambled up a narrow set of stairs, and came to a sudden stop. His upper body snapped forward and there was a terrible *CRACK!* as his leg fell through a false step.

His mind flashed in panic. He knew about haunted houses, of course. Everybody did. The false step was an old standby—like the pivoting fireplace and the torture chamber and the spiky pit. The spiky pit, he also knew, was just below the false stair. He closed his eyes and winced as a sharp pain shot up through his boot. His shin hit the edge of the next highest step with a second only slightly softer crack as his forward momentum was halted by the impact of bone against wood. He knew there would be a spiky pit, but that foresight did little to dull the rush of pain. He pulled his right leg out of the pit with his hands, and watched the blood well out of the tiny holes in the soles of his well-worn farmers' boots. All haunted houses had spiky pits and false steps, he knew that. He had to pay attention. He had to stop panicking.

It's lucky for him, he thought, that chickens thought small. If they had any sense of scale at all, he'd have been killed for certain. As things were, the false step only dropped down about a foot or so, and the spikes were little more than ten-penny nails. Favoring his uninjured foot, he hopped to the next good step and continued on his way. He needed clear thinking. Panic had a way of creeping back in, but he stemmed it off. The pain helped.

Until he heard it.

A rooster. Crowing. It came from up above—on the roof, probably. Damn! He was going the wrong way! He did not want to be going *towards* the rooster. He turned and ran down a long, bare, wainscoted hallway. It was dark, and Bobby barely noticed as he crashed through a small pile of skulls that littered the corridor. He was oblivious to the *swoosh* as something tiny shot past his left leg. The rooster, he knew, was the worst of the flock. Again, flashes of the past filled Bobby's mind. He fell to his knees as a montage of pain and anguish flooded his memories. The rooster, a monstrous black beast that blotted out all light and hope. Those beady, calculating eyes. The spread of its enormous wings. The distinct smell of creosote. The terrible sound that it made as it split the air with its thundering crow. The rooster stood taller than the rest of the haunted flock. He was more imposing, more intelligent, and much more dangerous. Even if the rooster stood alone, he would be a terrible threat. If he got too close to the rooster, Bobby knew, he'd be in real trouble. It could reach higher than the others, maybe even high enough to reach Bobby's face and eyes. His beak was sharper, and stronger, but the rooster had never attacked Bobby directly. He was the general of the undead poultry army, and was always in the background, commanding them, bringing strength to his feathered militia and bringing terror to his enemies.

So much for clear thinking. He stood again, and turned back towards a narrow staircase. A small part of Bobby felt the stairs were familiar, that there was something about them that he was supposed to remember … but his fear didn't let him dwell on it. Ignoring the pain that pulsed up his leg, he climbed the steps as if he might find freedom somewhere up high. There was another loud *CRACK!* as Bobby stepped into the same false step, already stained with his own blood, as he scram-

cluck

bled to ascend the stairs. Barely noticing the new pain, he climbed and climbed and climbed, one step after another. Limping with both legs, he looked like a circus chimp that had crapped in its diaper as he fled.

Clear thinking was well and good, but panic would do just fine if it meant running like hell away from the rooster. Reaching the next level, he emerged into another plain room. It was furnished with a large wooden hutch and a small round table. The softness of the floor told Bobby there was a rug underneath the layers of dust. The dust had been disturbed with dozens of tracks of both man and bird and then buried again beneath the dirt of time. So often had this cycle repeated itself that the floor looked like it had sprouted a dry, grey, mossy lawn. Bobby ran like hell across the room and slammed into a closed door on the opposite wall, leaving a cloud of dust swirling through the center of the room as he rocketed from the landing of the old staircase. The thud was loud enough that Bobby never heard the distant sound of a car door closing, or the stuttering of a reluctant engine. These new and less familiar sounds came from below him, from just down the long barren hallway where another door opened into a small entry parlor. Not that Bobby could have recognized the sounds of a car anymore, even if he had heard. It had been a very long time, and Bobby was no longer coherent; he was seized by adrenaline, fueled by fear. The hope of regaining any rational thought continued to dissipate with each soggy step of Bobby's wounded feet. He'd lost the opportunity to find his way back to the small entry-way (which was an old side entrance used primarily by servants), instead climbing the narrow staircase, running deeper into the maze of halls, dens, sitting rooms and studies that made up the ancient farmhouse's considerable interior.

As he metabolized the adrenaline, his senses began to return and he slowed a bit, fighting to catch his breath. He could hear them now. The rattle of chains, the whistling of mysterious drafts piping their way through mysterious cracks. He could hear the scuttling of tiny claws. He could hear the clucking and clacking of tiny beaks. He was in a small smoking room, full of high-backed velvet chairs, resplendent in their disrepair and stained with centuries of smoke. There were several doors leading off in several directions. There was a tiny coal fireplace and a large winged chair before it. By the looks of it something had made a nest in the fireplace; the wallpaper from one corner of the room had been scratched away and bundled up around the coal basket. The room, like most of the house, was dark. Light was rare, making day and night blend into seamless drudgery. It was so rare that the faint glow that suddenly appeared from the well of the narrow staircase drew Bobby's attention immediately. He crept forward and peered upward. At the top of the staircase, a small shape had appeared and was floating gently in the air. It was red, and round, with a green top. The ghostly shape of a ripe tomato bobbed just a few feet above the top step. It taunted him with the memory of fresh food, and the refreshing crispness of summer salads. It glowed slightly and yet was translucent; it was strangely fascinating as it wavered in the air, floating nearer, and then drifting backwards and up. It wanted him to follow it, he thought, just before he screamed. He turned and ran through the nearest door, into a musty parlor, leaving the light behind.

From its hiding spot behind the coal basket, a speckled red hen shook its head. This of course caused its gobble to fall off, and part of its lower beak to swing precariously as it hung limply from a small fleshless chicken-skull face. It didn't understand. It couldn't understand. The human never followed the tomato, and that just didn't make sense. A chicken would have followed the tomato. Tomatoes, as any chicken knows, are delicious. They are juicy and sweet and easy to gobble up even though some cosmic power had the sense of humor to give chickens neither hands nor teeth. Hell, they didn't even have lips! How unfair was that? Humans had all three, of course, but yet they turn away from a

cluck

perfectly ripe tomato and go running off in the completely wrong direction.

Maybe, the chicken thought, it should use the tomat-o-wisp to scare the human away, rather than trying to use it as a lure? Naaaw. The chicken knew that wouldn't work. Nobody could refuse a nice ripe tomato.

Chickens aren't very smart. Not even when they're dead.

Bobby wasn't thinking very clearly, but he knew that tomatoes don't float and he knew that he was scared as hell. He ran through a long hall—was that the long hall that connected the kitchen to the barn, or the long hall that led to the guest room?

Thwack! —and Bobby was on the ground again. Next to his head was a small pile of skulls. Tiny skulls. A small puff of dust rose from one evil socket, and a small spear was sticking out of his right calf. It was so small it might have been cute if it weren't for the blood. He pulled the little spear out—no bigger than a toothpick—and brought it close to his face for a better look. It had little markings on it, and little feathers at its base. Not chicken feathers, though. Probably pigeons. The little freaks were keen enough to hurt other birds, all right. They'd even eat one another, he knew—they weren't smart enough to know better. He honestly couldn't put two and two together to figure out why they had such a grudge against him. Why wouldn't they leave him alone? He knew that he should remember. He knew that he *would* remember, if they would just leave him be for a moment. If he could only calm down and concentrate, he could sift through what was left of his sanity and find the reason behind it all. Not knowing, Bobby assumed the memory would be a painful one. Everything in Bobby's life was painful, so why should this locked away memory be any different? After all, whatever had caused his once-magnificent home to become infested with the ghosts of chickens past couldn't possibly be something happy. Despite whatever morbid circumstances were behind the haunting, Bobby needed to know, and yearned to resurface those memories.

From where he lay, Bobby could see that several of the small skull piles lay in wait all down the length of the hallway. No doubt each had a spear for him, and he'd trashed his right foot and leg pretty badly today. He managed to get a grip, and took stock of himself.

His right leg hurt a lot. There was probably some sort of poison on that spear, he thought, or at least some disease. Chickens are filthy beasts, he always thought. His boots felt clammy because they were full of blood from the several small holes in his feet. The boots themselves were near ruined, but he'd be damned if he was going to take the things off. They'd pecked his pants clean away from the knees down, after all, digging into his exposed shins every chance they could. The boots were the only reason he still had toes. He scratched at his face and head and legs. He itched all over, and ached too. His knees had grooves in them from repeated falls, and scars from pecking. He remembered the stairs. That would explain the knees. He couldn't remember much from minute to minute, but he had a feeling he'd fallen for that one before. His thighs were relatively unhurt, and the remains of his pant legs covered them still. Denim. Good choice. Nice and sturdy. Farm stuff, denim is. Like his boots. He rolled over and stood up, continuing his self-examination.

His arms were scratched and bloody, but there didn't seem to be any wounds to worry about. Not clean though. He was almost as filthy as everything else. It's amazing, he reflected, how a few chickens could trash a place. He lifted his shirt to find more scratches and some fleas. A tick had lodged itself not far below his nipple, and he clawed it off and scrambled backwards. Ticks freaked him out. He hated ticks. With his best foot, he stomped the nasty insect as it crawled nonchalantly across the dirty floor, and then lifted his shirt again to check for others. He was clean, relatively speaking, and so he moved on to his hair. His head hurt, and his hair pulled away freely in his hands. Mange? No, chickens didn't spread mange. Probably lice, though. And more ticks.

Bobby shuddered. He stood up, and shuddered again. Just for good measure, he shuddered a third time.

At his feet, where he had just been sitting, was a small clutch of five large brown eggs. He stared gape-mouthed at them, and then backed uncertainly to the wall as they began to swell, and crack, and rot. Before his eyes they smoldered into a small pile of unborn decay. He wretched, but nothing came up. Despite the disgust, Bobby realized he was ravenously hungry.

At the end of the hall, two wicked hens watched Bobby as he stared down at the eggs. Like the tomato, the eggs never seemed to have the desired effect. The first hen—a large buff colored oven-roaster—was trying to get a small black fancy bantam to explain why the human wasn't acting right. She scratched in the dirt, and pecked the ground.

"*Cluck*," she clucked. "*Cluck, cluck cluc-kaaaaaaw. Braw braaaaaaaaaw. Cluck,*" which of course meant "I don't get it, this big stupid human isn't acting right. How are we supposed to haunt this idiot if he doesn't behave properly?" That really was the crux of the dilemma. The first chicken tried to explain, but was missing all of the toes of one foot and its head was completely absent. When it tried to scratch the ground, it ended up just hopping around and trying not to fall over. When it tried to cluck, nothing but a little wisp of noise and a tiny puff of dust would bellow up from the top of its neck. It made communicating difficult.

Of course, the second chicken didn't really understand enough of what was going on to care much that its companion was flapping about on badly deformed feet blowing gas out of its neck like some morbid smokestack. It assumed (rightly so) that the first chicken was trying to say the exact same thing that it was saying; namely, that man wasn't reacting correctly. The thing is that hens react in very certain and very consistent ways to eggs. If they notice one is there, for example, they eat it. Fast. Before the other hens notice it's there. The last thing you want to do, when you are a chicken, is share anything. The human, against all chicken logic, didn't eat the eggs. Not even after they cracked open and started to smell. That would have been a great haunt because he might get ill and die. They heard the farmer himself say that when they were still alive. "Sal-mo-nel-la" he called it, but regardless of his reasons and his fancy words, he never ate the ghost-eggs, stumping the chicken's futile attempts at gastrointestinal murder.

The most confusing part was that he never even seemed to get distressed about them. No chicken wanted to see its own eggs die. Unless of course you were eating them, but he wasn't, so why wouldn't he at least get upset about them? He did throw up, which is kind of like being upset, but not in the way they expected. It just wasn't right.

The first chicken started its demented little dance again, which would have meant "I just don't get it" if it could have pulled it off, which it couldn't. The second hen understood what the first hen tried to explain, though, although it certainly was hard to decipher the footless scratching and the wobbling of its neck stump.

"Cluck." The second hen confirmed.

"—" the first hen replied, and then fell over.

From a distant corner of the farmhouse, the sounds of screaming could be heard. Bobby had fallen through the step again.

Far away from the farmhouse, the crumpled remains of a FedEx package lay on top of a plain round fold-out table. It was covered with Air-bill stickers and several pale monochrome stamps from several pale monochrome government offices. On top of the envelope lay a report, and around the report, seated in metal folding chairs about the table,

cluck

were three very serious and very unhappy looking men. One was young-ish and strapping, though his posture was poor and he slumped in his chair. Two were older, with white hair and tired expressions: of these, one was meticulously kept and the other unshaven, although also well dressed. Only the neat, older gentleman sat without a slouch, but it didn't prevent him from hanging his face into his hands. The room was white and cheap-looking, almost clinical, although it smelled like the home of a longtime bachelor, with only the faintest aroma of fine coffee to make it bearable.

The report was constructed of several sheets of plain white paper with many creased and damaged photos glued and taped in short rows across the front of each. At the apex of the pile sat a heavier sheet that was adorned with letterhead. The impressive font and style of it would have suggested an almost royal importance if it had not been wrinkled so badly. The crest, which emblazoned the top of the page, showed a circle of feathers, with one more elaborately stylized feather standing below the initials "E.V." Beneath this, in fanciful logotype, were the words *"Ordre du l'Exorciste de Volaille"* and the date 1604 AD expressed by the roman numerals "MDCIV."

"If you're so worried, I can go and help," offered the youngest of the three. "I mean, it looks like a big enough job for two, and I've been thinking of taking a short vacation back home anyway. I mean, it's been a while since I've been back to America." The request was made a little too eagerly, and it made the others suspicious, enough so that the oldest man lifted his head from his hands long enough to snap *"Laissez-moi penser!"*

"Speak English, already, will ya?" The youth retorted.

"He said 'Let me think'," the other interjected, "but no, I don't think that you're going to America, on vacation or otherwise. We're more likely to recall Armand—

"Recall him? How can we recall him!" The eldest gentleman's face had quickly risen again in defiance of the suggestion. To the youngest he added "Well, Patrick, how is my *Eeenglish*?" The last word was stretched out and laced with both sarcasm and an unnaturally thick layer of French condescension. The two older gentlemen did their best to feed the growing cloud of pungent smoke with several quick puffs on their respective cigarettes.

"Your English is just fine, Jean-Pierre, just fine. What I don't get is why you two are so upset. I mean, is this report really so out of the ordinary? Dirty, crumpled, and ominous. Maybe I haven't been around as long as you two have, but it seems that everything that crazy old bastard sends us looks exactly the same."

"Crazy? Maybe, but don't underestimate Armand, he is ..." the statement trailed off because Jean-Pierre couldn't think of adequate words to finish it. How is it possible to describe Armand? Smarter than most, or at least well educated. Strong, enduring and for the most part fearless. Of course, he also had something else that only he possessed, but they didn't like to speak of that. Not knowing what to say, he turned to his partner.

"Claude? Maybe you can say it better," but Patrick was tired of waiting for an explanation, and he interrupted before Claude could answer.

"Besides," Patrick interjected, "he's the only one who can really do this anyway, right? I mean, the only one who can really do anything." It was an innocent enough observation, but it struck a nerve in Jean-Pierre that made the thick vein in his forehead throb noticeably.

"Shut it boy!" Jean-Pierre slammed his fists down onto the table as he stood up, punctuating his movement with a crash. "Are you saying the rest of this place is nothing but some giant hoax? That we are all pretending to be something that we are not?" The boy shrank back, and looked apologetically at Jean-Pierre. The other man didn't move at all—he'd seen plenty of rants like this one and knew that it would blow over in a few minutes—but the boy wasn't sure what he'd done or what the result of his master's anger would be. Jean-Pierre gave Patrick the willies.

cluck

It was something about the way the aging Frenchman refused to use contractions, then filled each overly long English phrase with sneering derision.

"I'm not implying that you're pretending anything. I mean, you practically came right out and told me during the so-called 'recruitment' that all we had to do was investigate a few anonymous calls—not even to really investigate but just to look close enough to decide when to send Armand in to clean the mess up – or to figure whether it was a hoax. Although come to think of it, we haven't even had any false reports since I've been here." The boy grinned, like he felt that any chicken-related activity was laughable, whether or not the chicken that perpetrated the crime were living or dead. Truth be told, when Patrick joined The Order he thought he was auditioning for a TV show, and he'd only gone along with things thus far because of the chance to see France, and the free room and board.

"You've only been here a year, rookie. We get plenty of pranks. Well, at least we used to. We used to all have to get our hands dirty too, let me tell you, until—"

"Until what, Claude? Why won't anyone tell me what the Hell is going on here, anyway?" Patrick's interruption silenced the room, and after an uncomfortable pause Jean-Pierre sank back into his chair.

"Je devine qu'il est probablement temps de lui dire ..."

"Probablement," agreed the other, and then before Patrick could begin to complain about their use of French, Jean-Pierre turned back to him.

"There is a rite to ascension, as you have been taught. An ancient and powerful ceremony that hands the power and wisdom of the *Exorciste de Volaille* from the Grand Master of our Order to his apprentice, so that it may in turn be taught to future agents of The Order." It seemed to be the start of a long tale, so Patrick felt it necessary to interrupt again.

"I know the story already. The Changing of the Guard—"

"The Passing of The Charge, you idiot." It was said with calm contempt of the type only possible from a Frenchman.

"Whatever," Patrick continued, unfazed. "The Grand Master of The Order of *Exorciste de Volaille* passes his life essence—containing all of his knowledge and power and memories—to his most worthy pupil. Blah, blah blah, and so The Order has survived for over four hundred years."

"Well, then you know as much as the ancient texts say. You know what we taught you. You know that much, so you might as well know the truth, too." He reached instinctively for a cup of coffee that wasn't there, and then jammed the cigarette hastily into his mouth as some sort of surrogate, feeding one addiction with the other.

"The truth is, that the Grand Master of this order of ours had about as much power as me and you. Sure, old *Monsieur Biddéon* looked menacing enough, but most of it was show. With some training he could see the things, or at least learned to recognize the signs of where they had been. He knew how to drop his psychological inhibitions enough so that he could find the bastards when he needed to, and kick them clear out of purgatory with a heavy boot—but that was it. There hadn't been a proper exchange of power for generations because there simply wasn't any power to transition between each master and his successor.

Then, a few decades ago, when I was a kid … well, this scrawny kid wanders in. He was an American kid, like you. We had no idea who he was or why he was here, at first, but he just waltzed right in— into secret headquarters—and started talking about being able to see ghosts. Chicken ghosts."

Claude picked up the story before Patrick could interrupt again. "It turns out that one of our retired agents, a priest now, sent him to us. The kid had power, and it wasn't long before the Master figured that out and took him under his wing. Heh. The Order really beat the crap out of that kid, never gave him any rest. At first they, *we*, persecuted him

cluck

because we thought he was a fraud, and then later on for *not* being a fraud." The two old men shared a quiet look of repent.

"Anyway," Jean-Pierre continued, "The Order kept him in the old temple almost all of the time. You have seen the old temple, have you not?"

"Yeah, they showed it to me when I first got here."

"What did you think?"

"I thought it was a joke. Still do. It isn't a temple, it's an office building. Sure, it's full of stone archways and cobwebs, like a real ancient temple might have had, but they're just plunked there on the linoleum. It looks more like a yard sale, to tell the truth. When I first saw it ... honestly, it kinda freaked me out." The older gentlemen shared a disapproving look, but decided to let this blatant blasphemy pass for now.

"Well, it freaked Armand out, too. He lived and trained there for years, until old master Biddeon fell ill, and began to die. Until he called Armand to receive the ascension ..." Claude's hand started to shake, and having just finished a cigarette began to fumble for another.

"What we are trying to tell you is that the Passing of The Charge was always ..." again, he turned to Claude for clarification.

"It was bunk," Claude explained. "For a long time, it was, anyway, but when Armand took the honor, something strange happened. There was a light, which was new, and this hollow rushing sound, and well ... Armand was different after that. A little more arrogant, and a little more bold. There was something different in his eyes, too, from then on ... like they could see things nobody else did. It was like he was always laughing behind everyone's back because he knew things that nobody else ever could, too."

Patrick was on the edge of his small, metal, folding seat. "So did he? You know, did Biddeon really ... you know, pass himself into Armand? Like they say?"

Knapp

"*Master* Biddeon," Jean-Pierre corrected, "and we do not know for certain because Armand is and always will be a pain in The Order's collective asses. Oh sure, we have all asked him, but he never gives anyone a straight answer. It doesn't matter, because whether he really took The Charge or whether it was just another ceremony of lies, we lost the last Master of The Order and things have gone downhill ever since. Armand refused to fill the role of Grand Master, you see? He packed up his stuff and hit the road. The only time we ever hear from him is when we get one of these crumpled, largely incomplete reports. But although he is a pain, he is also the greatest treasure that The Order has ever possessed."

"A treasure ... I suppose, but at the same time," Jean-Pierre added between puffs of smoke, "he holds the most flagrant disrespect for us. He left. We only know where he has been and what he does because of his piecemeal reports."

Patrick leaned forward. "Exactly," he said with the trademark lack of respect typical of the young and ignorant, "which is why I asked what the fuss is about. He always sends reports, and you've never worried about him before. So what the hell is the big deal?"

Jean-Pierre looked at his partner, and let his head fall back into his hands. "We don't know yet. Not for sure." The words were muffled by his hands, his face buried there in the dark while the others remained silent in thought. Eventually, he raised his head again. "Claude, we have work to do. We need to be certain." Claud looked first to Patrick, and then to Jean-Pierre, his gaze finally resting upon the tattered report.

"Until then," Claude said hopefully, "let's hope he doesn't get into too much trouble ..."

chapter 11 into the fray

The faded black car returned. It tried to resist, of course. It hadn't liked this place at all, the last time it was here. Cars don't have much along the lines of feelings, but what this car had was a mystical, mechanical aversion to inherently dangerous places. It did its best to break down; it was an attempt to communicate to its crazy chicken-chasing driver that they were going in what the car felt was the wrong direction. A tire went flat just a few seconds after the car's driver sat down—he hadn't even left the drive. Later, the muffler dropped off, but the driver simply stopped, picked it up, put it in the back seat, and continued on.

The windshield cracked for no reason. The driver drove on.

The passenger door opened, came slightly loose, and clattered against the road sending sparks everywhere. The driver drove on.

The fuses all blew. The driver had spare fuses in the glove box. The driver drove on.

He was a determined man. You had to be if you wanted to be *L'Exorciste de Volaille*. For those who are mono-lingually English, or who are unfamiliar with the inner circle of this particular sect of spectral warriors,[7] that roughly translates to "Poultry Exorcist." At least, it did centuries ago, when the title had been devised by the first Grand Master. A champion against the undead. Defeater of demons. He who protects mankind from the ways of liches, mummies, ghosts and zombies. Of course, like any career, those who fight against the undead have specialists. Saying "I fight the walking spirits of the fallen" is somewhat akin to saying "I work with computers"; the truth is there's just way too much to know for anyone to be a jack-of-all-trades when it came to the non-living. *L'Exorciste de Volaille* specializes in chickens; he would be at a disadvantage if put up against a human zombie, for the fundamental life forces that drive humans (lust, knowledge, power) are completely different from those that drive poultry (hunger, things that are red, unfocused caution about everything). It sounds like a cushy job ... and it had proved to be a cushy job, or at least cushy enough, for the several generations of exorcists that preceded him. The Order, until the arrival of Armand and his rather unique abilities, was little more than an elaborate charade of impotent Frenchmen; poseurs protecting the population against pretend poultry poltergeists. For a long time, The Order—though well intending enough—had largely been a con.

Now, with The Charge embodied into a man with special, spectral abilities, the work had become all too real. Armand lived in a constant battle against filth, disease and danger. They're filthy beasts, after all— and clever. Stupid, but clever. And beaks, even dead ones, could be dangerously sharp.

The car shuddered to a halt just in front of the old farmhouse. It considered blowing a valve or something as it turned onto the road by the creek, but thought better of it in the end. There wouldn't be any tow trucks out this far. There wouldn't be any tow truck drivers this crazy.

---

[7] Or for those who simply haven't been paying attention up to this point.

cluck

No, it needed to be in running order for a quick retreat. So it putted semi-reluctantly up towards the house, pulled over, and sighed audibly as one door clunked open of its own will. Armand got out. He thought for a moment that car doors weren't supposed to open themselves, but shrugged it off quickly; he'd seen far stranger things, after all. Hell, he had the voice of an ancient anti-poultry power living in his head, and you don't get much stranger than that. Without giving it another thought, he walked up to the stoop.

It was business as usual; the driver—the first legitimate exorcist in ages—would enter the half-world of the spirits while the car waited patiently outside in the fog. It wasn't glamorous, but it beat going in there with him. The car settled with another sigh, this one resigned.

Armand, on the other hand, did not settle. Nor did he sigh. Instead, he reached into a pocket and produced a small metal badge, bearing the same emblem that had been handed down to him years before. A circle of feathers, one upright, and the initials "EV." He felt the cold metal in his hand, and remembered that it was also cold back then ... long ago. He could feel the cold of the small emblem as it touched his forehead so many years before, and changed his life forever. He turned it over in his hands, feeling the embossed design against his rough and scarred skin. It was the same emblem that all chicken exorcists wore. It was a badge of honor.

Without further thought, he hooked it onto the lacings of his left boot, and he immediately felt more at ease. The ancient piece of metal served two purposes: one, to let the little buggers know who he was as he kicked them solidly about the room; two, to keep them from pecking away at his laces. Its main power was the confidence and the authority that it endowed upon him, which allowed him to breathe a bit more calmly as he prepared for battle. It was armor for his mind and for his sanity, just as much as it was armor for his left foot. Of course, his right boot was unprotected, but that was okay as he did most of his solid kicking with his left leg (he was a lefty). With the badge in place, he stood tall and proud before the front entrance to the farm. He was transformed from the shabby man who visited this place just a few days before. He was still shabby, but also ... *powerful*.

His costume was simple. Heavy boots that came nearly to his knees. That was important—everything less than a few feet off the ground was an easy target for a beak. He wore heavy canvas coveralls to protect his legs and to keep himself clean. Cleanliness is Godliness, the exorcist knew, and you needed Godliness. Ghosts didn't like Godliness. They didn't like it and so it gave you a leg up. Even though a belt is entirely unnecessary to hold up coveralls, his uniform included a wide belt made of heavy leather. It was his utility belt, and around his waist several small bags hung from it. They contained: foods and grains of various sorts and in various conditions; a small stone egg; his car keys; Band-Aids; and other typical baubles and trinkets of the trade. His shirt was longsleeved and he wore workman's gloves, but there was no special decoration to the attire. It was a working uniform, not one of pomp nor circumstance (although he always felt it would be both ironic and symbolic if his hat had a feather in it). The only pretense was in the badge, hanging from the boot.

He also carried the proverbial Big Stick. It was about six feet long, a bit knobby and built from sturdy stock. Its shod tip held a dark patina from years of use.[8] At the opposite end was the only item other than the badge that might give away the man's profession. It was the shrunken head of a small red fox. It had been stuffed by a local taxidermist but had still shriveled a bit, making it look like it was halfway between a corpse and a leather handbag. It was only a few inches long at the snout, and it

---

[8] What caused the patina is too unmentionable to, well, mention. It's not too hard to imagine though, considering the line of work its wielder is in.

cluck

perched atop the staff like a silent warden. The exorcist gripped the staff just below the fox head and looked it in the eyes.

"Ready, mate?" The fox didn't answer, being only a small part of a fox (and a dead stuffed part at that). Bracing himself, the gruesome figure of a man lifted up his heavy, adorned boot and kicked the door, which made a brief crunching noise as the wood bent and the lock popped. As it swung inwards, it passed through the ethereal shape of a small plump guinea hen. She was perched there, guarding the door. Most of her feathers were caked to her side, and her head and neck were blackened. With one talon, she gestured behind the man, who turned to look. He found, floating behind him just off the stoop, a wispy red tomato. It bobbed enticingly down the road, back towards the car.

"Christ, I'm not about to fall for the tomato trick," he sighed while stepping closer to the door. His left boot was already drawn back, but before he could land a solid kick, the little guinea had already fled into the protective darkness of the house.

"Chicken!" he called out after it, stamping his boot and causing the little badge to jingle satisfactorily. He grinned, and shook his head. Tomatoes. As if he, of all people, would fall for the oldest trick in the book. "Stupid bird."

Turning his back on the lonely, levitating vegetable, he stepped inside.

Chickens, generally, are indeed very stupid. It is hard to make that point clear enough. Where one will typically think, "Yes, so I've been told several times already; chickens are stupid. I understand," they will then go straight to imagining a level of stupidity that, in the end, gives the entire species far too much credit. They are stupid, unintelligent, lacking in intellect and devoid of logic. These particular ones had been dead for a long time. What their biologically active brains weren't able to deduce at all, their spectrally active lumps of rotting grey bits were able to understand ... somewhat. It wasn't a huge improvement, but it was an improvement, and it made them dangerous. While live chickens weren't capable of retaining more than a few thoughts and memories, dead chickens had a literal eternity to learn from their mistakes. Of course, being dead they were even able to learn from what would otherwise be *fatal* mistakes. This particular batch had been learning for years. They learned from poor Bobby, and they learned from each other, and their traps had slowly evolved. Their spooking became spookier.

At first it had just been fluttering around in chains clucking a lot. Eventually they learned to dissipate before a boot could hit them, but even that small bit of refinement could take up to a year of slow, undead chicken evolution. The tomato was typically the result of massive bird-brained experimentation, as it required a chicken to both imagine and create something out of pure will. The tomatoes were usually followed shortly by the eggs, as the two tricks used similar spiritual mechanisms. Those had become staples by now, tired poultry parlor tricks that the exorcist knew well, as most flocks came up with those.

The chickens in this farm, however, had more. They had leadership, and they learned, albeit slowly, that they could affect more than just themselves and the eggs and tomatoes. They were in a spirit world and they could will things to happen within their immediate surroundings, to a degree. That's how the false steps became false. One hen, who had always been drawn to the prints and patterns found within newly scratched dirt, had found a library on the third floor of one of the main houses, and had gotten into some old books. It couldn't read, of course, but the illustrations were straightforward enough. Shortly thereafter Bobby had nearly lost part of his leg to a tiny guillotine. This trap was a huge advancement in complexity, although it also lacked subtlety, so

cluck

Bobby had always been able to avoid it. [9] But the point holds true; these chickens were dangerous and cunning, and drew ideas from their surroundings, finding new and terrible ways to torture the farmhouse's old proprietor.

Armand stepped through a narrow doorway, and around the contraption that lay in wait for him on the other side. It was obviously a trap, but in the dim light, it was difficult to discern what it was exactly. Leaning close, he could barely make out two short posts, about two feet high and ten inches between, with a small inadequate blade poised at the top to decapitate any tiny intruders who could fit within its breadth.

This is an improvement, Armand thought as he inspected the hen's handiwork. *It might even cut through a boot ... well, maybe if you pushed down really hard on the blade.* Glancing at his own heavily clad feet, Armand wiggled his toes in morbid appreciation of what he'd just avoided.

"[Gosh darn] chickens are [really no good] and I [just don't like them]!" translated the exorcist's voice. As usual he intended to say something a little more colorful, but his voice was a firm believer in keeping things clean for the kids, and so the words came out just as censored as they usually did. He kicked another half-rotten zombie hen out his path as he struggled from room to room.

---

[9] For such an ill-conceived trap to succeed, the victim would have to lie on their belly and forcibly stuff their head through the too-small opening. Even Bobby wasn't stupid (or dexterous) enough to do that, but even if he had, the blade was barely heavy enough to cut through soft cheese, and barely sharp enough to open old letters.

"Look," he growled. "We don't have to do this the hard way. Just give me what I want and you can stay in here and [poop] and smell until the end of time."

He waved yet another tomato out of his way as he trudged through a teeming mass of the waddling undead. He kicked another and another. For every hen who was able to vanish before impact, two more were caught unawares.

"This is a fiery lot," commented Armand's inner companion.

"You can say that again, smartest bunch I've run across too."

A hen suddenly cocked her head, causing a bit of loose flesh to slide onto the floor. *Cluck?*

"Well, what do you know," Armand said, staying his boot as the little inquisitive hen shuffled closer. "Hey, did you actually understand me?"

"No way, chickens aren't capable of it. You're talking crazy—hey! Hen at six o'clock! Kick it! Kick it!" but Armand ignored the voice in his head and did something that went against all of his instinct, all of his training and experience. He shooed a few feather aggressors away, and then leaned down, close to the hen. He was too low, he knew, he was within range, outside of the safety zone.

"You understand me?"

"Um, Armand? You're talking to a chicken," The Charge complained, but the words did seem to sink in; the thing did understand him, he knew it. You could tell by the look in that tiny beady eye, dull with decay and death, yet bright with understanding.

"Look," Armand continued, "you're obviously a smart group of, um … chickens. Maybe we can settle this—"

"I can't believe you're parlaying—"

" … Look, I can fight you, I've got time, but we can do this the easy way—"

"There is no easy way—"

cluck

" ... Just hand him over, and we'll both get out of here, I've got no bones to pick with you." Armand held his hands out in some bizarre misplaced gesture of peace, honestly wishing he could talk his way through this and be done with it. The chicken tried to fluff its feathers and hissed, retreating from the exorcist. In an instant the tenuous connection was gone and the treaty ended before it could begin.

"Poor choice of words ... 'bones to pick' ... I think you've upset the thing's sensibilities," his voice taunted. Unlike its physical host, the voice seemed to remember that these chickens, like all chickens, were dumb. They were also dead, and completely beyond reason. Whatever the reason, Armand jumped quickly back to his feet, on guard against the next wave of attacks, which predictably came just an instant later, as the would-be ambassador hen disappeared into the onrush of maggoty assailants.

"What did I say?" He shouted, and rattled his staff at them. He succeeded in scaring some away, but others filled in the ranks. Reaching into a pocket of his utility belt, he produced a fat handful of sweetened grain, throwing it into the far corner of the room. More of his fetid, feathered foes ran out of his path, eager to feast on fresh feed, but there were just too many. Despite trick after trick, Armand's way was still blocked with shambling, decayed feathery forms. They approached, slowly closing in around him, as if a George Romero film had collided with a commercial for KFC.

"[...]" He tried to say. His voice couldn't think of any way to say that particular phrase without being rude, so nothing had come out at all. *I've got to see a doctor about this voice of mine*, he thought, as they advanced. He fought them, kicking and stomping, but the chickens kept coming. He was getting nowhere. He could plod against the wave of hens for days, he knew, and they would never relent.

"Great," his voice groaned, *"the hard way it is."*

Armand turned the staff upside down, and held it out like a long broom. Throwing a few real tomatoes like grenades, he pushed them back with his staff.

"Shh— Shh— Shh— Shoo!"

The shrunken fox skull that perched at the end of the staff worked better than any normal broom ever could. The chickens, upon seeing and smelling the fox head, were sent into an immediate state of panic, and he succeeded in herding the majority of the little ghouls into the corner. The flock became confused, slow and disoriented, [10] and Armand was able to turn the tide, containing the small angry mob. It was a technique he thought of as "coop sweeping" and it typically worked. Typically. In this case, the hens towards the rear of the pack began to spill out, flanking him and closing in behind him again. Moments after he had swept them away, the room was crowded again with miniature corpulent zombies. The more alert ones were keeping a safe distance from Armand's wildly swinging staff, but some were too rotten to know any better, and soon they pressed in, dumb and shambling, as zombies do. Armand was up to his knees now in the worst of the horde, and he was at serious risk of losing his footing.

If he tripped and fell, he'd be done for. Everything under the height of Armand's boot-tops belonged to them. Flightless, sightless, brainless and lifeless demon birds that would peck you to death (if they still had intact beaks) in the slow rhythm of the undead. The stench would be enough to kill some men, triggering a gag reflex that would soon suck down loose feathers and filth and bits of flesh and cause simultaneous spasms of coughing and retching. No, you didn't want to end up down there ...

---

[10] Sadly for chickens, this is a fairly typical panic reaction, which is often deployed when faced by a predator. There is a reason not many chickens survive contact with their natural enemies.

cluck

A plump, headless corpse waddled unknowingly behind Armand and wedged itself between his boots, briefly, before its wings plucked free and it was free to stumble on. One wing fell to the ground and dragged behind it for a bit, the other stuck in a rather unpleasant way to the inside of Armand's left leg. He shuddered, and ran his hands over the various pouches of his utility belt. Finding what he was looking for, he snapped open a pouch, and reluctantly pulled forth a handful of small, ripe cherry tomatoes.

"It's too early ..." Armand's voice said the words without his invocation, but he agreed completely.

"I've got no choice," he said to himself and to his voice, both of whom had serious misgivings. This was an ace-in-the-hole chicken-dispelling prop, which he usually reserved for emergencies. By throwing this trump card down so soon, he might find himself in trouble later, with no escape plan—but throw it down he must. With a final, momentary pang of regret, Armand scattered the small red fruits into the thickening throng.

The results were immediate, as they often were. Chickens simply *love* tomatoes. Chickens are also greedy. They also lack any useful appendage with which to hold on to something that they desire, to protect it from their greedy, stupid, opposable-thumb-lacking peers. In unison, dozens of chickens dove recklessly towards each bouncing tomato, as if pulled helplessly forward by some sinister electromagnetic trap. [11] A few of the softer, *squelchier* chickens were torn asunder by the reckless force of their more solid flock-mates. Some were trampled, some were spun about, and some were sent fluttering in that I'm-a-chicken-and-I-can't-really-fly way that chickens flutter in. A few made it clear across the

---

[11] It was not a sinister electromagnetic trap, though. It was just a bunch of irresistibly edible red tomatoes. Don't try to figure it out — it's best to leave chicken psychology to the experts.

room before hitting the cracked plaster walls with a thud and falling into little broken chicken piles.

Then the fun started. Again, in unison, a dozen of the fastest zombie hens picked up their heads. Pierced by the tips of their beaks perched a dozen red, ripe cherry tomatoes. Though the results were entirely expected, Armand couldn't help but shake his head and chuckle softly. It always reminded him of a small chicken circus, when they did this, running around with their little red rubber clown noses. The tomato-clad clowns then began to run in circles, hotly pursued by those of their naked chicken compatriots who hadn't been trampled or driven off in the chaos.

"You can't pay for entertainment like this," the voice in his mind opined, and he agreed. Entertainment and salvation, all in one, was priceless.

Elsewhere in the house, Bobby had stopped running. He had fallen again. His foot was so swollen in his boot that he couldn't balance on it. He couldn't really feel it anymore, either, but that was probably a good thing. He was pretty certain that if he could feel it, it would have hurt like the dickens. So instead of trying to perform difficult tasks like standing up he decided it was much easier to just fall over. His fall was broken by a large egg. This one cracked open when he crashed down upon it, sending a dozen wailing spirit yolks drifting up towards some light that mortals could not see.

Bobby tried to remember what was real and what wasn't, but he was distracted by a small, feathered thing pecking at his face. He brought his hands up in front of his eyes. He couldn't see that there were other hens about, in addition to the pecker. One had a piece of paper. It was filthy and worn, and it's a good thing Bobby couldn't see it. He was going crazy as it was, and he was plenty scared enough. He flailed as the hen tried to peck his face.

Other hens were gathering. There seemed to be two factions: the hen with the paper was large and plump and seemed to be some sort of leader. Not to Bobby, of course, who was far too busy to notice any of this, but to anyone else who might have been there it would have seemed that she was a leader. The paper was a simple illustration: There was a stick-figure of a man, with a circle for a head above two straight lines, crossed to form the body and arms. A third line formed an inverted "V" which completed the caricature by making the legs. How the chickens managed to scratch the lines precisely enough to form the rough image of man was a mystery. How they knew to label weak-spots of human anatomy was of pure animal instinct. Go for the eyes. Peck out the groin. The jugular, carotid and other blood-ways were also marked. The childlike drawing of a stick man became morbid as it was carefully dissected, made into a war map against human life. This is how a chicken might kill a man, the picture clearly illustrated.

She sent another chicken over to Bobby. The instructions were clear enough, even to a chicken, but as other hens gathered close for a lesson in farmer anatomy, the second faction raised a protest. Several tomatoes floated away from Bobby and towards a door that lead downstairs to a pantry. The pantry was off of the main kitchen, and the main kitchen was just a few doors and a short hallway away from the guest lounge. In the guest lounge, a confused and grumpy exorcist was swatting flying ghost chicks out of the air with his staff. Several of the chickens—including one of the few that were now pecking at Bobby's private areas—instinctively chased after them, but some resisted. They knew the rules; they had to kill the farmer. They had to do this before they could get any of the wonderful tomatoes. The smart leader-hen had told them this. The leader-hen had a big tuft of feathers growing out of her collapsed and burnt skull, and she took orders (it was rumored) from the Rooster himself. Also, the smart hen was smart and therefore, the other birds felt, if they did everything that she said it must make them smart, too. If they were as smart as the leader-hen, maybe the Rooster would give them direct orders, instead of her—and so they obeyed. It was flawed logic, but simple logic, well suited for small chicken minds. Especially suited to those who had been bashed in and were missing their brains.

The new group of rogue chickens was clearly agitated at the defiance.

"Cluck bock cluck braaaw!" she proclaimed. That is, "Are you stupid? Leave him alone! We have a bigger ferret to fry!"

"Ferret? We aren't scared of ferrets! We must kill the human!" To make the point, a spectral illusion of a ferret appeared and started to dance up and down the whimpering Bobby's back and legs.

Struggling to contemplate the subtleties of metaphor, the chicken rebutted: "The ferret is not a ferret! It is a man! A strong man! A man who is not a ferret but who acts like a ferret—he has killed many!"

"We can not be killed. We're dead already, remember?"

That stumped the newcomer for a moment. She had a point, they *were* already dead.

"Kicks us with boot" it corrected. Maybe it didn't kill them when it did it, but still wasn't nice to kick a hen when it was down. Or dead.

cluck

Bobby moaned.   He had rolled onto his face and passed out. Thinking he was dead the few hens that were still pecking him wandered off to join the debate.   That was the normal way things played out, of course: he would eventually pass out, and the chickens would then leave him alone, thinking he was dead.   Chickens are pretty lacking in intellect, and more or less devoid of any of the really high thought processes.   Forgetting all about Bobby, they started to *cluck* and *braw* angrily at each other. Their disagreement grew in volume, making quite a racket.

To anyone who was through one door, down some stairs, through a pantry and a kitchen and down a short hallway, it would have seemed strange.   So strange, in fact, that it would have attracted that person's attention.   It may have even drawn that person through the small pantry, down the short corridor and up some stairs (which it did).

There had been a huge commotion of clucking and scratching, but it stopped suddenly when a curious exorcist suddenly popped his head into the room.   A few dozen zombie chicken heads, caught unawares in the heat of their debate, looked up in unison.   Somewhere in the back of the flock, there was the soft thud of a beak as it fell free from its last sinew and dropped to the floor.

Armand suddenly found himself staring into the eyes of an army of cornered zombies.   "[Poop]!" he exclaimed.

Knapp

cluck

chapter 12   irrefutable facts about chickens

It was different once. It was better. In the pocket of the shabby coat of *L'Exorciste de Volaille*, there was a crumpled photograph that showed much better days. Days before the mist had come, and covered the sprawling acres of the farm with its mysteries. Four years ago—give or take—it was even better, for the house in the photograph had already aged and fallen into a rut of neglect by the time it had been enveloped. The gutters, plugged with leaves and debris, had spilled over, leaving long stalactite stains down the white facades. When the paint was fresh, back when the narrow country road was clean and clear of debris, the farm burst from the embrace of pleasant woods, bright and shining, magnificent and inviting. The tree lined road was mottled with sunlight, which sifted through a canopy of green to play little games of light with the road, the brook, and the fieldstone walls that marked the boundaries of the estate. The largest of three monumental maple trees stood proudly above and between its brothers, with heavy and powerful branches shielding the homestead from the whims of nature. The two younger trees tried their best to stretch over the road to the mighty rooftops, but the house had grown much faster than their boughs ever could, and before they were able to stretch that far, the house had grown a full story at least, well out of their reach. It was a race, but a playful, happy race. A race that the house was winning as it continued to grow.

Families came and went. Some were born into the title, others won their place through real-estate conquests. With each transaction, each new generation that had arrived, new rooms had been added. A workshop for farmer Millents was added during the years of prohibition. It had a hidden cellar in it, which was later expanded by farmer Brock's wife as storage for use in an ill-planned jam business (several hundred jars of jam could still be found there, if anyone cared to look). A decade after the Millents had died, a rich executive from Kentucky added a row of new stables off of the main barn, and they in turn were later converted into a hobby mechanic's shop through the addition of several crossbeams and one huge hoist. Just one winter later, the Kentucky horseman took his money south, and the house was left in the care of a gardener who added several hoop-houses. When he sold the place, one of the hoop frames was turned into a Victorian glass house, and the rest were torn down to accommodate a small in-law apartment. During all of this, there were other changes as well.

The addition of the workshop added girth to the original foundation, which made the proud farm feel squat. Discontent with stoutness, the roof of the main house stretch upwards, adding an inch here and there. The windows, for the sake of symmetry, rose a foot overnight, and a new clapboard emerged from between two others to fill the void below it. The cellar, once emptied of gin and filled with jam, grew stuffy, and a new window appeared just a month later. Nobody remembered clearly if there had been a window there before, but assumed that there had: after all, windows do not simply grow out of bare walls. Nor do chimneys, feeling spindly and small in the center of a vast roof (which must have always been that big, although no one recalls), broaden themselves, top themselves with a delightful soapstone chimney cap, and give themselves a nice pointing while they're at it.

It was a very particular magic that kept the place growing. There was an energy about it, an ego. It crackled in the air. Any normal farmhouse would have maybe a half-dozen small outbuildings; a smithy or a cobbler's shop, a henhouse or maybe a small lean-to for the tractors. But this house wasn't content with a few small improvements. It grew addicted, like a Beverly Hills glamour queen becomes addicted to tucks and lifts. A slightly wider dormer here, a taller window there, and suddenly the whole look of the place was wrong. Why be content with just a *few* different roof-lines? It needed more, and it channeled that need into each successive occupant for over two hundred and twenty years. What it couldn't manipulate its occupants into building on their own, it would construct in its own way—from will, and from power.

When Bobby and his wife Janice moved in, the house already had two complete in-law attachments, three kitchens, several workshops and two separate staircases leading down into two separate basements. No less than four sets of stairs lead up to the second floor—and in one case to a third half-floor. And the attic—oh, what an attic! The space below the house's roof was taller than most by twofold. It was so large and spacious and dry that it had once been used to store hay, at least until the construction of the second barn by the place's second owner. A barn was so much more suitable for hay, and the attic was so grand, that the construction really was necessary. The new barn had a loft along the back of one wall to better accommodate the bails, and could almost be considered two stories of its own. Of course the attic needed to be cleared, to facilitate access to the belfry, and a large bronze bell ... and that was just the main house.

It wasn't long before the chimney, with its splendid soapstone hat, required company, and no less than four magnificent chimneys rose from the various roofs. The first and original chimney was nearly five feet square by then, and was a strong reminder of the way things had been two hundred years ago.[12] The newer chimneys stood taller and were all narrow, though they each had a unique style and crown. The house saw nothing wrong with this: it would have cost a fortune to heat the massive house without them, although most occupants quickly learned that it cost a fortune to heat the massive house even with them. While certain people are attracted to large homes, the place had a knack for outgrowing its tenants. It was one of the reasons this beautiful house created so much activity at the local real estate offices of Boombard and Swallows, located 20 miles south in the closest thing to a town within many many more miles. It just cost too much to heat the place. Most would close off all but the original structure, and let the bulk of the place freeze in the worst part of winter. The plumbing was bad in some places, and worse in others. The electricity ranged all the way from "Master Electrician" to "Scary." When Bobby had moved in, he hardly ever lit the wood stoves in the main house. He was lazy at heart, and it was too much work to cut, stack, haul and burn wood. For the Bed & Breakfast business, which of course was Bobby and Janice's own addition to the unstoppable expansion, Bobby had installed a state-of-the-art furnace, with radiant-heated floors and even steam-warmed towel hangers for the guest baths. No expense was spared for the B&B.

There was also the barn—a massive structure—which stood four-and-a-half stories high and loomed above the estate. There were other barns as well: the horse barn; the equipment barn; and four or five sheds.

---

[12] The house liked to think that each improvement left behind "a reminder of the old way" when in fact almost everything had grown far beyond historical relevance, and very little of anything was original. The chimney, especially, was not a reminder of the way life used to be, except perhaps among Nordic halls where a single fire was expected to heat an entire village.

cluck

Most were attached to the main house by some means; a porch, or a catwalk, or more typically an enclosed mud-room or pantry. There was a carriage shed, and another carriage shed, and also a more modern garage, built by Bobby's immediate predecessor the Lampers. The coop was there, as well as several lean-to's for the livestock, which consisted of only a handful of sheep, a goat and of course the prize flock of chickens. Before the new section of the house had been built in its place, there was the chicken yard; sloping away from the midsection of the old house and around to the back of one of the smaller barns. It had been a microcosm of the farm itself, weaving in and among the outbuildings. It stretched this way and that way, around a tree, down a slope—wherever it could go. The wire fence was loose and shabby—as chicken fences often are. It meandered about the back sections of the house to provide its resident hens a variation of sun, shade and shelter. The coop itself had been built about a dozen paces off of an old milk room, which connected the chicken yard to both the servant's kitchen and an old decommissioned boiler room. Much to Bobby's eternal regret, that was all gone now, irretrievably so.

The farm was an amazing and unique place; even castles had to admit that it was impressive, even though they typically scoffed at timber constructions. What it wasn't, was easy to live in. Several of the previous owners had tried—in addition to the hidden distilleries and a small engine repair business—to use the house itself to supplement their incomes through opening a bed and breakfast, or an inn. A tavern? It had been tried by the Swanzees in the early 1900s. The problem wasn't that people were unwilling to drive for hours to reach the house (it had a reputation that had grown so strong it was able to retire and live off of the proceeds—in fact, the house's reputation could now be found in a secluded resort on the western coast of Mexico reminiscing about the good old days). The problem was that the house just wasn't accommodating once they got there. It was uncomfortable. It wasn't dirty, but it wasn't clean in the popular sense either. With several dozen halls, countless rooms, and more nooks and crannies than an English Muffin it was impossible to ever get that floor "so clean you could eat off it."

Of course, there were the chickens, and the lore that went with them.

Being a poultry farm of sorts, the old farm had a library stocked with books, guides, papers and notes describing the various conditions, qualities and attitudes of chickens. In this wealth of knowledge, several commonalities were evident. For those who have never had the honor of living with chickens, a few of these irrefutable facts about chickens will now be presented as they appear in *Chickens and You, or, What to Do Now that You've Bought the Chicken Farm*, by Bell Pitt. It was a very rare book. The edition in the farm's second-smallest library may be the only remaining copy in existence. If one were to find one's way to that library (which is on the second floor of the third addition, behind where the old tanning room used to be), and were to find the book, and open it to page 213, one would find this excerpt. It is from a chapter which is aptly titled, "Irrefutable Facts about Chickens," and is highlighted in yellow ink, which at some point faded to a dull taupe. It reads:

cluck

IRREFUTABLE FACTS ABOUT CHICKENS

1. Chickens are dirty. The feathers, by the very laws of nature, will work themselves into every crevice and crack they can find. Chickens are both covered with feathers and prone to fluttering around recklessly at the slightest provocation. The feathers fall out, usually into several decades of dirt, and flutter about everywhere. Everywhere. The "dirt" isn't really dirt, either. Chicken "dirt" is what ordinary dirt turns into when it has been lived upon by chickens for several decades.

2. Chickens are loud. The noises produced by a chicken range from the standard "cluck" to the more fanciful "bock" and even an occasional "bu-craaaaw." These noises are made constantly from one hour before sun-up to about one hour before dusk. And then there are the roosters. Roosters, unlike the hens, will attempt to out-loud each other for the sheer enjoyment of the exercise. The sound is anywhere from a squawk to a bawl, or even sometimes like a low growl, but it is always LOUD. A rooster out-louds a hen by about a hundred decibels, keeping the same hours (i.e., godawful).

3. Chickens are stupid. A chicken, when confronted by danger is likely to run straight at it for lack of any better ideas. They sleep soundly in full view upon any suitable perch, in defiance of any laws of self preservation. They may grow to understand concepts such as "food," and may even recognize dangers such as the "fox," but if you were to attach a small bowl of seeds to a foxes' tail, the chickens would most likely run happily, one by one in single file, to their deaths.

The list goes on to include "4: Chickens are often hungry" and "5: Chickens rarely evolve" and the more popular facts #12 and #32 which are, in turn, "Everything tastes like chicken" and "Never eat anything offered to you by a chicken."

The book had been around for a very long time, and it was no coincidence that it had arrived to its current place in the farm after being owned by several previous members of the chicken-exorcising order. [13] The house, in its vanity, knew that it was home to birds as well as to men, and that Janice's flock had been worthy of praise. Near the end of normalcy, when the good times were drawing to a close, it found a way to bend its will towards Janice. She sat down at the computer she and Bobby had bought to manage the B&B, using her cell phone to dial up a relatively high speed connection to the Internet, [14] and found a copy of the book in an online auction. She'd had it shipped all the way from France, but never got to read it; the house had it secreted away in the library before anyone knew it had arrived, and then ... well, and then not long after that, the mist came, and everything changed.

---

[13] Fact number 32 had been added mischievously by an elderly *Exorciste de Volaille* by the name of William Cousteau, nearly a hundred years ago when he stumbled across the text in a small local library in Broken Arrow, Oklahoma. He'd added the words in red ink with the bitter memory of a six-day struggle with intestinal cramps after eating a floating tomato while on a particularly nasty job in Las Vegas (it was just bad luck that an entire collection of the showgirls' costumes had been built from the feathers of a single flock of prize Silver Duckwing Phoenix hens. He had fond memories of the mission, though. He was backstage interviewing the girls when their costumes leaped right off them and started to flutter around the room angrily. It had been a rough fight but the background commotion of a dozen beautiful women running about the room and leaping onto chairs wearing only their skivvies and the occasional tassel was worth the effort.)

[14] There was no cable access to the remote farm, and satellite dishes had a disturbing tendency to fall off, disappear, or—in one case—become entirely encased in concrete overnight.

chapter 13 The rooster King

The Rooster with a capital "R" was the sole remaining male of the once proud collection of fowl. In life, having been blessed by the mysterious ribbon of cosmic and spectral power, the Rooster was easily the largest, strongest and smartest of its species. He was huge—*enormous*—a dark Cornish cock that through a combination of genetics and a rough chick-hood was already on its way to greatness. By the time the ribbon hit it, it was already nearly a foot tall—unheard of! The Rooster's growth was accelerated, of course, when the ribbon snaked its way in and amongst its wispy little bird-soul. It grew larger, and larger, until it put others of its kind to shame (and to death) with their insignificance. It looked more like a wild turkey than a mere chicken, although he and his shambling harem would take offense at such a comparison, for chickens thought themselves above turkeys, which they felt were loud, dirty and dumb.[15] If there were ever a chicken to be accused of pride and

---

[15] The irony is typically lost outside of The Order: when the pot calls the kettle black in such instances, the pot is also often cooking the chicken.

snobbery, it was a rooster. If a rooster could be considered arrogant, even among its own kind, it was the King. Its wingspan, if it had been capable of flying, would have nearly blocked the light of the enormous moon that hung over the haunted farmstead. Well, a good half of it at least. It was a veritable giant of his kind, and a champion to the adoring gaggle of hens, which were instinctually drawn to its sheer survivability. It had a trim, fit body and looked prehistoric as it patrolled the chicken yard with confident long-legged strides.

In death, the Rooster remained the largest and strongest of all the zombified birds, and quickly reestablished its place as the dominant member of the ghost-flock. It remained proud and tall of stature. There was only the smallest amount of flesh missing, despite the many scraps it had been forced to endure since its demise in the fire, so many years ago. Even though the flesh that remained was dark and rotting, it managed to maintain a grip on its reputation of beauty and grandeur (largely due to its magnificent plume of feathers, which had somehow survived the fire). Its eyes were also intact, beady and black, as was its pendulous red wattle, which hung nearly to mid-breast, and swayed majestically as the rooster strut about its domain. The rest of its head was a different matter; being largely devoid of any real skin, the Rooster's head itself was little more than a skull. The eyes, the beak, and the handsome wattle were there as if attached directly to the bone, and it gave him an impression of irrefutable evil and unstoppable power.

Power. Another differentiator for this particular bird: it had *power*. It was aware of everything that went on around it, and could sense the other spirits of its flock as they pattered, limped and hopped one-legged around the farm. It understood its flock as if it were a system, and kept a very close eye on things. The Rooster believed (rightly) that everything had its place, and that life—or death, as the case may be—was best when everything was kept in order.

cluck

The hens thought he was absolutely splendid. Beyond the handsome and powerful figure, they were drawn to the Rooster's immutable cockery. This was a bird with confidence! It was a chicken that never walked, or scratched. This chicken *sauntered*, and if it were hungry it would *dig* at the ground, slow and deliberate as if it hadn't a care in the world for what it might or might not uncover. Unlike any other roosters alive or dead, this one understood the hens well enough to manipulate them. It knew which hens it could mount at will, and which of the girls first needed to be kicked into submission with his long, hard nails, or buffeted soundly with its powerful bludgeoning wings. Roosters, above all else, had certain needs, and this was one rooster who would never be denied them. It was of little concern to him that the hens, which were undead as well, were completely incapable of laying real, fertile eggs. It was more a matter of habit, and of a certain pleasure, and of course *pride*.

For their part, the hens couldn't get enough of him; his long silvery-black feathers, his heavy long neck and keen gaze. And the crow! The Rooster could *cock-a-doodle* better than any they could remember. Of course, it was the only rooster they could remember at all, having memories that lasted no longer than four or five days, but his crow really was inspiring. It was also of little concern to them that *the* rooster was *the only* rooster—he was still their favorite. Being the lone male among them only made the decision simpler, which was good for their simple minds. It didn't matter that there had once been other cocks, nicer cocks, and that they had been killed off one by one by their new King. Things like that simply don't matter to a chicken.

Knapp

To be accurate, it wasn't entirely true that the Rooster was the only male, but the hens barely remembered the trio of handsome roosters known as the three musketeers. They were the last roosters to survive the chicken lord's reign of dominance and terror, long ago when the flock could still breath air and their bodies still pulsed blood through still-intact veins. Now they shared the same fate as the rest, but being bantams the three were only a fraction of the size of the Rooster King. They were not a physical threat to him, and so the Rooster showed mercy. He allowed the three tiny cocks to remain, although not before plucking every one of their magnificent feathers and emasculating them before the flock. Still, though stripped of status and exiled from their nature to live as hens, they were alive. Well, not alive, but they were around in a *not-alive* kind of way.

The Rooster was simply too strong to stand against. Partially because of its size and partially because of the strength it had possessed in life, but mostly because of that other power that it bore. The power that made it special. It didn't know where it came from, exactly, but it knew it stood alone above all others of its kind. It was the first to discover writing, and though the hens were slow to pick up on any form of real communication it was able to train them to scratch simple pictures, and to use common clucks and specific rhythms that could be interpreted as simple words. [16] Beyond a basic intelligence and cleverness, the Rooster was also able to change things, manipulating things with mind or body or spirit. It learned to summon its will into the physical. It made memories of the things it knew and understood to become real: a floating tomato, for example, or some other sinister interpretation of its

---

[16] Those who have been paying close attention might contest that it was a hen that had first discovered language. However, in a patriarchal society as well established as this one, the discovery was credited to the Rooster. The Rooster, of course, supported such claims. And nobody questions the Rooster, *capiche*?

relatively simple existence. The only true limit to the Rooster's power was that it knew so little of what the world had to offer. In life, it lacked the fullness of its power and simply couldn't understand. In death, the Rooster had been largely confined to the farm. Sprawling and expansive as it was, the experiences to be found within were limited, and so thus imprisoned his repertoire of abilities was likewise limited to things that were largely irrelevant to anyone other than another chicken.

To those who understand the habits of chicken zombies, ghouls and ghosts, this type of power often developed. However, where one chicken might unknowingly summon a torrential rain of infertile eggs, or some other horrific manifestation, it was extremely rare for such a skill to be calculated and deliberate. In that regard, the Rooster was alone, and it made him strong.

The Rooster was strong enough that, when it had sauntered into the very gates of Hell, it had been able to survive. It was strong enough that, like the earthly fire that ended its life, the fires of Hades were unable to extinguish the bird's soul. The Rooster had been able to invade Hell itself, and had been spat out again to return here. It was this power, most likely, that had drawn the other chickens' souls back also, at least at first, and so the flock grew, became fixed in this place, haunting it and tormenting the idiot farmer Bobby.

In the remains of the ghostly coop, the food had eventually run out. No longer needing to eat, spiritually displaced birds still felt an instinctual desire to fight over what little remained. Had there been other roosters fit to challenge left in the flock they would have soon fallen before the king Rooster's might, as he was an indomitable and merciless leader; able to kill other roosters so easily that none, regardless off how desperate for feed or how tainted by evil, would dare challenge him. When the Rooster fought, it struck quick and hard. Its beak and talons were sharp and deadly, and it knew how to use them. It attacked before its prey even realized they were in danger, and it ripped their souls out of purgatory and shoved them mercilessly down into whatever eternity awaited them. A bird of action, it held no remorse for this. It was the way chickens lived, when times were tough. Kill or be killed. It was of little consequence that in this case they were already dead. To this magnificent creature the others were nothing more than stupid, hungry birds. Without a thought it killed them before they turned on him, as it knew they would. The Rooster, confident in its superiority, ate their meat and drank their blood, and they, though vanquished, remained (albeit a bit deader).

Yes, there was something special about this kingly, Cornish cock. There was something foul about it, too. It was magical itself, but there was also an abundance of magic in and around the farmstead, and some of it—perhaps more than just a small part—had found its way into that tiny poultry brain. An evil part.

During life, the cockery was muted, and it hadn't been so mean-spirited. Perhaps it was the subsequent entrance into (and expulsion from) Hell that had changed it. After all, in just a few moments within the fiery depths of damnation, it had suffered an eternity of torment. In the Rooster's mind, things were different. It wasn't Hell that made the Rooster strong; the Rooster was already strong, and Hell was simply something that happened. It was the Rooster's own strength that had saved it from brimstone death, not the other way around. Again, this was an unusual trait for a chicken; self-reflection was typically reserved for higher mammals. The Rooster knew that it was a bit higher, a bit grander than the hens. Noble enough and proud enough to consider itself better than that *man*. Not all men, perhaps, but certainly *that man*.

"That man" was a thorn in the Rooster's side that could not be plucked free. The two were locked in an eternal battle of wills that the Rooster, despite all of its advancements and accomplishments, could not seem to win. It thought, and planned, crafting new ways to end the life of the farmer who had ruined the flock and brought it kicking and

cluck

scratching into this eternal, apparitional prison. How to kill this man was a dilemma to the Rooster, and it occupied its every thought. It pumped with every empty heartbeat, and it filled its lungs with each unnecessary breath.

Knapp

cluck

chapter 14 this olde house

The farmhouse looked upon itself and several loose shingles on top of the front-most porch realigned themselves in what could only be described as a smug expression. After all, the old estate had reason to feel self-satisfied. While it was an architectural bravura, the old building's magnificent construction wasn't even its only interesting quality. There was the landscaping, for example: while the gardens were somewhat neglected, they still contained an amazingly diverse collection of native plants and wildflowers. There were artifacts and textiles from the height of several eras built within it and into it. Not by design but by circumstance, the house had lived and grown through several generations of human progression. It had areas of roofing made of cedar, clay, and asphalt shingles. It had walls made from hand-split logs, milled lumber, lathe and plaster, and drywall. The same mighty and expansive walls, where one such board had been pulled free by time or where a hole had been dug by pest or rodent, had created a home for several families of various small animals. The house took great pride in knowing that the small clutch of white-billed woodpeckers, which fed routinely upon the termite-infested wood of the old dilapidated well house, was none other than the near-extinct species *Campephilus principalis*. The house liked the birds because they ate the termites that itched its frame, but there was also a bit of snobbery about their rarity.

The root of its vainglory, however, came from the place's history. It was built in 1793 on nearly five hundred acres, originally consisting of dozens of outbuildings including outhouses, a carpentry shop, a smoke house, cobbler, washroom and of course quarters for the slaves. This original collection of buildings occupied nearly five acres on their own, and most were clumped just behind the main house. The remainder of the estate was devoted mostly to woodland, an arena of sport for the original owner, who enjoyed hunting above all else. A relatively meager space was kept as lawn or garden, such that many of the outlying buildings were hard to see among the encroaching copses of the forest.

The remarkable thing was that despite its size and the obvious wealth of its original owner, it was not a mansion—not as would be commonly considered a mansion in those days, at least. It was finely constructed but empty of pomp, frill or filigree. A large yet simple home of the colonial design; three stories tall and completely lacking any wainscoting, mantels or pillars. There were no buttresses nor cupolas nor gables. The outbuildings were likewise plain. Most of them—the ones that were closest to the house—remained intact until nearly a full century later, when the lot of them had either fallen over and rotted or (as was more common) had been swallowed up in the rapid expansion of the main structure. It was a marvel of history, and yet, largely due to its humble and secluded beginnings, the huge estate had never once been mentioned in relation to any major historical event. Not once, not in the whole of the country. Of course, private records were kept. The house itself knew exactly where such documents could be found: in a locked trunk in one of the original bedrooms, at the foot of an old rope bed.

cluck

A few stories below in the small parlor of the main house there was more evidence of the place's past—a huge guest-book that dated back to the domicile's first days. A book crowded with the names of owners, guests, family and friends. By the time its first hundred years had passed, it had already seen nearly four separate inhabitants. The second tenant had signed the guest book "New proprietors Earnst and Emilee Trast" and the tradition had stuck. Between pages of partygoers and visitors, each new family signed themselves in as the dwelling's new proprietor, keeping a record of over one hundred owners by the time Janice signed her and her husband's names into the ledger. Janice had made colorful tags to mark some of the more interesting names, in an effort to add ambience for the few guests that their ill-fated Bed & Breakfast ever lodged. There were no celebrities, but there were several interesting stories the book told to those who knew were to look; Janice, having a knack for the quaint, felt the initial impression of the book might hook guests the moment they signed their own names. Not all the tales were happy, but they were certainly intriguing, and they showed the history of the place through their half-finished tales. For example, there was Monroe Beaty, an Englishman who stayed as a guest during the ownership of the Sventlovs at the request of his doctor, who felt he could use some weeks of country air to cure his lungs. Mr. Beaty had scrawled a note beside his own name, dating the annotation September 23, 1916, nearly two years past the date of original signature, and (the crafted bookmark explained) just after the Sventlovs had sold the estate to a Mr. & Mrs. Gint. The note read:

Whilst the clean air here heals my breathing, I must leave at the protestation of my olfactory senses. For the clean breezes of this beautiful country home have been spoiled—the air now stinks of Gint, a scent that I cannot endure! ~M.B.

Janice's note indicated that the story continued, found at another bookmark, which she carefully placed a few pages ahead, where Jonathan and Olena Gint had signed their own names into the book as the new proprietors, shortly after their purchase of the estate from the Sventlovs. In the margin of that page, written in an angry slant, was the rebuttal of Jon Gint. It said simply:

"Happy to have driven out that freeloading Brit!" after which the word "Brit" had been scratched out and a more feminine hand had replaced it with "git." There were many other such annotations and personal messages hidden within the registry, and Janice hoped that their intrigue would be enough to add five dollars to the inn's nightly rate.[17]

Yet through it all, the house had remained largely plain and each expansion—of which there were many—was simple in its design. The house simply had no flair for fashion, taking pride in the craftsmanship of its frame rather than the decoration of its walls. Individual owners tried to change things with fancy furniture, paint, and any number of interior additions, but the sheer frugality of the farmhouse's will quickly drove those occupants away. New families would arrive and stay a while, and eventually—like the Sventlovs—leave. Of course, vacancies weren't always caused by the house's influence or personality. People typically loved the farm for its homey and welcome demeanor, and the house made a concerted effort to love them back. It was almost as if, as many previous owners had explained to potential buyers, the house itself was making an active effort to make the place comfortable and warm. Yet churn remained high.

The sales were often private, simple contracts between buyer and seller. For some reason unbeknownst to them, each owner felt it best to keep the place out of the limelight of real estate moguls. For similar rea-

---

[17] "Intrigue," like "patina," can command a premium price from customers who will gladly pay extra to be reminded that they are not the only ones forced to endure lives full of "gossip" and "filth."

sons it was never gifted to the county or legally formed into an estate. In 1872 it was sold through Boombard and Swallows for the first time. The next year, after it had sold through the same realtor three more times, the realtor had opened a branch not twenty miles away, and a small excuse for a town had sprung up around its profits. The house welcomed this change, as it meant more activity overall. The villagers would often ride or hunt on the property, and as time progressed horses were replaced by families in automobiles, out to see the beautiful old farm during a Sunday drive.

"Sold the farm yet, Ned?" It was a common way to greet the various realtors of Boombard and Swallows. Where one would say "How're your shingles feeling today?" or "Nice weather lately, isn't it?" to any other person, it was always "sold the farm yet?" to an agent of B&S Realty. This was primarily because said agent would most likely retire from the proceeds of a sale. While the buyers were never rich, there was always enough tied up in overhead expenses to set a savvy realtor up for life. The intricacies of the estate were such that it trained each agent in every subtlety of the industry just before, ironically, allowing for them to pack up. Of course, at the beginning the house did sell for a fair amount. It was, after all, huge.

"Not sold it yet, Bob," the realtor would always reply. If it had sold, the realtor would be gone, not standing around for gossip.

"Well, there's always tomorrow," Bob would most likely answer. Bob in particular always liked to have the last word.

This particularly irritated Mr. Boombard. Mr. Boombard, one of the senior partners of Boombard and Swallows, had taken management of the farm account to "get the feel of it again" (although everyone knew it was just so that he could justify reaping the huge commissions for himself for once). It irritated Mr. Boombard because, after his first sale, they continued to ask him every single day.

"Sold the farm yet, Mr. Boombard?"

"Yes, twice now, actually."

"Well, there's always tomorrow." Mr. Boombard figured it wasn't worth the aggravation, and another agent was assigned to replace him. The money was great, but Mr. Boombard simply couldn't adjust to what he called the "country nature" of the villagers.

It sold again, and again. The town, like the farm, started to grow. Convenience stores and diners sprang from the ground. They were the types of establishments that catered to tourists, only it wasn't tourists that flowed through the area each season, but buyers. Farmers looking for a new place to set up shop, or romantic homeowners looking for a quiet getaway place, or in the case of Bobby and Janice, romantic home-owners who thought they might be able to live mortgage free by using most of the place for business. Other types were attracted too, of course. There was a constant need for surveyors. It seemed that every sale found some confusion with the property lines. It never occurred to anyone that each of the conflicting surveys, maps and appraisals could be accurate, and that the house itself was changing slowly over time. No one ever imagined the house could reposition itself so that the little pond was just a few feet closer to the old grain silo, or speculate that it did so because it liked the sound of the frogs in spring. No one questioned anything, as long as the slight discrepancies kept the town folk employed.

A few years into the twentieth century, however, and the town started to shrink. Shrink may be too kind a word, *implode* being more accurate. The house continued to sell, but each sale was for less and less. The population of honest architects, engineers and surveyors became weighted with an unwelcome number of lawyers and bankers. The farm-house itself began to develop a reputation, and by the twenty-first century the thriving township was a meager village once more. The farm had dwindled in market value to the point where it could hardly sustain itself, never mind an entire community.

cluck

The house's shutters flapped angrily as it remembered the circumstances of its decay. It should have been worth millions then! It should be worth millions now! It wasn't the house's fault that one thing after another gouged its value. First, the land had all been sold off to a nature conservatory. Newly unspoiled, the five hundred acres became overgrown, and then wild. Then there was a bear attack. Despite the house's silent insistence of blamelessness, it certainly contributed to its reputation: newly sub-divided and sold land would come under scrutiny as the house crept without care across the new borders. It knew it should have played by the rules, but who were these people to tell it where it could or couldn't grow? Tensions built up as quickly as the house itself. Superstitions entered the debate. Nobody stayed for long after that. The house was evil, creepy, haunted. Some stayed for as long as a year, but most left within a few months. The tourism—what little of it there was left— shriveled and died on the vine, and the house found itself alone.

Instead of growing outward, the tired old farmhouse began to run down. Seams opened up, breezes blew more freely through the rooms, and rain found its way inside the once-tight places. It became too much work for most people to even consider owning it. However, Bobby and his wife Janice were just ambitious enough (in the case of Janice) and stupid enough (in the case of Bobby) to give the place a try.

They were the last owners of record. Bobby had been there for five whole years, although he had been trying to escape for four of them. Only seven of those months were kept in the company of his lovely wife Janice, and only three of those months were spent managing the "Rambling Estates Bed, Breakfast and Country Inn." The B&S Realty agent stationed locally had long since been reassigned elsewhere, and no one ever drove by on Sunday.

The shutters ceased their ruckus and the house fell silent again. It brought this all upon itself, really. There was no sense getting upset about things. Sure, it wished that Bobby would leave. Sure, it wished the chickens would go, too. Despite the current infestation of human and non-human inhabitants, it was still the biggest and best damn farmhouse the world ever did see. With a sniffle of wind through a leaky gutter-spout, the farmhouse regained its composure and puffed itself up again with pride. *Yes*, it thought, *I am still magnificent*, and it smiled again.

The farm's feelings of resignation were not shared by the birds and men who lived within it. They too remembered the rise and fall of events that brought their fates before them, and were most displeased. They too remembered how good things once were.

The happy hens of yesteryear liked Bobby. They didn't know him as Bobby, of course. They couldn't speak or understand English. Not even the Rooster, who was large and strong and so much smarter than the rest had come fully to terms with human speech. They knew him simply as the tall wingless pink animal that brought food and water. They weren't smart enough to realize that the days when there was no food and water were the result of that same animal's laziness. They were simply grateful for sustenance when it was provided. They didn't know that the animal was a human, nor that the animal's wife was the only reason they hadn't all been slaughtered and barbecued. Chickens are stupid, in life. They get minutely smarter in death, but in life they're pure dumb. Pea-brain-at-a-legume-soup-factory kind of dumb. Definitely lacking the grey matter required for logical deduction.

The only idea in their collective feathered heads was "we love the animal that feeds us." They held onto this idea as Bobby waved goodbye to his wife, and then walked out to the small shack that had been built up against the outside of the henhouse. Bobby's wife was going to be away for three weeks; she was to attend a seminar on successfully marketing your B&B while Bobby stayed behind to meet with the architects and town planners to determine the best way to fit modern guest rooms into the ramshackle and random construct of the farmstead. After the seminar, she was going to make the most of the money she'd spent on the plane fare and visit her mother and sister, both of whom she hadn't seen in several years. What she didn't know is that he had already met with those people, and that he had also met with a general contractor, a wholesale supplier of furniture and fixtures, and his insurance provider. What the chickens didn't realize was that in the shack behind their hen-house, which had been mostly emptied the night before, there was a five gallon red metal canister of gasoline. They also didn't know that the stuff Bobby was sprinkling around on the ground wasn't food—at least not until they tried to eat it; it tasted acrid and smelled strange, so they only lapped up a little bit of it.

They also didn't know what fire was. Not until it was much too late.

Bobby had set the fire to create a low controlled burn, like when burning the fields in the spring. Bobby was a farmer. He knew all about this sort of thing. The fire crept in from just a few feet away from the furthest nooks of the hen yard. He had raked away the grass near the buildings to prevent the fire from wandering too close. The chickens smelled something, and a black cloud blew into their eyes. When they wandered over to the bright light that was flickering up from the ground, instinct told them to stay away, and so they gathered in a confused rabble in front of the henhouse. One curious hen, who had eaten more gasoline-soaked grass than the others, got too close to the fire and exploded like a big, feathery firecracker. [18]

Eventually, one or two of the smarter hens leapt inside the coop. It was safe inside the coop. Every chicken knows that.

Bobby was not a chicken. Bobby knew a bit more about things like *circumstance* and *intent* and *context*. He knew exactly what he was doing. He knew chickens loved tomatoes, so he threw a large juicy fruit into the

---

[18] An event that was later expanded by fast food restaurants into the idea of 'popcorn chicken'.

coop, luring the slower birds inside to join the others. The door was closed and locked only after every bird, greedy for food, had raced in after the prize. Bobby splashed a bit more gasoline around the base of the coop and then hopped back over the slowly advancing ring of fire to watch the conflagration. Just as the Rooster himself remembered things, Bobby thought that it smelled more than a bit like a barbecue.

The best place to build the guest rooms, of course, had been in the chicken yard. The shit-covered squawkers had always been an annoyance to Bobby, and now they were in the way of the business as well. So he took care of them. For good. The next day, the contractor showed up to find Bobby raking away a last pile of ash. The work was to start immediately; the goal was to have the expansion framed by the end of that week. He'd paid a premium to get a full crew to work long hours for the week, because he wanted everything done before Janice returned. He had it all planned. The bank loan for the construction was already secured, and he had some of his own money tucked aside, unknown to Janice. The furniture, bathroom fixtures, lights, rugs and even wall decorations were already ordered. They would arrive in two days, and were to be stored in the expansive equipment barn just behind the construction site. With materials on hand and the framing done in the first week, he hoped to have the first guest room finished and furnished as a surprise for Janice. The rest of the rooms would be completed over the next two months, but the first one had to be finished in three short weeks. To save money and time, there would not be a full foundation below the guest rooms. Instead, It would stand on concrete corner-posts with a two-foot crawl-space beneath it. They got to work immediately.

The haunting started not too long after that.

As the workers began to fill the spaces around the lonely farm, Bobby heard a chicken clucking. It was definitely a chicken, he thought, and it shouldn't be clucking because all the chickens were dead. He must

cluck

have missed one. He grabbed a net and worked his way through the activity, hunting for the survivor, but he never found it.

Later, when the frame was up and they were installing the plumbing and electricity, he took up the hunt again. He kept hearing something—a scratching sound now. Or a *tap, tap, tap* from beneath the floor. He obsessed about the sound, and scoured every inch of the massive estate trying to find its source. He prowled around constantly straining to catch hold of a sound or some telltale clue.

"What's got you so nervous, Bobby?" teased a large man. He was wearing painters' overalls and a flannel shirt.

"Nuthin'," insisted Bobby, although he was definitely starting to get jumpy. He hadn't found the stray chicken, but he knew he wasn't hearing things. "Did you hear that?" he asked the carpenter.

"Nope. You're the only one who hears ghosts, Bobby," and they all laughed. The plumber, the foreman—even the fat guy with the battered old ball cap who didn't seem to do much of anything.

"Ghosts ..." chuckled another worker, shaking his head. "That's a good one. Ghost chickens." He slapped his knee, and they all started laughing again.

Tap, tap, tap.

Was he going crazy?

Scratch-scratch-scratch. scratch ... tap.

Bobby didn't believe in ghosts. He thought maybe he was hearing things, though. He needed a vacation. He didn't get one. Janice was furious, and she grew more upset each time her loser husband started to obsess over "them noises." When he sprang awake in bed one night to the piercing call of a rooster which shouldn't exist, it was the last straw. Instead of a vacation, Bobby got something else. He got exactly what he deserved.

Knapp

cluck

chapter 15 the prophecy of the charge

It was just another day in the office. The two white-haired men were slumped in a semi-catatonic state at the same small round table, in the same cheap, cold office in the secret headquarters of the *Ordre du l'Exorciste de Volaille*. In front of one lay a small meticulously arranged cup and saucer, containing a fragrant cup of *café au lait*. A small antique spoon was propped on the small porcelain plate, most of the silver having worn off over the past years. It was now somewhat dull but it remained a formidable heirloom piece. The rich scent of darkly roasted coffee wafted through the small room. Both men were lost within the private spaces of deep contemplation, though their thoughts were focused on a mutual quandary. Next to the cup lay a short, trim stack of papers, neatly arranged.

Placed less meticulously before the second, slightly more slumped gentleman there was an abused ashtray, spilling ashes over one side and onto another crisp folder, which though clean and new was unable to hide the crinkled edges of Armand's rumpled report.

Knapp

The two objects, like their owners, sat motionless in perfect contrast to each other. One pristine man with healthy posture and an appreciation for fine coffee and a stack of papers so much in order that they practically glowed with authority. One slouching, rumpled man with an overflowing dirty ash tray and the creased and wrinkled source of their concern. A few new wrinkles were concentrated at one corner of the report, where Claude had been nervously grinding the pages between finger and thumb, off and on, for nearly an hour.

"Vous savez, nous pourrions être complètement confondus. C'a pu être une coïncidence." Claude said. He remained slouched as he spoke, not moving a single muscle in his body or even his face; the words simply dribbled out of his slack jaw. The rough English translation is "You know, we could be completely mistaken. It could be a coincidence," although without the benefit of the natural eloquence of the French language, it would translate more closely to "Maybe this is just a waste of time, and I can go home and sleep off this headache." His partner didn't seem to agree.

"A pu être," he said. "Could be. You know something is happening, though, just as well as I do. We knew it from the first moment we saw his report. We have been in this business for a long, long time. Someone less *préoccupé* might accomplish something great in so much time, written a *concerto,* or fed the poor perhaps. Instead we do this. Nothing but this, for a very very long time. So call it a hunch, if you will."

"Yeah, I know."

"And you *also* know, because we have been in this business for such a sufferingly long time, that when one of us gets a hunch, it's usually right. When *you know* something is going to happen, and *I know* something is going to happen ... well, there is little point in hoping that we are wrong, *n'est pas?"*

"Yeah, I know."

cluck

"And you *also* know that whenever *he* is involved, nothing is ever as it seems."

"I know, I know! That's why we dug into this, done all this research ... and that's why we still have that blasted report there in front of us. So don't be a stupid bastard and try to pretend this isn't happening, okay Jean-Pierre?"

"It is just that my head hurts. I mean, of all the people ... of all the places ... of all the *chickens* ..." He tried to think of another way out of realizing the truth, but it just made his head hurt more. Who would have thought the same weird little kid who turned up on their doorstep, long ago, would end being involved in the prophecy? Claude produced another cigarette from somewhere with the casual dexterity that only comes with professional circus training or a serious nicotine addiction. He shuffled through the papers again, this time with only one hand, as the other held the cigarette to his lips. A second envelope—air mailed from the states only a few days after the first report – was momentarily exposed, as was the new stack of Polaroids that accompanied it. It contrasted Armand's report in its cleanliness and formality, but it was that document's equal in terms of the unease that it caused its readers. Jean-Pierre eventually found the page he was looking for and slid it away from the rest. It contained minutely recorded data that only select, highly trained people could hope to understand. In the letterhead, a small crest was embossed into the heavy paper: a circle, surrounding a single feather.

"Armand's report is plain enough. This is a cataclysmic event and it seems to have unnerved even him ... at least a little bit. Although I'm not sure *he* realizes what he's going up against here. It's hard to tell with him." Opposite Claude, a weary Jean-Pierre nodded in agreement. "I'm not sure he was ever told about the prophecy, was he?"

"I certainly did not tell him. Back in those days we were all secretive. You know, so it was easier to hide the fact that we were *fraudes*." The meticulous man looked down his nose at Claude and shot him full of ice.

"Well, it is true, we are—were!" he added in his defense. "I do not know why it continues to upset you." The tension relaxed, and the stoic posture of the Frenchman slumped for a moment as he put down his coffee with a sigh of resignation.

"I suppose we were, yes, yes ... and it all changed because of this one stupid kid, and now this. He grows old and ... and all of these events, of which Armand himself is so closely connected ..."

"Are you saying that you think he knows?"

"Well ..."

"Hell, he can not know! How could he! We have just figured it out ourselves!" The exclamation was made as only a native Frenchman could promulgate, with both an animated passion and a calm still demeanor. He sipped his cup and leaned back in his chair. He did have a point, they had only recently uncovered solid evidence of the Inter-spectral Rift and it was unlikely that Armand had any knowledge of it. Armand was, by reputation, more of the "storm-in-there-and-kick-it" type of personality. They were lucky to get reports out of him at all; he typically couldn't be bothered by conjecture or supposition.

"Yeah, yeah, I know," Claude conceded, "but if he really is everything the master thought he was—"

"He is."

" ... if he really does possess The Charge—"

"He does."

"Well, then maybe he knows a lot more than he should. Maybe he does know about the prophecy. Maybe he does know about the events, and even this rift thing. I mean, why else would he be there fighting that chicken? It just doesn't make sense. It can't be coincidence. It's what you might call *merde.*"

"*Merde.* Of course. Yes, it is all very unlikely, that is for certain. Then again, that is to be expected with anything that Armand is involved in. After all, Charge or not, the stupid American is, well ... special."

cluck

"I know, I know. He's the only one of us that has any goddamned worth, how can I forget that? To think we've been in this job for so long and only one of us has any legitimate power!"

"Ah, but perhaps we are too quick to condemn The Order. We have knowledge, and knowledge is power."

"Yes, I'm familiar with that rationalization too. It helps me sleep at night. It keeps me from wondering why I didn't become a banker? Or a tobacconist!" He waved his cigarette in the air, leaving a thin trail of pungent smoke. "Think of the money I would save if I were a tobacconist!" He sighed and shifted uncomfortably in his seat for a moment, and then grinned across the table at his friend. "At least that fool Patrick isn't here to listen to us, to see us act like this." The newest initiate into The Order, so inferior to what Armand had been, had won his argument, and had gone home for a "short" vacation. To the two disgruntled agents of the disgruntled order of chicken exorcists, it was just as well. Patrick's winning excuse had been some story of a family obligation, but it was really a matter of Jean-Pierre and Claude wanting to get the foolish kid out from under their feet while they tried to sort out the mess of events occurring around them.

The two men settled back into their silence. The more sophisticated of the two continued to sip at his coffee, eventually finishing the cup and replacing it carefully on the small saucer. The other smoked, finished the cigarette, lit another, and inhaled deeply a few times before mashing the end into the innocent ash tray, which did not deserve his abuse but accepted it willingly. On the table before them, the papers stared silently upwards. A neat stack of clean white pages, neatly typed and embossed with the appropriate stamps of their order. To those who understood, the documents outlined several important matters. The first was the history of The Events, of which both men had just recently mentioned. The second was the circumstances of Armand himself, his initiation into The Order, and a jagged record of his various exploits on behalf of the organization. The final affair that the papers documented with special care and attention to detail was the most recent of said exploits: an incident concerning a certain house somewhere in the rural backwoods of the northern United States.

The Events that were being discussed had occurred many years prior, and had just recently been discovered by the two men. Each event involved the Inter-spectral Rift, that momentary rending of time and space that stretched the barriers between life and death so thin that something had popped between the two realms. One involved Armand himself, when he was still very young, and it had left him with an inexplicable fever and a lasting second sight. To these men (and all in The Order) it explained a lot; there was finally a justification and a validation of Armand's powers. They also just learned that the same rift had appeared on a stretch of highway not far from Armand's childhood home. It went largely unnoticed—again, a sudden brightening of the sky that rippled quickly to the horizon. It had been mistaken by many drivers as a heat mirage or perhaps some odd reflection from the tarmac ahead. One truck, a poultry truck, had actually driven straight through the rift. There was no effect to the truck or its driver, but a young rooster, barely a year old, was caught for a moment between realms, just as young Armand had been. The chicken had grown faster and stronger and smarter. From what The Order had learned, the details were fuzzy, but as best they could tell, the rooster had survived and grown into a magnificent bird. There was a record of a woman entering a rooster matching its profile in her local town fair, winning a blue ribbon. Through the fair organizers the two sulking agents of The Order traced the bird's owner, Janice G., and were shocked when they discovered where she lived.

The last incident—the one concerning a rather special farmhouse—involved an unexplained well of power. They were fairly certain this wasn't related to the rift, as it seemed to have occurred hundreds of years prior. There were a few very old reports of mysterious weather and

cluck

"unnatural, unholy lightening" that led The Order to suspect that perhaps another rift had occurred long before. The file was full of similar reports of odd weather, mysterious noises and lights. Many such claims surrounded the house; reports of a thick dense fog on otherwise clear and breezy days, and that sort of thing, which had caused the place to develop a strong and believable reputation for being haunted. There were also rumors that a murder had taken place on the farm and that the place was cursed because of it. That was distressing enough, but what was of real concern was that the pictures of the farm matched those attached to Armand's most recent report perfectly. The address of the mysterious farm matched that of none other than Janice G., and her prize-winning rooster.

The evidence was clear, when examined by experienced supernaturalists such as Jean-Pierre and Claude, that two souls had been touched by the spectral rift. It would seem that both were altered into something almost supernatural, gaining more power and insight than was their due. The two souls were Armand and the Rooster; one who can see into the soul-world and has taken possession of an ancient power known as The Charge, and the other who grew physically strong and painfully clever and who now roosts amidst the thickest nest of poultrygeists ever to be seen.

There was no reason to suspect it a coincidence that they had come together in place of mystery and power. Those of The Order did not believe in coincidences. If a second rift had opened and had altered the farm itself, why not assume that everything was interconnected? Spiritual events often were, after all. When strange reports began to appear from Armand, and when rumors spoke of local farmers who mysteriously disappeared, never to be seen again, The Order launched a full investigation. All the facts had been checked and rechecked. The conclusion was now presented before them neatly and concisely. The fulfillment of the prophecy was at hand.

"How long has he been gone?" Claude's words again came through an unmoving jaw, from the general direction of the shabby man's face, which was again buried in his hands.

"Who knows? Armand's original report came in ... what? Three weeks ago? From air mail. So, he was probably already in the house by the time we read it. Another day before we sent our dispatch to the States, another four days until the reply ... and another day between then and now. And we can not contact Armand. Why will he not use a cell phone, damn him! He is like some prehistoric idiot, refusing to use the tools that we give him."

"He's old-fashioned, that's all. Of course that means the whole thing could actually be over by now, and we wouldn't even know it. Damn, I wished he'd contact us. I'm about this close to getting on a plane and flying my ass down there myself." He made a gesture with two fingers, indicating exactly how close he was.

"Patrick is there already, we could send him ..." The suggestion was only half serious; in Patrick's first days on the job, it was clear that he simply wasn't going to work out. It was a major disappointment because Patrick had reminded them of the very young initiate Arnold, so long ago, before he had taken The Charge and adopted his new name. The two major differences between Armand as a young boy and Patrick were: one, Patrick was old enough and confident enough to find a loophole that would get him back to America; and two, he lacked any sort special attributes, least of all any supernatural abilities. The only common feature that remained was Patrick's ability to annoy both Jean-Pierre and Claude—often to the brink of insanity.

"You're dreaming. That kid's not coming back. We've shattered whatever delusions of heroism brought that loser here. And you know what? He's right." They both nodded, and quietly mulled things over for a moment in their minds, privately.

cluck

"Well, we are the only two left now besides Armand, so I am sure we would know if he was dead." Jean-Pierre was fishing for encouragement, anything to help counteract the dread and uncertainty that they both felt.

"How do you figure that?"

"I believe that The Charge would return if he was dead. Would it not? It would float back here on its own somehow, certainly. That is some comfort, *n'est pas?*" The thick French accent sounded pathetic, making Jean-Pierre's words sound more pleading and needy than he intended.

"I suppose ... if it's true. But I don't have to tell you, he's —"

"—the only one with any real power. Yes, I know, you keep reminding me. So when The Charge does get here maybe one of us will have some power too." There was no ambition in the claim, only sarcasm. It was Jean-Pierre's way of pointing out to Claude that, if the ultimate responsibility ever fell to them, The Order was done for.

"Or maybe not. It just might die with him." The dregs of an empty cup of coffee were swirled, and yet another cigarette was mashed unceremoniously into the pile.

"Jean-Pierre?"

"Yes?"

"What the hell are we going to do?"

"I have no idea, my friend. No idea at all ..."

Knapp

chapter 16   saving bobby

"Let him go!" demanded the timid yet mindful boy. He wasn't a boy anymore, of course. He wasn't the confused child who stumbled into strange situations as a result of his peculiar second sight. He wasn't even the blindingly observant youth who excelled at football. He was the exorcist, now. Or "The Exorcist"—with capital letters—according to some. He had many names, echoing through centuries of memories that he should not, realistically speaking, possess. "The Banisher of Bantams" was one of his favorites. They were especially colorful in the twenties ("Bird Purger") and the seventies ("Cluck Busters"). In the eighteenth century, he recalled, the names were always stuffy and formal, like "Surveyor of Extraordinary Incidents Concerning Fowl, Game Birds and Domestic Poultry", and then of course there was "L'Exorciste de Volaille," which was his official title now. He recalled these things from his education at The Order, and from deep within the dusty recesses of his own mind. He remembered many things that he had never experienced firsthand. He was the bearer of The Charge and thus possessed generations of memories and experiences and the wealth of knowledge and understanding that came with them.

His inherited awareness gave him memories of a day long ago, a day of odd coincidence and mystery. A special day. The Charge was inhabiting the body of a young kilted exorcist by the name of Fergus, who was in the process of investigating one of the strangest haunts The Charge had ever witnessed. He was far away at the time, in a small corner of Ireland's northwest. A poultry farmer had gone to collect eggs one morning only to find that each and every one of his chickens had laid a fully cooked rack of mutton. It was a subconscious, psychotic and rather symbolic plea to the farmer that he should eat more sheep, and fewer birds, as they were tired of laying eggs all day just to lose their friends and relatives to one of the farmer's dinner parties.

That had been a strange day across the world. Armand could only remember those bits that The Charge had seen through the eyes of young Fergus, but many such spiritual contests had been held. In a remote part of Russia, several tons of prize caviar had fallen from the sky like rain, much to the distress of the local shaman.[19] In a small village in a distant jungle, a stone—which looked a little bit like it could have been a person performing semaphore—had started to bleed, causing their current religious leader to be sacrificed and replaced with a less tangible but far more entertaining notion of a deity. An entire river in the south of England had turned to cheese, leaving the piper (who had been hired to rid the area of rats and mice) with a lot of explaining to do.

In America—far away from The Charge, the kilt and the mutton—a common mason lowered a massive stone into place, forming the foundations of a new farm. While caviar and cheese and other curious events

---

[19] Also to the distress of the townspeople. Caviar is *not* considered a delicacy when it is in you hair, in your boots, and other more intimate places. It proved a record day for the local bath house, although many of the bathers suffered a lasting phobia of chowders.

occurred around the world, something odd happened here as well. A force descended into it, and took hold of what would become the closest thing to a living structure to ever be built by man. It wasn't evil, or dangerous or even intelligent. It simply possessed an indomitable will to grow. In that, it shared a commonality with many beasts. In that, it was very much like mankind. On that special day centuries ago, it began its outward push.

The Charge hadn't been here to see it, when the farm came to life, and so images of the foundation, like those of caviar and bleeding stones, failed to flicker forth from the memories of the exorcist's ancient predecessors. Armand was forced to pause and contemplate the more limited addition to his own memory; the single, sudden strange feeling that something bigger than mutton had been afoot that day. Was it an epiphany? The effects of something he'd eaten? Whatever it was, he—like all exorcists of his line—was used to strange memories and odd premonitions. Fergus had mopped up bits of lamb and helped to convince the souls of past-stewed hens to peacefully cross over to the other side, and The Charge hadn't given it another thought. Until now. When Armand had stepped into the house, the memory and the strange feeling that went with it had been thrust to the surface of his thoughts. He could feel the power of the house with every step he took across its creaking pine floors, and the feeling was ... familiar.

"Let him go!" he called out again. He was speaking to the flock, of course. His enemies were still close, concealed. There was nothing in response save his own words echoing back amidst a distant and evasive clucking. They were teasing him. Whispering to themselves from the shadows, laughing at him.

"Come and get him," said a whisper—it was faint, the sound darting about the corners of the room in the way that only spirit voices could. There was laughing. Well, more of a "ba-braw-craw-cluck," but the exorcist knew what it meant. The hens shouldn't be mocking him.

Chickens don't talk, either. He must have imagined the bit about the chicken talking. Concerned, he looked down at his feet. The badge was still there on his boot, despite his having kicked nearly a hundred birds with it already; what kinds of chickens ignored the badge? Armand managed to remain confident, however; he knew what he was doing.

What Armand didn't know was that a long-deceased Porthos stood waiting just around the corner. Behind the pint-sized rooster, its companions Athos and Aramis stood ready. Each of the small bantam roosters had been completely stripped of flesh and feathers by their new lord, the Rooster King, and were nothing more than beaks and bones. Where there were once proud plumes of feathers, there was nothing but boney stumps and sticky, decayed tufts of down. Each of the musketeers had stuck a fresh feather into its tiny skull, in memory of their namesakes, and they gripped tiny, pointy swords in the calcified remains of their tiny, jointed wings.

In life, they were cast down by their King for their arrogance; they had attempted to gain the love of their King's favorite, confident in their collective beauty, and had been punished severely. In death, all was forgiven, and he celebrated them as his generals. While they were wee birds, they were still stronger than any hen, and the Rooster recognized this. He used them as a twisted sort of honor guard, often sending them alone to torture and maim Bobby, to allow the hens a bit of rest. It was not surprising, therefore, that the Rooster had commanded them to their current post, where they were poised to ambush the unsuspecting Armand. They had received the order and obeyed, like the whipped dogs that they were, for the Rooster had long since wrested any mutinous thoughts from their puny bantam minds. Their will had been ripped away just as their flesh had, until all that remained were miniscule, but extremely loyal, skeletons. Loyal and armed skeletons.

Armand stepped cautiously around the corner to feel a tiny prick in his leg where the miniature sword had barely penetrated the thick leather

cluck

of the boot. Porthos stood in an awkward *en garde*, the tip of his sword stuck firmly in the exorcist's boot. Behind him, Aramis and Athos flanked out, and struck slightly more successful poses, ready to attack.

"What the [heck] is this? Halloween?" Armand muttered, and with a deft flick of his staff Porthos was sent flying away, where he struck the wall and immediately dispersed. The little sword, still pricking the surface of Armand's leg uncomfortably, dangled limply from his boot. He shook his leg and the weapon clattered to the floor. The remaining musketeers backed away, their own swords still raised.

"Since when do skeletons wear costumes and carry swords?" Armand asked no one in particular.

In answer to his question, the mini-Aramis stepped forward, and brandished its sword high in salute. Tentatively, Athos shuffled forward, joining his own sword into two-thirds of the musketeer salute. Porthos' spot, of course, was vacant, and the two remaining roosters glanced nervously into each other's eyeless sockets.

"Feathered hats, swords ... no ... it couldn't be," Armand groaned, shaking his head in disbelief. "Well, in that case—"

He spun the staff around quickly and caught Aramis under the bony cleft of his small bony beak-hole, snapping the bird's tiny skull clean off its neck.

"All for one ..." He turned on his left foot in concert with the motion of the staff, and spun around to catch Athos square in the breastbone. Before Armand's right foot touched the ground again, the three musketeers were no more.

" ... and one for all."

Armand regained his composure, rubbing at the spot where the tiny sword had penetrated his boot. Again, he called out, "Let him go!"

A breeze picked up and then died, and then, as if the chickens were presenting Armand's prize to him in surrender, he heard the man he was looking for call back to him.

"Hu-hullo?" Bobby cried. He was still huddled on the floor, his face turned towards the dark corners of the room. He was covered in scratches and dust and feathers and blood. His voice was weak, as if it were an effort to create sound. It was a whimper that carried the entire weight of his ongoing persecution. The exorcist approached him, but before he could draw close, a sudden swarm of dark feathered forms spilled out over him, dragging Bobby through to the next room like ants might flee with picnic contraband. As he disappeared through the doorway, Armand could just make out the farmer's collapsed form amongst his avian captors. A matted, feathery fiend turned back to gaze upon the doorway, which began to melt and swirl as reality began to twist. With practiced calm, Armand reached into one of the pouches on his belt and pulled forth a thin, rigid shape. With a flick of the wrist it snapped open into the form of an eagle, built of wire frame with taught polyester wings. Another flick and the predator kite glided through the swirling doorway, instinctually scattering the flock and revealing Armand's prize. In a clearing amidst a circle of panicked poultry, Bobby lay curled into the impotent posture of a fetus, shaking.

The exorcist ran after him as the kite crashed into the far wall and slid to the floor, breaking the spell. The doorway tried to twist away again, closing itself in that mysterious way that doors in haunted houses sometimes do, but he was too fast and he was expecting it, now. He ducked through easily ... although he felt the back of his shirt collar pull a bit as it brushed the turning and sinking door frame. Something wasn't quite right, he thought, as he dashed over to the quivering form of Bobby.

The eyes that looked up at him were at once sunken with fatigue and bulging with horror. The effect made him look quite crazy. Coincidentally, that's just what he was.

"Hu-who ... wha? ... Who are you?" he babbled. He started to rock gently back and forth. Mysteriously, the chickens were nowhere to be seen. You couldn't even hear the scratching and clucking in the distance, as was usual.

"My name is Armand," the exorcist replied, in as comforting a tone as could be mustered by someone who did what he did for a living. "I'm here to save you."

"Ar ... Armand?" He squinted stupidly. "Is that foreign?"

"Well, no. It's Arnold, really. My master was, well, he was French. He called me Armand, or Archibald, or Armandard — heck he even called me Jacque once. But I'm kinda taken to Armand. You can call me either Arnold or Armand, whichever you like." The truth was that the exorcist wasn't really fond of either name. He had given in to The Charge's desire for his new name largely because he himself was so indifferent to the matter—and when you have voices in your head addressing you in a certain way, it's hard to ignore. Probably as a result of the same multi-tenant qualities of his mind, he had grown more accustomed to thinking of himself in the third person, anyway: as "the exorcist," or "the driver," or "the whatever-he-was-doing-er."

"I—, I— ... I'm—" Bobby attempted.

"It's all right. I know. You're scared. You're confused. There's a lot of those [things] out there. Sons 'a [female dogs]."

"B—but you're here. You're not even a—afraid. Why?" There was a look of surprise and awe on the wounded farmer's face; a once mighty hillbilly who was now reduced to envying the strength of other men.

"Me? Scared? Sure I am, but you can't show 'em your fear, man. That's what it's all about. You can't let 'em see it in your eyes, or hear it in your breath. Between you and me? Yeah, I'm scared. This is a tough one, this is." He wasn't looking at Bobby, but was instead padding at his clothes. "Who else is in here?" he asked, without looking up.

"Nobody!" Bobby answered just a bit too quickly.

"Are you sure?" Armand pressed, suspicious of Bobby's reaction. "I only ask because there were rumors of disappearances. Plural ones. Then

again, there was more than one rumor that you'd been murdered."
Bobby's reaction was one of confusion, fear, malnutrition and probably a
good deal of blood-loss. Was there guilt in there, too? It was hard to say,
with all of the psychological background noise.

Bobby laughed, nervously. "Nope. Not me. Heh heh." He looked
past Armand to make certain there weren't more chickens there.

"What about your wife? Janet?"

"Janice," Bobby corrected.

"Yeah, Janice. Is she in here somewhere?"

"No no no no no no." Bobby started rocking again, bobbing his
head limply from side to side.

"Are you all right? You look—"

"Janice left me. Left me here alone. With ... *them*." Bobby stopped
rocking and looked up at Armand, who had just found what he'd been
looking for in a zippered pocket on the inside of his coveralls. He produced a small bag of baby carrots from a pocket, and began to crunch.
Feeling Bobby's intent stare, he looked up.

"I'm just asking. Want to know how many people need saving.
That's all." Bobby's stare didn't falter.

"I'm ..." The words trailed off, but Bobby's gaze remained locked on
Armand, staring him in the ... mouth? Armand followed Bobby's eyes
more carefully, and realized the crazed glare was aimed at a small piece of
carrot that Armand had been holding in front of his mouth, ready to eat.

"Hungry? Here, have a carrot." Bobby dove into the bag with
gusto.

"I'm not hungry, I'm starving," he said through a mouthful of carrot,
his words accented by the crunching of the crisp vegetables. Flecks of
orange dribbled from the corners of his mouth. "I'd kill for some meat,"
he whimpered, thinking back to the last time he'd had a proper meal.
His mouth watered, adding to the existing stream of orange drool, and
he became more famished at the thought of succulent flesh.

cluck

"Meat? Nah, not me. I'm a vegetarian."

"Vegetarian?" It was obviously not a familiar concept to Bobby. "You mean, you don't eat meat?"

"That's what it means, yes," answered Armand a bit condescendingly. Of course that's what it means ... idiot.

"So you don't even eat ..." the words trailed off. The oldest cliché, known to vegetarians the world over, is the tired question "Not even chicken?" Bobby was dumb, but even he managed to spot the irony of the retort and stifled it prior to completion.

"No, not even chicken," Armand confirmed, regardless. "Not that they don't deserve it, mind you. Hell, they eat each other. They'd eat themselves, if they could figure out how. In this line of work, though ... well, I've seen enough to turn my appetite off just about everything. Especially chicken. Don't feel bad though, everybody always asks that. I don't know why, chicken's not a vegetable." Neither is fish, but people asked that too.

"W-what line of work?" Bobby managed.

"Hmm? Oh, this, of course. Rescuing people like you from undead chickens like them. I mean, look at this place. It doesn't exactly whet the appetite ... all filth and shit and rot." The words struck true enough that Bobby was forced to suppress a bout of nausea.

They sat and ate in silence for a moment. Had the dingy room been replaced with a green hillside, and the smell of decay with that of flowers, and had the two men known each other and been friends, it would have made a nice little picnic. It was none of those things, however, and once the small bag had been emptied, there was nothing left but an uncomfortable quiet. Bobby broke the awkward silence first.

"A tough one?" He peered hard at the rough and dangerous vegetarian. The confusion that swarmed and replicated inside of Bobby's fragile mind was itself confounded by the appearance of the strange man, clad in what was obviously some sort of costume or uniform and speaking calmly, but as a whole beyond all comprehension. "A tough one what?"

Centuries of spirit-fighting knowledge and power manifested itself momentarily to suppress a chuckle. "Chickens," Armand explained. "Ghost chickens. Never seen this many at once, really. There's something strange about the whole thing that I can't quite put my finger on." He held up his finger, which was missing the last digit due to a bad pecking accident a few years before. Looking at it he realized it probably wasn't the most comforting gesture; he lowered his hand again and stuffed it into one pocket. At about the same time, an angry feathered body thumped against the closed door. It just wasn't right. Chicken spirits didn't act this way. They didn't pursue, not more than a few yards at least. They never acted as a group. The door thumped again, and again. It sounded like an army of chickens was bashing its way in, and—

The door wasn't closed, he thought. Not like that. He had dashed in and thrown himself down towards Bobby, scattering the hens as he did so, and certainly not bothering to stop and close the door behind him because it had been closing on its own, the straight panels swirling and twisting into impassable wall. The next thing he remembered, the two men were sitting alone, eating carrots in peace and quiet, behind a normal, untwisted and unswirled door. Something was very wrong.

"Wait here," the suddenly alert warrior advised, tossing the words gently over his shoulder as he slowly approached the door; it was at once a command and a warning to remain calm and quiet. The door, in contrast, was rattling in its hinges now. The noise was deafening. He lifted his boot, and paused just a moment as his eye caught the glint of his badge. That badge stood for many things. Experience, for one. Not just his own, but generations of it. Experience that was handed down over and over again. Experience that told him that chickens didn't haunt this way. Sure, they can lay traps. They can flutter and peck. They can shower you with phantasm feathers and spiritual scat, but they don't

haunt like this. They don't play mind games because they—quite simply—don't have minds sophisticated enough to play games with. With a
breath of determination, he kicked the door outward.

Silence.

The source of the noise was gone, as suddenly as it had appeared. A
faint stirring in the air—a swirl of dust and down—was the only indication that something ... something had been out there, but all that could
be detected now was a distant scratching. No, a scrabbling. As if hundreds of taloned feet were scampering away in the distance, eager to be
out of sight lest they be caught at their mischief. Then—suddenly—a
scream. Armand's heart jumped into his throat, startled as the horrible
shriek washed over him. He froze, and turned ... slowly. It had come
from right behind him, right where—

As the scream continued to echo around him, he watched helplessly
as Bobby's struggling form sank slowly through the floorboards. It swallowed him amidst dirt, feathers and screams as his unlikely rescuer
looked on helplessly. Lamely, the seasoned exorcist tried to pull himself
together in time to reach the wailing bumpkin, but it was no use. He was
gone. Armand, *L'Exorciste de Volaille*, dispeller of displaced poultry souls
and calmer of ghoulish grouse, knew suddenly that he was completely
out of his league.

Again, silence.

Then something ... a door opening? A floor creaking? The distant
noises were too muted to identify clearly. Armand looked at the floor,
which was again intact. There was no sign that a human being had just
been swallowed up by some unholy mouth of wooden planks and square-
ended nails. The wood was dirty and worn, like any floor would be in a
house of this age, but there was no crack or seam. Nothing.

The exorcist sat down. The chickens were gone. He'd been in this
room for several minutes now, so they should have migrated towards
him. They should be here, pathetically attempting to spook him with

feather-brained clichés and tired, ineffectual traps. It was strange, but not the strangest thing had happened since he first heard the rumors about this place, about the prize flock of birds, about ghosts and ghouls. He had decided to investigate when he'd heard the even stranger rumors surrounding the disappearance of a man named "Bobby G." Bobby Garfundephelt, a name which is hard to forget in general but almost impossible to remember in specifics. Understandably, people just called him Bobby. Never mind what they called him, they even *thought* of him as just "Bobby" because he had a last name that was even hard to visualize, never mind pronounce. Probably Swedish, Armand had thought when his early investigations had first uncovered that name. Not that he was any expert on names, but that's what he thought, although Bobby didn't look Swedish. He looked ... backwoods. Backwoods American. *Homosapiens Redneckus*, through and through, and he just sank through a perfectly sound floor in a house, which is haunted but only by chickens. Chickens: stupid dirty beasts that should be completely incapable of scaring up anything of this caliber.

It didn't make sense. Armand struggled to orient himself, so that he might begin to work his way downward and find Bobby again. He was pretty sure he was still on the first floor. Had he run upstairs? He might have ... yes, he did but then he went down another flight after that, didn't he? Did he really? He didn't remember clearly where he'd been in the house. At first it seemed like he had just opened the door, kicked his way through a few ghost-infested rooms, and then found Bobby huddling in a corner. After thinking about it, it felt like he'd been running through that house for days ...

He shook his head to clear his mind. Was the house itself the force behind all of this? While houses were known to develop spirits of their own, they rarely cared about mortals enough to manifest anything noticeable. He'd never heard of a malevolent house-spirit before. Then again, this was decidedly not Armand's area of expertise. What he did

cluck

know was that chickens couldn't possibly be behind all of this—doors that close on their own and floors that eat people. Then again, he had seen the hen look very deliberately at the door before it began to melt shut. Against his instincts and better judgement,[20] he settled down to the floor, badly needing the rest. With a sigh, he took stock of what he knew.

Bobby had been trapped in this house for a few years. The house was huge—it was certainly the sort of house that one could imagine might develop self-awareness. When Armand had first stepped up to the house during his reconnaissance he knew this place was special. He'd done a considerable amount of research on the place. He'd found maps (which proved inaccurate) and deeds, and a lengthy history of the place, which contained more maps and illustrations but was clearly missing entire pages because the page numbers had jumped from three to seven. At the time, he'd written it off as the mere incompetence of small-town governments and amateur book-keepers, but now he suspected there might be some grander conspiracy. Each map showed a different arrangement, each deed contradicting the last.

One thing was certain, though: the house was definitely infested with chicken-ghosts. Dozens if not hundreds of them, from what he could tell. Yet somehow this ignorant hick had survived for years—no easy trick even if it were just the chickens he'd been dealing with. There would also have been hunger to contend with, and thirst, and—by the looks of the place—disease. Armand thought, not for the first or last time, that something was definitely wrong. What was it? He couldn't put his tip-less finger on it to save his life, which is just what he had to do: he had to save his life. And Bobby's, if he could. Bobby Garferwhatizname. The man, according to record, wasn't much of a man to begin with, and he was gibbering mad by now, but he had to save him anyway.

---

[20] Both of which told him "stay above beak-level."

Knapp

He had a badge of honor on his left boot that told him that much for certain. He had to save everyone. He was the hero. The Charge.

"Shit," he exclaimed. Thankfully, his voice didn't bother to censor that one. It must have known how deep they both were in it.

cluck

chapter 17 a calculating spirit

Outside of the "real world" there are several other places that people either aren't aware of, or—as is more likely the case—they are aware of but that they refuse to acknowledge. It's safer for the mind to blot things out that don't make sense, and these other places don't make any sense at all. Not by typical mortal standards, anyway.

One such place is a holding area for spirits. A waiting room, if you will. There the various life essences of the recently deceased, freshly departed from their hosts of flesh, wait to learn about the many possibilities that exist for them in the afterlife. Of course, there are no clear instructions, no maps or guides. There are no shiny counters, and no bells labeled "ring for assistance." If there were, the social workers (who don't exist) would likely all be on break. In the afterlife, there's a certain expectance of self-discovery, a reliance upon postmortem curiosity, and a reluctance (if not outright distaste) for any sort of spiritual nonchalance. If a soul is content to just hang around, then so be it. Of course, sometimes a spirit wants to progress further along the trans-existential timeline, but is—as they say—dumber than a bag of nails. Sometimes, said spirit would stare for eons at blatantly obvious clues—like a long tunnel with a light at the other end, or a glowing vortex that smells faintly of brimstone—but simply not get it. Sometimes, the spirit would get tired of trying to figure it out and simply drift around trying to communicate with still-living beings instead of simply moving on. In short: ghosts. Stupid ghosts. More often than not, chicken ghosts.

Not all ghosts are stupid, of course. Sometimes, a more intellectually endowed spirit would just be unable to find a suitable path—although there were plenty to choose from. There were worlds full of indulgences such as chocolate and cream and buttermilk biscuits. There were worlds full of action and excitement. There were whole planes of existence dedicated to such specialized things as lying in the sun, eating gravel, balancing atop high poles, and places where things could fly that normally couldn't fly. The belief shared among many human religions that there were only two choices—the very good and the very bad—was the understatement of an afterlifetime. There is always the person who, even in death, looks at the menu but simply can't make up their mind. The lack of aforementioned social workers or a suitable (i.e., dead) dinner date means there is no one around to make these types of hard decisions for them. Yet still, some souls can't find a place amongst it all, and are left to wander back among mortals, yearning for a place to fit in. They don't necessarily listen to gothic music and dress in all black and chrome, but it helps with the whole "ghost" image if they do.

There are also souls that do have a place. They do fit in. They know where they want to go, but there is something that deliberately keeps them from it. A strong emotion—often hate, lust, greed or malice—can be more binding than a bowl of oatmeal, sticking the bearer between life and death in a similarly constipatory manor. It happens this way because an indomitable thirst to quell the emotion keeps them from whatever

cluck

thing they want most, that which they search for, forever after. They *see* the light at the end of the tunnel, they *recognize* it, but they're too damn caught up in themselves to do anything about it, because when the chips are down their emotions hold more power over them than the promise of eternal rest.

Chickens definitely fit into the first category. They're often simply too stupid to find their way out of the spiritual antechamber to somewhere better, so they go home. They haunt people, but typically in a more indifferent manner than what most people think of as "haunting." They simply act out their own stupid, dirty and neurotic lives as they normally would, only more dead. A chicken fluttering through the house isn't terrifying by itself, but if you replace the chicken with a rotting chicken zombie it's a different matter altogether.[21] Chickens, while living, rarely form an opinion about humans, being unaware that there is anything more of us above our knees. Food shows up in frequent coincidence with the arrival of human feet, and so there is a positive hunger-association to counteract the only other two instincts that chickens possess: terror and panic. Sometimes chickens develop a hatred for humans after death, typically as a result of some epiphany concerning the two species' relative positions on the food chain, which itself is usually triggered by the cause of their demise: that is, being eaten. In such instances, a chicken in death will resort to simple tricks and traps: feeble, uninspired, and largely ineffective attempts at revenge. Things like the rotten eggs or the dancing tomato—consistent, yet spontaneous and disorganized. The thing that was haunting Bobby's country Bed & Breakfast was harder to classify. It fell into the first category (stupid) but also the third category (angry, vengeful). It hated. It hungered. It yearned for revenge. It wanted to make Bobby suffer, and it had plenty of opportunity.

---

[21] The difference between a zombie, a ghost, a ghoul, etc., largely depends on the amount of leftover flesh and the degree of opacity. The common denominators are "dead" and "walking the earth" and "terrifying."

Though the souls of departed chickens were abundant, this thing was not a chicken. Like the chickens, It didn't fully grasp the situation around It, but was far more intelligent than a hen and far more cunning than a rooster. It was perfectly aware of its non-chicken-ness. It knew that It was better, smarter, stronger. The loud and pestilent bird spirits were a constant annoyance to It, with their stupid gags and inadequate traps. Yet they were also Its ally. Unwitting accomplices, they were Its only true vessel through which to torment the one called Bobby: the wretched soul who deserved, above all others, to suffer forever. The one that It wished it could torture, dismember, peel like a grape. Him, the one who set fire to wood years ago and burned a chicken coop to the ground. The one who had grown so fat, stupid and lazy over the years that everything good had been driven from him. The one who had let the beautiful house fall into decay, and had driven his beautiful wife away from him. The peace of the farm had been spoiled with the noise of constant arguments, as his wife's soft demeanor hardened. He had ruined her kind spirit just as he had ruined everything else that he had touched, and her voice, once a calm serenade drifting on the country air, had turned to incessant screeching at the end. For that and so many other reasons It wanted to hurt him. It imagined red-hot pokers, sharpened screwdrivers, and other instruments of pain ... but it wasn't whole enough to use them, not corporeal enough to attack Bobby directly.

It lived in the house. A house which, like most things that lived across spirit realms, was sapient to some degree. It was surrounded by the lifeless wisps of the flock. It shared many things with both, yet It was entirely alone in the severity of Its anger towards Bobby, and It possessed a power that was incomparable to the rest. Even the Rooster could not challenge It, for the Rooster, like the hens, was Its unwitting slave. It had long since pressed the house's will down beneath the weight of Its own mighty ego.

cluck

Though it yearned to, It couldn't hurt Bobby directly. It lacked physical form, so despite Its power It couldn't touch him without some outside help. So It lured the chickens to do Its work for It. Only they were so ... well, they were chickens. They fell solidly into the first category of undead spirits: they were stupid in life, and were now stupid in death. Left to their own, they produced nothing but eerily floating tomatoes and a lingering fetid smell. They weren't much good at following orders. They only listened to the Rooster, and while the Rooster was smarter than the others, perhaps smart enough to issue complex commands, the Rooster didn't listen to anybody. Of course, if it could be coaxed into ordering the hens into launching some master plan against that fat bastard Bobby, they weren't likely to understand. It—this new power, possessing a greater understanding of things than most—knew that if It wanted anything done, It would have to trick the Rooster. It would use the Rooster to attack Bobby piecemeal, using simple commands, which could be easily followed by the flock.

Luckily, It had ideas. Good ideas. Evil ideas. Thoughts that a chicken could never have. Thoughts about pitfall staircases, and spikes, and spears. It knew about terror. It knew about being swallowed up into floors, eaten alive by floorboards, bones crunched and chewed by wooden teeth and bodies swallowed into rooms below. It knew about monsters under beds, and the terror of the unknown. Oh yes, It knew. It couldn't act on this knowledge directly, unable to shape reality with Its will to such a degree, but It held the knowledge, and It held that knowledge dear. The chickens, ironically, had power that It did not. They could make the spears appear. They could make the stair fall through, forcing the man's leg onto sharpened spikes. It wished they were capable of thinking on a larger scale, perhaps making a pit that Bobby could fall into entirely, but It would take what It could get.

It also understood that this newcomer was a threat, this bizarre booted warrior with his heavy coveralls and his arrogant, dangling badge.

He had to keep this new man away from Bobby. It had to do something to remove Bobby's potential savior so that It could keep Bobby trapped here forever. Bobby was not worthy of salvation. It alone had the drive and the power to ensure Bobby suffered adequately. It alone was duty-bound to torment him until the end of time. It lusted for that.

Then this newcomer came, and walked through the chickens like they were a pack of friendly kittens. The crow of the Rooster hadn't frightened him off, but rather served only to put him closer on guard. This thing, this bitter malevolent sentience that dwelt among the sprawling rooms of the farmhouse had to do something about him, and soon.

It wasn't really an evil spirit, despite Its capacity for evil. Rather, It was a good spirit turned evil through years of ignorance and hatred, guilt and self-doubt. It meant this Armand no harm. It held no personal grudge, but the chickens were afraid of him, and without the chickens Its power could not reach Bobby. Without their feathery corpses to do Its bidding, It was unable to touch Bobby, or to hurt him. Yet, even now, they were gathering among themselves, formulating a plan, attempting to find a way to defeat this new chicken-warrior-man. Instead of focusing their undead fowl fury upon the cursed hillbilly, they were focusing their attention on Armand. Bobby deserved the torment more! This newcomer, however good his intentions might be, had become an unfortunate distraction. The hens had even gone so far as to appeal to their king, the Rooster, further interfering with the persecution of Bobby. The eternal, painful, and—most importantly—*uninterrupted* torment of the man It hated so strongly was paramount. With the Rooster commanding his harem to act against Armand instead of Bobby, the damned hick would be left untroubled. Each minute that Bobby was left in peace was a minute of anger, hurt, and despair left un-dealt; a minute of satisfaction denied to It. It had to give the chickens a new idea, a new way to scare away this newcomer, some method of eliminating the distraction. It had to act soon!

cluck

Suddenly, like a new sprout in early spring, the idea pushed forth from the darkness of the spirit. The thought grew within It, straining upward towards the real world until it was strong enough, and then branched outwards and took shape. The idea coalesced and once it was whole the spirit grabbed onto it: it could control the chickens, and even the Rooster, in order to hurt Bobby; it could do the same to hurt this newcomer, only he seemed unaffected by and unafraid of the flock; therefore, if It couldn't control the chickens to hurt Armand, It would control Bobby, and make him do it. Bobby was large, strong, and best of all stupid. It had never thought to turn Its attentions to Bobby in this way, to make him do Its bidding. The idea was wonderful, refreshing, magnificent ... and so It spread Its will outwards, looking for the man It hated so much.

Being incorporeal, It was unable to make the sinister chuckle manifest into real sound as It turned the full power of Its will towards a meager, helpless, hillbilly brain.

Knapp

cluck

chapter 18 to defy the laws of tradition

Bobby was throwing up again. He didn't remember sinking through the floor a moment ago. He didn't remember wetting himself, or landing on a pile of bricks. He didn't remember much of anything. He didn't recall eating anything, but the vomit was there. It came up, wave after wave, a grossly brilliant orange bile. Every time it subsided he would stand up to find another pile of festering eggs beneath him, and he would start the cycle of regurgitation all over again.

Armand the exorcist was a distant memory, maybe something Bobby had imagined. There was some more vomit, and Bobby forgot about his rescuer completely. Armand wasn't imagined, though. He was still sitting cross-legged on the floor of whatever room Bobby had disappeared from. He was lost in thought about what to do, focused inwards. Zen priests often meditated in such a manner, looking within themselves to find some inner balance, some untapped power of mind and body. Yogis, stretched into demanding poses that forced the body, breath and spirit into one place, meditated in a similar way, looking for internal harmony that would relax them and give them strength. Armand, neither a monk nor a practitioner of yoga, was simply lost in thought, looking for answers. He rolled facts about in his brain, he contemplated his situation, and he planned for various eventualities. He didn't understand what he was up against, and he knew from experience that he was unlikely to ever figure it out. Yet he also understood he would never find Bobby again, he would never save him, unless he did manage to discover what it was that he was truly up against. His posture relaxed into a slouch, synapses firing away, his gaze lost in the distance.

What did he really know? Not much ... He had found this place, done some simple research. He didn't look too closely into things, just enough to learn that the place wasn't ordinary, and that it contained a spiritual power that was chicken-related. He knew enough that he had to come here and save Bobby, but not enough to learn why. He didn't care why things were extraordinary because everything in his life always had been. All he knew was that he was in a house, a strange house. He knew the house was haunted by chicken ghosts, zombies, ghouls and lich. Nothing outside of a typical day's work, really. Then he'd found Bobby, and lost him again. He knew there was a power at work above anything he'd ever experienced before, and for the first time in his life since accepting The Charge, he was truly afraid. He waited, hoping his inner voice might offer some suggestion, but it too was lost in silent contemplation. He leaned back further, resting his back against a small nesting box made of dirty wooden slats, fixed low on the wall behind him.

Nesting box? He thought, *That wasn't there a second ago.*

"*Uh oh,*" his voice murmured, also roused.

The exorcist hopped up from where he was sitting directly into a low crouch, listening. This at least was familiar territory; the appearance of a nesting box out of thin air meant that a spirit hen was nearby. He peered inside, expecting to see rotten eggs nestled within the hay, but there were none. Armand attempted to curse, and steeled himself. Chickens were

cluck

largely unimaginative, which meant that if they weren't angling for the rotten-eggs trick, the floor was about to drop out from beneath him.

He braced himself, and it did: all sense of weight leaving him as the floor disappeared with a faint "pop." A scant moment later a shock rippled through his legs, knees and back as his boots encountered solid ground again, his weight catching up with the sudden acceleration and deceleration of the rest of his body. His head snapped back and he bit his tongue badly as his teeth were jolted together.

"You should've rolled," his inner voice criticized.

"No thit!" Armand cursed, a small trickle of blood drooling from his swollen tongue. His voice giggled silently inside his head.

"You thound tho thilly!" Armand spat, and then cuffed himself hard on the head, hoping that The Charge would be able to feel it. Though the fall startled him, and he was now bleeding freely from his mouth, he couldn't help but smile. This was more like it! Predictable and chicken-like. To a chicken, one of the worst situations imaginable is that you can't reach your nesting box. Luckily for Armand, he didn't care one bit about nesting boxes. He knew the only way he was going to lay an egg was if one of these undead hens tried the making-you-think-you-were-laying-eggs trick, and he knew that if they did play the making-you-think-you-were-laying-eggs trick on him that he wouldn't fall for it. Instead, he looked for a way to reach the door (which had risen out of reach along with the newly manifested nesting box). Luckily, any qualified *Exorciste de Volaille* carried a set of tools that had been carefully refined through the centuries for situations just such as this. Leaning his staff against the wall so that the fox-head was just below shoulder height, he used it to gain the scant yard of extra reach that he needed. With one hand, he grasped the base of the doorway while he hitched the staff up with a

boot, caught it with his other hand, and then chinned himself to the door. He stood in the doorway, [22] and pushed the door open.

He took a moment to collect his thoughts and catch his breath, and then opened the door. Warily, Armand exited the room and found himself in a hallway, and was relieved to see a window that overlooked the inner courtyards of the sprawling estate. He tried to get his bearings, attempting to make out which building was which and where the front of the house might be, but it was all too jumbled and disjointed.

"Check the map," his voice suggested.

"No use, those maps aren't any good. I mean, one of them might be but how am I supposed to know which one? They're all different."

"That's a good point, I suppose. Well, try to think from the pictures, and from what we've seen with our own eyes."

"They're *my* eyes," Armand noted, but his voice trailed off as he searched his memories. The outside of the place was just as confusing as the inside. About the only thing he could clearly recall was—

He stopped looking around on the ground and turned his attention skyward. He knew there was only one way out of here, and that was to go to the top. That is, to the roof. The grand old cupola atop the highest barn. To the Rooster.

"Um, are you sure that's a good idea?" Eavesdropping on Armand's thoughts, The Charge felt it best to interject before they were both killed. In all the history of his trade, the Rooster was the arch nemesis; the ultimate challenger who was to be feared, and to be fought. Now, for no reason that Armand could understand, he knew he needed to meet this Rooster on different terms.

"No ... no I'm not sure," he replied. This is no time to embrace the predictable, he thought, as he realized ashamedly that he had been as

---

[22] This was only possible because chickens, being roosting birds by instinct, are incapable of imagining anything that you can't roost on.

much a product of weak ceremony as all of the rotten eggs and ridiculous tricks. *Screw predictable*, he thought, and he opened the window, and began to climb.

The problem with a person breaking tradition is that traditions are built from more than just one person. When one person turns from the defined path, they can lose sight of this fact, and expect that whatever epiphany had freed them must also have enlightened everyone and everything else involved. Sadly and more commonly to the immediate detriment of the enlightened individual, the rest of tradition is more likely to rebel and hold even tighter to the frameworks upon which they are built. Traditions do not like to be broken. They resist it. They fight back.

High upon the highest rooftop of the expansive estate, two proud, clawed feet[23] gripped the loose shingles of a watchful cupola. The talons were strong, each cloaked with a brilliant hood of feathers, from which strong scaly legs stood tense. The legs widened into magnificent downy thighs and then widened yet again into a feathered chest: arrogant in its cockery, mighty and powerful. At its side stretched a span of strong wings, crafted from a myriad of colors and patterns, as thousands of individual feathers—each artfully painted—converged into a tapestry as complex and beautiful as only chaos could arrange. The tapestry was so elaborate and rich with hues that upon a cursory glance it seemed to have no color at all, simply a glistening black like the void space of nightmares. The neck was thick and powerful, ready to challenge a butcher's axe or even the bite of a fox.

---

[23] One foot lacked actual claws, being burnt and mostly missing, but it was still proud.

The Rooster had just one thing on its mind. Combat. It had to defend the flock, and the person it had to defend it from was the fire wielding farmer who committed genocide against his harem. He'd been crafting ways to cause this villain pain for thousands of sunrises now, and today would be no different (or so thought the Rooster). In actuality, the day turned out to be a little bit different. It started with a car, and then "The Driver," who turned out to be something called "The Exorcist."

The Rooster knew about the exorcist, or at least it had a dim conceptual understanding of him. It held a mysterious memory that made this strange spiritual warrior familiar, much in the same way the exorcist held inexplicable memories of the Rooster. Due to events that a chicken could never hope to comprehend, some pearls of knowledge had been passed down from cock to cock. The historical teachings of chickendom had transcended death, and it now also knew things prior to its own life—much like Armand understood all of those things that The Charge had experienced before his time. Thus the Rooster held the collective wisdom and intelligence of many undead roosters before it.[24] Again, it wasn't entirely sure how, but it knew. The knowledge and awareness had come to it in the flash of brilliant ribbon light that cut through its soul so many years before. The memory was vague, but chickens aren't particular about details and not overly concerned with knowledge at all. What they did know, however, they trusted and to summarize this particular thread of weak chicken logic, this Rooster knew that the exorcist was its enemy.

The exorcist entered his house, and made demands from his hens. He kicked them, he defied them. The Rooster knew something had to be done. With a flourish and an angry shake of his less matted feathers, he turned the hens away from the devilish farmer for just a moment, and

---

[24] That is, very little.

pitted them against this new foe. Everything had been going according to plan, too, until this. This man—dressed in full garb of his trade and even wearing that accursed metal mark on his boot—began to act strangely. He is supposed to avoid me, thought the Rooster. He is supposed to find a way to banish me *without* conflict—for I alone can hurt him! *He knows this!*

The Rooster hopped from talon to nub, stomping back and forth, swaying like a drunken ship captain in a storm.

So why is he climbing the roof?

It fluffed its broad breast skyward and roared at the silent sky. Stomping, and screaming, suffering the indignity of this man's assault on the familiar patterns of history.

He must be crazy! He should be fleeing!

It simply wasn't normal for a weak human to show courage, to charge headfirst into battle. Though the Rooster could sense this new man had power, it was still foolish of him to approach. A battle on the rooftop—on the Rooster's terms and within its own territory—was witless. Tradition dictated that the human should be behaving differently.

Tradition.

Content with his part in this long established ritual, the Rooster steeled itself, waiting, ready to attack. Death had been good to the Rooster. It was much larger than it had been even in life. It had the added strength of undead muscles. It had a horribly twisted reality about it that made talons sharper, beak harder, and wing more bruising. Its kicks could kill lesser mortal animals—even dogs or fox—with a single terrifying blow. It also could not die—a decided advantage to already being dead—and it could feel no pain. Yet the man climbed clumsily up the side of one of the equipment barns. He was using the thick coiled wire of the many lightening protectors to pull himself up and among the many roofs, buttresses and gables. This was a challenge, a slap across the face with a white glove, the throwing down of the proverbial gauntlet.

Knapp

The Rooster didn't like it. The Rooster liked tradition. If something had changed that meant it had to be allied with this crazy mortal, then it had most definitely not received the memo.

Watching both the Rooster and the man from the ethereal spaces that transcended the old farmhouse, the other spirit force, evil and brooding, saw Its window of opportunity closing. The man and the Rooster would fight, one would win. The Rooster was likely to win, but It couldn't take the risk that this strange man, with his strange powers, might prevail. It would need to intervene. Now. It reached out, intent on putting Its plan into action. It searched for the soul of Its nemesis, and found him cowering as usually in the face of some new feeble attack by the flock. With a flick of Its will, It poured through the halls, spilling under doorways and steaming through the cracks in walls and wood. Debris was stirred with the force of Its passing, dust was lifted. There was an audible hiss—almost a sputter, like cold water dripping onto a hot stove—as It flew to Bobby.

cluck

chapter 19 battling bobby

Bobby woke up from a deep sleep screaming and trying desperately to escape the inferno. The panic kept him from immediately realizing that he wasn't in his bed, but on the floor of one of the old milk rooms. Rooms like these, scattered throughout the areas of the sprawling structure—usually in those areas where "house" met "barn"—had rarely if ever been used for the storage of milk, but had often been used for the storage of junk. Every unwanted thing imaginable had been collected here over the course of many years: bottles, both whole and broken; those little plastic trays that plants come in; odd pieces of string; scraps of wood that were put aside for some future project that never happened. There was nothing resembling a bed, at least not for a human. Only rats and mice—and, more recently, lifeless shambling chickens—made their homes here. It was therefore a futile effort for Bobby to beat at the flames with his bed sheets, as neither the flames nor the sheets actually existed. The panic couldn't be blamed entirely, for if Bobby had been a little bit more acute, or perhaps more brave, he might not fall for the same hallucinatory tricks over and over again. As it was, his unique cocktail of ignorance, lack of will, and cowardice combined nicely with the shock of the hallucination, keeping him from realizing that he wasn't on fire at all, and was in fact a bit damp. It was just a dream—carefully inserted into his frail psyche by one of the more devious hens—but a dream all the same. Being a bit mystical in nature, and Bobby being past the point of relative sanity, the dream stuck for a few full minutes before he finally realized he wasn't burning alive. He gasped a few times and shook his head, and then finally calmed down.

There was nothing new about this dream. There was nothing new about being tormented by the lost souls of that cursed flock, but there was something that was new. There was a new force brewing in the old farmhouse. New emotions: hope, courage, pride—foreign things that stood out against the pale of the grey and dim feelings that had made a home within the farm, and within Bobby. There was hatred and anger as well, but within the framework of the new power, such emotions held more purpose than normal, and it was disconcerting. It had an effect on just about everything including poor Bobby. He felt It drawing near. There was another, older force as well, and though it filled the air like smoke as it rallied in defiance against It, boiling up a last wave of defense, it was but a thin veil before Its ageless desires for revenge. The result was tangible; the air was charged with the conflict of the old and new powers. Hairs, normally plastered flat against Bobby's neck with years of muck of sweat and blood, stood up. Bobby checked one last time to make sure he wasn't still smoldering somewhere, and then climbed shakily to his feet.

"Hello ...?" he called out meekly, hoping nothing would answer. He spun around, expecting a hen, or a spear, or more fire—but there was nothing. He spun around again, twice as quickly, with no more success. Uncertain of what else to do, he cocked his head to listen. There was

cluck

something different about the new flavors of hatred and anger in this place. Though Bobby didn't know it, even the Rooster was emoting new tastes of spiritual energy. Of course, the challenging aura and power of the exorcist was new here, though Bobby couldn't grasp that there was anything special about Armand, even if he were able to remember his would-be savior at all. While the forces surrounding the Rooster were changing slightly with the ebb of the spiritual winds, its attitude was fairly static. It was simply waiting, redirecting some of its significant spectral force towards the exorcist as the ragged and rough ghost fighter clambered his way slowly up the many tiers of the master house. The exorcist's will was equally fixed, focused solely on reaching the Rooster (though not yet aware the Rooster wasn't mindful of his plan for a truce). The other forces were not so docile. There were strange things afoot in the ancient and tired old manor. You could say (with that eerie tone that people use when reciting ghost stories) that a storm was brewing. A terrible, cataclysmic storm. Melodramatic, but appropriate. Especially when the air started filling with a distant hiss and sputter, and the dust began to stir around Bobby.

It was moving. Fast. Crashing through the invisible forces and spirit tides of the other powers of the farm, It sloughed and spilled forth, filling the small room, slowing now and spreading like an oily tide, glistening with hate. It was the same evil spirit that It had always been, but now It was an evil spirit with work to do, and It did Its job through the mind of dear old Bobby Garfundephelt. There was a momentary deafening noise, and then just as suddenly there was silence. The dust settled again. Bobby, agitated as if struck by a sudden chill, paused mid-scream to ruffle his hair with his hands. His hands reached up, working their way over his face like the hands of a blind man, trying to read the features of a stranger. His left hand slapped him in the head, and again, and then the right hand did the same. He hopped in place, and turned around. He looked at his arms as if they were foreign, and then rubbed his two, thick grubby hands together as a single, malicious and inexorable thought landed within its mind. It was a seed, planted within the feeble nut-like mind of Bobby Garfundephelt. He remained Bobby, but something more than Bobby as well. He flexed his mind around his new thought.

Kill.

Bobby wasn't aware It had found him, and had settled over him like morning dew settling onto a crisp spider-web. That It had enveloped him, and that Its will seeped inside him. He was only aware of his new desire.

Kill.

Bobby grinned, his crooked teeth barely showing white through the cake of grime that covered them. In his mind, Bobby saw the image of a man, dressed boldly in boots and carrying a staff. The figure seemed strangely familiar, and a fleeting memory told Bobby that the man was a good man, until the recollection finished fleeting, and he was left with nothing but the hollow, empty hate that It had imposed upon him. Whoever this man was, Bobby was going to kill him.

The good forces, those that tried to stop the wave of hate as it crashed into Bobby's mind, receded. Perhaps with the help of other benevolent powers it would have succeeded, but those would-be allies weren't participating. Armand, oblivious, was climbing dutifully to the rooftops. There was also a goodness, which could almost be called power, in the car. It, unfortunately, was too far away to be of any real help. It was also insufficiently brave. The evil had been able to force Itself upon Bobby relatively unhindered: in this skirmish between these particular archons of right and wrong, wrong had been the victor.

Bobby, not knowing that his new idea *Kill!* was not entirely his own, stood up and began to walk through the long corridors of the ancient estate. The force which motivated him didn't like Bobby. It didn't like being inside the corporeal body of a wretched, no-good hillbilly. It pre-

cluck

ferred to float free of him, watching from afar as he suffered. Now It had to take a more active role, in the only way It could, by entering Bobby's mind and making that despicable place Its home.

Kill.

With a blank stare, Bobby walked on. There was a hen out in the hall waiting to scare him with a small beaked head on a string, but Bobby simply walked past it without taking notice. One deliberate step after another moved Bobby upwards through the vast estate. He didn't whimper, or cry, or shrink away from the rotten assault of impotent zombies and ineffectual tripwires and spears. He simply advanced, in a slow methodical manner that would have made a proper human zombie proud.

Outside, the old run-down car, having grown both nervous and a bit bored, became suddenly alert as it felt the wave crashing through the house—but then it was gone and the car settled easily back into boredom. It began to cycle through its meager selection of pre-set radio stations, finally settling on the static-filled sounds of Michael Jackson's "Thriller" from the All-80s Radio Network. The rest of the hens, also detecting that something was up, had dispersed. The ever-present noise and dust and fetid smell subsided towards normalcy, and the tune was just barely audible from the high halls of the farmhouse. Bobby cocked his head again, though with more certainty now that he was filled with Its spirit. He heard the song, faintly, from somewhere far away. It was an appropriate enough tune, but Bobby didn't stop to listen, he didn't hum, he didn't dance. He simply walked on.

Kill.

He walked out of the milk room and into a kitchen. There were several kitchens in the house, so it took him a moment to realize which kitchen he was in. For some reason, his mind was allowing him to remember; he knew exactly where he was, and he followed the most immediate path he could towards his goal. He left the kitchen through a stout wooden service door with large creaking hinges, and strode calmly up a back staircase, stepping lithely over the third step, which was false.[25] The stairs rose steeply between thin walls, each step scraping its mark into a thick layer of dust. Another small thick door lead to the East servant's quarters, and then another, until the stairs reached the top and turned to present a small archway, wedged at an odd angle between two thick beams. Bobby entered another smaller kitchenette (presumably added ad-hoc by the servants themselves, so they wouldn't have to climb three flights of stairs every ten minutes), crossing quickly and nimbly, avoiding the debris of long forgotten feasts, ducking into another small landing, and then up yet another service stair.[26] He emerged into a rather impressive sitting room, which connected to a landing on one of the largest formal staircases in the house.[27] This stair led downward, growing as it went until the staircase swelled to almost eight feet in width, and sprouted a plain but impressive wooden banister, decorated at the bottom with some sort of long neglected statuary. Bobby paused, looking downward at what could have been the bust of some well regarded but very ugly ancestor, or it could be that the carpenters had found their way into the brandy that day; regardless of its intrigue, Bobby ignored it, turning instead to face the wall behind him.

It was a wall, and like all walls it was generally flat and featureless. There were no paintings, nor tapestries. There was no loose piece of wainscoting that could be wiggled just so, and a distinct lack of large ornate candelabras that could be swiveled in just the right way. There

---

[25] And the tenth, which was a regular solid stair but which had something nasty stuck all over it.

[26] With another false step, full of spikes, but he avoided it without seeming to notice.

[27] With some of the largest false steps in the house, which were full of spikes and rotten eggs and tomatoes.

cluck

was nothing at all to indicate to Bobby that if he were to push right ... *there,* that the wall would fall back ominously, and with a short belch of stale air and dust, swing inward. Bobby pushed the spot anyway, and it fell back, and belched, and swung. Squinting, Bobby could see the darkest, narrowest, steepest flight of stairs ever encountered. Mountaineering gnomes with a fear of open spaces couldn't have designed a stair less inviting. Upwards he went. Legs that moments earlier could barely keep from shaking in fear now ascended with confidence. The stairs rose steeply, and turned at regular intervals. It was as if a stairwell and a tunnel had, in a moment of illicit passion, spawned this horrid, enclosed offspring. It grew smaller with each turn of the well. Bobby climbed, and then climbed more. It was four full flights before the steps alighted him into a tiny hall, which presented a single nondescript door.

Through the door was an attic. In the attic was a window. Bobby walked into the room. Like the other chambers in this surreal abode, it was covered in dust, dirt and a scattering of downy cobwebs and feces. The window was a tiny dormer, with wavy panes of glass that were barely held in place by strips of wood and cracked putty and peeling paint. Bobby walked past stacks of old cardboard boxes, broken and neglected window fans, and a dusty plaid suitcase, moving straight along the single sunbeam that pierced the gloom. He made straight to the window, took hold of what was left of the wooden frame, and pulled it upwards. The window crumbled under the effort of opening, and panels of glass fell both inwards and out. Fresh air rushed into the room, carrying with it what sounded like a voice saying, "Ow!"

Bobby's boot ground the broken glass as he leaned forward, sticking his thick head, topped with his unwashed mat of hair, through the opening. Looking down, he saw a tired and slightly nervous exorcist was clinging to a shutter for his dear life, sprinkled with bits of broken glass and wood. The exorcist was looking back up at him, no doubt wondering what had caused the small avalanche of debris. "Hello?" he called upwards. "Bobby, is that you?" but Bobby had ducked his head back inside, and was too busy scanning the contents of the attic to reply. A broken television, a pile of mouse-eaten books—and an old coat rack, with four carved feet and a crown of chipped chrome hooks. He ran to it, snatched it up, and rushed back to the window. The dusty coat rack was nearly six feet long, and wide enough that it tore away the remains of broken glass as he thrust it through. His eyes glimmered red as he wriggled his shoulders through the window, leaning outwards. Below him Armand stared upwards with a confused expression that turned frantic as Bobby reached down with the heavy coat rack and nonchalantly struck at the exorcist.

"Holy [feces]!" the exorcist yelped, nearly falling from surprise as the crook of a hat-hook was prodded rather painfully into his shoulder from above. Looking up, he could see Bobby inside, taking aim for a second assault, and so he clambered sideways as far as he could to avoid Bobby's reach. He slipped downwards a few inches, bringing him further from Bobby's reach but also placing him in a precarious position: his left foot was stretched upwards and out, barely reaching the sill that had previously taken his full weight, and his right foot reached down as far as it could go, toes pointing downwards to an even smaller dormer. His arms splayed outward and his chest pressed flat against the loose clapboards, hoping desperately that he would be able to lean in towards the house, and not outward towards thin air and then ultimately the ground. "What the [devil] are you doing, Bobby! Hey! Stop it!" Bobby wriggled further out of the tiny window, stretching downward.

The coat rack was clattering around in the area where Armand had just recently been, but as Bobby squeezed himself further through the opening, it drew closer and closer to its elusive target. Armand, his face pressed flat against the house, could see little more than the tip of the coat-rack as it swung about.

cluck

"Dohd you thig we thould dalk aboud thid?" Armand pleaded, his face pressed firmly against an uncomfortably protruding nail and rasping his dry lips across the cracking paint, filling his mouth with dust. The bludgeon retreated from view, and there was a pause, a moment of silence, and Armand risked moving his head enough to glance upward. From above, Bobby's head poked out of the window again, followed by both arms.

"No talking," Bobby muttered matter-of-factly as he heaved himself through the window. With his chest and both arms on the outside of the small opening, there was no way to reach back in and retrieve the weapon. He hesitated another moment, and then scraped himself back inside again. Armand risked a grab for the shutter of the window below Bobby, upon which he had been perched earlier, and managed to pull himself into a slightly more stable position. There was a cramp forming inside his left thigh, threatening to spasm, and he considered kicking in the window, escaping inside to solid footing.

"You'll never make it," the Charge whispered inside his head. *"Look in his eyes, there's something driving him. Look at the intelligence in there."*

"I don't think Bobby is as stupid as he pretends," Armand answered.

"Stupid? Maybe not, but that's not what I mean. There's knowledge and purpose in there beyond what a man should be capable of. He'll be on us in no time if we play on his terms. The only reason we're safe now is because he's too big to fit through that little window."

"What do you think it is, then? Why the change? He was a gibbering mess when I found him."

"I don't know, but ..."

"But what?" The cramp eased away as he shifted more weight onto the window, and was replaced by a dull ache. Armand didn't like the tone of the voice in is head.

"Well, what do you think people see when they look into your eyes?" his voice asked him.

Knapp

"I don't think people generally look into my eyes at all, so I don't suppose they see much," he answered testily. He peered upwards, but still couldn't see any sign of Bobby. "—and I'm trying to listen, if you don't mind!"

"They see an intelligence that shouldn't be there." His voice answered for him.

"I wonder what he's up to ..." Armand wondered out loud, and then, inside himself he said, "What? Are you suggesting he has something inside of him like you? ... Not the Rooster."

"I don't think so. It doesn't feel roosterish. Just be careful—" and before he could even finish talking to himself the flayed tip of the old coat rack burst through the window beside him. Armand lost his grip with his left hand and swung dangerously outwards. After a moment of flailing he found himself stretched out again, back towards the flat nothingness of open wall, his right toe stretched to its limit to gain a tiny toehold on another sill. The cramp snapped back, and started to argue with the dull ache over who had squatters rights to his groin.

He was a little bit afraid of heights, but he knew about making decisions. He knew his only choices right now were to take charge and fight back, or to eventually get battered downwards. He couldn't cling to the wall like Spiderman forever, and he couldn't climb—either up or down—without using the windows for purchase. It was only a matter of time before Mr. "I'm inside on solid ground with a coat rack" managed to pry him loose. He imagined bouncing and rolling off of the gables and gambrels, mansards and modillions and the various other elements of the mansion's many roof-lines, being tossed about by architecture like a mouse being tossed by a petulant cat before his pulverized body eventually hit the ground with a dull squelch. The decision was an easy one. It was made easier when Bobby climbed easily through the window, weapon in hand.

cluck

"Oh great, he fits through this one ..." but Armand wasn't listening to himself. His groin hurt, and he was tired, and he didn't know why Bobby was attacking him and he didn't care. He let go of the shutter with one hand, willfully abandoning the only firm hold that had left. Grabbing his staff from where he had secured it in his belt, he swung it around as soundly as he could and struck Bobby's hand. The fox head that topped a Cluck-Buster's staff might look plush, but the softness was an illusion hiding bony snouts and pointy little fox teeth.

"Atta boy," his voice cheered to him inside his mind, as Bobby pulled his hand back fast. *"Let him have it!"* Teetering precariously, scraping his fingertips deep into meager handholds, Armand pressed his advantage. He swung back to the window, towards the estranged farmer, and as soon as his toes found a solid hold he used the momentum to swing the staff around again.

There was a yelp, and the coat rack took the path that could very well have been Armand's. As he had imagined, it struck the eaves of a small overhang, rolled down the steep roof-line of a gable, clattered momentarily against a rather pointy lightening rod and was sent spinning outward to fall the remaining several stories uninterrupted before exploding on the gravel of an interior drive, far below. *That could have been me.* There was a pause, a moment of reflection on the side of both combatants. Bobby was only inches from Armand, with one leg entirely inside the house, and one hand holding a firm grip on the inside framework. Armand, on the other hand, was entirely outside the window, with only one foot on the sill. One hand was jammed painfully up under the weather-beaten shutters, and the rest of his limbs were hanging free. Bobby grinned.

"You've got to go," Bobby said, and The Charge shuddered inside of Armand, sending a chill through his spine that almost made him fall. It looked like Bobby, but it didn't sound like him, and there was definitely something else, something that neither Armand nor The Charge could put his finger on. His voice was deeper and more resonant, his back less hunched, and his eyes ... Armand couldn't help but notice that everything about the man who he had been trying to rescue seemed, well ... less *ignorant*.

"I have to go? Great. I'd love to. If you don't mind, I'd like to take the stairs."

"I can't let you." Bobby asserted.

"You can't let me take the stairs? I can't see the harm in it—"

"I can't let you get to The Roof." Bobby clarified. Armand wondered briefly what warranted the capitalization of The Roof.

"Ah—you know I'm going there then, to the roof?"

"You're climbing there."

"Well ..." Armand began. It was hard to avoid the fact that he was indeed clinging to a shutter, that he had climbed several stories up the outside of the house already, and that he would reach the roof. He thought desperately of excuses, that he was washing windows, or trying to catch his escaped parakeet, anything at all that might justify his presence on the wall. A presence, he couldn't help but notice, that was in serious risk of being an absence: the shutter was beginning to pull away from the house, and one solid push from Bobby would send him plummeting to his death. He tried a different tactic.

"Why would I want to climb to the roof?" he asked. Simple denial, confounded by anti-logic. It was a method his parents had both used on him when he was a young boy, before he left home and apprenticed himself into the bizarre line of work that was apparently about to be the death of him.

"You're trying to reach the Rooster. You can't do that. At first I thought he might destroy you, which would have been okay. I thought it was a clever enough idea to let him do it. Yeah, it was a good idea. Now things are different. I don't know why. I don't think he's going to kill you at all. I think that *you* might kill *him*. I can't have that."

cluck

"Well, he is already dead, you know."

"You'll destroy him."

"Not *destroy*. What I do is more like ... *putting to rest*."

"It's killing! You know it is! I can hear the doubt in your own voice, as you try to deny it. You know it's wrong." Armand was taken aback. A few hours ago, Bobby was an ignorant, red-necked hick. A wounded one, even. Now he'd suddenly turned vicious and cunning and insightful. He'd just managed to hit the only nerve that Armand had that was worth hitting. The question boiled in his mind: is what he was doing here wrong? What he's been doing for most of his life? He'd always wondered, deep down inside, but the thoughts rarely surfaced.

"It's necessary." The Charge proclaimed, within his head.

"It's necessary," Armand repeated aloud, although his heart wasn't behind the words. It was the main reason he tried so hard to repress his doubts: it's very difficult to possess an inner ideologic conflict when there is a very biased voice in your head.

"It's necessary if you want to stop this idiot from killing you." Sometimes, The Charge could be very hard to argue with.

"I really have to point out that I'm doing this for you," Armand said, turning his attention back to Bobby. "I think that's important to mention, seeing as how you haven't seemed to figure it out. In fact, you're coming darn close to getting me killed." Bobby was pushing towards Armand, unnervingly close, forcing Armand to inch along an inadequately wide piece of molding.

"I don't think he's listening," the inner voice observed.

"I'm trying to save you! Why in the world would you want to stop me from doing that?" The toe of his boot barely had any grip left on the narrow window-ledge, forcing him to rely once more on the weathered wooden shutters, which creaked ominously under his weight.

There was a strange look in Bobby's eye. "Save me?" he said, quietly. "Oh no, you can't save me. I can't be saved." He reached out his hands towards Armand, menace in his eyes.

"Jump!" the Charge screamed inside him. Bobby's hands, fingers stretched out like claws, were inches away. "Are you kidding? If I jump, I'll—"

As Armand screamed his protest aloud, Bobby hesitated, just for a moment.

"Jump or be thrown! Aim for that—"

Before The Charge could finish, before Bobby could recover from his surprise at the outburst, the exorcist jumped.

As he fell, Armand thought of his mother. There was no reason for it. Hell, there were plenty of other things he could have thought about. For example, trying to catch a hold of something, to save his life. He could think about some of those internal things that possessed him—his powers, and the spirit of The Charge—that were nested safe within him. He could have watched his whole life flash before his eyes, in fact. Watching your life flash before your eyes was a popular choice among people who were about to die, these days, but for some reason it was his mother who filled his mind as the air rushed passed him and the ground screamed upwards towards him.

Sentimentality produced a distant thought, somewhere on the edges of Armand's consciousness, but it was protested. *I never knew your mother, but I'm sure she'd want you to try to catch that frieze—*

Though he hadn't thought of her in years, the image of Armand's mother was etched deeply into his mind as a figure of purity and love. He always remembered her wearing a pale blue sweatshirt with an embossed picture of a cartoon dog on it. The dog was blue, too, which was

cluck

odd, and it had long draping jowls. The sweatshirt was exceptionally soft, and it made an impression because it is the same sweatshirt she always wore when Armand was a very small boy. She would wear it around the house while doing the daily housework: cleaning up; vacuuming; and other chores, right up to when she would make a lunch to share with her son. After lunch, she would disappear for a while and tidy herself up, getting ready for when Armand's father came home. She would come back downstairs wearing something slightly nicer by most standards, although Armand preferred the sweatshirt. It marked the beginning and end of comfortable mornings. When he had grown older she had gone back to work, and the sweatshirt was rarely, if ever, seen.

... or maybe that gutter, that might hold us—

His mother was uncommonly pretty. He knew that, even when he was young. He hadn't seen her in dozens of years, but he guessed she was probably well into her seventies by now. Maybe even her eighties. She could be dead, but he felt that she wasn't and he had learned to trust his instincts when it came to death. Two people, mother and son. Few have loved each other so deeply as they, and then it all changed. His visions began. And the trouble. She always approached the "incidents" with the same calmness and affection with which she embraced the rest of her life, but the guilt had settled into Armand's young mind regardless. Why was he different? Why were these things always happening to him? Why did his mother feel the need to bring in outsiders like Mr. Thurmond? As he fell, the fond memories had already begun the familiar transition to betrayal.

She sent you to a convent!

True, she had. How is a boy supposed to deal with that?

I suggest that we figure that out after you catch hold of whatever that thing is, jutting out—

Images did flash before his eyes now, but it wasn't his life, not all of it. It was the blue shadow of a beloved dog, the eery glow surrounding his schoolmates, the terrible storm of blue light seen from the monestary. The avenue of fond remembrance had turned to bitter regret, a transition that was familiar to him. It wasn't that he blamed her for what she had unwittingly done to him, it was that he had loved her so much, and that it was over. The air rushed past as thoughts, old and new, churned violently together, and then, suddenly, something extraordinarily strange happened. Somehow, somewhere deep inside Armand—even deeper than the bizarre consciousness of his voice that was The Charge—Armand found a way to forgive. To forgive his mother and himself. His mother, despite her faults, had known the difference between right and wrong. What he was doing now *you're giving up* was wrong. Maybe, just maybe, if she had been around, he'd have figured that out sooner *that would have been nice* and none of this would have ever happened. Maybe, if she'd been here, he wouldn't be falling to his death right now. Maybe, if he'd looked back just once over the years, she would have been there, waiting. She'd abandoned him, sure, but he'd abandoned her, too. He'd abandoned the normal life that he'd always coveted. As the circle of blame completed, he knew he could make it right again, if he lived long enough.

It gave him power.

He unclenched his fists and forced open his eyes as he fell. He saw a dirty, unkempt hick peering down from his place half outside of the open window. Beyond him, and higher up, was the silhouette of a magnificent black bird. Images and memories clicked into place, giving him even more power.

"I love you mother," he said out loud. "I'm going to see you again. I promise ..."

cluck

To say that the eaves hurt when he crashed against them would have been an understatement along the same lines as "the ice caps are a bit nippy this time of year" or "standing buck naked and hip deep in snow at the ice caps while drinking ice water in front of an enormous air conditioner is a bit nippy." He tried to pull his wits about him as he rolled down the steep roof-line. There was a pointy lightening rod coming up, he knew, but he had also fallen quite a bit to one side of where the coat-rack had fallen. Spinning wildly as he rolled down the roof, he tried to catch sight of it ... There! Using his staff for extra leverage, he hooked one arm over the lightening rod. Just a few feet to the left, he realized, and that eight-inch steel spike would have been intimately acquainted with his bowels. As luck would have it, he managed to stop himself at the much more reasonable price of some bruises and—he felt inside himself for other pains—probably a dislocated shoulder. And his side ached. Hurting, he grabbed the staff tightly with both hands and hung from the edge of the second-highest roof of the house.

"Are you going to let me swear?" he asked his inner voice.

"I think it's probably appropriate, yes," answered his voice.

"Twice in one day, huh? Halle-*fucking*-luiah!"

The car had been around the block a few times, so to speak. Over the years, it had driven nearly three hundred thousand miles. Armand knew that at some point along the way the car had picked up some of the magic that Armand himself was always surrounded by. Maybe it was the habit of parking the poor thing in or near haunted places. Maybe it was Armand's own supernatural essence, imbued upon him by The Order of Volaille long ago and since rubbed into the car through the worn driver's seat. His posterior had certainly spent many hours there, giving osmosis as fair a chance as any. If he wasn't up to his eyeballs in feathers and filth, he was driving that tired automobile. If he wasn't driving it, there was still a good chance he was sitting in it, watching someplace, taking pictures. Or sleeping in it. His apartment was a crappy little place, unwelcoming and unclean; his travels kept him away from it, with little regret.

Wherever it came from, the vehicle had something special. It could think and act on its own to a certain degree. At first, Armand hadn't believed, but eventually the little discrepancies and coincidences added up. He would park the car on one side of the street, only to later find it parked in the opposite direction. He would leave the windows open when working on a hot day, to avoid returning from some horror scene to sit in an oven, and find the windows closed regardless. He couldn't have known that while he was inside a large commercial hatchery attempting to banish the spirit of a rogue turkey[28] that there had been a short spell of rain, and that the proud old clunker had simply meant to keep dry.

It was several such occasions before Armand fully understood that his car had motives of self-preservation, and to an only slightly lesser degree of loyalty to Armand and his duties. Even after fully believing and accepting that an inanimate object had powers of its own, Armand hadn't guessed the full extent of the situation. Could a man-made machine possess feelings? Intellect? A sense of humor? A sick sense of humor that sometimes crossed the lines of irony and was often entirely

---

[28] Armand did not typically work with turkeys. However, the haunting in question involved a turkey that was haunting a chicken-egg farm; the stupid gobbler *thought it was a chicken* and wouldn't leave its nesting box. Its presence had upset the ladies and egg production had halted. The owner contacted the Institution for the Incarnation of Unnatural Turkeys, Emus and Ostriches (IIUTEO), but the resident cluck-buster had been pitching for a holiday, and had insisted that the problem lay squarely in the EV's jurisdiction.

cluck

inappropriate? The answer to these questions, of course, is yes. The car was black, made of metal, and possessed one bench seat and two buckets, both made of cloth. There were mirrors and floor mats and chrome. There were wipers and even a small but proud nub of metal where a hood ornament once stood. Yet it was so much more than that. It even had a name.

Of course, it couldn't tell anyone its name, being unable to speak. If it had known Morse code it might have felt inclined to communicate through short and long honks of its tiny flatulent horn.[29] It did not, however. It learned all that it knew of human ways from watching Armand. Due to long nights staking out potential hauntings, and Armand's tendency towards cheesy dime-store fiction, it had learned to read and its view of the world was also influenced by the poorly constructed fiction of discarded paperbacks, along with the more certain but less believable mysteries of Armand's everyday adventures. It preferred the soft-bound stories to the real ones, and had just recently named itself "Fleming" after the author of the same adventurous MI-5 agent James Bond whose novels littered the back of the car, as well as most of the space beneath the passenger seat.

Fleming didn't feel well. It—*he* was distressed for several reasons, not the least of which was the laundry-list of self-inflicted maladies he had used in a final effort to keep Armand from this place. Armand didn't know better, the sturdy black car thought. He was human. Sure he had powers, but it took one spectral anomaly to fully appreciate another, and Fleming knew this house was special in so many ways ... probably all bad. He could feel it. It wasn't just the chickens. It wasn't even the house itself, which had a good deal of its own power, but something ... *else*.

---

[29] It would have sounded something like this: ..-. .-.. . -- .. -. -. --.- .. / .- .-.. / -.-- --- .- / .- .-.. .-.. .. --. ..... - / .. .- . / - .... . .-. . .-.- . / ....-.. .-.. .-.. --- --.- . / --- .-. . / -.. .- -- . / .. .... / .. . .-.. / .-.- .-.. . -- --.- .. -. -. --.- / . .-.. . / -.-- --- .- / .- .-.. .-.. . / .-. .. ... --. .... - / .. .. .-. / - .... . .-. . . .-.-.. / / ....-.. .-. ...- --- /

247

A stronger force than even the ancient sentience of the rambling mansion could muster. This force was definitely evil. Spirits can talk to each other—well, not talk so much as they can communicate on a different level, a form of communication more focused towards the intangible aspects of a disembodied soul than upon the physical receptors of a mammalian ear. If it were possible to translate this empathy into English, the house would have said, "Beware. Turn Back. There are powers here that should be feared." Typically when spirits speak of powers that need to be feared, they mean one of two things: humans, which of all other creatures have developed the skills to exorcise them; and a place of damnation that any sensible spirit wants to avoid at all costs: Hell. Despite Fleming's reluctance to return to this place, where he had already been boldly warned away from once, he had obeyed Armand and in the end sat parked outside, again, on that terrifying country road. Armand had been inside for a while, and his trusty steed was getting nervous. The house, which had been a noisy beacon of warning during the first visit, was now silent. The extent to which this was just not right was so obvious that a blind man could see it. A blind *alive* man, even.

Eventually, the waiting became painful and Fleming's thoughts drifted towards the house.

"Are you there?" he ventured, expecting something horrible to happen in response. There was an immediate flood of noise from the chickens, alarmed at the sudden presence of another spirit-force the way that a live flock of birds might be surprised by the sudden appearance of a hungry dog. It was a jarring reply, certainly, but not unexpected.

The car's will bent closer to the house, listening for something. The house felt asleep … or maybe restrained. The radio turned on and off and flickered through the stations again as a chill ran down the poor car's drive train. Just as he could hear and speak he could also see, in a sense, and right now a small point of motion caught his attention. Up high on the side of one of the larger additions, his master appeared. Armand had

cluck

just crested the roof of a lessor structure from somewhere at the back edge of the inner courtyard, so all that was visible at the moment was the silhouette of his head above the roof-line. He was climbing along the roof, as far as Fleming could tell from way down by the road. Hmm ... that was certainly new.

Fleming watched with interest as the head suddenly bobbed and weaved. The car could hear distant shouts as his master tussled with something just out of sight. From what Fleming could tell, there was something attacking Armand from the direction of a nearby gable. Then, as Fleming watched helplessly, his master fell.

That wasn't good. Normally, Fleming the Faithful could feel his master in much the same way he could feel the presence of other spirits. It was due to Armand's own powers and his attenuation with the "other side." In the noise of the place, however, any faint signal from the tiny human was drowned out by chickens, the house, and of course that mysterious *other thing*. All Fleming knew was that the frail human had fallen from a high place, and had disappeared from view. This was bad. This was worse than usual. Armand was not James Bond, who the car knew was capable of surviving such a predicament. Armand was likely to be dead. This was the worst of things that could ever happen to the tired old automobile.

With timing that would have made a Hollywood monster-movie director tingle with delight, the house chose that exact moment to speak.

"Abandon hope," it began. Its voice, if that's what you wanted to call it, was weak. It finished the phrase as cliché dictated, *"... all ye who enter here."*

Fleming freaked—the sound of his horn droning in the closest approximation of a scream he could muster. Abandon hope, all ye who enter here. He knew those words. All spirits did, even the most pure (which the little car was not). Those were the words that could be found at the gates of Hell, scratched into the arches on a signpost made of bone.

Hell. There were only those two powers that spirits fear, humans and Hell, and while sometimes humans turned out to not be so bad, Hell was rather more predictable. The trusty little auto had grown used to humans, but the thought of having the remainder of his faded paint boiled off in the ovens of eternal damnation was terrifying. A bit of gasoline trickled from his tailpipe. This place, somehow, was tied to the very gates of Hades, and that—no matter how you looked at it—spelled trouble. Too much trouble for his master (who was dead) and too much trouble for him.

From the top of the manor, Armand's tattered form tried to speak. The wind had been knocked out of him by the fall, and he'd used what little breath he'd had left on his initial exclamation of profanity, leaving him at a literal loss for words. He composed himself enough to climb the nearest gable, and pull himself across the crest of the roof-line to rest. As he dragged his body—abused and broken—up the loose shingle roof, he could clearly hear the horn-blast of his old banged up Ford. He could hear the engine start. The radio clicked on and off rapidly, with the volume turned up full. The sound of National Public Radio snapped in and out of his ears as it did so, "—partisan attack—*click*—a statement—*click*—unconcerned—*click*—tonight's report—*click*—"

Armand listened to his only means of real escape perform a neat three-point turn, on its own with no driver, and tear away down the road. The engine hummed, which was atypical. It purred like a kitten that had just out-run a particularly nasty neighborhood dog. He called after it, weakly, gasping for breath and fighting the pain of what felt like a broken rib, but it was no use. His words were drowned by the noise of the horn, the radio, the wild clucking of chickens, and now—to put icing on the

cluck

cake—the sounds of redneck-entrepreneur Bobby G. calling to him from above.

"Hey! You're alive!" Bobby shouted in disbelief, his voice trailing off as he ducked back into the house—no doubt descending through stairways, hidden doors and hallways, intent on finding Armand so he could finish the job.

"Thanks for caring," thought Armand, gasping. He didn't get it. It didn't make sense for Bobby to turn on him like this. Then again, nothing was making sense today. It wouldn't have surprised Armand if his broken bones began to dance and sing burlesque. There was a moment's pause ...

"Nope, I don't hear them singing," said The Charge. Armand wasn't so sure: it felt like his ribs were doing high kicks. Why were the chickens acting so strange? Why were they so smart—or at least, why were they so smart relative to how smart chickens normally are, which is not at all? Was Bobby possessed by them? That was highly unlikely. Possession usually took three ingredients: power, will, and intellect. The chickens had more power than normal, certainly. They were also willful, stubborn creatures. What they lacked was intellect—and that was a critical piece of the equation. To take control of a mind, you had to be able to convince it that it wanted to be controlled. It was the job of a master negotiator, a salesman or a politician. Not a chicken. What else, then?

The house? Possible. It had power ... the whole thing reeked of an ancient force, but then why work through Bobby? It could certainly have stopped him on its own. A window could have slammed shut on his fingers, or a shingle could have slipped loose at the worst possible moment. That is how inanimates—such as houses—typically worked. If they could be bothered to manifest their powers against humans at all, which they typically couldn't. He tried to think it through, ignoring the pain in his torso. The house was certainly like none he had ever seen before, but even if it wanted him dead, it still didn't fit. Armand always felt that things should *fit*. Logic was like mathematics in that regard: if everything was in its place, things would always snap together neatly. This wasn't neat. It didn't make sense. It wasn't logical.

"You're trying to reach the Rooster. You can't do that. You'll destroy him," Bobby had said, and then, *"I can't be saved."* What did that mean? It was like he didn't even want to be saved, like he wanted the rooster alive just so the rooster could go on haunting him. The rooster would probably kill Armand, if he ever made it to the roof. The flock was too large, and the rooster was too clever. While it hurt to think that, it was true. A clever chicken. It was unprecedented, unpredictable and extremely dangerous. So, if Bobby wanted Armand dead, why not just let him climb?

It just doesn't make sense! The exorcist screamed the words inside his head—it hurt too much to scream out loud.

He knew one thing, though. Whatever this new power was, if it was all about stopping him from seeing the rooster, then that was the one thing that Armand was even more determined than ever to do. His shoulder was starting to swell, and he was still a bit out of breath. He didn't think he could climb any farther. He looked around. From his lofty position—flopped over the top of the gable like a dead trout—he could truly appreciate the chaotic nature of the farm's construction. There were angles, lines, chimneys, joists, mantles, buttresses, and all manner of things jumbled together like one of those ransom notes, where the letters are all cut out. Back towards the window, there was another gable. Below him, between those two, there was a third—it was the one that had nearly skewered him on the lightening rod. Further along still, there was the start of a long roof-line which extended back towards the tallest of the barns. The roof-line zigzagged around the nearest corner of the barn, making it look as if the whole gabled structure had been thrust upwards through wood and shingle, the sharp tip of its cupola piercing through first, and the rest of its bulk pushing aside the old house as it rose triumphantly above all the other structures. The zig-zag of the roof continued along past the huge barn and back again towards a smaller barn, and then—

Armand's eyes snapped back, and up. A cupola. The highest point on the tallest barn, over six full stories above the ground. Atop it there was a simple weathervane in the shape of a country rooster. He stared up at it. It stared back down, and scratched its talons in an unmistakable challenge. That was it, Armand realized: that bird was the key to it all. It stared intently at Armand, and then looked away, and then back again, and then away. Armand's eyes darted back down, following the black cock's gaze, back along the zig-zag, and there! There was a small window just above the roof-line, cut into the front side of the massive barn. If he could make it there, he could get in through the window. Maybe, once inside, he could find another way up into the cupola, one that would be easier on his ribs. There would surely be a ladder to the top, he knew. Barns needed to be repaired. Barns this old had been built by hand, and that meant you could always get anywhere to repair it by hand. Taking a deep, painful breath, he started his way across.

"Do you have any Advil in your utility belt?" his voice asked, *"it hurts in here."*

"Can you shut up for a second?" Armand answered testily, "I'm a bit busy right now."

The Rooster, watching from his noble perch, crowed approvingly and struck a pose fit for royalty: his exposed spine thrust upwards, the rotten meat of his breast pushed out, and his beak pointed upwards in the arrogant posture of his kind. He ruffled his features and crowed again, and waited for the exorcist to arrive.

Armand groaned. His voice was right, his insides hurt like hell.

Knapp

chapter 20 hunters hunting hunters

The King of Chickens, *Gallus Regalus*, the Rooster. A mighty spirit that had grown powerful in a neat parallel to Armand's own development. Though semi-flightless and somewhat domesticated, the bird perched high and still on top of a distant roof, lording over those below him. Despite its arrogance (which was somewhat justified), it watched quietly from the lofty perch at the far end of the rambling estate. It looked past dormers and crooked sills, falling gutters and splintered cedar shingles. It ignored the wafting scent of decaying leaves as it rose upwards on the warm currents generated by the ancient metal roofing.

From the Rooster's point of view the fight between Bobby and Armand was curious. The King of Chickens remained perfectly still as it watched, partly due to the intensity of its focus and partly so as not to be seen. It was doubtful, the Rooster thought, that the humans would notice from such a distance. Humans have weak eyes, and rarely seemed to pay any attention at all to their surroundings.   Not like a chicken. Chicken eyes aren't as acute as, say, an eagle's ... but bird eyes are bird eyes, and any self-respecting cockerel would always be alert for any sign of danger. The Rooster's eyes were better than average, as well, and beyond mortal sight he could *sense* the two men as they moved about the catacomb halls of the farm.

I doubt that a human could ever do that, thought the Rooster, mentally patting itself on the exposed vertebrae of its back. A flutter of wings and a ruffling of feathers accentuated the Rooster's glee; it, like any cock, took pride in its abilities.

Still, the one human was remarkably perceptive, and had proven himself worthy of caution. The other one, the bastard man who had bullied his wife and burned the flock to death, setting this whole despicable affair in motion, was there too. The Rooster had been watching them both for some time. They had been cooperating at first, which was most peculiar. It was because of this that the newcomer was seen as an enemy as well, at least in the beginning. The man's attire didn't help him, as he was obviously dressed for combat, and he bore the insignia of one of poultry-kind's oldest and most feared enemies. In the recesses of its rotten chicken brain, however, it knew the man held some sort of connection with him.

What was the word? An "exer-something..."

There was a familiarity to him, something that stirred a distant memory from long ago, from when the days when the Rooster had still been alive, perhaps? No, it wasn't that ... the feeling was too distant, and continued to elude the Rooster as he watched. They were fighting now, the two men. Quite brutally. If they had been allies before, they certainly weren't any longer. If forced to judge, the Rooster would bet several of his finest hens that these two were bitter enemies. The farmer, that vile and violent backwater fuck of a human, was the Rooster's enemy. Rooster logic began the slow, rhythmic churning that would eventually lead to a decision: any enemy of *that* man was a friend of the Rooster.

cluck

Logic was a difficult thing for chickens, and this logic in particular proved taxing, pushing the Rooster's mind to the limits of its ability. The idea of "friend" was foreign to it, and the contradicting motives of both men confused it.

It continued to watch as the man in the coat clung precariously to the steeply pitched roof. He was sidling away from an open window, and the farmer was climbing out after him. There was an exchange of words and then—

As the man fell from the roof, the Rooster hopped a bit to one side, and then fluttered across the small courtyard in that special, almost-normal-flying way in which chickens fly. [30] With much effort and even more flapping, it came to perch upon the sill of a hayloft door, where it was able to get a clearer view. Just as its talons alighted on their new perch, the exorcist, looking tired and sweating through his heavy coveralls, let out a loud curse. Perhaps the Rooster *had* misjudged this shabby and dirty stranger, after all, with his long coat and his even longer scar. Perhaps this new man really *was* a mortal enemy of the farmer. Perhaps, then, he really *was* an ally to the Rooster?

A few bird synapses fired, and the Rooster made up its mind. There could be no other option; to the Rooster, life was black or white. If you were an enemy to an enemy you were at least partially a friend, but it still wasn't entirely sure if this meant it had to help the man or not. Instead, it watched from a distance. It watched as the man scrambled away from Bobby, and it watched as Bobby scrambled after him. Armand had climbed higher. He was in and among some of the high dormers now,

---

[30] "The Introductory Teachings of The Order of Chickens (Canadian Chapter)," by Melvin Stromm, describes chicken flight as "looking like a midget in a straight jacket, with a huge winged hat, trying to swim against a strong current, only in the air and without the involvement of water." Mr. Stromm was largely correct, and a decent enough *exorciste*, but he was discouraged from writing further texts for The Order, regardless.

and it was again difficult for the Rooster to see, so it flew again, this time to the top of the highest cupola. It was farther away, but the view was unobstructed … and the Rooster really didn't want to miss anything.

Perhaps alerted by the motion, the man looked up and across the way. As if his eyes were drawn there by some cosmic chance, Armand's gaze drifted until he was looking directly at the King. Armand's eyes met the Rooster's for a brief moment as he struggled to survive. It was as if a huge shroud had been lifted. A memory flashed inside the small pea-sized brain of the Rooster. There was smoke and fire, a familiar scene that the Rooster often relived in his quest for retribution against the farmer. Then the scene changed: there was still heat, and there was still fire, but the sky changed and the wind settled. A huge doorway loomed before the Rooster, inviting and yet repulsive. The Rooster stepped closer, and the door slammed shut. It had teeth around its frame, and these teeth were now clenched shut. The Rooster, still inexplicably drawn inward, squeezed between two of the giant stone teeth, but then … what was it? A taste? A scent? The Ruler of the Roost wasn't certain *what* the memory was, what sense it was recalling. It was a power … the same power that had sucked him up and spat him from the depths of Hell, so many long years ago. Something had pulled the Rooster's soul, tugged it back into the world of the living. It was—

In the moment of epiphany, the Rooster could see the connection as if it were a glowing leash of power. The cord stretched away in long meandering loops of spectral essence until it finally led to Bobby Garfundephelt, where it was held tightly in his sinister hand, anchored by that terrible man halfway between life and death. Another strand, somewhat kinder in its essence, trailed away towards Armand, but this new cord was not a leash but rather a *connection*—a dotted line that linked the two. Logic tried to distill itself within the confines of the Rooster's muddy brain. What did these wisps of power mean? Was Bobby the victim of the Rooster's revenge, or was the Rooster trapped by Bobby?

cluck

Armand was what? His saviour? Or his creator? Was the tiny form of the pitiful exorcist, clinging desperately to the roof, the cause or the cure of his pain? The Rooster blinked, and the vision of the epiphany was broken. The lines that brought the three contenders together vanished, leaving the Rooster even more confused than before.

It knew one thing, though. It was an incontrovertible truth, a fact of solidity that was stubbornly fused to the interior of the gaping skull where the Rooster's brain should have been: it must save the exorcist. Until the Rooster could meet Armand on its own terms, the man had to live. The Rooster broke Armand's gaze and glanced instead toward a small window in the roof-line. If the man knew anything, he'd make for that window, thought the Rooster. Sure enough, Armand followed the glance, noticed the window, and then turned back to the Rooster for only a brief moment before scrambling away towards safety.

Bobby had killed the Rooster, long ago. The Rooster was now hunting Bobby, so that it could finally rest in peace. Bobby was apparently hunting this newcomer, although the Rooster wasn't sure why. The exorcist, in turn, was hunting not only the Rooster but all of his harem. The Rooster and Armand were joined by their own morbid history, and now some new connection had been formed between the Rooster and the filthy ignorant hick named Bobby. All of them hunters, all of them prey. Isn't it strange, how souls and spirits can become so intertwined with fate? Most chickens are incapable of understanding irony, but the Rooster could. It thrust its chest out and ruffled its plumage, grinning with pleasure at its own superiority. Whatever happened it was certain that it, at least, would survive. Cocky bastard.

Knapp

cluck

chapter 21 the charge of the order

A brief excerpt from the Book of The Charge[31] —

Upon the high places and hills of old, The Charge stands overseeing all. From places high, above the mundane and material things, his eyes do see the spirit world, where souls are oft to dwell. From lofty perches, akin to the place of fowl and hen, his mind doth know the ethereal place of bird and man, and his ear doth hear them and his words are heard by them. From very high up he feeleth as spirits do, his hands thus able to grasp at them and his clad feet able to kick at them, for his body too knoweth the spirit world of poultry and beast and

---

[31] The Book of The Charge was originally published in Paris, France, 1642, using old-timey French, but has since been translated to old-timey English for convenience.

woman and man. But mostly poultry. The Charge has an affinity for chicken, and is most attuned to them above others.

The Charge's eye is sharp. The Charge's mind is clear. The Charge's arm is strong and muscular. The Charge's aim is true. The Charge is first to act. The Charge is last to be deceived. For The Charge is eternal. The Charge has seen it all before. The Charge stands against all of the evil that the forces of Guinea, Bantam, Leghorn, Wyandot, Brahma and Grouse, who art dead, yet returned to the world of the living. The Charge is not to be fooled by his foes. After all, thou art rather stupid, being chickens after all. The Charge's nose doth shield him from the smell of seces. The Charge's power is magnificent and immortal. It is not bound by the limitations of thine host, but when called upon doth touch upon the heavens.

Silly as it seems, The Charge still manages to keep a straight face somehow, since this is actually some pretty serious stuff.

cluck

chapter 22 hostile reunion

With great relief, Armand clambered through the small barn window and fell panting onto the dusty floor of an old hay loft. It was honest dust, free from the filth of the chicken horde that covered the rest of the farm with a darker sort of dirt. There were several abandoned swallow nests, and some signs that a family of gulls (or perhaps pigeons) had lived here at one time, but now it was quiet and neglected. Any bird-related refuse had disintegrated over the years into much less disgusting piles, and the scent of slightly punky wood filled the airy loft. After resting for a few minutes, Armand stood and peered over the loft's single railing, exposing the grand interior of the resplendent barn. There were five clearly visible levels, each connected with a wide spiraling staircase that left the interior of the space open all the way to the peak of the enormous roof. Almost every surface was covered with some sort of old tool or implement in varying states of disrepair. A single pathway, just wide enough for a man to navigate, wound its way through it all; a jigsaw of efficiency that let no space go unused. Far below, an old rusty rim from an antique tractor leaned against the slotted door to an abandoned stall, and Armand could barely make out what looked to be the remains of several empty burlap feed bags. They had been emptied and shredded and made into nests—no, not nests but colonies. Rats, Armand thought. A good sign, it meant at least one place within the barn had been held against the chickens. Chickens didn't like rats, although these were a better breed of bird than most, and it surprised Armand that something as simple as a mundane rodent would deter them. It also surprised him that the Rooster didn't seem to care at all that there were rats in the barn. Many rats, by the look of it. It was just up there, around the spiraling insides of the old barn and up, not far from where Armand was now. As he suspected, there was a set of stairs—really no more than a ladder that had been built permanently against the inside of the rafters—that lead up to the final heights of the cupola. Atop the cupola, the Rooster was waiting. Without much additional thought about rats, Armand clambered over a small pile of cedar roofing and made his way towards his destiny. Inside the cupola the dust of decaying wood and the dirt of moths and bats and birds was lessened. On each of the cupola's four sides, at waist height, were evenly spaced wooden slats, angled to keep out the rain and weather but to allow a breeze through. The slats were held inside diagonal grooves, and he easily removed one and then another, opening one whole side to the outside air. Gingerly, being careful to avoid scraping his already bruised chest and back against the panes, he climbed free of the weather-torn cupola, and stood—shakily at first—on the roof top.

He steadied himself, quickly finding balance on the roof's peak, his staff held before him by one wavering arm. The pain in his side was in the past now—or, rather, it was in the present but Armand himself had transcended away from it. He was in a zone, drawing upon strength that his mind and soul knew he had, ignoring that other strength of his physical being, which had nearly abandoned him. He inched slowly backwards, away from the cupola. It was only four or five feet high above the peak of the roof, but Armand had climbed out onto the steep pitch of the roof's southern edge, making the top seem that much higher. The cupola was wide and capped with copper that had turned green and brown with well over one hundred years of tarnish. He couldn't see the top from his current vantage point, but he knew what was up there. He could feel it. He moved further back along the roof-line, so that he could see his nemesis, and the first sign of the beast came into view almost immediately: a brightly colored plume of feathers, spraying up from somewhere near the center of the cupola's shallow peak. The colors shimmered with what little sunlight was able to penetrate the unnatural fog which still loomed over the entire estate. In a way, it was beautiful, a fountain of prism colors, fireworks perhaps, or a sunset caught and compressed into a tiny space in the sky—and yet when the light changed the tiniest bit all color fled into blackness, giving the prism feathers the impression of coal-black death. A few steps further back, and a red-crested face appeared. A few more and the long, thin-but-strong neck was revealed, each vertebrae turned grey with age yet stark against the rich blackness of the Rooster's plumes. Then the chest, and legs, and talons. Talons, Armand noticed, that could crush trained fighting cocks, tearing them through, shredding them like cheese. Those talons were sharp, powerful, huge.

Several centuries of memories, mystically imbued into Armand, *l'Exorciste de Volaille*, coalesced into a single frightening thought. *"This is the largest rooster, living or dead, ever known to walk the face of the planet."* The Rooster was the size of a large dog, broad and brave. It held that special sort of rooster-pride that can only be described as *cocky*. It was noble, fearless. It was missing one eye, and one toe, and a large portion of its hind quarters. Instead of the eye, there was a spot of burnt and rotten black against its skull. In place of the toe was a white nub of bone. At the base of that magnificent tail was a festering hole. Not festering with disease, but with evil ... with magic. The culmination of a skeletal spine bridged the gap, holding the bird together with only minimal assistance from sinew and gore. With a grace that defied its terrible visage, the cock hopped nimbly down onto the rooftop to face Armand on equal ground.

They were like two gunslingers, hands hovering quietly above holstered pistols. Much unlike the dusty arena of an old-west duel, the barn held the two contestants far above the world; a sloped and dangerous confine for the inevitable battle between two great opposing powers. The barn, being as large as it was, had required special construction to allow it to drape over previous rooms, stalls and stairwells, and as a result one side of the roof had a comfortably shallow pitch. Armand stood at its zenith, the steeper face falling quickly away to his left. Shaking away the spaghetti-western cowboy analogy, Armand took the pose of his preferred genre, replacing the wild west with ancient Japan. Fixing his eyes upon the beady red orbs of the Rooster, Armand shifted one foot forward into a low stance. Keeping his knees bent to maintain his balance, he lowered the tip of his staff and looked down its length directly into the Rooster's eye.

The inner voice again broke the sanctity of Armand's thoughts. *"It reminds me of a verse,"* it said, and then inside Armand's mind it read to him:

> *Open here I flung the shutter, when, with many a flirt and flutter,*
> *In there stepped a stately raven of the saintly days of yore.*
> *Not the least obeisance made he; not a minute stopped or stayed he;*
> *But, with mien of lord or lady, perched above my chamber door -*
> *Perched upon a bust of Pallas just above my chamber door -*
> *Perched, and sat, and nothing more.*

"What are you going on about?" Armand asked the question of himself, as he often did, out loud. Just a few steps away, the Rooster cocked its gruesome head.

cluck

"It's called poetry. A bit high-brow for you, I know, but it is a classic."

"I know what it is. Shared consciousness, remember? I mean, what's with the sudden urge to herald my approach with words? Words that, I should add, nobody can hear but me."

"It seemed fitting."

"Fitting? Well, what about Bond? I like to think of myself more like old double-oh than some stodgy poet."

"You do think that, but Bond, well, he dresses better. He's handsome, suave—and British, of course. There's no comparison. I'm sorry to be so blunt, there's really no other way to put it. You should be happy you've got poetry. Besides, it's fitting:

> This I sat engaged in guessing, but no syllable expressing
> To the fowl whose fiery eyes now burned into my bosom's core;

"Yeah, fitting and distracting. And it's a rooster, not a raven. You know, giant mannish sort of a chicken? Size of a large dog? Right there, in front of me, ready to attack? So how about you watch my back instead of rambling on inside my head when I'm trying to concentrate?"

"Like I said: low-brow." Yet the voice, being sensitive to the challenge at hand, sank into nervous silence.

"I know this isn't right," Armand sighed to himself. Then, stronger and with conviction he repeated himself. "I know this isn't right, but I've got to stop you!" He screamed. It was primal—not his own voice but the collective voice of his master and his master's master before him. The Rooster stepped closer, its sharp nails *tick*-ing against the metal flashing at the roof's peak. With each alternating step, the tick was replaced with the scratching of the one bony nub. *tick ... scratch ... tick ... scratch ... tick ...*

"You're strong," Armand confessed, "But I'm stronger. Whatever holds you here, you have to let it go. I can help you. You can be at—"

Knapp

He had meant to say peace, but he was quite interrupted by the Rooster's sudden ghostly laugh.

"Fool," it hissed, "you can not free me!" The Rooster's earlier thoughts of truce vanished into instinct and it lunged—a quick flash of movement that was stretched and prolonged as time slowed and Armand's mind raced. There was a flash behind Armand's eyes: a memory of Armand as a young boy, when he was still known as Arnold. The thought snapped against the inside of his eyelids and ricocheted through his brain. There were summer smells: cut fields and apple blossoms drifting across the dry air. There were friends, too: Carl, Nate ... and there was a glow by Matt's foot, a horrible blue feathered thing—and pain. The memory flooded back in the stretched and wretched span of time within which the Rooster flew towards him, its sole talon flaring before it like the boney tusks of a dragon. And then time returned. Armand stood fixed, lost in the past, as the talons struck hard into his thigh. The canvas of his heavy coveralls failed and pain screamed through Armand's leg, waking him enough to push the creature back again with his staff and regain his composure.

"I ... I know you ..." Armand looked closely at his foe, at the feathers that were at once black as night and at the same time like a rainbow, at the steady red eye, at the sheer size of the thing. "I—"

"You do not!" the Rooster interrupted, positioning itself for another attack.

"No, wait— yes, I do ... you were at the mall, it was years ago. You were in a crate, and you attacked me then." The two combatants shuffled about, on guard, as Armand tried to find the words. Surprisingly, the Rooster listened.

"I was just a boy," Armand continued, and then the pang of the memory subsided as Armand realized what it all meant. "I killed you— or almost did. I *beat* you. I beat you then, and I'm a lot stronger now."

cluck

The Rooster ruffled its feathers in protest, making itself look large and menacing.

"Crate?" It hissed. "Mall? You are a fool. That was not me, that was ..."

Armand stopped listening as his mind reeled. It wasn't the same rooster? It had to be, it was so terrifying, so strong. Armand's legs grew unsteady. This had to be that bird. It had to be.

"It's not, Armand. It's not."

It has to be, Armand thought—it was more than a thought. He was pleading to himself. There couldn't be anything worse.

"Everything seems bigger when you're a kid," The Charge whispered inside him. *"You were right to be scared then, but you're not the kid you were back then. You have me now. You have power!"*

Power, yes ... Armand had power. A lump was forming in his throat, but he pushed it down, suppressing his fear, controlling it.

"Another," Armand concluded. "So there are more like you."

"No, just one like me. I am the King. There are others who are dead now, yes. Like me, they scratch at the ground between life and death, but they are puny. The rooster at the mall ... that was, regrettable. I tried to save him, as I tried to save Helena, and the others ..." Armand crouched defensively and warded off the Rooster's tentative advances. This so-called Rooster King just laughed off the monster that Armand fought as a child, and that had haunted his dreams ever since, as weak. But The Charge was right, everything seemed bigger then, when he himself was so small. There was something else, too, hidden in this rooster's boasting. There was the sound of ... regret? It wasn't typically the type of emotion to expect from a rooster. Roosters don't save other roosters, they challenge them, often to the death. And who, or what, was Helena?

"No time to think about that now," his voice urged, *"because that thing is about to jump."*

Armand took a quick inventory of his remaining weapons, and realized woefully that his belt, hung with tricks for dealing with spirits such as these, was largely depleted.

"Shit," his voice said to him, inside his head, *"we're in trouble ..."*

"Quoth the raven, nevermore."

As if on cue, or perhaps sensing Armand's faltering courage, the Rooster attacked. "You can not defeat me!" it crowed, and, using its powerful wings to lift it upwards, its strong thighs kicked it forward into a powerful leap. Armand's eyes were only a margin away from a painful introduction to the rooster's needle-sharp spur before he deftly redirected the bird to one side with a short flick of his staff. Like Big John during his fabled showdown with Robin Hood, Armand put the rooster momentarily in his place.

"I can," Armand insisted with confidence, but there was a deep uncertainty. These chickens had surprised him already on many levels, but this was too radical. Roosters, even grand cocks like this one, simply did not talk. It was another indication of the flock's power, and a cold reminder to Armand that he had never encountered anything like this before. Was he prepared? Did he have the power to win against this majestic, splendid animal? No training could prepare him for this type of force. Ghouls rarely spoke, even human specters. More advanced animal spirits might communicate with gestures, or with the silent empathic spirit-talk, but they never spoke out loud. Not in English.

"Your fight is not with me, human."

The ghostly words barely completed before the second assault. This time, the giant Rooster evaded the staff long enough to crash with a thunder of kicks and a tornado of beating wings into Armand's forward leg. It was the left boot, complete with his badge of position, but any significance thereof was lost on the Rooster's wild rage. Armand stumbled backwards a full step, and then another as he struggled to distance himself. He spun the staff around deftly and with a crack it struck the bird squarely on its back, pushing it downward and then backwards with what should have been a fatal blow. Too bad it was already dead—fatal blows don't mean much to the dead. Still, it had the desired affect of increasing the gap between the two combatants, and Armand—like some morbidly costumed fencer—advanced again, positioning himself further from the barn's edge and offering him the more favorable footing of the roof's shallow northern pitch.

"Do you know who I am?" Armand asked, honestly not certain of whether the ghost-chickens he had fought for so long were aware of what he was. He lunged himself, and kicked the rooster squarely in the head with his emblazoned left boot, as if to drive the question home.

"Yes, I know you," it hissed. The words came out of its narrowly opened beak like steam from a tea kettle. "I know you. For all eternity, from before the first moment of time until the end of days I know you." The tone suggested this knowledge was a dirty secret, and that to this spirit Armand's own existence was somehow unavoidably tragic.

"If you know me then you know that my fight is with you."

Not the greatest debater, Armand, but he had a point. Why would the Rooster deny it? Was it smart enough to be purposefully misleading him? Was he simply trying to bargain for his own safety? Chickens weren't supposed to be smart at all ... never mind capable of diplomacy. Armand, with practiced form and the rough strength of a lifetime of hard work, continued to press the attack. Feathers began to drift about in small eddies as the two stirred the air with attack, parry, retreat.

Any concerns about the Rooster's unwillingness to fight, however, were cut short when the proverbial gloves were taken off. Armand's attacks were capable of hurting the undead, even this exceptional example. If he hurt it enough, it wouldn't die (being already dead) but it would lose its ability to hold a form in this world. The spirit would be forced back into the non-corporeal planes, where it would (hopefully) wander off to some better place away from mortals. The Rooster, however, was not defenseless. It had so far been attacking with claw and wing and beak—Armand would have several bruises as a result—but it had more power than that, and as Armand pressed him hard back towards the cupola, it used it.

The pain in Armand's ribs returned as the rooftop suddenly opened up, swallowing him up to his armpits before snapping shut around him again. The steel flashing that was creased atop the roof's spine rolled and pulled back like a monstrous silver tongue. From the rafters below hot, humid air wafted over him like breath. The cedar shingles splayed outward like rotten hobo teeth, grinding against him as the roof closed up tight around him, pressing the breath from him and sending new spasms through his body. His left arm was trapped completely, as was his staff. His right arm, wrenched into an uncomfortable angle by his attempt to catch himself, was free but its range of motion was limited. He could only flail it wildly without much effect. The gesticulations were certainly of no concern to the Rooster, the King of the scariest flock Armand had ever seen, as it leaped forward again and landed with a painful biting grip on Armand's trapped shoulder. The sharp talons, the razor teeth that tipped the Rooster's one whole leg, bit deep. Armand's coveralls failed again, tearing open as the Rooster's claws sunk deep into the muscular flesh of his upper back and arm.

Armand screamed. The pain of the massive talons holding fast into his flesh was excruciating and brought back the deeper pain of his shoulder's earlier dislocation. For a brief moment that seemed eternal, the mad fowl stood there, *gripping*.

"I tried to warn you," it hissed quietly in his ear. Armand had to wonder why the Rooster—his ancient arch-nemesis—would want to warn him of anything. He didn't have time to think about it for long, however, as new pain struck into the side of his face. Trapped and helpless, Armand was being pecked to death. Slowly. He could feel blood running down his neck and into his shirt. The first strikes had been to his temple, and soon Armand felt a tug as a small piece of skin was pulled away.

"Damn you!" Armand managed through clenched teeth. He didn't want to die this way. If the ghosts ever got him, he at least wanted to know how, and why. There were too many unanswered questions for him to die here, now. Not yet.

"Look, it's not like I want to fight you," Armand pleaded. After all, the Rooster had been hesitant to fight, and now that Armand was losing that fight he felt it prudent to revisit that possibility. The Rooster paused, considered.

"No, I do want to fight you!" Armand shouted. It wasn't Armand, it was his voice—the voice of The Charge. Damn it! It was going to get him killed! The Rooster stepped closer.

"No, I really don't, honest!" The Rooster stepped back.

"I do!" It stepped forward. *"I have to!"*

"I don't! It's not right!" ... and back again.

"He's just saying that because you're winning!" The Charge shouted through Armand's involuntary lips. "No kidding!" came Arnold's own reply, though through the same orifice, as the Rooster moved in once more. Just as The Charge had censored Armand's attempts at obscenity over the years, it now tried to directly alter the words coming from Armand's mouth. The resulting fox-trot of unwilling edits as Armand fought against himself was confusing enough to distract The Rooster, at least. It stopped its advance again.

"I do not [I want to] fight [anybody but you] no I do not [I don't] want to fight you [hah—that's a double negative!] no it isn't I don't want to fight [yes you do!]"

The Rooster had given the negotiations his best effort, but this was ridiculous. It stepped forward once more, deciding to end this stalemate conclusively by pecking Armand in the face.

"No!" Armand began to whip his head around frantically. He couldn't afford to loose an eye, and it would be harder to hit a moving target. The Rooster, realizing that Armand had some fight left in him, tried to kick him. Now, a chicken can kick. A normal hen could crush a gourd with a well-placed stomp, if it were so inclined. Think about the shape of a drumstick: it is a mass of muscle, the sole mobilizer of its flightless host. Like an ice-skater or gymnast, chickens build enormous strength in their thighs, simply from what they are. In this case it was even more-so; the King Chicken was much larger and much stronger than a normal hen. A single thigh from the King could have fed a family of ten for three days. [32] The first kick echoed through the exorcist's skull with a deafening ache. A second one might prove fatal. Unlike his unnatural enemy, to Armand, fatal meant fatal.

The Rooster kicked again, but Armand was ready. He had power of his own—not the least of which is the human ability to think under pressure and adapt to adversity, even when he was being constantly distracted by voices in his head. As Armand felt the claw loosen its grip on his shoulder, he knew the kick was coming, and he turned his head quickly to meet it. Mouth open, with an awesome and terrible look in his eye, Armand caught the leg in his teeth and bit. They were now at a standstill: Armand, trapped in the mystically warped wood and shingles, and the King, held fast in Armand's clenched jaw. Armand closed his eyes tight against the onslaught of beating wings as the rooster tried to free himself, and bit down harder. The bird gave up momentarily, relaxing, and then turned back to its immaterial methods of attack.

A tomato appeared ... but Armand did not open his mouth to bite it. Rotten eggs materialized above him, dribbling filth onto his head, finding its way into the corners of his mouth. Armand did not free his grip. He knew these tricks. He knew the King was capable of more, and

---

[32] At least in life. In its current state, the Rooster's leg was still massive, but it was also massively unappetizing.

if he was falling back into feeble habits such as these, it meant he was desperate.

"I'hhb neht gahging do leht ooo gho!"[33] Armand insisted through tight jaws. The taste was horrible, but it was better than the alternative. He shook his head, sending pangs of hurt into the worried incarnation of poultry. Could he break its will simply like this? If his boots could hurt the undead, and his staff could hurt them, then why not his bite? He had never learned the tactic in The Order—nor had any of his predecessors.

Not surprising, Armand thought, *this thing tastes like—*

He had to cut the thought short to prevent himself from retching. If he vomited now, the rooster would be free. He bit harder still, and there was a crack as long-dead and brittle bones, well guarded under a thick layer of decaying muscles, snapped.

The King Chicken, the Rooster with the capital "R" panicked. In a sudden, adrenaline-fueled effort to free itself, it opened the roof once more and they both fell. Armand barely had the will or the energy to fight, yet the two clung together and managed to continue their struggle as they fell. They hit the lip of the topmost loft and crashed painfully through the flimsy rail along its edge, rolling outwards and down. The floor of the next loft below hit them harder, stopping them completely. Armand coughed up something thick as he hit the ground hard but he didn't spit out the leg. Soon that floor too became soft, and opened up as the roof had. They sank through it like unfortunate pioneers in a bog of wooden quicksand. They fell through a small bookcase full of mason jars and old paint cans, causing a cymbal crash of broken glass and banged aluminum. Again they hit the floor, and again it opened up, although this time the exorcist did spit the cock from his mouth, freeing him to

---

[33] "I'm not going to let you go." Well, you try to talk with a live chicken leg in your mouth. Err, make that a *dead* chicken leg.

gag and scream. The panic was simply too much, and wasn't likely to subside as they fell, side-by-side again.

Through a moldy bail of hay littered with tangled wire.

... and again,

Onto a much harder surface that opened up in turn to spew them inside of the house. [34]

... and again,

Into a butcher-block countertop covered in old skillets and pans, through that, and onto a chipped tile floor.

... and again.

Finally, they stopped with a dull *thud*, a short metallic *screee*, and a relatively quiet but very distinct *crack*. Turning his thoughts towards himself, Armand did a quick damage check. If that rib wasn't broken before, he thought, it was now. No ... not rib, *ribs*, plural. There were at least two, if not three broken bones biting at him from inside his chest. The pain throbbed throughout his body like a hangover headache that didn't know it was supposed to stay in your head. A bad hangover. A three-day-drinking-binge hangover.

Armand moaned. There was blood in his mouth, and another different-and-horrible taste. He spat, and felt with his tongue that he was missing some teeth. Well, at least it's my blood, he thought. Thinking about it at all made him contemplate the other substance inside his mouth, however, and this time there was no stopping it: with the cruel contraction of abdominal muscles against broken ribcage, he spewed a steamy bloody broth across the dirt floor.

---

[34] The barn was attached to the back of the house proper, but being taller than the house by several stories it sagged over the top in such a way that on one side, falling through the bottom floor of the barn put Armand and the Rooster inside the top floor of the house. The other side of the barn continued down several more stories before ending in a dirt floor on ground level.

cluck

Dirt floor, he thought, *Where am I?*

Not in the barn—they had fallen into the house. Looking around, he could barely make out a stack of boxes in the dim light. The air smelled musty, a dank yet somehow comfortingly familiar scent. Potatoes.

I'm in a root cellar.

He staggered, trying to get to his feet. His head was filled with a blinding pain, making it even more difficult to find his bearings. He rolled onto his side in a futile attempt at standing, and felt his ribcage compress unnaturally.

"Christ, I'm only supposed to have one floating rib." Armand wheezed. The damage was more severe than he could guess, but the adrenaline in his blood and the acid in his throat willed him to stand regardless of the pain.

The dirt beneath his feet was soft ... probably the only reason he survived the fall at all.

The King, being dead, was largely undamaged from the fall. Thus it was quicker to regain its composure and resume the fight. Shaking its newly broken leg, it wobbled about, forced to balance on the feeble nub of its unbroken leg as it did so. The outline of Armand's teeth could be seen clearly on either side of the break, and the leg gushed something not entirely the same color as blood, and not entirely the same consistency as puss.

Being dead for several years, these types of setbacks were inevitable, and the Rooster floundered about for only a few moments before learning how to adapt the handicap into a functional lurch. His attention returned to the exorcist just in time to see him stand. Like the prize fighter, looking in the eye of a well-matched foe, the Rooster examined Armand. He was strong, but he was also the loser of this fight.

A fight, the Rooster was forced to remind himself, *that they should not even be fighting.*

After all, Armand was an ally of sorts, and though the Rooster wasn't entirely clear on the logic behind its internal friend-or-foe debate, it knew the battle had to cease before the man was killed. The King let Armand get to his feet fully before he extended his will again. The dirt around the Rooster began to rise, slowly swirling about like an angry fog. The dirt around Armand, like several stories of flooring above them, suddenly softened and churned, sucking him downward. He sank to his armpits before the ground hardened around him again.

"*Well, isn't this a fantastic bit of déjà vu?*" grumbled the voice in Armand's head. It was right, of course: Armand was trapped, again. Unlike the last time, however, he'd been hugging his chest when he sank, trying to hold his ribs in place as he struggled for breath. Now, arms pinned underground, he was completely helpless. Nothing remained visible of Armand save for his head and shoulders; a struggling and frightened bust of a once calm and confident man.

"You looooooooose," the King said, drawing out his declaration of victory into a long and sinister sigh. The bird, who like Armand had once stood proud and strong, lurched up to the man's face. It looked him in the eye, staring him down, and then turned his gaze to his own broken leg. Wobbling the limb before Armand's eyes, the Rooster teased him.

See, he was saying, *you can break the leg, but you can't kill me.* Armand stared back into the one beady eye.

"I don't understand you," Armand gasped. The pain in his chest was slightly lessened thanks to the support of his earthen prison. His grave, potentially. He tried to hide the fear as best he could, and held the stare as steady as he could. The Rooster lurched closer still, and leaned forward—careful to stay out of range of the human's mouth—pressing its pimply head within inches of Armand's face. The stare continued, a minute gap between the two eyes; one human, one chicken; one live, one dead. Armand gasped again, trying to keep his breath shallow, and

cluck

waited for the blow to come. The Rooster, standing so close, seemed even larger as it loomed.

"You are a fool," the hiss continued, "You can not feel it? You can not taste the power?"

He could certainly taste something. He spat again, afraid of what he might swallow if he wasn't careful.

"Power? Yeah, I feel it. It's ... weird. But I don't understand," the pain was subsiding a bit, or perhaps shock was setting in. "I'm a bit of a specialist. I only know chickens." He managed to throw the Rooster a short, crooked grin. The Rooster looked up a bit, bringing its beak directly in front of Armand's right eye. Armand remained still. The sharp beak was so close that he wasn't even able to focus on it. He could feel the slight breath from the two tiny nose-holes as the damned chicken exhaled.

"You have both of your eyes, but you do not use them," muttered the King. It was just Armand's luck to conduct his last conversation with a chicken that spoke in riddles. He meant to say something along these lines, but before he could summon a retort, the Rooster looked up suddenly and turned away as if startled by something undetectable by mortal senses. With a flash of light, the Rooster disappeared, and Armand lost consciousness.

Moments later, his eyes—delightfully still intact—opened. He was in the root cellar, alone. His ribs ached, as if he'd been stepped on by a horse (or worse). He lay sprawled on top of the dirt. *On top!* That was a definite, although mysterious, bonus. He searched his memories, unable to explain his newfound freedom, unable to explain while he was still alive.

Remembering the Rooster's last words, Armand blinked his eyes, intent upon using them. Whatever the stupid cock's motivations were, it had left Armand alive and he intended to at least humor the bird's warning. As he opened his eyes to the power of his second sight, however, the value of the bird's portent faded as the rest of Armand's senses were overwhelmed with brilliance. The blue light was so powerful here that he couldn't see anything with his eyes, whether—as the Rooster had put it—he used them or not. It was just as it was when he first looked upon this place, from the road, during his initial reconnaissance—a blinding, rippling light of souls that threatened to disorient him and break his mind. Reeling against the force, he quickly shut his vision off again, suppressing it behind his dimmer, but much less taxing, sense of normal sight.

You have both of your eyes but you do not use them ...

"Stupid words," Armand muttered, considering how unwise it was for him to have listened to a chicken in the first place. "Stupid words from a stupid chicken."

> Much I marveled this ungainly fowl to hear discourse so plainly,
> Though its answer little meaning — little relevancy bore;
> For we cannot help agreeing that no living human being
> Ever yet was blessed with seeing ...

Armand shook his head against the sound of his inner voice, and seethed as much as possible without breathing too heavily, for his ribs ached with every inhalation.

"Remind me," he said with each shallow breath, "if we get out of this ... to rip you from my head ... and kick ... your ass." The world grew dim, and Armand nearly lost consciousness again.

"You're just grumpy because you're almost dead," said his voice.

chapter 23   good night sleep tight

The mysterious malevolence which had manifested itself within the haunted farmhouse-turned-coop hovered above Bobby. For the first time since the arrival of the exorcist It felt satisfied, looking down upon the pathetic creature It had just departed to see him unconscious, a puddle of drool and blood beneath his slack jaw as he lay helpless and limp upon the grubby floor. It enjoyed seeing Bobby like this, when the stupid bastard passed out from fatigue, or fainted from fright, or get himself knocked out cold by a particularly well-engineered chicken trap. This time, however, he'd collapsed when It had ripped free of him, after using him to fight Armand. That had been fun, It thought. It took some additional pleasure in noting that Bobby had hit his head when he slumped suddenly to the floor, and if It had been able It would have laughed and spit at the man while he was down.

Instead, the enigmatic evil spirit fluttered with anticipation as it loomed above Its prey. Bobby's face was pale and his cheeks were matted and wet from tears that suddenly and inexplicably leaked from his unconscious head, like the gush of a cut garden hose or sprung plumbing. The force hovered there, for a moment, above the human that had so recently contained It. It hated this man. There were no words to describe the intensity of the emotion; it was as if an insatiable desire to kill was constantly at war with a driving need to postpone Its victim's suffering. The contradicting desires clashed with tangible electricity, drawing power from the spirit world with the heat of their sincerity.

The spirit force reveled in Its regained freedom, taking a moment to extend Its senses outwards through the house. The walls shrunk away from the probing essence of It, cringing from the sheer hatred and primordial evil of this monstrous and disembodied soul. It looked through the rooms and saw something It did not like at all. The other man—the *Exorciste* who possessed powers of his own, who was dressed so oddly in garments of an unknown but obviously spiritual persuasion—was alone in the basement. The Rooster should have finished him. Still, he was prone, barely alive, and it would be easy to remove the annoying bird-hunter from the picture, It knew. Armand was so badly hurt that he couldn't cause much interference at the moment, and the Rooster was undoubtedly back to work organizing the hens against Bobby.

The feeling of satisfaction increased, spreading with It through the narrow passages of the house. Armand was a threat, the entity knew, and would need to be dealt with eventually ... but being so injured and alone he was of no immediate concern, allowing It to focus on the incapacitated idiot farmer. Whatever evil plan It had in store for Armand, It could wait until after It dealt with Bobby. The anticipation mounted. Its obsession with the redneck was enough to coalesce Its anger, melting hatred and malice together into a primordial, evil plasma.

The shape glowed, brilliant like the fire of the sun, and yet It cast no illumination into the dark and cold room. It was the light of hate, guilt, regret. It floated in the air above Bobby, turning Its attention solely onto him, and plotted. Eventually, content with a plan, thin tendrils of power

cluck

reached out from the aggrieved specter. From the far corners of the farm, the evil presence pulled forth the ingredients of Bobby's newest torments. From the darkest places and most sinful realms It mined the hate with which to build Its malicious scheme. When It was finally content, the bright cold fire dimmed and the spirit shrank back into itself. Just as suddenly as It had appeared, It vanished from the physical world as It settled back into the helpless body of Bobby G.

What happened next was like a stage-play: as if on cue the chickens emerged at the poor farmer's periphery: a hen suddenly visible, perched on top of a dresser; the scratching of a talon in the hallway; a flutter of feathers at the corner of his eye. He was slowly encircled by decayed meat and tainted poultry as the final act began.

There were no tomatoes. There were no rotten eggs. There were no tiny traps and tricks, feebly insufficient in their lack of scale or creativity. There was nothing but a calm and growing crowd of feather-crested heads and crusted scabby combs. Soon, Bobby regained consciousness to find himself alone in a small circular clearing amid dozens if not hundreds of chickens—each in some various state of decomposition, such that all their parts together might only piece together a handful of complete hens, yet their numbers seemed to be double or triple their actual count due to the grotesque quality of the mob. Bobby started to gibber as he became aware of his situation; he had no memory of his combat with Armand. Adrenaline levels reached a point where all metabolic strength turned inwards, and his outward fear melted away to be replaced by a dry rasping ice that numbed his body. Fresh tears welled up behind his tired lids and he began to pant, hyperventilating uncontrollably. His skin was damp and cold, and his eyes were frozen wide, so that his lids were completely hidden beneath the edges of his fixed stare. The one rational thought that Bobby managed to muster presented a small taste of curiosity to the rapidly boiling stew of terror.

"Why aren't they attacking me?" the thought asked him. It was his own thought, certainly, but it was as if it originated from somewhere outside. Because it seemed the right thing to do, Bobby answered it.

"I don't know," he said. His words lisped slightly through a deep laceration in his lip; he had bitten through it without realizing ... although he must have done it some time ago as there was no fresh blood.

"They should be attacking you," the lone rational thought persisted. *"They hate you ..."*

"I said I don't know," Bobby insisted, calming slightly. The conversation did some good in that it distracted him somewhat from the crowd of angry barnyard birds.

"Why aren't they attacking ..." the thought said yet again. Bobby—despite his mental and physical condition—knew his single rational thought was far too singular to provide any more additional information. If he wanted information, he would have to go to the source. He turned his head upwards, and the tears that previously fell straight from his hanging face to the floor now dribbled down his cheeks. They tickled his chin, causing him to wipe one arm across his face as he looked forward into the mass of hens.

"Why aren't you attacking me?" Again, it seemed the right thing to say. He needed to know what the hell was going on, after all, and there was no one else around to ask. So he asked them. He knew they were only chickens: dirty and stupid and hardly worth the grain they ate; useless, flightless and disgusting; prone to cannibalism; bereft of any thought above a vague instinct of survival. He knew this, but he asked them anyway. They weren't normal chickens after all—which was evident in their uncanny ability to walk about and torture him despite the fact that they were most definitely deceased.

Lacking any one else to turn to, he turned to them, and directed his question at them. As he did so, the scene moved forward as if it had been waiting for this cue. The stage began to move again, like choreographed death. The chickens before him parted in a silent flurry as a larger shape approached. A much, much larger shape. The reverence that the hens gave to their King was evident in their ghostly quiet and unearthly calm. Towering above them—nearly as large as Bobby's own frail form—the rooster approached. Somehow, it managed to swagger and lurch at the same time, adopting a gait that was at once jaunty and eerie, and not entirely unlike that of John Wayne. The arrogance of the animal was tangible. Bobbing its head from side to side, it fixed first one eye and then the other eyeless hole on the farmer. It strutted to the inner edge of the circle, and then paused as the sea of chickens closed in behind him.

"Why do we not attack you?" It hopped upon its unbroken leg, so that the sharp, bony knob of the other clacked menacingly against the floorboards. The walls tried to shrink back from the culmination of events. The dresser, now a perch for four fat zombie hens, caused a slight commotion of feathers as it flinched backwards against the wall and broke the silence with a loud thump.

The rooster stepped closer, so that it was just inches from Bobby's face before it continued. "The answer is simple, human. We *do* attack you!"

There was the sudden rush of hot, damp air and a flash of red, and then suddenly Bobby was alone again. The hens and their King had vanished in an instant and the uncomfortable quiet of a mob of irreverent birds was replaced with the real silence of solitude. Pure silence, like the dark.

...

Click.

...

Bobby was uncertain whether he heard the sound, and he strained his ears searching for some confirmation.

...

Knapp

Clickety-click-ity-click-clickety— The sound danced at the edge of his perception again, but it was a more certain noise this time. It was a clattering sound, almost like the claws of the chickens but different ... smaller, and more numerous, like ... like insects.

An excerpt from The Farmer's Guide to Raising a Flock, by Burnaby Slump:

> The aspiring Chicken-farmer should be alert for bed bugs. Bed bugs are a nasty insect that has qualities similar to both a tick, a flea, and a vampire bat. That is, they suck blood, move quickly, and are difficult to eradicate. They're also creepy (hence the vampire bat reference). Bed bugs were once a common public health issue. The pest, which proliferated worldwide, began to decline in incidence through the mid twentieth century. This decline coincided with a slight increase in personal hygiene that also occurred through the mid twentieth century. There is a direct parallel between hygiene and bed bugs. In regard to the poultry industry, bed bugs are an irritation. Most readily available farm pesticides and fumigation products will stifle any population of bugs before the situation gets out of control. However, if the coop becomes compromised, bed bugs can spread easily into the main house on a farmer's clothing or in his hair.
>
> Bed bugs have undergone occasional resurgences during various periods of history; most notably during the 1960s in America and almost seasonally in certain backwater areas in Europe. Worldwide reports indicate a recent increase in the number of infestations, particularly in the dirtier corners of the world. Luckily, with recent social evolutions that distance mankind from filthy hippies and other demographics with sub-par standards of cleanliness, concerns of infestation have been more recently limited

cluck

to small micro-environments in the world's farming communities. That is, bed bugs are often found in filthy, dung-filled corners of styes, stalls and (of course) coops.

Bed bugs are wingless insects, roughly oval in shape, and creepy like nobody's business. They average about 5 millimeters in length when fully grown, and are fast runners. Their nasty exoskeletons are rust brown, changing to a deeper red brown after feeding. The red tones come from their source of food, which as has been mentioned is blood. Bed bugs are flat, like a tiny land-flounder with an attitude, and as such they can hide in even the narrowest cracks and crevices, making detection extremely difficult.

The two main species that bite chickens include the common bed bug, Cimex lectularius, and the tropical bed bug, Cimex hemipterus. There are five juvenile stages of each, known as nymphs. These smaller versions of the adults require at least one blood-glut to molt to the next stage and it takes from 5-10 minutes for complete engorgement to occur. The entire nymphal development takes from 6-8 weeks, while the adult bed bugs can live on average for 6-12 months. Regardless of the nymphal stage and sex of the insect, all bed bugs require blood. Many leading agricultural scientists conjecture that they lust for blood like horrible, albeit tiny, monsters. After mating, each female lays 2-3 eggs a day, until the end of the wretched bug's life. The cream colored eggs (the size of a pinhead) are attached the interior surfaces of a bed bug nest, and they will hatch quickly if kept warm.

The mouth-parts of bed bugs are especially adapted for piercing skin and sucking blood, furthering their association with vampire bats and also with other despised critters such as wolverines and sea monsters. Unlike sea monsters, bed bugs are well adapted to penetrating the protective layer of feathers and down to feast upon chickens. Like most blood sucking arthropods, they inject an anticoagulant saliva during feeding, which stimulates bleeding and can cause lasting damage to afflicted birds.

Bed bugs hunt in response to warmth and will be drawn to any detection of carbon dioxide from the breath of a host. Once a feeding site is located, they will build nests that can grow into a serious infestation in mere days. They tend not to live on their hosts, and the only actual contact is for a blood meal. Most blood feeding occurs at night, and they generally seek shelter during the day and become inactive while digesting the blood meal. However, bed bugs are opportunistic and will bite in the day especially if starved for some time. They can survive for long periods without feeding. They will feed on any warm-blooded animals including rodents, rabbits, bats, people, and of course chickens.

Being a foul and dastardly species, bed bugs shelter in any variety of dark and dastardly locations, mostly close to where their prey sleeps. This includes: under mattresses (hence the name "Bed Bug"); between floorboards; behind paintings; under carpets; in various cracks and crevices of a wall; and in the hardened crusts of feces that are found in and about many farmyard locations, but most especially in an around chicken coops. They are smart enough to hide when not feeding. They creep out of their nests only at night, when their prey is sleeping, and they can easily feast undisturbed.

Bed bugs tend to stay in densely populated colonies, and heavy infestations are accompanied by a distinctive sweet sickly smell. Mysterious blood spotting is often a clue that a nest of bed bugs is nearby. Bed bugs may also be traced by the presence of small, round, black droppings.

cluck

Everybody knew at least one thing about bed bugs: they were used to scare children into staying in their beds and sleeping. Everybody knew the twisted (and hardly sleep-conducive) rhyme, "Good Night, Sleep Tight, Don't let the Bed Bugs Bite!" Most farmers knew, as Bobby did, that bed bugs were real.

Bobby knew all about bed bugs, having fought with a small infestation of them personally, in his own flock. He had puzzled for months over the lessening production of eggs, but thought little of it until the birds began to die. Even then, he didn't really care that much, but his nagging wife loved the dirty flightless birds and eventually motivated him towards a solution. Bobby didn't like to expose any evidence of mental ability or intellectual pursuit (for the sake of his image), but he could read and often did. He had read plenty at the time—including the colorful passage in Slump's *Farmer's Guide to Raising a Flock*—and he had worked tirelessly for several weeks to remove the infestation completely. The answer ended up being the full-scale fumigation of the coop and chicken yard. The whole place stank like pesticide for weeks afterwards, but the coop had been rid of them. Not before some hens had passed on, and many of his birds had become emaciated and sick, but that was no bother to him. It had cost a pretty penny in pesticides, which did irritate Bobby, but he had largely put the incident out of his mind.

Until now.

Click-click-ity-click-ity-click-clickety-click—

The sound continued to dance, closer and closer to Bobby as he trembled, all alone in the middle of the vacant room. *Click-ity-click-click*—the sound grew louder, spiraling around him now, a pirouette of terror that was quickly joined by a waft of humid air and a distinct smell; the scent of molasses and salt, or of a mixture of too-sweet tea and human tears. The clattering intensified to a cacophony of clicks; the sound of an army of insect feet marching in some drunken, flitting rhythm. The sound was familiar.

"*Sounds like bugs,*" thought Bobby. "*Naw ... bug sounds aren't that loud ...*" A feeling welled up within Bobby's chest, a cocktail of confusion, fear and doubt. Things never went right for Bobby. He was a tortured soul, and could only ever expect the worst. He had no way of knowing that something larger and more sinister was at work around and within him. He had no awareness of any other power than that of his suffering. He had no knowledge of It, hovering above him, watching the scene, fixated with glee at his suffering.

Silence fell fast like a guillotine as the chattering ceased, waking Bobby from his worrisome self-reflection. He nervously spun around on the floor, trying to look in all directions at once, afraid of what was coming. *Knowing* what was coming, and wishing to any God who would listen to save him from his fate. Then after a hideous pause, pregnant with malcontent and malevolence, a lone chitinous claw emerged from the darkness. It scraped the floor as it dragged the bulk of a great beast into view. More legs followed, and a tiny head, hard like iron and covered in black bumps and protrusions and a multitude of thick wiry hairs, quivering madly as they scented the air for Bobby.

As the monster clawed its way closer, Bobby froze. There was no longer any need for nervousness or fear. It was here, now. He could see it clearly as it loomed before him, *Cimex lectularius.* It stood no more than three feet from the floor, but its vast flat abdomen spread out far behind it, and filled the room to both sides like a well-fit carpet. A large, chitinous, man-eating carpet. Its hardened sides scraped deep groves into the failing plaster of the old house's dusty walls. Its rear was lost in shadow; its front, prominent and poised before the still man, held fast as if he were frozen in ice.

The creature's maw presented itself as a warrior might present his arms before a battle, a salutation of two large swords crossed before its

cluck

head in an exoskeletal tribute of sharpened bone, affixed to the dark wet hole of the creature's ingestion. The mandibles were large enough to reach around Bobby's waist and take hold of him entirely, he thought. Behind them, a sucking rim of insect lip surrounded a lone proboscis, which wavered before the monster like a blind man's cane. As his scent finally isolated him, the proboscis shot towards him, straining against the giant bulk of the creature's mass to reach him. A second later, the bug shot forward with shocking speed and grace, chasing after the pointed, sucking organ, towards its prize.

Bobby returned to his senses just as the bed bug lunged, and he was only able to avoid it by throwing himself sideways. The shock subsided and his senses returned to him. Where was he? He had dodged the attack just barely, and his amateur attempt at rolling free had landed him with his face on the floor, with something sharp—presumably the bottom landing of a staircase—pressed painfully in his back. There was a pain in his shoulder as well, though he didn't know why or where from. The floorboards, just inches from his face, were wide and the spaces between them were wide as well, the result of years of seasonal expansion of the untreated pine boards. The spaces were once clean, but now they were packed with dust and dirt; home—it would appear—to a host of monstrous parasites. Atop the resident debris was a newer assortment of refuse. There was something dark that looked like rough-hewn marbles scattered about, and larger chunks of something else that was porous and rough, like some pale crumbling lava stone. A small stick of splintered wood, covered on at least one side with a cracking red glaze, garnished the debris.

Plaster, he thought. From the wall.

He looked up. The wall behind him was in a state of disrepair, the horsehair plaster walls crumbling in many places. The layers of dirt on the walls were exemplified by a pale rectangle where the finish was cleaner. Behind him, held between his shoulder and a loose baseboard, was the remains of a portrait. It must have fallen as he crashed unceremoniously into the wall, and struck his shoulder.

Not too bad ... he thought. He was sure that something far worse could have, should have, happened. His imagination held up a vivid scene of his disembowelment by insect incisions, of being ripped apart and sucked up, until all that was left was an empty sack of skin. He imagined—he could actually feel—the pain of the pincers as they bit, the salty metallic warmth as the hideous lips attached themselves and the proboscis sank deep inside him. Despite the clarity of Bobby's imagination, in truth he was unharmed. The painting that fell on him caused some pain, but he wasn't consumed. He barely noticed the portrait's visage—misaligned within the broken frame, looking as regal as could be when one is long forgotten—before instinct forced him to scrabble further along the wall, avoiding a second clumsy attack from the giant bug.

The wall ... the portrait ... it wasn't his, and didn't look like anything he'd bought himself. Many decorations and wall hangings were bought at auctions when the new guest rooms were built, but this wasn't one of them, he was sure of it. The stairs ... it was a stair he landed on after all, a protruding first step that led sharply upwards. Behind the blood sucking insect, which filled the room like a carpet, he could make out bits of hearth and what might be a small brick alcove. He was in a kitchen. One of the oldest kitchens, used by servants long ago. The creature turned to face him again. If Bobby had been able to pause and reflect, he might wonder why rotten tomatoes and pranks with rotten eggs had suddenly evolved to such a frightening and sinister threat. Then again, he might not. Bobby wasn't prone to reflection, even on a good day. He'd already done so once and wasn't likely to again any time soon. He had watched plenty of action movies on TV, though, and he was able to react well enough to the situation at hand, in his own uneducated redneck way.

cluck

The creatures' legs and head were at one end, leaving the majority of the expansive, undulating torso to drag behind it.

It must be nearly ten feet or more across, he noticed, *although not very high from the ground at all …*

Bobby quickly devised a plan, as acute and sophisticated as a bowling ball. He grabbed the sharp stick of the broken frame and hurled himself clumsily onto his adversary's back. It reacted by backing up quickly and thrashing about as best it could, but other than rolling Bobby about and making it difficult to stand, there was no effect. Bobby stayed on his knees, riding the bug like some nightmare pony. Poised as best he could, he raised the stick above his head and plunged it into the insect's hide, where it squelched up something thick and pale. The bug, to Bobby's disappointment, did not die. He pulled the stick free and plunged it in again, and again, and again—all with the same result; welling spots of ick and some more thrashing, but nothing terminal.

Around Bobby, the dark spirit grew restless and unhappy. Bobby wasn't supposed to show courage—not even stupid courage! Nor self confidence! He was supposed to blubber and weep, to cower in fear and long for a quick and painless death that would never come—but Bobby's attack had proven hopeless. He had failed. That, at least, gave It some moderate pleasure. The spirit enjoyed watching Bobby's face as the dumb-ass farmer realized his failure, as the fear returned, and the confusion closed in again.

It's a bug, he might have thought, if Bobby had been practiced at thinking. Bugs have open circulatory systems and an internal anatomy that could (sometimes) allow them to survive a boot stomp or worse. Of course, this wasn't just a bug, it was an enormous creature that was built like a bug, a giant. It would be even harder to kill than one of its normal, tiny brothers. *The stick isn't going to phase it at all*, he realized.

I've got to get out—to escape ... escape ... He thought then, his mind reeling back into panic.   From the spirit ether around him, It watched, gleeful, delighting in Bobby's re-found misery.

Though his mind had faltered, he was right.   He couldn't stay there forever, perched on the hideous bug.   He had to run, to hide.   The room offered only one answer: the fireplace was too shallow to escape the reach of the thing's massive maw, so it would have to be the stairs.   He slid off just behind a writhing leg and fell forward onto the stairs, scrabbling up them quickly with no concern for his shins and knees that banged against the hard wooden steps.   Free of its rider, the bug spun around quickly to face him again, but it was too wide to join him in the narrow stairway.   He slumped back against the stairs and let the adrenaline subside as the overgrown bed bug snapped pathetically at the empty air below him.

As he stumbled further up the stairs toward freedom, the physical manifestation of the insect colossus drew back and grew still, as It shifted Its attack back into the world of illusion and delusion.   The specter of the bug faded away.   Bobby continued to wriggle stupidly upon the stairs, staring downwards with eyes stretched wide, unaware of his attacker's mysterious disappearance.   In Bobby's tortured mind, the legs, shell and yearning proboscis remained, fighting upward, squeezing into the impossibly small stairwell.   He felt the creature's bite in his mind as clearly as if it were real.   He felt his flesh being pulled away, consumed.   Screaming and kicking at the imaginary beast, Bobby struggled, flailing against empty air, climbing higher onto the stairs.   Then the vision left him, suddenly.   The creature was gone.   He was alone, panting, wincing against the lingering pain left behind by the gnawing of his imagination.

He picked his nose against the foul-smelling dust, and spat the foul-tasting dirt from his mouth.   He ran his fingers through his hair, and was momentarily chilled as he drew back his hand to find it covered in a thick red juice.   More blood?   Bobby wondered how his head could have

cluck

been cut. The bug had been gnawing on his leg, and he didn't remember hitting his head when he'd fallen, earlier. Turning around cautiously, he searched for the cause of his new wound. Half expecting to find another of the beasts squatting above him, chewing on bits of hair and scalp, Bobby squinted up into the darkness. Was it the chickens, pecking at his head while he had been fighting to escape the bug? As the bright blue spots of adrenaline faded from his eyes, he peered more clearly into the dark. The entire stairwell behind him was filled with silent, hovering tomatoes, bursting with ripeness. The chickens *were* back, and up to their old tricks.

Bobby had two choices: back down to the kitchen, or up to where the chickens waited. Shaking, Bobby crawled slowly up the stairs to where the giggling, infantile prankster hens had gathered. He swatted a tomato aside, determined to distance himself as much as possible from that horrible, infested kitchen. Not so easily dissuaded, however, a number of the fowl drew from their dark places of hiding and filled the top of the staircase. The entire angry mob of hens, in various stages of death and decay, pressed down on him, stopping his ascent, threatening to push him back down into the terrible hallucination. Above, the chickens which had tormented him for so long. Below, the awesome power of It, manifested into a nightmare reality that threatened to devour Bobby whole. What happened next surprised the chickens. It might have surprised the bug, if it were real. Hell, what happened next even surprised Bobby, and he's the one who did it.

Bobby stood up. Not in the normal manner of clambering slowly to his feet, the way he might have done in his current state of health, but rather the manner of standing up typical of someone who had just had a powerful and sinister spirit slam into his body like a metaphorical (and metaphysical) ton of bricks. With insane clarity and a newly possessed calm, Bobby rose like a vampire from its coffin at the fall of dusk, and spoke:

"I am afraid that I can't allow you to defeat me today." His voice was deeper than usual, and reverberated unnaturally within his larynx. His eyes, too, were different. Both cloudy and sharply focused, all at once. "As much as I enjoy our little games, I have a more pressing matter at hand." The chickens leapt down one step, openly hostile. They were angry. They did *not* enjoy these games. They wanted blood. While they often tried to kill Bobby, and while he often mysteriously escaped them, they did not see this as a game.

"You see, as much as I deserve the pain, and as much as I cherish the threat of death, there's an outsider in our midst. I'm not sure who he is, or why he is here, but he's taken it upon himself to rescue me. How funny is that, really? I mean ... he wants to rescue *me*." He skipped gingerly down the steps, chuckling eerily with each step, and walked calmly through the small kitchen. There was no terror, not even the tiniest bit of apprehension, as Bobby turned to address them further.

"Of course, he can't realize that I don't *want* to be bothered during our playtime. He can't realize the true scenario at all, really. Whatever his powers are, they are not over me, they are only over *you*. He is getting rather meddlesome, however. I thought he was taken care of, but ... well, let's just say that he's hitting a nerve, or is about to. He's hurt so badly I'd thought I'd have some peace from him, but noooo ... he keeps on coming! Hell, I'm amazed he isn't dead. I'm not sure how he does it, but he's getting too close, and I'm not about to let him kill you. I still need you, I'm afraid. So I'm going to have to interrupt our fun so I can stop him. I think there's some soft dirt in the old root cellar that I could bury him in. Maybe I'll bury him alive. He can haunt this place with the rest of us, and give us all some company." The laugh that followed echoed deeply up the narrow staircase, scattering the undead flock back into hiding. "It's too bad really—that bed bug thing was awesome! I'll have to remember that one ..." Still laughing under his breath, Bobby strode to the center of the old kitchen, crossed his arms before his chest, and vanished ghost-like into the floor.

In the darkness up above, there was some mad scratching amidst a flurry of feathers and the occasional dropped beak. Hens were frantically scratching the floor, *clucking* and *brawing* in a frenzy. The rough translation went something like this:

"Somebody run and get the Rooster ..."

Knapp

cluck

chapter 24 chickens aren't stupid

You have both of your eyes but you do not use them.

Armand turned the words over in his mind.   Uncertainty had replaced everything he thought was certain. He had come to this place to free a man, and found the place infested with chickens that were so ... odd? Different? Powerful?

Scary.

He had found the most disturbingly potent haunting of his career—of any career of any of his line, whose collective conscious had made him what he is. He had found chickens that could talk, and a rooster that could fight like a mother. He had found Bobby G., the goal of what should have been a simple rescue. Only Bobby didn't want to be rescued. Bobby had fought him, sent him falling from that window.

Pangs of pain surfaced at the recollection of the fall.

Why had Bobby fought back? Why had he refused to be saved? Armand searched for an answer in his mind. Why the hell was that redneck even alive? That was a good question. How could that stupid ignorant hick fight off these chickens for years? Another memory flooded through Armand's aching brain: Bobby, huddled and afraid, devouring carrots like he hadn't eaten for days. He couldn't have eaten anything at all, thought Armand, not just for days ... but for years. It just didn't add up. And then there was the fight, and the Rooster—the King Chicken himself—who had not only spoken to him, but had given him ... what? Help? A clue, perhaps, but a piss poor one.

You have both of your eyes but you do not use them.

Armand tried to think about what that could mean. Was it a simple boast? Chickens were simple creatures after all. The Rooster could have taken both of his eyes out with two swift pecks and left him for dead in the cellar. If he hadn't bled to death, he probably would have wandered around blind for days or even weeks before finding his way out of this place and even then his car had abandoned him. Instead the Rooster had made a point to *not* blind him.

He calmed himself. He recited some of the irrefutable facts about chickens that he had always known. Facts that had been drilled into him by the "priesthood" of his youth. Facts that his life was based around, and that let him predict the motives of the departed. There had to be a clue in there that would decipher this riddle.

Facts about chickens. There was a list:

1. Chickens are loud.
2. Chickens are dirty.
3. Chickens are stupid.

And so on ... but the answer was right there. Armand was obviously over-thinking things. Giving a chicken too much credit was one of the classic blunders among new initiates. "Thinking like a human will get you killed by a chicken," he had been taught. It was a lesson that was

cluck

important enough to be passed down in books, and it was a favorite among The Order. The only problem is that after years of squatting powerless in their secret offices The Order had lost touch with the true meaning of most of its teachings, and this lesson was no exception. The saying had turned into a daily idiom that was more likely to be used in the context of house chores or card playing than chicken hunting. After taking the helm and absorbing The Charge into his body, Armand had learned that lesson firsthand on more than one occasion. Over and over again it had proven relevant, such as the time when a small highway rest stop was overrun by possessed chicken McNuggets. The little brown things were hovering all over the place, dripping hot grease and causing a general nuisance. It was so easy to assume it all had higher meaning: a statement against the mass production and slaughter of meat birds for the fast food industry and all that. Chickens, however, simply couldn't operate at that level because they lacked the capacity to think beyond the familiar concepts of food, water and sex. It turned out to be nothing more than the spirit of a confused hen that had been processed for finger food. The poor girl's soul clung to the frozen products after having her physical body pureed, shaped and frozen, but the air conditioning in the delivery truck had gone bad and the whole shipment was thrown unceremoniously into the dumpster. From that point on, every time a new delivery truck would arrive, the spirit that now dwelled in the large green garbage receptacle would attempt to regain some semblance of self by coalescing inside each fresh new package of frozen chicken bites that was carried past it on the way to the loading doors. It was never anything political or planned, it was just a simple chicken soul following some simple chicken desire.

If he was going to figure out what was going on with the Rooster now, Armand knew he had to think like a chicken. Did the Rooster think like a chicken? Maybe not. Armand was stuck in the conundrum of trying to think like a chicken that knew how to think like a human.

Knapp

What did the riddle mean? Exactly what it said? If it wasn't a riddle, or a metaphor, or anything else then the Rooster wanted him to find something, wanted him to see something. It had brought him here, and left him here. Alive.

Suddenly aware of what he had to, Armand began to search around him in the dark. It was small—at least when compared to the massive sprawling expanse of the farm—but it was still a sizable room. There was only one small window, set high in the wall, letting an insufficient amount of light strain through dirt-stained and cobwebbed glass. He needed light. There had to be a light down here somewhere. Even the oldest houses managed to have power installed into their darker corners, and this had been a working farm. There was no way farmer Jo and Betty-Sue-Backwoods operated a farm of this size by mucking around in the dark.

Making his way to a wall, he followed it around, feeling the rough stone foundation with one hand, groping for some wire or conduit or any indication that civilization had been added to this ancient cellar. As he moved along the wall, he used his free hand to hold his guts still, trying to ignore the pain as he concentrated on finding a light. Sharp needles shot up through his leg, crackling around his kneecap as they fired their way up to his brain. Realizing how dependent he was on the wall for support, Armand decided the leg was probably more than just hurt. It was most likely broken. Reaching down in the darkness he ran his hands up and down his leg and felt a distinct swelling just below his kneecap, and as he probed the spot a feeling of sharp knives raced up his leg. Several choice words began to formulate between his brain and his voice-box.

"Can I have the satisfaction?" he asked himself. "Just this once?"

"Just once my ass. I've given you too many concessions already," his voice replied, tritely. It drove him absolutely crazy when he used that tone on himself.

cluck

"[—] you!" He told himself, and was momentarily surprised by the
bluntness of the censorship. His voice simply suppressed itself, rather
than providing a helpfully euphemistic synonym. In response to his own
curiosity, he told himself, *"Well, you took me by surprise. And besides, I'm
a bit preoccupied!"*

His voice was right, there was more important work to be done.
There had to be a switch down here somewhere ... there! His hand felt
something. He fiddled with it for an embarrassingly long moment before realizing it wasn't a switch at all. It was metal though, he was certain
of that, and there weren't too many reasons why a small square bit of
metal would be mounted at shoulder-height on a basement wall. It must
be a junction box, he thought, and sure enough there was a narrow strip
of hard conduit leading away from it. He followed it up the wall, and
with great pains he managed to stretch one arm up to trace its path along
the ceiling. The conduit ended, and he felt a short length of greasy wire
that disappeared into a smooth, round object: a light. He'd found a simple electric bulb, hanging near the center of darkness. More searching
produced a pull-chain, which *clicked* satisfactorily as the basement
flooded with bright incandescence. Luckily, the ceiling was low, and
even dipped a bit near the light; because if he stood straight with anything resembling correct posture Armand was certain he would split in
two, or died from agony ... possibly both. Luckily, the light was low
enough that he could reach it while hunched up, bent over in agony.

Once the place was lit, Armand was able to survey his surroundings.
As he suspected, he was in a cellar. As he also knew, from his recent
moments crawling and scrambling around, the basement had a dirt floor
that was highly uneven. The pitch of the floor rose steadily towards one
side of the basement, and dipped suddenly in several places where some
trick of time and atmosphere (and the footsteps of rodents) had formed
shallow potholes in the dirt. The dirt was dry and cracked, and mostly
smooth except for small scraps of wood that had fallen from the rafters.

There were rickety cupboards built along one wall, long inhabited by spiders and covered with cobwebs. One cupboard, its hinges sprung with age, hung open and revealed an assortment of old canning jars and rusty metal lids. The sole source of light hung frugally from a nail near the center of the cellar, and the wire that fed it went towards the back wall, where it split and circumnavigated the room in either direction. Two wires fed the bulb, Armand noticed with a shudder. Two poorly shielded wires, one positive and one negative, probably left over from an old knob-and-tube electrical system from a hundred years ago.

"Way to go, Einstein. It's lucky you didn't electrocute yourself."

Internally, Armand nodded in agreement.[35]   If there had been a break in the brittle sheathing of those wires and Armand had connected the circuit as he had followed the lines with his hands, he'd have been in for a nasty shock; the perfect end to a night of being kicked, pecked, gouged, crushed, and broken. From the direction he came from, the wires first encountered a small square junction box and then split to run the circumference of the room at waist height in either direction. One of those wires disappeared from view behind the stairs, but the other eventually joined a small fuse box. It was open, exposing several old fashioned gas fuses and a good deal more cobwebs and dust. In the other direction, the wires wandered out of site, their progress blocked by the thin wooden stairs that descended from the ceiling just in front of where he stood. Anyone coming down those stairs would be just a few feet from the front wall, facing away from him. Under the stairs themselves there was a collection of trinkets and debris. There was an old ceramic jug, a rusted garden spade, some pieces of hose, and several tin pails containing assorted nails, screws and various bolts with mismatched nuts.

---

[35] Many people talk to themselves in their heads, but only one who is truly practiced at communicating with inner voices can nod and gesture to oneself with any measure of success.

cluck

Armand moved toward the stairs, leaning heavily on the rail. His ribs hurt, and his breath was hot. As if he needed any more complications, he tripped in some of the soft dusty soil and pitched forward onto the ground. He caught himself with his hands, causing a new wave of pain to pour through him like boiling water.

"More broken ribs, I bet. Better take it easy," his voice speculated. Damn voice wasn't good for anything but conjecture.

"You should know," Armand said out loud. He was talking to himself, of course, but for some reason he felt the words should come out from his throat. "You're in there. Can't you tell?"

"I should be able to, but to be honest I'm not sure. You're a mess. I'm a mess. You really need to take better care of ourself." Armand tested the bottom stair and it felt strong, so he put his weight on it, pulling himself slowly up.

"Thanks for the advice. I don't suppose you've got any ideas about what's going on around here? I mean, something useful."

"Well, that rooster didn't kill you. That rooster is different from anything I've ever seen, and I've seen a lot of roosters. Centuries worth. I get the feeling it wanted to ..."

"Wanted to what?"

"Well, it's almost like it wanted to help you, but that just doesn't make sense." Armand put his hand on his side, slowly massaging the swollen area. He hated to agree, but The Charge was right this time. Nothing made any sense. *"Although, now that I think about it, there's ... well, there's something familiar about it all. It's like, that Rooster reminds me of you when I first passed into you. You already possessed power that you shouldn't have had, and I think this Rooster is the same. You never act normally, so maybe it makes sense that it's not acting normal either. Maybe it really does want to help you."*

"Yeah, well it sure doesn't feel like it was trying to help me." He prodded a rib, and it jiggled. The pain was like a hot bolt of electricity shooting up into his skull.

"I know, but ... well you were rather confrontational, you know. Maybe this rooster is different. It seems intelligent. Shit, it can talk, after all." Armand winced at the word.

"I thought we had a deal? If I can't swear, neither can you ... but yeah, I know what you mean. It said I have eyes but I can't see ... what the heck does that mean? I can see just fine. Better than most, as you know." He hauled the next foot up, grabbed the rail, and painfully pulled himself up another step. "The obvious answer is to use my other sight, but I tried that and it was a bust."

"Well, whatever the answer is I think you need to find it fast. If you have to choose an ally, I'd choose him over that redneck farm boy. I'd say it's probably the safer bet, the lesser of two evils. The chicken doesn't make sense, but at least it's consistent. And it might be smarter, too. That Bobby guy is crazy."

"Why do you think I'm pulling myself up these [darn] steps?" He stopped, rolling his eyes internally. "You could have let me have that one. It might have helped to dull the pain."

"Sorry, habit." The two were silent as Armand pulled himself up another step, and then another. *"I think it's simple: the chicken wants you to see something, something specific that he wants you to notice. It doesn't look like Rooster-boy going to help us find the thing though, so we're on our own."* He reached the top after a long and agonizing climb, and put one hand on the knob of the door. He inhaled deeply, catching his breath before he turned it, opening the door.

"Why hello there!" Bobby said from within the newly opened doorway, startling Armand so badly he nearly fell back down the steps. The farmer's face was the owner of a highly disturbing grin. He stood

cluck

just on the other side of the newly opened cellar door, face to face with the crippled *Exorciste de Volaille.*

"You can swear all you want!" Armand's voice screamed at him, *"Just get the fuck outta here!"* The way forward was blocked by Bobby, whose face was twisted in an unnatural way. Whatever possessed the man was no longer making any attempt at hiding itself. His eyes bulged, and under the man's twitching lips a mouth full of broken and blackened teeth were visible. His posture was contorted, and his gaze was terrible. Armand had no choice but to retreat back down into the cellar. The pain was almost unbearable, but the new dose of adrenaline enabled him to keep it at bay as he bound down three steps at a time and came crashing into the cold stone foundation.

Bobby, recognizing the futility of Armand's flight, descended more slowly. He took just two steps down, and then turned to close the door behind him. While his back was turned, Armand shuffled back around the stairs. He could use the shovel as a weapon, if he could just reach it before Bobby, healthy and whole, caught up with him. As he ducked around the side of the stairs, Bobby called down to him.

"Run, run, but you can't hide. I know this basement well ... there's nothing down here but you and ... me." The voice came from the top of the stairs. He hadn't even felt it necessary to come down here yet, Armand thought. I've got time to lay a trap.

"Get the lights," his voice suggested, *"and when he comes around the stairs, brain him."* It wasn't a bad plan. Armand picked up the shovel as quietly as he could and limped back towards the light. It hurt like hell to raise his arm back up to the small pull-chain, but with one simple *click* it was dark again. In the cover of the blackness, he crept back beneath the stairs.

"Oh no! I'm afraid of the dark!" Bobby mocked, still from the top of the stairs. "Are you? Maybe I should turn on a light? No need ... I can still see you, you stupid fuck! These aren't your average old eyes!"

The laughter that followed made the exorcist's skin crawl. Partially because it was the eerie laughter of a madman, and partially because it was getting closer.

"You're going to have to get the light back on," his voice commanded. *"If he can see you, you need to be able to see him. You'll just have to fight him one-on-one. Man to man. At least you've got a shovel."* It was a small encouragement. Moving back towards the light, Armand was able to find the chain again by waving his arms upwards in the darkness. He didn't pull it yet, but listened as hard as he could. In the stillness and the quiet and the pitch black, Armand couldn't help but think that this might well be the end of *L'Exorciste de Volaille.* He had training, and power, and a weapon ... but he wasn't sure he would live. If he somehow got to a hospital, maybe, but if he stayed here, fighting ... even if he managed to push aside the pain he doubted if the effort of combat wouldn't kill him.

"Turn on the light you dumb-ass!" his voice shouted, waking him from his drifting thoughts. He pulled the chain, and with a mocking *pop* the fragile chain snapped away from the bulb and fell limp in Armand's hand. The light remained off. Broken. It had actually *broken.* The cellar remained dark.

"I hate the dark," his voice complained. *"Everything is usually so damn bright."* It dawned on them both at once. He could use his other sight to see in the dark.

"There's enough spiritual activity in this farm to light up Las Vegas!"

Though Armand knew the brilliance would be nearly unbearable, he also knew the voice was right. He steeled himself. *You have eyes but you do not see*, the Rooster had said. Armand knew it didn't mean for him to use his second sight like this—that was human inference again, and it didn't apply. Regardless of what the stupid bird meant, Armand had better eyes than anyone else alive. He no longer had the luxury of pushing the vision back, blotting it out, covering it up. He breathed deeply,

cluck

asked his voice if it was ready, and then—cautiously, squinting—he let his true vision free.

The brightness was everywhere, just as before. Everything was awash with a blue glow, each one a dim individual spirit but together it was like a sun. It was as if the place had its own enormous shining blue soul and he was standing directly inside of it. As he grew accustomed to the light, he began to focus, casting about for shapes. In front of him, a bright area was moving towards him, slowly. It stopped right in front of him, just out of reach.

"I can see you," Bobby mocked. So this was how it was going to be. The hick was going to draw this out, reveling in his victory over the man. "You realize I'm going to kill you, don't you?" Bobby circled him as he spoke.

"*Let him talk ... maybe we can learn something.*" Armand's voice suggested.

"You've interrupted everything ... Tomatoes! Eggs! You basically just fucked it all. You screwed the pooch, screwed my plans! You've ruined my penance! You were gonna help that dang-gum chicken-shit rooster, too! Weren't you!"

"Are you going to tell me anything useful, or are you just going to walk around in circles talking nonsense?" Armand asked.

"Talking nonsense!" Bobby shouted, "I am not—

The words were cut off by the resounding thud of the shovel as it crashed into the side of Bobby's head. The effort hurt Armand just as much, but it was worth it. Bobby fell to his knees. Armand couldn't see with his normal vision, so he couldn't assess the damage. He knew the blow had been a good one though. Still, all Armand could see was the bright ghost image of the man, and any detail that he would have normally seen was washed out by the sheer brilliance of this place. He took a step forward, raising the shovel again, but the hesitation had been too much. Bobby's foot caught the spirit warrior in the stomach. There was a crunch. Bile and blood welled up in Armand's mouth, and he stumbled backwards, tripping over the same patch of soft dirt and falling heavily onto his back.

Over him, the bright outline of Bobby loomed triumphant. Armand was growing accustomed to the light now, and the details were getting clearer. He could make out Bobby's features, the tightness of his muscles. There was something else, too. Something strange. "*Look at his legs*," Armand's voice urged him.

Bobby's legs, like the rest of him, were spirit-blue and bright. Armand had seen this blue light for most of his life, and it was no surprise to him to see people this way. To him, looking at someone's soul was the same as looking at someone's clothing. It was simply a part of them. If the person had a freckle, the spirit had a freckle. If the person got a haircut, so did the soul. Souls were a reflection of the physical being, and they duplicated a person's self-perception precisely. It was for this reason that Armand could see Bobby's baggy clothes, torn and stained. Bobby saw himself that way, and so therefore Armand did, too ... except for the legs. The legs were different. Where the rest of the crazy farmer was a clear representation of the physical man, the legs were stretched and blurred. His feet were no more than a distorted cloud of light, trailing away into the ground. It was as if, from the knees down, Bobby had no self-perception at all.

"*What do you make of it?*" his voice asked him, but he honestly didn't know. It was like this nemesis of his was rising out of the dirt like a mist, like some Djinni streaming forth from a bottle—and the answer struck him. The soul *was* rising from the dirt. From the soft dirt. In the basement floor. Armand had tripped over the spot twice, but hadn't stopped to wonder why there was loose soil in an otherwise hard-packed cellar. He blinked, and tried to focus more clearly. Tune out the rest of the light. Dim the overwhelming brightness, and concentrate on the one spirit before him. The spirit of Bobby, the man who he had come to

cluck

rescue. The spirit that wasn't clinging to a physical form like it should, but was rising like a plume of smoke from the earth.

"Hey, I've got a good one for you," Armand said to himself, and then he pulled himself a bit more upright, and recited:

Like the chicken, never thinking, always shitting, always stinking
of the rancid stuff of poultry dust that settles on the chamber floor;
And his beady eyes have all the thinking of a chicken who has been drinking,
And the soul-light from him streaming to this spot upon the floor
Shall be lifted —

"*—nevermore?*" offered his voice in conclusion, thinking the rhyme wasn't half-bad. Surely, a tribute worthy of Poe.

"Evermore," Armand hastily corrected.

"Evermore?"

"Yes, 'evermore', as in 'lets put an end to this for good!'"

"*Got it, big guy! Dig!*"

Armand clawed at the ground, dragging himself up onto his side, and began to crawl slowly towards the spot. It was directly between him and the stairs, and Bobby mistook his goal. "Trying to escape, are you? We can't have that!" Bobby jiggled with silent laughter and moved to intercept him by blocking the bottom of the stairs.

"Do you even think you can make it up the stairs? I mean, assuming I wasn't here to stop you from trying? I doubt it. There's a long way to go, even if you made it up there, before you'd be free. This is a big house. You could get lost in here. I'm lost in here, and I know this place like the back of my hand. Built a lot of it with my own two hands, after all ... or with my own money at least. Built the chicken yard myself, though. Burned it down myself, too. I never really wanted the damn birds in the first place, but my wife nagged and nagged and nagged. She wouldn't let it rest. Feed the chickens! Water the chickens! We need more chickens!

Knapp

We need a bigger coop! We need a bigger yard! Damn birds ... we just ended up with more and more of them until the whole freaking place stank. And whatever I did wasn't good enough! Before you know it she turned ... mean.

"So I killed them. Every last one. I had a barbecue, I did." He looked up in the direction of the old chicken yard, but being underground it looked to Armand as if he were simply staring into space. Taking advantage of the distraction, the exorcist crawled closer and closer to the shallow grave. He still had the shovel in his hand.

"You know, she never forgave me for that. Never forgave me at all. From then on I was nothing more than 'the chicken killer.' Like they were the most important things in the whole goddamned world and I was just some dumb-ass hick of a husband. You can't blame me for drinking, the way she treated me. You can't blame me for hittin' her, the way she was always blabbin' and bitchin'!" He had longed to tell his side of the story to another human for so long, that once he started the words kept coming. Forgetting that he wanted to kill Armand, for the moment, he continued to gripe, trying desperately to get a very heavy burden off his chest. Armand wasn't listening. While Bobby droned on, Armand crawled determinedly to the spot, and to the backdrop of Bobby's irrational ranting, he thrust the blade of the shovel inside.

As the ground broke, fresh rays of blue light shot forth.

"What the fuck do you think you're doing?" Bobby woke from his fugue and strode quickly to the trembling man. Armand's muscles were failing him, and he was spitting up large quantities of blood. Hardly a formidable opponent in his state, but Bobby showed no mercy. As Armand scratched feebly at the loose soil with his spade, Bobby's foot came down on him again. Armand fell flat against the ground, his face in the dirt not two inches from a newly exposed bone. A human bone. He braced for a second blow, but none came. What did was the sounds

cluck

of commotion, so loud he could barely hear Bobby screaming and cursing over the ringing of his own ears.

"Don't give up now, Armand! Not yet. Dig up those bones, do anything. Just don't die." The words were coming from inside him. His voice. A familiar sound. The voice of an old friend. It was telling him to not give up, to keep living. To keep digging. Armand managed to wriggle himself into a sitting position. One eye was now swollen shut. How had that happened? He couldn't remember being hit in the eye, but it was painful and tight. It would be black and blue in the morning, if he lived that long. The sounds of a struggle continued, and he tried to focus on them. There was a bright light streaming from the broken ground beneath him, streaming like rushing water to the thrashing form of Bobby. He was fighting something ... what was it? The Rooster?

"I knew it was trying to help us," his voice said, and Armand was forced to grin despite the pain. The Charge loved being right. *"Still not sure why, though."*

"It's got something to do with these bones." Armand ran his fingers through the dirt, and could clearly make out large bones, buried in the shallow and dusty grave. "Is this his wife, do you think? Maybe he killed her and buried her down here. These things do usually come back to guilt, you know, and murder is a sure-as-[heck] way to develop guilt." It made perfect sense; he kills his wife, goes crazy with guilt, and that somehow rubs off on the chickens, and—

"That doesn't make any sense at all!" his voice reprimanded him. *"How could her guilt lock them here? It can't be her, and if it's not her, then that only leaves ..."*

"Him," they both realized at the same time. The bones belonged to Bobby. Bobby had been dead all this time, one more ghost amongst so many. Suddenly, many things made sense. Bobby's strange possession, his reluctance to leave, his repeated references to punishment, penance ... and why the Rooster and the hens wanted him gone so badly.

Knapp

It was Bobby's own guilt that kept him here, and it was so strong that it kept the Rooster and his flock here, too. He wanted them to have their revenge on him as penance for what he had done. He wanted to suffer forever. By forcing them to stay here and torture him, Bobby's twisted needs were both satisfied and renewed: he suffered, yet he was making them suffer again as well. He was caught in a catch-22 of spiritual proportions. Bobby knew it, and he didn't even care. His madness longed to carry the spiral of guilt and suffering on into perpetuity.

Armand couldn't help but wonder how Bobby had died, and was contemplating scenarios in his head. Did the chickens kill him? It was rare for a haunting to turn fatal, but not unheard of. Suicide? A simple accident? *"Look at that!"* his voice interrupted, with awe. Armand allowed his thoughts to stray for a moment as he turned back to the battle that was taking place no more than a few yards away. Amidst the swirling vortex aura of blue, the Rooster and Bobby were clashing like two Greek Gods; each was formidable and powerful, and had a lustful hate for the other. Bobby was drawing energy from whatever force was causing the air to glow, and hurling it in waves at the bird. The Rooster, in turn, was using every trick in his book against the deceased farmer. Weevils and insects jumped at him from somewhere within the ground. Flames burst around them, filling the basement arena with the charred, murderous history of the old, innocent flock. Unrecountable illusions of horror were summoned to assault Bobby. At the same time as the spiritual war was waged, physical violence was being done as well. Fists met feather, talons tore flesh. It was an awesome spectacle.

Though the flames weren't real, they did light up the basement, giving Armand the use of his normal vision. No longer needing the spirit-sight (nor the headache that it imposed) he filtered it out again, pushing it back into the cold but comfortable corners of his consciousness. He let just enough of the blue light through to prevent him from being taken unawares by a spirit again. With the aid of real light,

cluck

Armand could see there were definitely bones in the ground next to him. Human bones. They were all loose and piled together, as if whatever body had been buried here had first been cut into pieces. Armand didn't know what to do. If this was a chicken spirit, he could exorcise it. After all he was *L'Exorciste de Volaille*.

He tried, but it didn't work: Armand waved his staff over Bobby's head, and muttered various incantations, letting the power of The Charge wash over him. Bobby's ghost continued to stream forth from the exposed remains, however, as strong as ever. It would seem that Armand's powers held no sway over human specters.

Turning to a more mundane approach, Armand tried hitting the bones with his shovel, as if it might somehow transfer the impact to Bobby himself. Every muscle burned with the effort to lift the utensil and strike with it. The pain of the exertion combined with a new wave of nausea and desperation, causing Armand's eye to twitch. He pushed past the pain. With a groan, the shovel rose high, arcing upwards, and then crashed back down again, raising a cloud of dust from the desiccated grave. It was a futile effort and didn't result in anything other than a fit of blood-speckled coughing. Armand lacked the energy to complain, so he simply rested, leaning against the shovel, grasping for a solution.

"How do you humans do it?" Armand was not sure if the question came from The Charge within him, or from the Rooster.

"Do what?"

"Put your dead to rest!" It was The Charge who spoke, from within him. He could hear it clearly now, his old familiar, internal voice. *"Say a prayer?"*

"Um ... yeah, say a prayer, I guess."

"Well, then say a prayer! Yeah, I know, he's already in a grave so say the damn prayer!"

Armand, already experiencing excruciating degrees of discomfort throughout his body, managed to look even more uneasy. He looked down at the grave, up towards the clash of existential titans that raged before him, and then quickly back to the grave again.

"Our, um, father," he began. A few paces away, the Rooster was being buried by flaming comets of evil, filling the small cellar with celestial steam.

" ... whose ... art is in ... Heaven?"

"Sounds good to me!" the Rooster broke free of the brimstone rubble and launched a dozen razor-sharp feathers from an extended wing, tearing through Bobby's flesh like knives.

"Hollowed be thy name ..." Armand ducked as Bobby recovered, his lacerations melting away as if by magic, and vomited a bout of flame past the Rooster towards him. The motion ground the tips of his broken ribs together, creating new definitions of agony inside Armand's midsection.

"Just say Amen! Just say Amen!"

"Amen!" Armand shouted. There was no discernible effect.

It was no surprise, of course. What God would listen to the prayer of a man like Armand, who had made a living in sharp conflict to just about every major religion?

"You missed part of it, that's it. There's a bit about 'delivering us from evil' ... you should've said that bit—

"Oh shut up!" Armand said aloud. Bobby and the Rooster, locked in immortal combat, took no notice. Still leaning against the shovel, Armand tried to clear the dust from his throat, and the webs from his brain. There had to be a solution. How was he going to get out of this? The ghost-Bobby was stronger than the ghost-Rooster, and it would only be a matter of time before it would be able to turn his attention back to Armand. If it did that, Armand was a goner. Very few pieces of Armand felt up to another challenge.

"Bobby!" Armand shouted. "Bobby, I've got your bones here. I know your secret now, so what's the point?"

cluck

"I'm busy!" was all that Bobby could muster for a reply. He was trying to avoid being battered by the Rooster's gigantic, heavy wings.

"Really, what's the point? You're here haunting yourself, don't you realize that? You're *dead*, Bobby. If you kill that Rooster, and me, you're still going to be dead. You're going to have even more to regret. It's not going to solve anything."

"Good thinking," Armand's voice encouraged him. *"Keep him talking,"* but Armand wasn't trying to distract Bobby. He was beyond that. He just wanted to know why. He wanted there to be some sense made of it all before he died.

He picked up one of Bobby's femurs and threw it at him. It passed harmlessly through the blue shadow of Bobby's soul, but it made Armand feel better for trying.

"Let's take a moment, shall we?" Suddenly, The Charge was speaking to Armand with a disturbingly calm demeanor.

"What? I'm kind of busy!" It was true. Armand was busy trying to futilely attack the ghost of a dead man who was fighting the ghost of a dead chicken.

"It won't take but an instant—

"What!" It wasn't a question, it was a one-word summation of Armand's current feeling, which was: "You'd better get to the point or shut up, because the last thing I want to experience before I die is any more frustration on your account." It wasn't that Armand held anything against The Charge, or that he hadn't appreciated the countless times it had saved him, comforted him, or simply helped him pass the time. It was simply that people wanted to conclude their existence with something more. A memorable, poignant utterance that would end up on a plaque somewhere. A heroic and courageous deed that could be carved into a statue. Something epic, poetic and proud. Nobody wanted the last moment of their lives to be spent checking the answering machine, or looking for a stamp, or listening to some incessant internal force—one which felt it had some right to ruin your moment of parting simply on account of it being an eternal spiritual power—blather on, going "um," and "by the way," and "did I mention." In this case, Armand really wanted an answer, from Bobby. After that he could die happily. Well, *satisfied*, at least.

"Sorry to bother you, your self-absorbedness, but it really will only take a second. That's how these flashes work. An instant. Before your eyes. Are you ready?" Despite the fact that Armand had at this point more or less given up, he resented the implication.

"Flashes? We'll have none of those! I'm not dead yet!" Armand jabbed his best fingers deep into the dirt floor, pulling himself to freedom with renewed vigor. Bobby paused, and cocked his head, his redneck brow furrowed in honest confusion. Armand had said that last bit out loud.

"Well, you're just about dead, as far as I can tell. But don't worry, I'm not starting unless you're going to pay attention. I've saved up some great bits, over the years. There's the lady at the Value Quick — remember her? You were buying sugar." Yeah, he remembered. She was standing behind the counter next to a large window, and wearing a skirt that, with the light shining in the way it was, and the material being as it was ... well, it was a nice memory. Despite the pain it caused in his teeth and gums to do so, Armand smiled.

Armand wasn't dead, so he pushed the memory aside. He was a fighter. He'd survived one of the most interesting childhoods imaginable. He'd survived the French internment at Camp Weirdo. He wasn't about to give up now. He wasn't going to lose, not to Bobby, not this way. Suddenly, knowing wasn't enough. Feebly, he fumbled with his less-good hand at his utility belt. He regretted not having a proper belt, full of exploding pellets and boomerangs and vials of useful liquids and gases.

cluck

"Batman ... now he had a utility belt," the voice of The Charge muttered into his head, rubbing salt in the wound. All Armand's belt had was pouches full of Blue Seal feed pellets, a vial full of Ivomectrin, and no boomerangs at all.[36] There was a single cherry tomato left, bruised and small. In desperation, Armand flicked it at Bobby. Like the bone, it had no effect, simply passing through Bobby's jutting, angry chin before falling to the dirt. Bobby turned to look, but other than that was unaffected.

"So, who killed you then? I mean, you didn't bury yourself down here, did you?"

That did the trick—Bobby stopped and turned back towards Armand. "He did," he said, pointing at the Rooster. The unexpected accusation stopped the Rooster fast. The big, feathered bird-king hopped from talon to stub, looking wildly about the room, roving its beady red eyes of fire around the cellar like a lighthouse beacon. "Who, me?" the gestures said.

"He killed me by turning her against me. She used to love me before those blasted chickens came along and fucked everything up between us!" Despite the blood and the pain, Armand had to suppress a chuckle.

"Oh," he replied. "It had nothing to do with you beating her, then, for—how did you put it? For 'blabbin' and 'bitchin'? It was the chicken's fault. I see."

"Way to go, Arnie, piss him off!"

"Not my fault at all!" the Rooster boasted, confirming its indignant behavior with words. It was smart for a rooster, but it was still, at heart, a chicken. It didn't understand the true depth of the conversation. "It's him that keeps me here, because of nothing that I did. Nothing *we* did!"

---

36 Ivomectrin is a useful farm medicine capable of stemming of all sorts of scaly chicken infections, including various worms and mites and all sorts of bacterial growths. It did not, however, have any documented effects upon ghosts, and it rarely returned to you if thrown.

It lunged at him again, and tore open his guts with his talons. Like the Rooster, Bobby was nothing more than a shadow of his former physical self, and the wounds sealed themselves immediately.

"It is your fault!" Bobby screamed. "It's your fault that she—"

"Killed you? Is that it Bobby? Is that what you were going to say? That she killed you and that somehow it wasn't your fault, or hers, but the fault of some chicken? I hate to disagree, but if anyone is to blame it's your wife for not killing you sooner. I'm not an expert in these areas, but I'm sure you deserved it, you stupid sonofabitch." His inner voice, The Charge of The Order of Volaille, cringed.

Bobby was deflated a bit by the reality of the words, and he stepped back from the fray, momentarily defeated. Armand pressed harder, despite the pain, and turned to the Rooster.

"This is about guilt! It's *always* about guilt!" Armand spat the words out with a fresh mouthful of blood. "You ..." he searched for a name, but there was none. "You ... rooster! He's only here because he's guilty about what he did. You want to kill him, it's easy. *Forgive* him!" It was true. Somehow, from somewhere deep inside, Armand knew it.

"You're not going to get all soft on me again, are you? This is a battle we're in—" his voice began, but it was cut off by Armand's blood-speckled shouts.

"It's only a battle because we're making it a battle! Can't you see?" Bobby, the Rooster, the house, and even his own voice paused and turned their attentions to the mad, raving exorcist.

"I can see that you're about to get our ass kicked, and if you get a chance to sneak out of here while they kill each other, it might be a good idea. That means not screaming and waving your fists around like that, by the way."

Armand knew that The Charge was wrong. There was no escaping this without solving the conflict, and there was no way to solve the conflict without removing the source of enmity between them all. Again,

cluck

The Charge cringed inside Armand's head; in the exorcist's mind, The Charge was the source, or at least one of them.

"You know what you have to do," he said to the voice inside him. "You have to be the bigger man. You have to end this."

"I suppose I can forgive Bobby, but I can't forgive The Rooster," the voice replied, sounding scared. *"I was created to oppose him. It's why I exist."*

"You have to." They both knew it was right. Inside Armand, his power shifted, and the entity known as The Charge came to terms with its fate. The Rooster was still staring at Armand, who now looked directly at the bird, as an ally and, perhaps, as a friend?

"We've forgiven you, and now you need to forgive him. You see, what we've been doing all along is wrong. We create our own ghosts. They're born from our guilt and from our fears. It's why I'm here, and it's why you're here, and it's definitely why he's here. All it takes is forgiveness, and he'll simply cease to be."

"It's not that easy," Bobby barked as he threw himself at the King of Roosters again, but Armand knew that it was. Every exorcist knew if you removed the cause, you would banish the ghost. Bobby's ghost was caused by his guilt, and the best way to remove guilt was through forgiveness. Unfortunately, there's another rule that every exorcist knew (at least the chicken exorcists): All chickens are stupid. Most are stubborn, too. The Rooster dodged Bobby's attack and countered, driving the dead man backwards.

"How can I forgive him for what he did to me, to us? How can I forget what he did to—" the name, unspoken, quelled the fire in the King's black sockets, the undead equivalent of welling tears. The Rooster regained its composure and readied itself for a fresh attack. Armand couldn't help but to think that he, personally, had killed more chickens over his lifetime than Bobby ever had. He hoped The Rooster was too distracted to come to the same conclusion, or maybe wouldn't care.

Armand had fought chickens according to the rules, at least, and maybe that was good enough.

"You can forgive him because he did what he did out of ignorance." He wasn't getting anywhere. The Rooster began to circle Bobby, who was still stunned and silent near the center of the cellar.

"You can forgive him because it's the right thing to do!" Armand shouted, but this tactic had even less effect. The Rooster didn't care what the right thing to do was, it was the Rooster with the capital "R." It was strong, and noble, and proud. It didn't give a rat's ass about right or wrong. It only thought of itself. How could you convince something as proud as a rooster to think selflessly, especially in the heat of battle?

Pride. That was the ticket! Armand played to the weakness he knew all roosters possessed, and attempted to persuade this one, now, with flattery.

"You can forgive him because *you're better than him.*"

There was a tangible silence, as bird and Bobby both froze.

"I am better?" The cocky rooster pondered. His large beaked skull wobbled from side to side, the red fiery bead of an eye wandering about in a staccato flicker of thought. Finally, coming to the conclusion that it was the superior being,[37] the Rooster threw its head high and proclaimed, "I am better!"

"You are," Armand agreed, "and because you're better than him, you can forgive him for being an inferior creature. When you forgive him—this is the best part—he'll go away!"

" ... *then maybe someone could call an ambulance,*" his voice added, weakly, "*it's getting cold in here ...*"

The Rooster stopped hopping and stomping about, and drew itself tall, breast thrust outwards. It was superior. It could do this—it could do anything. It could ... forgive.

---

[37] Not a surprising conclusion, if you've ever known a rooster.

cluck

"You are a strange human, who can persuade my ancient enemy to forgive me. That is why I did not kill you. I should not trust you, but I do." The Rooster circled again, positioning itself between Bobby and Armand. "I must know: if you are right, what will happen to him?"

What would happen to Bobby was largely unknown, but Armand had a hunch. The pain was fading, and was being slowly replaced by a tingling cold feeling. He had to take a slow shallow breath before speaking again. "His ghost will have ... no reason ... left to stay here. It will be forced to go ... away?" What did that mean? By the look of The Rooster, it was wondering the same thing. "Some people believe ... good people go to Heaven. A place of peace ... and beauty. Bad people go to Hell. Fire and brimstone ... eternal suffering." The Rooster hopped from side to side, and shook its dead, leathery wattle in contemplation.

"This 'Hell' ... I think I know this place. Yes, that sounds right." Pictures of lava-red light, spilling from between large stone teeth, fluttered through the Rooster's mind. "It ... it sounds like a fate worthy of him. Worthy of my forgiveness."

No sooner had the idea been conveyed, than Bobby's blue brilliance began to fade. Like Armand's dog Boomer, whose soul had ascended to spiritual byways so many years before, Bobby's spirit was now moving on. Bobby's face twisted in disbelief for an instant before he began to fade, and Bobby drifted away towards eternity. At the end, before Bobby's soul left this world forever, his eyes dimmed a little, and looked inward. Armand wasn't sure, but it just might be that Bobby realized the consequences of his ways before the end. It just might be that he felt the full weight of responsibility for one fleeting moment. He might have saved himself, just in time.

"—*Or he could be on the fast boat to Hell,*" suggested Armand's less sympathetic voice. Sure enough, unknown to all of them, something happened far away: two stony rows of thick, fiery teeth curved upwards in a momentary grin of glutinous satisfaction before the mouth of Hell opened wide, and waited to receive a fresh morsel into its maw.

The Rooster King sauntered over to Armand.   Moments earlier, Armand had been battling the Rooster for his life. It was the Rooster who had brought him here. It had shown him what to do.

"I knew you would win," the Rooster said. "I knew that if you could see that man for what he was, you would be able to send him away. I saw you send some of my hens away, despite the spell that kept them here." Armand didn't feel like he had won.

"But I tried that, and it didn't work." Armand gasped as he tried to turn his head and a new wave of pain shot through his spine. "It was *you* who sent him away." The Rooster cocked its head to one side.

"Perhaps," it said, "yes." It scratched at the dirt around the bones. "I do not understand fully, but I am ... grateful?" the Rooster tested the word, which like the feeling it described was new. "Yes, grateful."

"He was guilt-stricken, because he killed you ... and the other chickens. By doing so he had ... driven ... his wife ... away." He stopped, and breathed slowly for a while until the pain ebbed away again. "He hated himself, and he took it out on her ... and she eventually killed him for it. He thought she had done it because he had killed all of you chickens. He held tight to that guilt ... used it as a source of power. With it, he kept you here ... on purpose. So that you could torment him ... for all time ... he wanted to ... suffer." It was really kind of sad, he thought. He couldn't help but notice the blue light, which permeated this whole place, was lessening slightly. The chickens were free, now, and as they realized this their spirits began to fade. "So, what happens now?"

"We are free to choose our paths, now. I will go away, with Helena, into eternity, as was intended. This is right." Armand shook violently, wincing against the pain of the spasm. "You are hurt." The cock observed. Armand laughed, causing more pain in his guts and making him spit up more blood.

cluck

"I owe you ... for some of that," but for some reason he was smiling. "Yeah ... I'm busted up ... pretty bad. I don't see how ... I'm going to make it ... out of this one ... alive. I'm bleeding. On ... the inside." Armand wondered if even his inner voice was hurt. It was being awfully quiet; normally, it would be saying something inappropriate, but instead it remained silent. The Charge couldn't feel Armand's pain directly, but it had lost its entire purpose for being, and felt it was best to contemplate that in the short moments left before its host body keeled over dead. Armand shuddered, despite the pain the movement caused. It was very cold. Pressed against the dirt floor, deep below ground, Armand attempted to shiver again, but only succeeding in awakening new aches.

The Rooster stepped closer. It prodded him with one huge talon, and Armand groaned at the touch. "Is there anything I can do? Before I go ...?" Armand smiled again.

"I don't suppose ... you know how to dial ... 9-1-1 ...?" Armand chose to pass his voice's recent joke on for the Rooster to hear. "Get me to a hospital?" he coughed, and then everything slipped into darkness. Floating in the dark, he contemplated what had happened. He and the Rooster were like mirror images of each other. They were a singular purpose, a unified will. They had been connected, somehow, all along. The day, the last day of his life, had been the culmination of all his powers and training. In the brief moment at the end he realized a kinship and friendship with the Rooster. The culmination of a centuries-long war between man and chicken was over. He would have shed a tear for all the suffering that had been caused, not by ghost chickens but by human kind, but his eyes were closed, and dry, and he doubted he would ever be able to cry again.

Knapp

Armand was unconscious when the hens arrived. There were hundreds of them, and though many were beginning to fade, and many more were weak, they were still able to lift Armand's limp and broken body, and just as an army of ants might carry away some massive prize of food, the chickens carried him up the stairs and through the labyrinth halls of the farm. Like a breaking wave, the hens spilled out from the front door of the farm, and as the wave receded the tired and broken *exorciste* lay washed upon the banks of the winding country road. The chickens sank back into the farm, and then one by one they vanished. The Rooster was the last to go.

Armand lay there, bloodied and still, for only a few minutes before a new light was cast upon his body. Not the blue light of the spirit world, but the white light of a headlamp as Fleming cautiously pulled up next to him.

When the exorcist finally came to, he was in a white, sterile hospital bed.

cluck

chapter 25 dimming the blue lights

Armand leaned against the driver's door of his reliable old friend and stared aimlessly into the nearby ferns. He took a breath, tasting the flavors and humidity of the country air. He savored the smell of the damp earth and moss, and the freshly budded trees. An old stone wall held back the forest, marking the boundary between land and road. The stones were freckled with sunlight, which also reflected coyly from the trickling surface of the narrow brook, and played among the wavering fronds of fern and shrub. The trees, mostly maple and birch, rose to form a thin canopy that was almost wide enough to enclose the road, like a tunnel. A few evergreens grew here, too, the lower branches broken and fallen among the ferns and needles of the forest floor. Enough light shone through to make it a happy scene, and Armand couldn't help smiling. He remembered the foreboding fog and that sinister moon that blanketed the narrow country road on his previous visit, and he inhaled deeply, letting the breath slowly back out again in a long satisfied sigh. He had done well here. There was something dark and damaged about

Knapp

this place, and he had fixed it. It was a suitable feeling, a comfortable one. A fitting last impression of Armand's long and unreal career. His retirement was going to be an easy one, he knew. Everything was resolved.

A bit further down the road, a blue light swelled up from behind the trees like distant city lights viewed from the countryside at night. A small ways further further down the road was the most architecturally amazing house Armand had ever known. It had seen better days certainly—after all, it had been infested with ghosts of several varieties for years, and ghosts were not prone to home maintenance—but it still had a presence about it. More than a presence, it had a soul. Armand could see it, glowing in the distance. Even after the exorcism of farmer Bobby and the release of all those chickens, there was still a power there, glowing blue and bright for no one but Armand to see. He patted the roof of the old faded black steed and the engine rumbled to life. He climbed back in and they rode slowly down the road together. The car enjoyed the approach, a nascent attitude towards quiet country places. Like Armand, something had changed within the car. It pulled up to the front of the house and into the drive.

"Whoah!" Armand stopped the car with the command as if it were a horse. His foot never touched the brakes, but the car obediently slowed to a gentle stop, just at the entrance to the drive. "I'll get out here," he said, and he did, pausing for a moment to look up at the old estate. It was magnificent now that the dangers had been expelled from it. He tried to count the buildings: The main house; an attached "L"; the newer section that was built as a hotel; one, two, three barns behind it all and one in front; the massive barn with the cupola that the Rooster had made his throne. There was too much, and Armand lost count. Shaking his head in amazement, he turned and walked to the edge of the drive where an old metal mailbox (painted silver but made mostly of rust) was propped up by a steel pole. Armand opened the mailbox, brushing aside

cluck

some cobwebs from within its mouth, and then took a small package from his coat pocket.

The package was a small brown envelope, overstuffed and wrinkled at the edges. He tipped it on its end and caught a small object wrapped in thin and supple leather. He hefted the parcel in his hand, judging its weight, and then slid the bundle back into the envelope. He ran his tongue across the glue. After sealing the envelope, he inspected it one last time before putting it in the mailbox. The address was written in English and then also in French. Being uncertain of what postage would be required, he had covered every free space with stamps. He raised the small red flag on top of the mailbox. Having contacted the post office already, he knew they would add this place to their route soon enough. It would probably put the postman out of his way by miles, Armand thought, and then he quickly rummaged inside his pockets again until he was able to produce a rubber band, a pen, a small scrap of paper and a ragged twenty dollar bill.

Please be sure this package is delivered safely. Here is some money for any additional postage and for your trouble, A—

He had begun to sign the scrap "Armand," but stopped himself. After some thought he completed the signature, as "Arnold." He was no longer Armand. That name and all its connotations were put firmly behind him.

Turning back to the house, he could almost imagine it in its earlier years. He imagined the crowing of healthy, living roosters from amidst the barns. The blue glow emanated from every square inch of board and beam, and it collected in the spacious farmer's porch like some spiritual greenhouse. He imagined a happy fat dog, lying there on the porch. Maybe he would get a dog, he thought. A bloodhound, in memory of old Boomer. It would make a fitting bookend to his life.

"You're quite the old house, aren't you?" he said aloud. The house couldn't speak to Arnold, but the man could feel the resounding *yes* that echoed up from within the structure. Arnold closed his eyes, and thought about where he might be able to hire a painter. He had money, which was good because it would take both time and money to bring this massive place up to snuff. A worthy challenge for an old exorcist's retirement.

When Arnold opened his eyes again, the blue light was gone. He suppressed it as he had done before, but not to blot out its prior overwhelming brilliance, for indeed the softer blue glow that remained after the other souls had gone was almost comforting. Rather, he simply wished to see it in the normal sunlight. "I hope you don't mind, but I want to see you for real from now on." It was quite a view, and after enjoying the scene for a quiet moment, he added, "Yes. I do think you look best in the sunshine."

He walked up onto the porch and turned the old marble knob, opened the door, and disappeared inside. His voice liked it this way, too, but it didn't say anything. They had agreed they were going to live normally for a while. Arnold began to investigate the house, a task that would occupy all of his remaining years. The lights in the kitchen were out, so he looked for a basement so that he might check the fuses. Outside, the old car pulled itself up further into the drive and, noticing an open barn door just past the porch, parked itself comfortably inside. The moving van would be here soon, so it would be best to stay out of the way, it thought.

Almost two weeks later, a grey-haired man in plain brown khakis and a thin cotton button-down shirt leaned on the edge of a plain, round table and opened a small brown envelope. Inside was a small heavy

cluck

object wrapped in leather. Peeling back the folds, the man contemplated the object held within. He closed his eyes and bowed his head. *"C'est l'aube d'un nouveau jour,"* he said quietly, to himself. "It is the dawn of a new day." What might have been a tear welled up within the old man's eyes, but if it *were* a tear, it was one of joy. Opening his eyes again he looked down at the small metal badge. It was scratched and worn to the point where the lettering was barely visible, but it had at least been polished carefully, so that it looked like real gold again. The simple crest was difficult to see without years of ground-in dirt to add contrast to the embossing, but it was clear enough in the old man's eyes. He had seen it many times before. One feather, upright within a circle of down, beneath the letters 'EV': the emblem of *L'Exorciste de Volaille,* the symbol of his order.

Soon, Jean-Pierre, the only other member of The Order, arrived. Seeing his old friend standing there, still, he too knew what had happened. There had been a conflict powerful enough to build generations of their kind, but that conflict, they both knew, had at last been resolved. Old Armand had done it. There were still spirits, of course. There would always be those souls who couldn't find their way, but there was an understanding now, and humankind had an ambassador of sorts in the poultry underworld, to keep things under control, at least for a while.

There's no need to fight anymore. Armand had found his peace, and like him, The Order would need to find a new life, with new adventures.

Close to four thousand miles away, Arnold hammered away at some loose clapboards on the front of the house. He looked up at the sound of an approaching car, wiping the sweat from his eyes. A young couple emerged, one of which held a small something wrapped in a red checkered cloth. The other introduced them as Arnold's new neighbors.

Neighbors, he thought. *Well, whadya know. Neighbors.* Introductions and handshakes completed, Arnold apologized for his appearance. He'd been working all day outside in the sun.

"Don't think twice about it," the young man insisted. "To be honest, we're glad someone's moved in whose fixing this old place up. It was dreadful here for so long, most of us in town avoided this road completely." Arnold smiled.

"Actually," the man's wife ventured, "we've always wondered what it was like inside ..."

The pleasantries ended with the exchange of some fresh baked bread and Arnold's offer of a tour, and the three soon escaped the heat of the sun to begin the long tour of the old farm. Before they reemerged nearly an hour later, a friendship had been forged. The woman was Emmy and her husband's name was Chris. They shook hands again as they left, full of smiles.

"We won't take up any more of your time, you're so busy."

"Not really, just finishing up a few of the more urgent projects before my mother gets here. I don't have to pick her up at the airport until two o'clock this Sunday."

"Oh how wonderful! Where's she flying in from?"

"You know, I'm not entirely sure," he answered truthfully. He had found her through less than normal means, and when he called her, there was so much to say that it had never come up. "I haven't seen or heard from her in a long time," he finally muttered in way of an explanation. "All I have is an area code and a flight number. I mean, I grew up in Detroit, but I don't recognize the number."

"You could always look that flight number up online and find out where it's coming from," Chris suggested. Emmy slapped him playfully on the arm to distract him, sensing they were trespassing into something that was maybe a little too personal. "Well, you tell your mother that we wish her the best," she added and then whisked her husband away. As it

cluck

turned out, they eventually met Arnold's mother and got along beauti-
fully. When the two young neighbors eventually began a family of their
own, Arnold's mother would watch the kids for them, if she was up (still
from Detroit, as it turned out). As the children grew, they often visited
the farm, fascinated by the wonderland that it was. Soon they grew
more, and when old enough would come to help old Arnold with the
chores. It was an easy farm to care for—almost as if it were taking care of
itself—and most visits turned into social affairs, no matter what the
original intention had been. The eldest son, Michael, eventually leased a
portion of the estate, and opened the old Inn again.

In short, life had returned, and all was well again.

"You know," Arnold told the new manager of *The Rambling Acres
Inn*, "they claim this place is haunted ..."

"You're such a joker, Uncle Arn," and the old man just grinned.

"Seriously. They say it was haunted by chickens. You could hear
them scratching at the dirt under the floorboards, and sometimes they
would set tiny little traps for people," and they both laughed at the
absurdity of an old town's superstitions.

Knapp

cluck

epilogue

"It's amazing, really, the way the place has cleaned up. It's all gardens and such, now, whereas before ..."

"I'd appreciate it if you didn't speak to me as if I weren't even here," the house complained. "I mean, it's me that you're talking about, isn't it?" The shutters of the front porch fluttered for a moment.

"Sorry, it's just that I'm not really used to talking to, err ... farms." It was true, Fleming wasn't used to speaking with anyone. He'd certainly tried to communicate non-verbally with the man he drove around, as he still lacked a way to speak out loud, but he always failed; and he'd heard the house speak to him before, but he'd never tried talking back.

"Well, I'd never imagined talking to a car," the house replied, miffed. Of course, consciously speaking through one's mind wasn't really talking. It was more like thinking, and so the house was able to pick up the innocent intentions of Fleming's thoughts. Recognizing that he'd spoken somewhat harshly in response to the car's flattery, the old farmstead quickly added, "You look better yourself."

"Thanks," Fleming responded, proud of the new paint job and thorough detailing. Arnold had been taking good care of both his car and his home, and both cleaned up well. "Do you think he's happy?" the old automobile asked of his new friend. "I mean, really?"

"Oh, it's not my place to wonder about those sorts of things. I mean, the last guy who was here was happy to live forever in between life and death, wasn't he?" The house was referring to the farmer, Bobby. "Who knows what makes humans happy ... but I'm happy. It's good to be full of clean air again, and to have a proper washing—and to be rid of that damnable fog. Not to mention all that chicken shit."

"True. Well, I think I might go for a drive. It's such a nice day for a drive."

"What if he needs you, then?"

"He's sleeping in the hammock, just behind the second carriage shed. I can see his feet from here. He'll be out for hours ..."

"So he is, so he is."

From down the pleasant little country road, a breeze picked up, scattering freshly fallen leaves. A family of swallows and a fat gray squirrel argued over a cache of nuts, and the bright green of lacy ferns rippled with the summer air. The birds continued to twitter and swoop at the squirrel, who eventually bounded off along the top edge of a low stone wall to find his feast elsewhere. There was the buzz of insects all around, but the breeze kept them at bay, making the scene a comfortable one for all. When the breeze died down and the rustling of the small wood subsided, the clear water of the meandering brook could be heard—barely audible over the sounds of life—and then it would disappear again as the air picked up once more.

"You know," the house added as the car began to back out of the drive, "I think he is happy." The car paused, and then flashed his headlights once in the automotive equivalent of a nod before accelerating rapidly down the winding country road, the summer air blowing wildly through the open windows. All was right with the world.

cluck

THE END

about the author

Writer and part-time defender of all that is good in the world, Eric D. Knapp lives on a farm in New England with his wife Maureen and a host of animals (including, you guessed it, chickens). Eric studied English and Writing at the University of New Hampshire and the University of London, and went on to become an expert in the completely unrelated field of networking technology.

A few years ago, Eric found his soul (which had apparently been kicked under the sofa), and began writing professionally. His first book, *Out of Place, Out of Time*, was recognized with an Independent Publishers Book Award, and has been lauded with praise consisting of words like "brilliant" and "unique" and "imaginative."

about the illustrator

Ian Richard Miller, New Hampshire designer and father of three, holds an Associate's in Illustration and a Bachelor of Fine Arts in Graphic Design. Ian constantly strives to augment his natural creative design and Web development proficiency with new materials and methods. Fervent precision and tenacity are clearly evident in each piece produced by this talented artist.